TOTAL IMMERSION
DARK WORLD

S.J. LARSSON

SEVERED PRESS
HOBART TASMANIA

TOTAL IMMERSION: DARK WORLD

Copyright © 2017 by Severed Press

WWW.SEVEREDPRESS.COM

ISBN: 978-1-925711-02-8

WELCOME TO MY OBSESSION.

I never get sick of the intro cutscene to Elora Online. Headband on, and then fifteen seconds of the most wicked graphics and exciting immersion in the greatest epic of battles, with *Ananta* causing complete mayhem. And damn if he doesn't look cool as hell.

Ananta is controlled by a Nuudle Mystic who summons him. He comes out of the little Nuudle's heart as a swirling blue mist, and then quickly gains form, floating in the air before him.

Ananta is massive. He fills the screen in defined, scaly detail.

He's blue, with nine snake heads that make up most of his body, which is that of a long, forked-tailed serpent. The eyes on the heads have glowing lightning bolts shooting out of them in sparks of silver. Their mouths are enormous, sharp-toothed, and open with hunger only flesh can appease. Surrounding *Ananta* is an aqua fog with black, wispy shadows dancing within. At his outer glow, water droplets spray in a mist.

An army of all races and classes stands before the Mystic and *Ananta*. One green, especially gnarly Mylop lizard can't stand it, the waiting. He raises his axe, roars, and makes a mad run at *Ananta*.

That's my PoV, point-of-view, in the cutscene.

Ananta's belly opens a hole and a golden-skinned man's face emerges. He has glowing, white eyes. That's why we all know *Ananta* is a *he*. The Mystic chants words, commanding the beast. *Ananta*'s mouth opens as all the snake heads turn toward our army of Elora, with gaping mouths brewing fireballs, and flames spew out. They are red, black, yellow, orange, blue, green.

I'm the first to get fried. Then, I'm floating above, and I see the army is wiped out, and Elora is slowing burning, city by city, territory by territory.

And now I'm logged in, in game.

I access my item menu and use my Comfort Ring. I'd been so tired last night that I logged out outside Baneswood in the middle of nowhere. I warp back to my home point in Cashmere, where I'm meeting the guys. And Sally, of course. She gets mad when I call her a guy, but she is.

Today is a big day. Today I get my revenge, and I'm confident. I'm ready. I've been working relentlessly toward this day for eleven months since The Seeker jumped me. I haven't told anyone, but today... I can't wait to get to Lucille's Brewery and tell them what I'm about to do.

They'll think I'm mad. I'm not. Maybe I'm a hero, and not the kind above some revenge. The hero who, yes, does it for revenge, but also because so many people would be free. All over Elora. Heroes are complicated.

No, I'm not one. I know deep down. What I am is a gamer who has taken on the biggest challenge in-game I could find because I can't resist. I made my own mission—I will defeat him where everyone else has failed.

1

CHAPTER 1: THE TELL

I spawn at the Kila Crystal, where I usually keep my home point, in Cashmere on Wet Eyes Isle. It's in the Marana Sea just outside the underwater Siren Territory. My mansion is on the east coast of the isle. Kila Crystals are for getting around faster, and you have to earn accessing them by finding them. Nobody ever knows if they've found all of them. They're also the only places you can set your HP before you get your first home. Otherwise, you go to your graveyard.

Cashmere's where everybody goes to hang out. Maybe because the auction house synchs up to all the capitals' auction houses, or maybe it's the taverns with the best stat boost brews you can get. It's beautiful, right on the water, peaceful, bustling. Everything is gray, moss-covered stone and quaint structures.

I'm a Dragonbane Maniac. Maniacs are hand-to-hand fighters. I gave myself red spikes down my back, three black spikes on my tail, and curling, big, black horns. White hair, dusky smoke skin. Dragonbane were created eons ago when the mad, power-hungry Bane bred humans and dragons into Dragonbane. It's a long story, the history of Bane, his brother Kane, and Dragonbane altogether. Once, there were humans and dragons, but now only Dragonbane.

Maybe it's because it's this day, but I'm reflecting a lot on my character. How I feel like he's the real me. In Elora Online, you must choose a first and last name, no special characters or numbers. I'm Sid Vicious. That's the real me.

Sometimes you see someone running around with just one name. Must be some secret quest, some item, some reward. No info on the wikis. My guildmates and I have speculated on it for ages, among other oddities of this world.

I'm anxious about telling the guys what I'm going to do—take on The Seeker and destroy him. I know I can, but will I choke and come back defeated, with all my loot gone, starting over? It would be mortifying to tell them after I boast my plans. Better keep it subdued. Like it's not the big, huge deal that it is.

I walk the gray cobblestone streets of Cashmere, watching the other players I pass on my way to Lucille's Brewery. The five races are everywhere—Sirens, the lovely ladies of the sea; Nuudles, the little people who are best at black magic; Mylop, the lizard men giants made for tanking; White Elves, best known for their healing and huge, beautiful territory; and Dragonbane, the best damage dealers in the game, in my opinion. You can pick what race and class you want, and each race has race-specific stat boosts when you start, but you get even more of a stat boost of the race-specific kind if you pick a race and class that are made for each other.

And stat boosts are everything.

I'm a level nothing. There are no levels in Elora Online. Everything is item and stat-based. My stats are through the roof, especially my strength, or STR. It's up to 346 now. When The Seeker got me eleven months ago, it was at 278. Every single digit of a stat boost counts. As a Maniac, STR is my most important stat to do the most damage. My two other big stats I work on to get stronger as a Maniac specifically are attack, or ATT as my secondary stat, and CRG, courage, as my third.

There are seven different stats for your character, and even if you don't have much use for stats like mind (MND) as a Maniac, you still work on all seven as you go. The more stats, the more power, the harder you hit, the more damage you can take, the more good loot you can get, especially when you get high enough to start running dungeons. Plus, Attack (ATT) and Defense (DEF) are must-haves we all grind. We get Attack, Defense, Strength (STR), Mind, Intelligence (INT), Concentration (CON), and Courage (CRG). In eleven months, I've gotten them all higher than they were before The Seeker got me. Yeah, I'm a determined man when it comes to righting wrongs done to me. Revenge, indeed. I want it so bad, I have lived for it for almost an entire year.

I enter the brewery. It has wooden tables and chairs, light wood floors, and a long bar with beautiful Siren NPC, non-player character, bartenders. Behind the bar, a large open window looks out at the water. I see my crew sitting at our usual booth, and they wave and call out to me.

"Sid! He's here! What, you sleep late?" says Peter Johnson, my RL, real life, friend, Jacob, who started playing the day I did. We've been friends since we were kids. He's a green Mylop Lancer. But really, he's a social player and crafts all the time. He's rich as hell from it, too. Tells me everything about crafting. I've tried to explain I like farming for cash, but he still geeks out on crafting so much that he can't help but talk to me about it like we are still eight.

"Be there in a minute, gotta get a drink."

A green-haired Siren NPC behind the bar serves me a huge mug of Blue Ice Ale. It costs a pretty penny. I need it today.

I sit with my friends and guildmates at our booth, between Good Deeds (Sally) and Koolio Koolaide. I see Koolio has the same brew I have but not as big.

I can't wait to tell them, but they are in the middle of talking about Koolio's quest for a new special Lord move that was in the update last week. He's a Siren Lord, a tank who uses healing to do his job, and as all Sirens are female, you know we tease him relentlessly. He always has something witty to say or downright puts you in your place in response. He leads the guild—Nowhere Squares, it's called.

I start chugging my drink. I can feel my body's heart pounding in RL. I don't want to interrupt, but at the same time I want to stand on the table and scream it. I chug instead until Sally notices my drink.

"What are you doing a courage stat boost for? And that huge?"

The drink is a CRG stat booster that lasts four hours, and the stat slowly goes down to your usual stat by the end. My base CRG stat is 271, but once the whole drink is in me, it'll be at 325.

"I was wondering that about Koolio, but I've gathered it's the Chain Heal quest. You have to fight a dragon from the past?"

"Yeah, man," Koolio says. "Need the CRG boost so I can have faster moves."

"Good luck."

"I ain't gonna need it." He sticks his forked Siren tongue out at me.

"But why you, Sid?" Sally persists. I know Sally in RL, too. She's a few years younger, a friend of my sister's. "I know your digital expressions. Your eyes are burning redder with every sip of the brew, and you're all twitchy. Spill." She's a Dragonbane Knight, a real hack-and-slasher. Silver scales and white spikes with red hair. Black, twisting horns.

Nottingham Rose, a UK player and a Nuudle The Black, says, "I see it, too. And how much did you spend on that monstrosity of a drink?" The Blacks are the nukers of the game. Black mage, basically, and big damage. He's slow, but excellent in dungeons. Thorough. Nuudles are small, skinny things, a little like gnomes, but they are proportionate. Nottingham has blue skin, long, black hair in a ponytail, and a red glowing spiral on his forehead. His race is well-known for Nuudle Eyes. Big, round, and oh-so-expressive.

The other Nuudle in our group, Raging Rampager, a Stylist class—the buffers basically—who's always dressed in fabulousness, speaks up. "You've been grinding hard since... you know. Your STR stat must be through the roof now with all the quests and missions you've done. What is it now?"

"346." I chug down the last of the blue ale. My red dragon eyes must be like fire.

"Damn, son," says Peter. "You're drinking all that, you're fidgeting, Deeds's sixth sense is kicking in. What's the game plan for today?"

They all stare at me. Now's the time. I pause. I could just not tell them. What if I lose? I'll be so crushed to tell them I'm doing it and then come back a loser.

However, a little gusto from my friends will help just as much as the blue ale.

In a quiet voice, I say, "I'm going after The Seeker today."

Dead silence. And then everyone talking at once. Lots of questions.

The Seeker is a Dragonbane Killer, basically a ninja. Got the Dragonbane stat boost like I did for picking a race and class that naturally go together. He's often invisible. He's black, has black spikes all over, and sports six twisting horns on his black-haired head.

They want to know how I can find him.

"I've been watching him. He has patterns. I've followed message boards of his attacks on other players, and there's a pattern. He picks certain places at certain times. I'm almost positive I know where he'll be in about a half hour. Plus..." I give them a cocky grin. "I got me a Seer Amulet last week."

"Seer Amulet! Where did you get that? Was it a hidden quest?" yells Peter. Players inside peek over at him with curious expressions.

A Seer Amulet, when worn in the necklace slot of my gear, lets me see invisible things, like an invisible Killer who will be outside the Mantle of Bliss in White Elf Territory ready to pick off mage fishers for their stat boosting items so he can sell them on the AH. All the while killing their progress from possibly years of playing, like he did me. Like he's done to many, many good players.

I hear Sally in the guild chat channel. "He's doing it, guys! Sid is going after The Seeker!" I don't get a chance to tell of the treasure map I bought and found it with, all after reading a Nuudle history book in a library in the Temple of Nuudlel. But meh. We've all done that.

"Dammit, Sally, don't tell everyone. It'll get back to him," chides Peter.

It's too late. Nowhere Squares' chat channel explodes with excitement, all the while Koolio and Peter telling them to keep it to themselves. On the downlow.

"When, Sid?" I hear my favorite voice in the guild say. Silvia Diamond, a blonde, pale White Elf Blessed class. Best pure healers in the game. I've had a crush on her for two years, but never had the balls to do anything about it other than join all her dungeon runs and help her with missions and quests. It's made us good friends, but she's not at our booth every morning, is she?

"I just had my CRG boost drink, and if timing's right, I need to hit the Kila Crystal and head to White Elf Territory's Kila Crystal in the Mantle of Bliss. I'll get him there. He should be lurking outside in the territory somewhere close," I tell her.

"Wow! That's amazing! I'm in the Mantle now. Want me to tele you here? I'll give you something for good luck," Silvia says.

Nottingham raises a blue eyebrow.

"Sure, thanks. That would be great."

"Give me a minute to run out of the Mantle. That is, you said you wanted to be out there, and it'll be quicker that way. I can use Swift Feet and I'll tele you in five. That stat drink will wear off."

"Well, thanks," I say. In RL, my cheeks are warm.

My friends at the table can't stop talking to the guild about it, so I turn off guild chat. It's making me nervous.

I reach up in RL with my right hand and adjust my headband's viewing to 50 percent. Now I see my apartment and the game equal 50-50. I set my character on auto-static movements. Better empty my bladder before all this gets going. I get up from my gaming recliner and walk to the bathroom, turning off my mic as I take a leak. Then back to my seat. I adjust the headset back to 100 percent and turn my mic back on.

I wonder what gift Silvia might have for me. Now my heart is really hammering.

Silvia invites me to a party. I accept. "Thanks, guys. It's time. Silvia invited me, and she's going to tele me."

Sally tilts her Dragonbane head. "You got this, you know it. If anyone can, you can."

"Yeah," says Koolio Koolaide. "You're the best in the guild. I never said that."

I grin at them. I haven't turned guild chat back on, but I hear Silvia in party chat channel. "Hey, Sid. Are you ready?"

"Yeah. Thanks."

Everything goes white, and then beautiful White Elf Territory surrounds me. Rolling, green hills, bushes, flowers everywhere. Small trees with buds and blooms that never die brush the landscape.

Even more beautiful is the image of Silvia Diamond standing before me, still sparkling from using her white magic to get me here. She smiles at me. I smile back.

"You look nervous. Is that why you got off the guild channel?"

"Yeah." I don't want to look nervous in front of her. I want to be a badass that she swoons over.

"Well, I know you have to get to it. Here. A gift." Her long, slender arms wave in the air and pale blue, sparkling light comes out of her hands. She's using a big move, with me as the target.

Silvia Diamond casts Blessing of Inner Peace. Sid will dodge all Special Ability attacks in next battle.

"That's incredible! Thank you so much, Silv." Blessing of Inner Peace, a Blessed's biggest move acquired through a near-impossible quest (I helped her with it), will allow me to dodge all Special Ability attacks in the next fight I have. She won't be able to cast it again for another day. I'm surprised she had been able to cast it at all. "I mean it."

"One more good luck charm," she says, then takes a step toward me. She leans up and kisses me on the cheek. I'd never wanted physical sensation in Elora more than that moment. She leans back down. "Copy the gameplay log, win or lose. I want to read it, and I want you to tell me all about it. Maybe we could go down to Siren Territory and hang out in a sunken ship or something?"

"I'd like that," I tell her.

"Now go. I know you'll defeat him."

I grin at her. She likes me, acting like it's more than friends. Hell, I don't know. Wow, this day gets crazier and crazier.

We say goodbye, and I'm off to lurk behind trees and bushes in Laninga, an area south of the Mantle of Bliss where, according to my research, I will find The Seeker. Thanks to Silvia's tele, it only takes about three minutes to walk there. I don't dare use my Chimera mount. He'd see me a mile away. Once in Laninga, I use a shadow potion and equip my Seer Amulet. The shadow potion will make me invisible, but if The Seeker also has a Seer Amulet, which he must certainly have stolen off someone, he could see me if he has it equipped. I'm gambling he's in true Killer mode, ready to cut people down fast, and for that he'd have a Stealth Choker equipped. I won't be able to examine his gear. He'd know I was there because he'd get a message saying he was being examined. If he is wearing the Stealth Choker, his Sneak Attack move will do devastating damage when he hits his unknowing victim while invisible at first attack.

Still, I stick to the trees.

I see a few players running here and there. None would be his targets. Too low of stats. They wouldn't have anything good. I can tell simply by looking at what they are wearing.

At sea's edge, on the farthest east side of White Elf Territory in Laninga, I see a shadowy figure crouched down by a Nuudle fishing off the edge. As I get closer, I read that the Nuudle's name is Fangs McGore, and his gear tells me he's a Magician. Wealthy, high stats. I can't imagine the jewelry he has on, but I know that's what The Seeker is after. He'll make a killing on the auction house.

A little closer still, and I can finally read the name in light blue above the shadowy figure. *The Seeker.*

I found him.

Adrenaline pounds through me. I think of Silvia's kiss.

I'm ready.

CHAPTER 2: THE FIGHT

I think. I'm going to stay calm and not be intimidated by the huge black-and-spiked Dragonbane Killer hunting prey. The same one who almost made me quit playing eleven months ago.

My mind goes blank of all plans.

Okay. Okay. Just refresh. You have it memorized, look at the moves real quick. Refresh.

I lower my game view to 30 percent and pull up a page in my browser with both of our moves. Killer against Maniac. I want to read them one more time, right now, in case one of my many imagined plans doesn't go as planned.

These are what we see as we get our moves, and we get our moves through quests and missions. The first move quest is always an easy one, and the weakest move. The last on the list is the once-a-week use, the big move. We can look at our moves list or spell list (for mages) and this is what we read. We can't use the same move over and over. Most abilities have to have an alternate ability used before it can be used again. It's not a complete list; some moves and spells can be learned through secret quests and missions, and Elora Online continually adds them in.

Maniac moves:
Punch—Punch target in the face, causing damage and stun for 5 seconds.
Gut Punch—Punch target in the gut, causing damage and -5% percent of total health every 3 seconds for 21 seconds. Some items and gear may affect this ability.
To the Throat—Hit in target's throat, causing high damage and root for 20 seconds.
Thousand Fists—Rain down punches by the dozens over ten seconds, stunning target and causing high damage +STR stat percentage. Some items and gear may enhance this ability.
Eye Gouge—Gouge out target's eyes, causing blind for 60 seconds and -3% health every second for 30 seconds. Some items and gear may enhance this ability.
Special Ability: Going Feral—Rage attack on target, causing 90% damage to target's total HP, but taking 40% of Maniac's total HP. Can only use once a week.

I read quickly, glancing through the words to make sure The Seeker is still there. He's prowling closer to the unknowing fishing Nuudle.

Killer moves:
Hacksaw—Manifest a hacksaw to attack opponent. Deals damage.
Head Slam—Manifest a crowbar and hit target on the head. Deals damage.
Bind and Gag—Root and silence target for 20 seconds.

Strangle—Stun target for 5 seconds.

Shadow—Go invisible and silent until canceled or using another ability.

Sneak Attack—Deal high damage at first strike when in Shadow mode. Some items and gear may affect this ability.

Stealth—Block target's attack 50% of the time. Some items and gear may affect this ability.

Slit Throat—Deal high damage to target +/-% ATK stat, and target loses 5% total HP every second for 20 seconds. Cumulative.

Special Ability: Instant Death—Pull target's heart out of his chest, killing him instantly. Some items or gear may enhance this ability. Can only be used once a week.

Instant Death is bad. Really bad. I'm hoping he's used it this week, but he probably hasn't. I'm not the only one who's tried hunting him. He would save it until he needed it. I know he has one of those special items for Instant Death—Blood Ruby Ring. When equipped, Instant Death can't be blocked by anything at all.

Maybe he had needed Instant Death sometime this week when I wasn't watching him, or maybe one of the online accounts of his attacks the past week left the move out.

When I first read abilities and moves, I didn't realize the percentages were for the total HP that the player has at maximum, and also for available HP in other cases, or what HP you have left. It delighted me when I figured that out because a lot of my Maniac moves have DoT based on total HP percentages.

I hadn't thought of catching him being about to attack someone. I can use this to my advantage. I can attack right after he kills the poor Nuudle, when his health will be lower. I know, I'm not a White Knight tank, doing good and saving the little guy. I'm not worried about it. I have his name. If… when I defeat The Seeker, I'll mail him all his stuff back.

The Seeker uses Sneak Attack.

I watch Fangs's HP bar drop 25%. He instantly equips all his fighting gear, getting rid of the fishing gear.

The Seeker uses Bind and Gag.

Oh, this fight will be over fast. The Seeker had targeted this guy. It's obvious. He had to change gear, giving The Seeker a chance to bind and silence him, so as a magician, he'll have no way to attack for twenty seconds without using a Breath Mint as a move. The Seeker wastes no time.

Fangs McGore uses a Breath Mint.

Fangs McGore uses a MegaPotion.

The Nuudle's HP goes up to full.

The Seeker uses Slit Throat.

Fangs's HP drops to 50%, and his HP is draining as I'm trying to keep up.

Fangs McGore uses a MegaPotion.

The little Nuudle's health goes back up to 70%, but then keeps dropping from Slit Throat's DoT effect.

The Seeker uses Strangle.

Oh, man. Now he's stunned and can't get rid of the silence with a Breath Mint. He chose a health potion over casting spells. He must have panicked.

The Seeker uses Slit Throat.

Fangs' HP drops to 35%, and because the move is cumulative in its DoT effect, he's now losing 10% of his total HP every second until the first Slit Throat runs out.

***Stun* wears off.**

Fangs McGore uses Enhance.

Now the DoT stops, but he's still rooted. That doesn't really matter for a mage.

The Seeker uses Stealth on himself.

He can't have the extras that have him at 100% ability to block moves. He'd need help from other players for that, and if I know anything, The Seeker has no allies in Elora.

Fangs McGore casts Drain Essence.

The Seeker's HP drops to about 50% and Fangs's is at full health.

The Seeker uses Bind and Gag.

Fangs McGore uses a Breath Mint.

The Seeker uses Strangle.

The Seeker uses Slit Throat.

Fangs is back down to 50%, but his stun wears off.

Fangs McGore casts A Thousand Needles.

That's a tough move for a Magician to get. It drains HP at 10% every second for 10 seconds, basically killing the opponent if he doesn't do something.

The Seeker has stopped playing around.

The Seeker uses Bind and Gag.

Fangs McGore uses a Breath Mint.

The Seeker uses Slit Throat.

Now Fangs is at 15% health and it's dropping fast.

Fangs McGore uses a MegaPotion.

His HP goes up to 50%, but is dropping so fast it's down to 30% as The Seeker makes his next move.

The Seeker uses Strangle. Strangle has no effect.

Fangs McGore casts Drain Essence.

The Seeker blocks by using a Marena Seashell.

It's over now. Fangs is at 1% HP and before he can make a move, he keels over, the DoT doing him in.

Once a fight is over, all effects go away.

I read my personal dialog box that only I can see as I arranged it in my gamer interface, but I watched, too. I could even see their facial expressions. Fangs McGore looked scared and pissed at the same time. He knew who The Seeker was when he attacked him. He knew he was about to lose all his loot— special items he'd spent hours, days, weeks, months, years getting.

The Seeker had a blank, almost bored look the whole time. Now, he bends over Fangs' fallen body, and his hands dig through the character's pockets and, not displayed, his bags.

Holy crap. He didn't use a MegaPotion before looting. His HP is at about 50%.

Now. It's now or never. I'll not get a chance like this again.

All I have to do is use Go Feral and it's over.

I sneak up behind The Seeker. My heart in RL beats irregularly. It's actually going to be this easy. I feel sweat drip down my RL forehead.

I drop my invisibility to attack. Unlike Killers, everybody else has to be visible for their attacks to work.

Sid Vicious uses Go Feral.

Boom! He falls over on top of the little Nuudle. I didn't even get to see his face.

I did it. I actually did it. All the gameplay strategies, all the plots and rethinking a real battle—useless. I got lucky and he got careless, not using MegaPotions and being taken over by greed and ego.

I have to loot fast or else he'll come back to his body, resurrect, in time to get me good. I have no idea where his grave is. Something tells me he's close, has some way to get to me fast.

So, I loot and loot. I don't have time to look at everything, and my bags are filling up, but I don't care. I've been playing for seven years. I know what looks like what and I grab it.

I put on my Comfort ring as my heart stops altogether. His body lights up and comes to life. How did he get here so fast?

The Seeker uses Instant Death.

I'm dead.

Blessing of Inner Peace blocks Instant Death.

Silvia's blessing icon in my active effects disappears. She must have somehow, somewhere gotten a Gilded White Elf Ring, an impossible drop in an impossible dungeon. If a White Elf Blessed wears it, their blessings always, *always* work, even on the big moves that say *never, ever*. She didn't even tell me.

Thank God for the beautiful Silvia, because her blessing saves my life, and not a drop of my HP spills.

Sid Vicious uses Comfort Ring.

And then poof! I'm in Cashmere at the Kila Crystal.

I did it. I did it!

I feel relief, giddy, and also a bit like I cheated. I hunted him, hacked him down in one hit, and warped right when he came back to attack me.

Oh my God, he'll be hell-bent on coming after me now, but he won't be able to for a long, long time. I made especially sure to get all his Killer special items. He's too weak without them to do what he does. I killed his high stats and enhanced abilities.

I know my glory story isn't that glorious. If it weren't for Silvia's blessing, I'd be dead and looted again.

Should I make it more exciting? I could brag that I was an epic fighter, that the battle took thirty minutes. No, an hour. I've planned fights with him in my head that would go on that long, so I know what to say.

But no. That's not what happened. I may be a non-hero seeking revenge and challenge, but lying isn't my way.

I head west to Lucille's Brewery to find my friends, turning Guild Chat back on. I hear them. They're speculating on how my progress with The Seeker is going. Peter is saying he knows I'll have no problem with it. I'm a master Maniac, he says.

I enter Lucille's. Sally, Peter, Raging, Nottingham and Koolio are still sitting there, unable to leave until my return. Now I'll tell them about my inglorious victory, and then I'll message Fangs McGore to see if I have any of his stuff.

I wanted it to be better. I wanted to put on a great fight. Oh well. His reign of terror is over for now, and I at least did that.

CHAPTER 3: THE BRAG AND THE SPOILS

They don't see me at first. Their heads are bent together in discussion they don't want overheard. In Elora, you can always hear those close to you, and the brewery is packed with players getting stat boost brews.

In RL, I fumble to the end table to the right of me for my keyboard and send Silvia a text message to meet me here. I then send one to Fangs McGore, telling him the same and that I have some good news for him.

They both answer with questions, but they both say they're coming. I answer only to say, "Hurry."

I approach our booth and they stare, mouths open. I guess it's because I'm not naked. The Seeker loves to leave his victims naked. Fangs would have gotten a cheap robe for now, and to be honest, I'm surprised he hadn't immediately logged out in a furious rage. I had when The Seeker did it to me.

"You did it?" Sally squeals.

"I told you!" Peter practically yells.

Koolio puts his siren webbed feet on the tabletop and hands behind his head. "So, spill. Tell us every move. Paste the gameplay display into a note and give us all one as you tell it." He smirks, but I see admiration in his eyes.

"We have to wait. Two more are coming, and I... I need to wait."

They make complaints and there's heckling, but I don't feel as high as I should. I only want to tell this once.

"Well, at least tell us who we're waiting for," Sally says.

"Silvia and another player I met out there. If it weren't for them, I don't think I could have done it."

"Who is this mystery player? Did he back you?" Raging asks.

"No, not exactly." Other people in the brewery are getting quiet, straining to listen to the loud table, knowing something is up. "Sorry, I want to wait."

They all seem peeved except for Peter, who just keeps grinning at me and shaking his head.

I start going through my inventory to see all the loot I'd managed to get from The Seeker. I have over 120 new items. Once I knew Fangs had his stuff back, I'd see what my friends and the guild wanted. Oh, damn. So many good things. And then I see my old Steel Knuckles, ones he'd taken from me so long ago. They had to be mine. It's an enhancing item for my Thousand Fists move, making the damage insane. I had to run the same dungeon forty times to get it to drop. Yeah, my friends are the best. They ran it with me many, many times. The Seeker couldn't sell it or use it because it was a rare item dungeon drop from a quest line. Those can't be sold or traded. Just looted. I wonder why he kept it, had it on him. A trophy? I had put up a good fight back then.

I equip it. My gloved fingers gleam silver.

I see stuff everybody would want, and some killer items I can sell. Many I can't. I see a Love Lily. I'll give that to Silvia. It takes up a hairstyle item slot.

It's great for Blessed class because it enhances healing spells' effects by 25%. High-end goldsmiths make them. Even Peter isn't rich or high enough goldsmithing level to make them, and on the AH, they cost around five billion. Who has five billion?

Well, I guess I could if I put it on the auction house, but this is for Silvia. Even if she hadn't blessed me, I'd give it to her. Shy or not.

Right as I imagine it tucked behind her ear, she walks into Lucille's and straight to us. Her White Elf eyes are glowing white with excitement. She actually hugs me, and I wish I could feel it. "Tell me everything!"

"I will. Just waiting for one more person."

She gives me a curious look. "Who?"

"You'll understand when I tell you what happened."

"You're back so fast," she says.

"Yep. It was really quick." I smile at her. She smiles back.

We wait a few more minutes and I see Fangs McGore walk in the brewery. He's wearing a white cotton robe, no shoes, no gloves, no hat. I wave to him. "Over here, Fangs."

He nods at me and makes his way to join us. He stands at the end of the booth, and I know how he feels from the look on his computer-animated face. I had that look once.

"Have a seat?" I ask him.

"I'm fine."

"Okay. Well, here it goes." I tell them the story, the whole thing, leaving out Silvia's kiss on the cheek, right to when I used my Comfort Ring and got the hell out of there.

Stunned silence when I'm done, and I realize it's not just our table that's quiet. The whole brewery is. Everybody had been listening and I never noticed.

"So, yeah. I have lots of stuff of yours, Fangs. I know, I took a cheap shot, but I saw the opportunity."

"How'd he get back to you so fast? Wouldn't his grave be in Dragonbane Territory?" asked Nottingham.

"There are quests you can find in graveyards that let you get a tombstone in different ones. Hard quests," says Koolio. "He probably did them all."

"Yeah, I thought so. Where I found him, in Laninga, well, that's close to a White Elf graveyard," I say, then look at Fangs as he finally sits down.

"Oh, man. Oh, man, man. I owe you big time. You're really going to give it all back to me?"

"Everything I have that's yours, yeah. I didn't have time to get all his loot. Here, I'll open my bags. Fangs, tell me what's yours. The rest of you, if it's not Fangs', let me know if you want it. Send the bag link to the guild. Same goes for them."

In game, nobody can see your bags except Psychics, a healer class nobody has a clue as to how to unlock, unless you "open" your bags to them.

"But first, for saving my life...." I turn to Silvia, who sits next to me. "For you." I hold out the Love Lily to her and she gasps, eyes wide as springtime windows.

"For me?" she whispers.

"If you hadn't given me that blessing and had that ring, then I never would have made it."

"Well, isn't that cute," Sally says. Dammit. That girl doesn't quit. She'd had a little girl crush on me growing up that never quite died like it was supposed to.

"Sally, you'll get goodies, too," I tell her.

"Don't call me Sally anymore. Call me Good Deeds. That's my name."

"Alright, Sally."

"Oh, shut up."

I open my bags.

Fangs freaks as I trade him the items that he says are his. I have no reason not to believe him.

Some people in Lucille's come over and ask to see. Why not? I offer them a peek.

The questions from strangers start.

"Did you really defeat The Seeker?"

"He's not going to be able to kill everyone anytime and take everything anymore?"

"What's your name? How long have you been playing?"

And on it goes.

I'm not feeling it. Didn't they listen to my story? I let a helpless Nuudle get jumped and took out The Seeker with my big move after Fangs already had him down in HP. Looted, saved by a blessing, warped. It's not glamorous, but everyone is acting like it is.

Silvia puts her Love Lily on. It makes her long, blonde waves push back behind her pointed elf ear, and she's friggin' adorable.

"I'm beat, guys," I say suddenly. Too many people asking the same questions. I want the strangers to go away. I know it would be different if I'd gotten him with pure skill, and it bothers me. I want to get out of Elora and take a nap. "Everyone get screenshots of the bags?"

They had.

"Let me know what you guys want, and what the guild wants. I need to sleep for a while."

"I understand," says Silvia.

Does she? I wonder.

"Thanks for all your support. You guys are the best," I tell them, then log out in Lucille's. The game visuals and audio blip off, and I remove the headband, putting it on top of my keyboard. I rub my eyes.

My apartment is a mess. I need to clean. I've been thinking that for four months, but I always get on Elora Online instead.

I go to bed and get in dirty sheets. It's around eleven in the morning. It doesn't matter. I don't have a real schedule because I don't have that high-paying computer programming job anymore. Hated it anyway, but I'd saved, and three years ago I decided I only wanted to play Elora. It is as simple as that.

I feel myself drifting into a sweet slumber, much needed. All that built-up stress from waiting, planning, and then finally executing what was supposed to be the hardest self-given quest in game eased out of me, and I thought of Silvia with the Love Lily in her hair. I wonder what she really looks like. If I'll ever get the chance to know. What would she think of my looks? Just saying. I'm not bad, but I'm not Mr. Wonderful. I'm twenty-seven, haven't worked in three years, and can hardly keep myself bathed and my fridge stocked. What woman in her right mind would…? Then again, she's been playing Elora Online as long as I have, when the price dropped to get new gamers in. I'd always had the money for it, but Peter, or rather Jacob, really wanted to, and he wanted me to do it with him. I had no idea I'd get so involved.

And I love it.

~

I sleep for a lifetime, and wake up after dark. I feel better about destroying The Seeker, no matter how it was done. It needed to be, and maybe that was the only way it could have been executed.

I actually did it.

I take a hot shower and change into a pair of sweatpants and a tee I've only worn a couple times. Then I'm in my gaming recliner, hooking up my headset. It sends its electronic impulses to my temples, where it engages my frontal lobe and puts me in Elora Online. I watch *Ananta* destroy Elora for the fifty thousandth time. Never gets old. That summon is a badass. I yet again wonder why I never see Mystics in random dungeon runs. Or anywhere, really. Seems like I saw one when I started playing, but not sure. Legend and memory get mixed up after so long.

Next, I'm in Lucille's sitting in the booth. Some players I don't know are at the booth and look shocked that I appeared there. Yeah, it is a weird place to log out, sitting in a popular watering hole's booth. Every gamer knows you don't do that.

"Sorry, sorry," I say. "I was tired and logged here." I get up and turn.

"Wait!" the blue Mylop at the table calls to me.

I look back at him. "Yeah?"

"Are you… *the* Sid Vicious?" he asks. By his gear, I can tell he's a bard. Mylop Bard, go figure.

"What? What do you mean?"

Another in the group, a Siren who's actually a girl, says, "It is you! I saw the statue!"

"What statue?" I'm so confused.

"I put daisies at the base," she continues. "The Seeker took out my husband over a year ago and he wouldn't play again for six months. Thank you so much. You have no idea. I can't wait to tell him I actually met you."

"Oh, uh, thanks." I smile, not sure how these players I don't know have heard about the fight. And what statue? They keep staring and grinning, and I feel uncomfortable, so I bow, thinking it feels appropriate, and run out of the brewery. I get on guild chat to see if any of my buddies are on.

"Hey, what's up?" I say.

It seems like all of their voices speak at once when they hear me. It's a garbled mess. I get a text chat from Koolio. "Meet me in Luminar at the Kila Crystal. ASAP." I turn off the chaos of guild chat.

I get to Cashmere's Kila Crystal, seeing other players wave and smile at me. A few thank yous in the air. Am I famous?

I access the Kila Crystal's menu of other Kila Crystals I can get to, and choose Luminar, the capital city of Siren Territory. I eat a Breathing Berry so I can breathe underwater for an hour and use the Kila Crystal's teleportation system.

White screen with gold-and-silver sparkles, and then I'm in Luminar. I've always loved this place. Everything has a sea-blue, almost aqua hue to it. The city is built in a spiral winding upward from the Kila Crystal. The path is made of pebbled sand and shells. The structures are giant seashells, seaweed bundles hiding buildings, sunken items from centuries ago that Sirens transformed into living spaces.

I see bubbles coming out of my mouth as I look at the ancient-ruins of Siren Territory. Sirens aren't born; they "become" from the Caves of Eternity in the territory, which is why they're all female. They are the only race that can breathe under water all the time.

The Caves of Eternity are also filled with end-game dungeons, but oddly, it's where you spawn when you enter the game for the first time if you choose to be a Siren.

"Over here."

I swim to the other side of the crystal. Koolio Koolaide swims in place before me, flippers flipping. His green hair floats out all around him. He's a beauty, but he's a dude. Gotta remember that sometimes, but when he opens his mouth, it's easy.

"We have to talk," he says. "Ever since you logged out, everybody's been talking about what you did. It went server-wide. Every player in this game knows your name. No, listen. They built you a shrine in the Player Hall of Fame."

I'm stunned. "They did what? Who? How could anyone afford it?"

"They had a three-hour fundraiser and I'm betting everyone but The Seeker paid tribute to have it built. That guy has screwed up a lot of people's gaming. I wanted to get to you first. Tell you."

"Why?" I plant my feet on the sand and glittering seashells.

Koolio shakes his head, hair floating everywhere. "I heard how you told the story today. I saw the look on your face. You wanted a big victory battle story that showed off your skills as a player, didn't you?"

I look down.

"Yeah. I wanted to get to you first with all this blowing up to talk sense into you. It doesn't matter how it was done. Someone almost as bad as the historic Dragonbane Bane was taken out by you today. You did that. Come on. Don't you see what that means to all these people? Take some pride. Enjoy this. I'm telling you to enjoy all of this. Even if you didn't get your epic battle, you did an epic thing. Remember the look on that Nuudle's face when you told him he could have his stuff back?"

I pause. "Yeah."

"Can you imagine if that had been you eleven months ago? You'd think whoever did it was your savior. He's the one that got the fundraiser going. The statue was up within fifteen minutes of the fundraiser being over. And man, they must've made a fortune because wait til you see it. In the Player Hall of Fame."

"Oh, wow. Just… wow." I have no words. I'm dying to see this. It must be the statue the Siren in the brewery mentioned.

"Yes, wow. That's what I want to hear. That's how you should be feeling. Now, come on. Let's go see your shrine. Get back on guild chat and we'll invite the whole guild. It's like everybody who plays Elora is online right now because of this. I think it's the biggest thing that's ever happened since the game went live in 2020."

"I don't want to get in guild chat. It's… overwhelming right now."

"Okay, okay. Who do you want to be there when you go? And you're going right now."

I think about it. I don't know. "The usuals, I guess. And Silvia."

"Well, of course Silvia." He actually winks at me, looking like a true siren from Greek mythology. "I'll message them. Give me a min."

His face goes into automode while he accesses menus. The way the game interface works is that you look at different areas of the virtual interface to make things happen. It's weird at first, but you get used to it fast. You don't even notice if someone is accessing menus or making notes because the game is smooth at covering up the RL eye motions. If you're going to lower your vision setting to see RL or you're going to be doing a lot of things, like Koolio is now, your face does the automode. Still animated and blinking and breathing, but no real expression on his face.

"Alright, they are on their way. We've been waiting and waiting for you to come back."

"Seriously?"

"Hell, yeah. Now, let's use the Kila to get to Sheala."

Sheala is the other capital of White Elf Territory and holds the Player Hall of Fame at the top of an Elven tower on a cliff overlooking the Marana Sea.

"Alright." I'm excited. Really excited. I'm glad Koolio got to me first. He has a way of making things right, good.

We warp through the Kila Crystal to Sheala. This Elven city is enormous. Lots of white marble and wildflower-lined walkways. The path we take up to the Player Hall of Fame is a wide, white marble spiraling path upward around a tower. Round and round we go. My anticipation grows the closer we get, and then we're at the top. The ceiling is domed and painted with a mystical mural of Elven artistry. Huge marble columns hold it all together.

I peer inside, wondering where my statue is, what it looks like. What it says.

"Sid!" I turn to my right. Silvia runs up to me, still wearing her lily. I hope she never takes it off. "Thanks for inviting me. I can imagine how overwhelming all this is to log in to. The story is everywhere, spread to every message board and chat room and guild chat in game within an hour."

"Damn," I say.

"Good Deeds, Raging, Peter, and Nottingham are already looking at the shrine, waiting for you. They've been here since it was erected. It's so funny. Peter keeps telling all the visitors leaving gifts that you two are best friends. He's so proud of you."

"We are best friends. He's trying to make me look good."

"That's what good best friends do." She grins and takes my hand, the one now wearing my old knuckles. "Let's go!" She pulls me into the shrine. I glance back at Koolio. He's smirking and nodding, arms folded like he knows all about it.

He probably does.

There are lots of shrines in the Player Hall of Fame. I've been here a bunch of times to read the stories of what these players did. The statues are gold, and can be as small as the player himself, or as large as three times the size of the player. Elora has been online for fifteen years, and I used to like to come here and wonder about its beginnings, who these first epic players were so long ago to be made the first of the Player Hall of Fame. The stories were great, but I didn't know a lot of what they referred to, especially if it involved other players.

"This way," Silvia calls back to me, glancing at me with a grin, tugging me along.

I toe the edge of the magic circle in front of the entrance. It's like a mirror, but your hand or foot passes through it. Sometimes players jump in it, and they hover at mid-waist, saying they feel like they're in space. The inscription circling above it reads, "A Link to the Past." It's a homage to Zelda and just a cool thing that makes you more excited to go inside. You're about to see history, a link to the past, inside. Stupid, I know, but I'm feeling pretty high.

The three of us go through a few halls of shrines, moonlight shining in from the open archways of the marble tower, glinting on the golden figures, making them gods.

We get to a large room on the western-most side, and Silvia leads me to the farthest arch overlooking the water.

That can't be... no. That can't be my shrine. I see ahead of me just the one, and it's enormous. Easily the biggest in the Hall of Fame. It reaches all the way to the painted, domed ceiling. Once upon it, I can't even acknowledge my friends congratulating me, nor the other players giving blessed flowers and other offerings to the shrine.

I see me, standing five times bigger than I am in game, with the pose I make just as I use *Going Feral*. But there's another figure. It's The Seeker, and he's face down on the ground before my figure, tail high in the air. He's only regular player-sized. Fangs isn't in the shrine. I move through the crowd to read the shrine's inscription, done on a golden block.

It tells the story exactly how it happened, but it demonizes The Seeker—and, well, he was a demon—and makes me a hero. A goddamn savior and legend.

The players in the crowded hall of my shrine recognize me soon enough. They thank me, tell me their personal stories of what The Seeker had done to them or someone they cared about. I am so brave, they say. I am so determined, they say. What a good heart I must have, they say.

I have to admit, in those moments, my attitude changes. I *did* do something good. Yes, I did. I mean, look at the shrine! For all of time while Elora Online is online, players throughout gameplay will see this and I won't be forgotten.

I have a nagging doubt I don't want to think about, but I'm not one to shy away from facing truths. The Seeker won't let this go.

He'll do something. I'll have to start tracking him on message boards and through hearsay again, just to be ready... in case. Who knows what he has saved in his vaults in his hidden mansions?

I think, though, that I can beat him in a real, fair match. That's the truth. Otherwise, I never would have even considered my revenge mission.

CHAPTER 4: GAME OVER

My new attitude on my kill feels good, and I do keep a check on rumors of The Seeker, read message boards, check with players in-the-know about these sorts of things. The Seeker hasn't been seen or heard from since the defeat.

It makes me uneasy, but at the same time, I'm having too much fun. I'm so rich it's stupid. Whatever the guild and friends couldn't use, I put on the AH and made forty billion. I have a mansion in every territory with stat boosters on tap in every one for my friends and guildies to use.

I play with the best dungeon runners in game now, and bring along my buddies who want to come. Silvia is a great dungeon healer, selfless to a fault sometimes from healing everybody before herself to keep from getting hate, and often runs them with me.

Nothing new has happened there. You know what I mean. We hang out a lot and did have a nice time talking at the Sheala Shipwreck in Siren Territory a week after the big fight. She opened up to me, telling me that her older sister used to play Elora Online with her when the game first launched fifteen years ago, but committed suicide while in game soon after starting to play, leaving a cryptic note. She'd taken a bunch of prescription sleeping pills, logged in, and just did it. Silvia said she herself had been fifteen at the time.

Her voice had cracked as she talked about it, and I had put my arm around her shoulders even though she couldn't feel it. Just was natural. In RL, she's just a few years older than me. I never knew that.

I can't imagine what that must have been like for her. I wonder if she keeps playing Elora Online as a way to somehow feel close to her sister. She had said to me twice they were like twins, even had a secret language being one year apart, as she spilled her most personal feelings about it. I was surprised she felt comfortable enough to talk so openly about it with me. I didn't know what to do, but I don't think she wanted me to do anything but listen and understand, which I did and try my best to do. Since then, Silvia has been on my mind more than ever.

Back to the meat. Now I have incredible gear. My STR is 413 from the help I get with missions and quests to boost the stat. I have items that enhance all my moves, and the confidence in fights to be a wicked force of destruction. I do serious damage. Like I always wanted.

I'll keep this short, because I still don't understand what happened to me. I was happy, I was a beloved player. I gave gifts to everyone. I played the AH like Nottingham taught me now that I had money. Made more money. Loved being a Maniac more than ever. Built another mansion in the black volcanos of Dragonbane Territory. And Silvia and I worked great together. It was a slow build, but there was magic.

It was all so good for a few months. So very good.

Then it happened. The thing I'm still trying to understand.

I'm in my gaming recliner playing late one night, running Kakalanee, an end-game dungeon in Dragonbane Territory. With Silvia, no less. I'm on fire. I destroy everything. I save other players. I own this game.

In RL, late this night, I have a physical sensation. Like I said before, there are no physical sensations in Elora Online. I feel something cold press against my forehead. I reach up out of instinct, not even adjusting my visual, but before my fingers can touch whatever is on my forehead, I hear a booming sound so loud my eardrums must be bleeding, and at the same time feel incredible pain in my head… and then Kakalanee Dungeon goes away, fades to black.

The pain leaves. Stops abruptly.

Blackness, just blackness is all I can see. It's all I can hear, too, if that makes sense. My interface is gone.

Then, in the distance, glowing red. It comes closer until I make out letters, and finally, they are close enough to read. Red letters on never-ending black. "Game Over." They get so close that they fill my vision. I swear I can taste them, feel their shapes, have empathy for their color. Blood red, glowing. *Game Over.*

There is no game over in Elora. You respawn at a graveyard if you die, find your body as a ghost, and resurrect. Nothing killed me in the dungeon, either.

I have no idea what has just happened to me. Am I playing Elora still? Is this some part of the high-end dungeon? Some secret quest?

But the cold thing on my forehead. I didn't make that up. The pain, the sound. The sound was with my real ears, not the headband implanting the audio.

What has happened?

The letters fade away to black melting into black. I close my eyes. Wait. Count to five.

I open them and see.

CHAPTER 5: DARK WORLD

Sure, I open my eyes, but I feel more than see. I feel... Elora. Smell her soft, moist, foresty scent. I feel her air, and even through the haze of looking at a rainy, gothic graveyard with red lightning streaking through the night clouds, I smell her. The rain makes me wet, and I feel a chill.

My interface is back.

What has happened to me?

I feel strange. I reach up to take off my headband, but I only use my character's hand and pluck at my hair. I can feel it. It's long, no horns on my head. Why can't I use my RL hands?

I turn on guild chat. Nothing. I'm not in a guild anymore.

Where am I and what has happened to me?

Why am I feeling Elora with my senses and actually getting wet from a storm?

I stifle the panic. I have to act, I just know it. I have this general feeling that's what I need to do, and I don't know if it's because of the panic or in spite of it.

I wipe rainwater from my eyes as a burst of thunder claps my ears. I look around.

Yes, this is a very gothic graveyard. The tombs have gargoyles, twisted characters of all races forever honored in stone statues on some of them. All around the medium-sized graveyard is a dense wood, only blocked from overtaking the cemetery by a black, wrought-iron fence.

It's so dark. I can hardly make anything out. I access system controls in my interface, but they won't open. I can't lighten up my visuals.

I walk, just to move, in the direction I had been facing when I opened my eyes after the bizarre event I can't explain. I wipe my eyes continually, trying to see through the downpour of rain. Ahead of me, near two gray graves that are simply arched, I spy an NPC Nuudle named Calla holding an umbrella. Her back is to me. Maybe she holds a clue as to what is going on.

I reach her. "Hey, hey you?"

She turns. "Why, hello there! I'm so very happy to meet you! Welcome to Dark World—Total Immersion Mode!"

"What is this place? What happened to me?"

"Welcome to Dark World!" she says again. She's my height, oddly, black-skinned, has silver hair down to her waist, and big, violet eyes. She has a Nuudle cryptic marking on her forehead, one I've not seen on a Nuudle before. It looks like a cross between a bird and a dragon, artful and colored yellow. "Come under my umbrella with me. We will begin your transformation!"

"What transformation?" The umbrella certainly looks inviting.

"It's the beginning of Total Immersion! How very exciting for you! I'm so very happy you are here. Come, come!" She gestures for me to join her.

The rain does suck, and I can feel goose bumps all over. Whatever is going on, the umbrella, whatever comfort it might offer, is too tempting and I step under it.

A blue-tinted bubble suddenly sprouts up around us. "What's that?" I ask, pointing at the bubble.

"I'm so very glad to have met you, but I don't even know what to call you! Let's pick a name now, okay?"

"I have a name." I try stepping back out of the bluish bubble, but it's like a wall. "Why can't I get out?"

"Because you don't have a name or class yet, silly thing!"

What? "I'm Sid Vicious, I'm a Maniac. Come on. What the hell is going on?"

She shakes her little head and holds a finger over her pink lips. "Now, now. No need to use foul language. You should be happy! You get to start all over! How many people get to do that? Now, in Dark World, you have one name. You can pick your first name or last from Elora. What will you choose?"

"What do you mean? I'm not in Elora?"

"We'll discuss that at another time. You are in Dark World for now. That's all you need to concentrate on."

"What is Dark World? What is this 'Total Immersion'?"

She shakes her head again. "So many questions. You'll find your answers once you begin your new adventure! Now, which name? Sid or Vicious?"

"I don't want to do this, I want explanations!" I'm angry, frustrated, confused.

"It's quite simple. You're either Sid or Vicious!" She grins and winks.

"Fine!" I yell at her to be heard over thunder. "Fine, I'm Sid. That make you happy?"

Her violet eyes widen. "Yes! Yes, it makes me very happy! You are Sid!" She grins again. "Now, to pick your class. Here, I'll make a mirror so you can customize your appearance."

"My appearance?"

She waves her wand and silver spouts out the tip.

Calla casts Mirror.

A shining, silver-gilded mirror appears next to me and I turn to look into it.

Oh, my god. I'm a Nuudle. A friggin' Nuudle! "What the fuck?"

She pats my shoulder. I feel it, a dainty pressure. "What did I say about the language? A true Nuudle doesn't say such things as every word and word placement has special meaning. Look, look! What hair will you pick? What color skin? Oh, and the marking!"

I glare at my image. I'm wearing a white cotton robe, have the standard Nuudle template anyone is given to begin making their character. "I don't want to be a Nuudle."

"But this is Dark World, where you are flipped! This is chosen for you. Someday, you'll see why. Or maybe now! But you can't change who you are." She shifts and puts her hand on her hip. "I think you'd look nice with black hair. Or purple. Or green!"

I don't know what to do. I think for a moment, staring into the mirror. A Nuudle! I hate Mage classes. I've never been one in this game, but have tried it in other MMOs. Not for me. Boring. I'm a melee fighter by nature.

And I'm so damn small!

"Take me back to Elora."

"You are in Dark World! You really should be more excited. Very few are given the chance to be in Total Immersion mode."

"But what is it?"

"You ask too many questions. Where's the fun in knowing everything? Now, select your image. You will make such a cute Nuudle!" She sways back and forth, smiling up at the red lightning crossing the sky.

I don't know what else to do, so I access my menu. Black hair, curly, down to my shoulders. That's fine. Silvery skin. Sure. Blue eyes. Man, I miss my dragon eyes. Nuudle eyes are big, round, and have enormous pupils. I make my Nuudle skinny.

"Very good!" says Calla. "Now, which mark for your forehead? This is *very* important!"

"Why?"

"Because it demonstrates your class, silly. Don't you know anything about Nuudles?"

"The marking has nothing to do with class."

She looks to the side. "Well, maybe not in Elora, but it sure does in Dark World."

"In that case, don't you think I should pick my class before choosing a marking?" I say.

"Well, now that's the attitude! Let's pick your class, then."

I go through my menu of choices. All the usual ones are there. I scroll to my stats.

Holy crap. All my stats are at 1.

Holy crap.

Well, INT, CON, and MND are at 15. Those are the Nuudle starting stats. If I want any chance here at all, I'll have to pick a mage job so I'll at least have some more stats. I quickly check my bags.

Empty. Not even a weapon.

Crap, crap, crap, crap, crap.

"Something the matter, Sid? You're taking an awfully long time." She puts her hand on her hip again, tilting the umbrella even though the blue bubble keeps rain far away.

"I have nothing! No stats! No weapon! What do you think is the matter?"

"Hush, hush now. It's okay, you can take your time."

"I don't want to be a mage. I want my old character back, my Dragonbane Maniac. I can't be a mage just for the stat boost."

"Well, that's awfully close-minded of you."

"Oh, shut up."

"There you go again. So rude! Nuudles have more class than that." She shakes her head in disapproval.

"Okay, fine. What class do *you* think I should be, then?" I ask. My irritability and confusion fight each other.

She taps her pink lips. "You know, I think you would make the best Mystic I've ever seen!"

I glare at her. "Mystic? Mystic! It's not even listed as an option, stupid NPC."

"Hey! I'm not stupid! I'm a high-level teacher in the Temple of Nuudlel. I just happen to know you'd make a great Mystic! The Mystic to tower over all Mystics!"

"Mystic. How am I supposed to select it when it isn't even an option?"

She leans in toward me. "Look again," she whispers.

I check the class options again. Lo and behold, Mystic is listed now, in light purple italics. Wow, I've found out how to unlock the ever-elusive Mystic class! I must be in Elora, some secret part of the game.

Sure, a secret part where I can feel… everything.

"Okay," I say. "Sure, I'll be a Mystic. Why not?" I need the stat boost, and I admit, curiosity has set in. Mystic? Really?

Would I someday be able to summon *Ananta*? By God.

"Excellent choice! I told you I wasn't stupid. I can see right through you, Sid. Now, you have a choice between four markings. Usually I offer three, but for you, I offer four. Here."

My interface shows me in the mirror with four different marks on my forehead. One captures my interest right away. It is a blue serpent, and *Ananta*'s made of blue serpent heads. "That one," I say, and point at myself in the mirror.

"Wise choice. Maybe you aren't stupid, either." She laughs wildly. "Here, a gift in your inventory. Also, check your quest log. I have given you your first Mystic quest. Use the rune tattoo on your left hand for the quest. You'll figure out how. May the blessings of Mystic and summons follow you, and be sure to make friends. They will help you more than you know, more than they did in your life before."

"What do you mean, my life before?"

But the blue bubble around us fades, as does Calla. "Don't forget to look behind you." She keeps smiling and waving as she disappears into nothing, and the rain pelts me.

I'm alone in a storm in an unknown graveyard. I look at my left palm. There's a marking of five men clothed in furs and baring horns, faces shadowy and twisted from untold lifetimes of deviant being.

I access my inventory to find a Shaman Stick, a weapon, and equip it. I don't know if it does anything special. No stats on it. I check my stat menu next. INT and MND are now 20, and CON is 32. DEF went up to 5, ATT +2.

Next, I look at my quest log.

Battle the Counts of Hell is the only quest in my log. I have to fight them to claim them to be able to summon them.

Calla said to look behind me, which I do. I read the names on the two black marble tombstones there.

Sid Vicious, one reads, with an etching of my old character's image on it, and beside it, I read *The Seeker*, with his image carved into the rock.

What the hell happened to me? What is this place? What am I to do?

CHAPTER 6: CHANGED AND THE SAME

First, I need to figure out where the hell I am. I open my map. My icon is in Sunset Forest, the supposedly haunted area between White Elf Territory and Nuudle Territory. Full of undead mobs. But it's not called Sunset Forest. It's called Forest of the Dead.

That's not the only difference this map has from Elora's map. Yes, the world is shaped the same, but some names are different. One stands out to me in particular. The Fallen Wall of Bane is simply the Wall of Bane. The Red Snow Mountains, the pass between Dragonbane Territory and White Elf Territory, is called Snowy Mountains. The legend in Elora was that the Red Snow Mountains were called that because of Bane's battle with the White Elves there when he tried to conquer White Elf Territory. That's where Kane defeated him, after allying with the Nuudles and White Elves. They hadn't done magical work together in 1,400 years at that point because it always ended in destruction.

The White Elves cast a spell over the mountains after the battle, which they won, so that no Dragonbane could ever cross it again. The barrier spell kept snow from falling onto the mountaintops, keeping the snow red from blood spilled in the historic battle.

All the capitals of the territories are the same, except that Kane, the capital of Dragonbane Territory, is called Bane. Is Dark World somehow part of the past of Elora? I seem to be where... or when... things that are world-building pieces of story in Elora are now fact. It doesn't make sense to me.

The quest for the *Counts of Hell* is marked on my map at a cave near Kleeple, the capital of Nuudle Territory.

How am I supposed to get through this damn pitch-black forest and to Nuudle Territory with nothing but a Shaman Stick with no stats?

I access my friends list, knowing nobody will be there, and I'm right. Blank menu. I can't even get my keyboard to send a message to someone I know... I have no RL hands.

Wait. I can access my interface with my eye movements. I am doing that, right? Suddenly, I'm not so sure.

This is too weird, too bizarre. What is happening to me?

The map is getting soaked, and I'm freezing in this weather. More thunder overhead, and then a spider web of red lightning follows. I look up at it and sigh in frustration.

Something at the far edge of the dark graveyard catches my eye.

I look to the corner of the wrought iron fence and make out what looks like a Siren player with silver hair and light gold skin watching me. Her name over her head is Anella. She's wearing black gear and robes, with the silver hair spilling out in front of her from beneath a hood. I've never seen that gear in game before.

Should I approach her? Tentatively, I wave.

She just keeps staring at me.

I slowly walk through the cemetery, bare feet getting soaked and water inching up the hems of my cotton robe. Anella watches, and as I get to the fence, she hops backward over it and ducks behind a tree. I get the sense she's timid, but I need help.

"Hello?" I call to her. "Can you help me?"

I move slowly as I climb the fence. My wet robe catches on a post, and I fall flat on my face in the mud on the other side.

I hear her giggle, and I look up. She's peeking around an enormous tree trunk and covers her mouth, and then disappears behind it. I get to my feet, wiping cold, wet mud from my face, and say, "Hey, hey, Anella."

She pokes her head from around another tree beside the one she had been behind. How did she do that?

"Can you help me?" I say softly. My instincts tell me to be wary. Or it could be that everything is so strange that I'm, well, terrified. I can feel everything, and if she attacks me, will I feel pain, too?

I'm betting I will.

"Are you Mystic?" she whispers.

"Yeah, yeah, I am now."

She smiles slightly and approaches me. "Not just anybody gets the option to choose Mystic. Nobody has that marking on his forehead. You're like me."

"What do you mean?" She's standing right in front of me now, and I'm afraid of the attack that might come.

"I am The Hidden, and that quest line only is an option for certain players. People. Situations." She reaches down and rubs some mud off my cheek. "You poor soul. Nothing makes sense, does it?"

"No. Can you help me? Explain what's happened here?" I rub water from my eyes. "Where am I?"

She backs away, eyes wide. "I can't help you. Not right now. You'll have to figure it all out like the rest of us."

"Why? I mean, if you know, why not just tell me?"

"It's… complicated." She waves her gold, webbed hands in the air. I get the feeling she's a little off in the head, but wicked intelligent.

Anella casts Shielding from Horrors.

A greenish hue of air surrounds me in a bubble. I reach out and touch it. It feels thick and slimy. The rain stops pelting me, and I realize she's cast a Hidden spell that protects me somehow.

"This will last for three hours. You will be able to get to where you need to go. And one more thing, one more gift, if you will."

"Thank you, but I need help figuring out how to get back to the Elora I know, the character I know." I'm grateful the rain no longer soaks me, but I can't understand why she won't simply explain what is going on.

She swirls her hands around again and they glow white. "Hold out your Shaman Stick."

I do.

Anella ignites a Lightning Shard.

Anella uses Enchant Weapon on Shaman Stick.

"That's all I can do for now. Good luck, Sid. Make good friends." She backs away.

"Wait, wait! Come back!" I follow her, but her eyes widen and she turns, using something like Blessed's Swift Feet.

Anella casts Scatter.

Her figure zooms away into the trees and splits into many images of her until they are all gone. I have nobody to follow.

Damnit, what the hell?

I look at my Shaman Stick, which now glows a soft eggshell white with little sparkles of silver dancing around the crooked, pale, notched wood. I look in my menu to see what enchantment she put on it.

Shaman Stick is enchanted with White Lightning, causing lightning damage to target equal to ATT stat.

I have a weapon. Wow. She really helped me out. I can do 2 extra damage every time I use the Shaman Stick.

If I'm remembering correctly, these woods are full of the lifeless. But they are high-stat mobs. Dangerous. One hit from them and I'd be back in the graveyard. Or would I?

I know nothing.

I am grateful to be shielded from the rain, though, and wonder why Anella didn't have one of her own. She'd been getting soaked, but maybe here, in Dark World, a Siren enjoys being in the rain. Maybe it feels good. It's an idea, that's all, but it settles my panic some to think, to figure.

I look at the map again. I'm going to have to hustle to make it to Kleeple, where outside I can farm the easy mobs and buy some real gear with what I earn.

I look at my Mystic moves.

Ability List for Mystic:

Spontaneity—Gives target random buff. Wears off in two minutes. Cumulative.

Special Ability: Seizure—Invokes summon's strongest attack. Cast once an hour. Some items or gear may enhance this ability. Summon's Seizure attack will appear in menu or answer to command once Seizure is activated.

Great. These are useless. But once an hour, not once a week? Incredible.

May as well try the one move I have and see how good it is. Can't use Seizure without a summon.

Sid casts Spontaneity. Sid gains +4 DEF.

A purple swirl comes out of my chest and twists around me. I feel stronger. I physically feel stronger. How the hell—?

My defense went up 4? I check my stats. Yep, there it is, with a timer counting down from two minutes. Because I can't cast the same spell twice in a row, or make the same move, I hit a tree with my Shaman Stick, and a bolt of lightning shoots out, marking the tree. I cast Spontaneity again, and this time it gives me +2 STR. I feel stronger, still, and an odd sensation of confidence. It's amazing.

Not too shabby. Throw in some decent gear, and I might have a chance with these *Counts of Hell*.

I have to think positively.

I have no choice.

I enter a weak trail into the forest, leaving the graveyard. I glance back one last time at mine and The Seeker's tombstones, where the rain almost seems to fall the hardest. Just then, a streak of red lightning jolts from the sky and hits right in between them. The sound is so loud I jump.

Creepy shit.

I turn and go onto the trail. It's going to be a long walk.

I keep my eyes open for undead, wishing I could see behind me. A few Skeletons chase me here and there, but I'm able to outrun them. Not even going to attempt fighting. I'm still too scared of what it will feel like to be hit. My glowing Shaman Stick helps light the way some, and I'm grateful for that. The trail takes me to a split in the dark forest, where two paths branch out. One leads north, and the other south. That's the one I pick, hoping it will lead me to the Pass of The Black, the pass made by an ancient Black Nuudle who wanted to map Sunset Forest. Or the Forest of the Undead now, I guess. The pass is marked on my map. I wonder how long that pass has been here if I really am in Elora's distant past.

My robes are starting to dry out, but my feet ache. The forest on foot goes on forever, and outrunning mobs leaves me breathless and achy. How long will this trail go on? The forest is known for magical mishaps, supposedly caused by haunted dead souls. What if I'm walking in circles?

I keep an eye on my drying map. It looks like I'm heading for the pass, and it might take another twenty minutes to get there. On I go.

One of the things that makes Elora Online so different and special is that there are mysteries in the game nobody could ever explain. No one could find answers on the Web, like how to unlock classes like Mystic and The Hidden, Anella's class. It's a healing class, solo class. Most important stat is supposedly CRG. I've never even met one. Also, there are hidden quests, and as I've learned, hidden parts of the game entirely.

Again, the questions rage through my head as I catch my breath from running from a Wakened Tree. Where am I? When am I? What happened to me? Where is my headband? Why can't I access my RL body? Do I have eyes and are they in control of my interface? It feels like it, but it kind of doesn't.

What was that feeling of cold hardness on my forehead, the loud bang, the pain, the *Game Over* I saw?

Am I dead? I can think, feel, breathe. I can't be dead. Has my consciousness somehow been put into the game? There has to be a solid reason for all this, but I don't know what it is. I have to go with the flow, stay cool, watch, check out this Dark World. The questions bounce around my brain, but there's one thing I do know.

I have no clue.

Finally, I reach the Pass of The Black and ease down the black-fenced pass warily. But nothing happens. Thank God.

I emerge into grassy, lush jungle as daylight starts filtering in from the east through hazy clouds. There's no rain here. I check the counter on the protective shield Anella had cast on me. It has two hours left.

The fields are full of low-to mid-stat Nuudle Territory mobs, like Mad Mushrooms and Daisy Chains, both of which would knock me out in one move. I sneak around them and have to outrun a few who detect me. I keep my map handy and finally hit a road leading to the Temple of Nuudlel, where the Nuudles study their magic and craft one-cast spells. Awesome library, if you're into that kind of thing. I've enjoyed it at times. I might have to consider that.

The roads are almost always safe. I'm grateful to be on one.

It takes about fifteen minutes of walking to get to the temple. I'm astounded by how different it looks than in Elora. In Elora, it's a shining, black, towering temple, jagged and elegant, with *Ananta* on top carved out of black rock. The Nuudles mined the obsidian from the cliffs to the east, where they block the Endless Sea. It's fantastic from afar. Here, it's in the same place, but it has golden gilding all over, and etched golden runes of magic on the shining walls and towers. Nuudles use runes and words for their magic.

I'm heading to it, but suddenly, as I see a player with one name run out of the entrance I face and invoke a Speedy Turtle mount, I get scared. I don't think I should go in that temple. Not yet. I think it's best to circle around the temple and hit the road to Kleeple. All roads in Nuudle Territory end at the temple, so I just have to dodge mobs to get a couple roads over, which I do.

First thing I'm buying after I get some cash is a pair of comfortable shoes. Don't care what stats they have. My feet are killing me.

I cross the long, sandy road toward Kleeple and can see it on the horizon finally when I'm atop the Grassy Knoll. Smoke billows up from the potion furnaces, just like in Elora. But even Kleeple from afar seems different than in Elora. Newer, more bustling, more exotic. The jungle flora seems bigger, brighter. I see a lot of one-named characters on mounts, flying or riding in and out of Kleeple's main entrance, which is a wide, sandy path with enormous black wrought iron gates that are always open. They are also gilded with gold, like the temple, but they aren't in the Elora I know.

A few of the players wave to me. A couple laugh at me as I enter the Nuudle capital. What must I look like? I don't even have a house of my own to look in a mirror. Covered in a damp, muddy cotton robe, no head gear, no shoes or gloves. Never had to clean myself in game before. Not even a Comfort Ring on my grimy finger. Greenish smog surrounding me doing God knows what that was cast on me by a Hidden. I must look like a little kid whose parents never take care of him. Nuudle, why?

The paths are more overgrown here in Kleeple than in Elora's Kleeple. I avoid eye-contact with others and head for the Kleeple magistrate's mansion. I want to see the NPC magistrate, hear what he says.

I pause right there in the path of sand, with a wide, purple flower hanging over my little head.

Maybe I should find out who the magistrate is. If I'm remembering Nuudle history right, in the time of Bane, an NPC named Jarana was magistrate. She joined the Mylop in overcoming Bane, talked the White Elves into helping.

Oh yeah. And the Sirens stayed out of the whole thing.

I should approach a player and simply ask who the magistrate is.

I admit I hate this. I don't want to be a newbie again. I don't want any other players to see how I suck here in Dark World. Plus, there's that fear of being attacked, the pain that might or might not come with it.

Nearby, there used to be Plapy's Playhouse, which was a stat-boosting watering hole. Surely someone in there will help me.

I go around the corner of the high-hedged path, but Plapy's Playhouse is a white stucco round building with a sign I can't read. It's in Nuudle. Runes.

I sigh, grip my Shaman Stick, and pull open the door.

Inside, bright morning light spills into a white-walled round room with an oak wood bar on the far wall. The mahogany tables scattered around are full of players, all with one name. They turn and look at me, and then go back about their business.

I look around, assessing who best to approach. Mostly, the place is full of Nuudles. It's pretty small in here for another race to be hanging around.

I spy a Mylop in dark heavy armor fighting gear, in a corner sipping a DEF brew, Nuudle Nerves Nicety. Sure, he's a Mylop, but he has black, forward-bending horns and black spikes around his eyes.

Fighting classes always put me at ease, and curiosity overwhelms me as I take in his appearance. Mylop don't have horns or spikes. They are smooth, big lizard men. This guy is dark green, and his gear is amazing. Shining black tank armor like a White Knight might wear at high levels, but smoke-like tendrils ease off the surfaces. His headgear is a chain-metal cowl made of the same metal as his body gear. His HP bar is dense with segments. See, the HP bars are chopped into little segments to show party members' stat strength. The more little blue segments you have in your HP bar, the higher stat you are all around. This Mylop's stats all around are very high.

Before I think about it, I examine him. Days is his name. I have to see what he's wearing and if there are any clues as to why he looks so different.

Dark Knight. He's a Dark Knight? Days is a Dark Knight, the tank class nobody can get?

Oh, crap. Now he's looking at me, knowing I examined him. He would have been notified in his game interface.

I freeze, not knowing what to do.

He waves. Smiles.

My shoulders relax and the air runs out of me. I weakly wave back.

"Come on, then!" he calls out to me.

The Nuudle with him takes one look at me and snickers. She's tan with a lightning bolt symbol on her forehead, and wears her blue hair in pigtails. Name's Simple. The Black. Not too much lower a level than Days, judging by her gear on the outside. Especially her rings. Only goldsmiths wear stuff like that. High level, craft specific.

I make my way across the tiled floor to the far corner where Days the Mylop and his comrade, Simple the Nuudle, sit on the same side of the bench with their backs to the door. But of course, in my case, they'd turned and not taken their eyes off me since I examined Days.

"Come on around to the other side and sit down," Days says, his voice curious. I feel more relaxed still and collapse onto the smooth, mahogany bench. Instinctively, I rub my aching, grimy feet with even filthier hands.

"Would you look at you!" says Simple. An actual girl player by her voice. "Mystic. How'd you get that gig?"

"How do you—oh. The marking."

"That's not just a random Mystic marking," Days explains. "That's *Ananta*'s marking. Never seen a Mystic with *Ananta*'s marking. You?" He turns to Simple.

She sips from her MND stat boost goblet slowly. "No. And that's common knowledge. Hey, who gave you the smudging?"

"The what?"

They look at each other and shrug, then look back at me. Days says, "The smudge, the protection. That's an expensive scroll. The green foggy shit."

"Oh. Oh!" I tell them about Anella, but leave out her name and class. Say she did something, but I couldn't remember what. I keep things very simple. I'm dying to ask questions, get every answer available to me, but these are high-stat players. The "smudging," as they called it, is wearing off, and if it had offered me protection against getting my ass physically harmed in the most painful ways, then I don't want to say any more than is necessary just in case I'm reading these two wrong. They might give me a nice eyepatch reason if they feel like it.

Here, it's like anything goes, everything is real, and you are completely alone without even a notebook to collect your thoughts in.

No time for that, anyway.

Days nods throughout my explanation of the disappearing Anella, and then asks, "So you are new to Dark World as of about four hours ago?"

I look down at the polished dark wood table and mutter, "Yeah."

"A Mystic with the only *Ananta* symbol I've ever heard of," Days says sarcastically.

"Sorry, it was rude of me to examine you. I've never seen a Mylop who looks like you, or a Dark Knight." I slide off the bench and stand.

"Wait!" Days grabs my upper arm and I meet his eyes. We're eye-level, with his sitting and my standing. "Don't get your G-String up your twat. It's weird. That's all. Come on, sit back down. I'll buy you a beer." He smiles at me, but whenever a Mylop smiles, it just looks scary, especially on him.

"Yeah," says Simple. "I'm sorry. We got off on the wrong foot. It's been a long time since I've met someone fresh out of the cemetery." She smiles too, and hers makes me more at ease. Her purple eyes glow slightly and then she points back to my bench with them. "Go on. Have a seat. And a beer. Maybe I'll throw this garbage Mind drink out and have a beer, too. Not as good as a Siren Ale, but Nuudles have second best." She hops up and goes to the counter, where several Nuudle barmaid NPCs wait.

Days turns to me. "I know you have no idea what's going on, but I'm going to get you moving fast. If you don't, that's your fault. A Mystic with *Ananta*'s glowing mark on his Nuudle forehead? You're a target. Hey, what were you before?" He leans in toward me.

"Dragonbane. Dragonbane Maniac. You?" It seems like the right thing to ask.

"White Elf Blessed. Guy char. Wanted to hit on all the girls playing White Elf healers. Learned later that was the Dragonbane guys' job." He laughs and now his grin isn't so scary. I can't help but smile back.

"There's nothing like beer in Dark World. Nothing like it. Once Simple gets back, I want to hear your story. If you'll tell it? And don't leave a thing out. Beer's on me the whole time." Days waves his clawed, dark hands. "Look, I have a good feeling about you. It was a Mystic who first helped me when I found myself in a Mylop graveyard. Deep in the caverns, too. No light there. But suddenly, I could see in the dark when she summoned *Varengan*. Her name is Shell, a Siren. She's in our guild now, too." He grins again. "Enough about me. Here's Simple with our beer."

Simple places three foamy pints in front of us, the hourglass-shaped mugs frosted over and with glitter sparkling off slightly smooth white.

Days says, "Go ahead, there's nothing like it that you've ever known."

CHAPTER 7: BATTLE OF THE COUNTS OF HELL

I can taste it, and it's heaven on earth. Real beer, high quality! I can taste as well as feel here, and I can smell the alcohol in the brew.

Instinctively, I invite them to a party and we chat within the party group, unheard from others, with a quick eye movement from me through my party menu interface making it so—or did I use my eyes? Enough of that for now. They smirk at each other as though my obviously badly hidden paranoia of what it will feel like when I actually get hit with a crossbow/spike/tiger claws/lightning bolt is so typical when I mention it. Like I will have anything to say that they haven't heard before. Thought themselves. Maybe I won't. Still, this makes me feel better, and they comply, and there it is. I don't ask about if I'll feel actual pain. I don't want to know. Not yet.

I tell them everything about my experiences with The Seeker. Right up to where I saw his tomb next to mine. I leave out everyone else. I do tell about the shrine. It's the only good point of the story. Even when I speak of Silvia giving me the blessing, I tell them it was a Blessed White Elf guildmate with the Gilded White Elf Ring.

I don't hide how everything went down with The Seeker. By now, you have to realize that's not me. Of course, who doesn't like being appreciated? The thing is, I want to have that from merit. If I know it isn't, then it's shit.

The shrine is different because I saw how many people were relieved that I had done it. They all knew how. They didn't care. I saw my efforts' merits in what I had done, not in a well-fought, skilled and successful battle, which is what a shrine should be built for, but merits in how players repeatedly told me thank you, bemoaned their stories, and I listened carefully to every one. I got pissed all over again each time for them. It was a good deed.

Some part of me still feels like I'm hunting The Seeker, and knowing about that tombstone, well, I feel pretty sure that means The Seeker, now Seeker for sure, is in Dark World too, and the game is making our fates intertwine for... what?

I don't know.

My God, Days and Simple aren't kidding about the Nuudle beer. Light as champagne and bitter enough to dry the sweat off you midday in the jungle. I've never been physically affected by any stat boosts I've taken in game, but I feel this, and yes, it's like beer, but colors stand out. My body feels good, no pain in my feet. Days and Simple's faces move and swirl as I drag on with my story of eleven months of hunting The Seeker. I've gone back to that part of the story for some reason, and I'm not sure why.

Days and Simple want to show me the cliff off Kleeple over Paradise Sea for the upcoming sunset. Sunset?

Days carries me on his back. My feet are grateful. He tells me I'm a gross mess and laughs. I can't walk if I want to from the odd beer.

None of this is a big deal. Right?

I can't wait to see the sunset.

Kleeple Cliff is a flower garden in Dark World, but all the flowers, like fat orchids, glow their unique colors ever so slightly. It is truly a paradise sea. Nuudles have it good. When I think of my beginnings in Dragonbane Territory, all the black volcanic glass, dragon bones, and black sand. True, I loved it, but this, right now… it's perfect.

We watch, quietly sitting on glowing tropical growth.

Once the sun dips until no shine is left, Days turns to me and says, "I'll put you up in an inn. You'll need to sleep Nuudle beer off and take a shower. Don't worry—won't feel a thing in the morning except a boost in Defense."

"Don't I need DEF now?"

"This way." He heaves me up and Simple takes my left hand. She keeps me level as we walk away from the glorious sea and into the darkening city of magic. They take me to a little hotel with a bedroll on the floor in a small room, a shower stall without a curtain by the sheet separating my box from everything else, and I'm in that bedroll before I fully acknowledge its existence.

Simple bends over my face and tweaks my nose. "Check your quest log in the morning, cutie." She winks. I wink back but forget to open my eye. The other eye thinks that's a fine idea.

I wake up in the inn bedroll from a sleep like I haven't had since I was a little boy who played hard the day before. I feel focused, alert, ready. Ready for whatever, because that's all I am faced with in Dark World. It wasn't as good as real sleep, and I remember some night sweats, but that was probably the weird Dark World beer.

What was that about DEF boost? I check my stats. My DEF is 9. Nuudle beer is very good for low levels! I wonder if the effects get higher as your stats demand more.

Quest log. Check the quest log. I remember Simple saying that to me through the Nuudle beer haze before I passed out.

That stuff is something else. Makes me curious about the Siren Ale.

There are now two quests in my log. One is pending, from someone named Shell, Mystic, guild Faithgamblers. That's the one Days was in when I examined him. He said the Mystic who helped him was named Shell.

I accept the quest.

Nuudle The Black Master Gronai has lost his desire to make up new runes for advancing The Black students. Shell thinks you are the Mystic for the job of bringing Master Gronai's spirits up. You can find Master Gronai in the Nuudle Temple west wing, top floor, south turret on the wall.

This is a hidden quest but can be given to a Mystic by a Mystic who deems you worthy. Do not let Shell down.

Rewards:
+3.3 CON
+1 ATT
+2.1 DEF
Gain Mystic Ability Contemplation.

I can't see from the quest description what the ability does, but those are high stat boosts for a quest, especially a beginner's quest. Stat boosts can be as slow as .1 gained per event you do to boost that stat.

I wish I knew more about Mystic. I mean, I spent some time reading, asked players, close friends—just out of my love of watching the intro where *Ananta* burns me alive, and then everybody. I looked and looked. Nobody had any answers. Now I'm opening a gifted, hidden quest from a Mystic to me, who myself is now a Mystic.

I remember the sunset, and the feel of the hangover from the beer makes me focused again. So much energy. I never felt anything like physical energy in Elora.

Can't sit on my hands. Got to get to that temple… but first, I'm going to try out my Shaman Stick with the lightning boost enchantment on some Wild Onions outside the gate. Stats are in the 1-5 range, and they drop planting bulbs, which gardeners use and will buy a stack of at the AH for enough to get me a piece of low-level gear—shoes.

I'm about to find out how bad it hurts when I get hit, because I got to get this shit learned and done, and done right.

I exit Kleeple—lots of players watching me—and head into the fields in front of the jungle. All those Wild Onions hopping around with pissed-off looks on their pale faces, grassy, green hair flopping side to side.

Here goes. At least I'll get to experience how all the stats *feel* to me. Something to look forward to.

Sid casts Spontaneity. Sid gains +4 CRG.

I hit the ground with my Shaman Stick. A spark flies up at my face.

Sid casts Spontaneity. Sid gains +6 ATT.

Are you kidding? My CON, MND, and INT stats won't help me hack down Onions because I have no spells or summons. But look at these! Onions are at the highest +5 DEF.

Oh, I gotta quit thinking about it and kill one before the timer runs out and I lose my nerve. +6 ATT! Add in the lightning…

I give a battle cry to the sky as the first Onion I charge faces me. I slam it across the face with the Shaman Stick. Lightning shoots out of it and the Wild Onion's hair fries into ash. The Onion sticks its yellow tongue out at me before fading away, leaving me a pile of treasure. I dig through it. I don't think about how easy it was, nor that I still don't know *how bad it's gonna hurt*. Just not thinking.

One bulb, two leaves. I might be able to make something with these leaves, come to think of it. When I first started Elora Online with Peter, who then I still thought of as Jacob-my-bestie, he'd been into crafting almost from Day One. He used to ask me to hold onto odd drops that don't sell because he could level crafting stats with them. They took longer but cost nothing. They take up inventory space to everyone else and are usually dropped to make room for other goodies.

Kleeple must have a clothcraft station where I could learn the basic skill, maybe a recipe with this grass…

So, the time went. I don't know how long. I covered myself in buffs and destroyed every Wild Onion before it had a chance to even think about me existing. I went into Dragonbane Maniac mode when I farmed for cash. Some people craft, some people hunt mobs with high-priced drops, some just run dungeons, some do raids on The Notorious to get rare, pricy drops, some garden, some do favors with their magic, some make and sell scrolls of magic... and I farm. I zone out and hack and slash and collect. That's what I do all morning with the Wild Onions until my interface tells me my robe pockets won't hold any more Onion bulbs and leaves.

And then, of course, I go to the AH, put the four stacks of bulbs I have up for sale—and when I think about how much the stuff I put up in the AH used to be priced at!—then hunt Kleeple for a weaving instructor who might show me a use for the leaves.

At this point, I'd like to take an aside. It's mid-afternoon by the time I'd leveled up weaving to 3, and I get enough cash for a pair of shoes from a stack of bulbs that sell—very comfy, no stats—gloves with +1 INT, and a Crystal Headband from two more bulb stacks. I thought it would look stupid, but it somehow ends up being the same color as my forehead symbol. Glows the same hue ever so gently. It wraps around the front of my hairline and gives me +2 ATT, +1 CRG, +2 CON, +1 MND. I made sure to go to what I knew (would know?) as Plapy's Playhouse from the day before to examine myself in the mirror behind the bar.

Instead of regaling you with my first farming attempts to get myself out of the mud and at least heading somewhere gear-wise and stat-wise, I'll sum it up even more. I spent the whole day farming those damn Wild Onions, and never once did one so much as brush my shoulder. No knowledge yet on the pain front, but I had ten stacks of bulbs, some random low-level gear drops that I couldn't wear, and leggings I'd crafted with the grass on the AH, and I actually feel physically and mentally tired. I think of the inn from the night before and the bedroll. I won't have anything like that tonight. Every time something of mine sold on the AH, I bought. I'm broke.

I leave Kleeple at sunset and head toward the Temple of Nuudlel up the northeast road from the capital. There's a mailbox at the Temple of Nuudlel if my AH stuff sells, and that's where the money goes for pickup.

I sleep in a thick jungle tangle of briars a little way off the path where it winds in an unusual pattern.

I sleep instantly and wake with the sun. I have no drowsiness like in RL when I wake up. Nice, but weird.

~

The spell-making chamber in the Temple of Nuudlel is packed with players making spells on parchment. Instant, one-time casts, abilities from other classes, stat boosters, damage, healing, protection... you name it. Called Scrolls.

I find Master Gronai in his turret. He's a white-haired Nuudle Magician with a gnarly staff. I'll skip the NPC BS for now, but I'm offered options to answer as he discusses his loss of interest. I guess to the best of my knowledge, keeping in mind that Nuudles are particular about the importance of each and every chosen word.

When he asks me to show him an example of something that might renew his love for the art, I'm stumped.

In my interface, a one-minute timer pops up and starts counting down.

He stands there, watching, waiting with a depressed look on his wrinkled, yellow face.

I start to talk, but he interrupts me.

"No, no. Enough of words. I'm so tired of words. I want to feel something again."

I look around the turret. Bookshelves full of magic books, torches. I can't figure this out.

I look back to him. He seems even sadder as the timer reaches ten seconds.

I run to face him, and do the only thing I can think of.

Sid casts Spontaneity. Master Gronai gains +40 CRG.

I hack a torch with my Shaman Stick. It tips over and starts burning a bookshelf. Two seconds left.

Sid casts Spontaneity. Master Gronai gains +75 CON.

The timer stops at 00:098.

Master Gronai stands tall, looks away from me and out of a window at the sunny morning. "You know, I suddenly feel somewhat focused, as though in the past when I have been focused, I'm focusing on negative things." He turns to me. "You have shown me with your magic that there is magic in the world that can mentally make someone feel better. What is this magic?"

"It's a Mystic spell."

"You're a Mystic. Of course."

"Yup." I grin. I did it!

"Interesting. Interesting. I knew a young Mystic once. She taught me one of her spells—or rather showed me—and I made a scroll that has the ability to grant that particular Mystic spell to any Nuudle I choose. I happen to have one of those scrolls, and I'd like to thank you for helping me." He holds out a scroll, the Nuudle-written one-timer spell, and it looks like a rolled-up piece of yellowed parchment. These are the things the herd of players are making in the room downstairs.

I happily take the scroll. "Thank you, Master Gronai."

"Use it. I'd like to see it and feel it again. If you will indulge me further?"

"Of course," I say as I'm already unrolling it. I select to use the item, and then I physically feel a surge of high energy, like a shock, run through me.

Sid learns Contemplation.

I rush to my abilities list.

Contemplation—Protection for target. – Damage, random. Wears off in 45 seconds. Cumulative.

"Now, if you will, young Sid," he urges, looking excited.

Sid casts Contemplation. Master Gronai gains Protection.

Silver shoots out of my hands and coats him like a suit of shining body armor, and then he sighs. "Thank you. You, now."

I forgot about the fire. I turn, and the bookshelf I hit is smoldering. It seems to have taken care of itself. I whack the blackened bookshelf. Lightning shoots out. No fire this time.

Sid casts Contemplation. Sid gains Protection.

The silver flows from my fingertips and spreads all over me. Inside and out, I feel so very safe, warm, like being held by my mother when I was a toddler. It's amazing, and fades quickly, but leaves a general good, smooth mood after.

"Holy shit, Master Gronai. Thank you so much!" I hug him. He hugs me back. We're in-the-know right now.

"Remember your language, Nuudle Mystic Sid."

"Okay."

"Words are beings—they are the only way we convey meaning to one another, which gives them ultimate power of union."

"My way conveys how I feel pretty well," I tell him.

He chuckles. "You may write some interesting scrolls with that attitude."

~

I'm waiting for Days outside the cave where my quest for the *Counts of Hell* is. For three days, I grinded for cash, crafted, and spent some time in the history part of the Temple of Nuudlel's library trying to figure something out. Lots of stories I didn't know, but nothing helpful to explain my situation.

Master Gronai is an unusual NPC. They make NPCs compelling now compared to how stiff and repetitive they were, say, twenty years ago. But I genuinely like him and visit him when I'm in the temple. I make sure to cast Contemplation on both of us every time. I've even helped him phrase some scrolls I found him working on one day.

It's been three days, and I messaged Days about an hour ago telling him I had the spell and new gear. He said he'd meet me at the cave in an hour, so that's what's going on.

I have much better gear now. My robe is blue with white trim, and +2.9 CON, +1.2 INT. My shoes are upgraded to flip-flops with +2 ATT, and I made sure they were comfortable. I have three rings. Altogether, they give me +7 CON, +2 INT, and +2 DEF. It was the best I could do with what I could afford. I think I look kind of cool for a Nuudle, but maybe that's compared to what I looked like three days ago when I walked into Kleeple for the first time.

Days flies in on a red and black dragon, along with a Siren named Sorry riding a pitch-black sea serpent. She's blue, black curly hair, has a crazy, colorful headdress, tight see-through red robes, and sparkling sandals. Yet again in Dark World, I'm seeing gear I've never encountered in Elora.

They land, put their mounts away, and approach me.

"Looking good, looking good," Days says to me and claps me on the shoulder. I'm so small that I tumble to the side a little.

"Sorry, you really don't seem like a Nuudle."

"I know, right?" I shrug.

"This is Sorry. She's a Voodoo Lady. I know, never seen one, thought the class was a myth. Like all three of ours, but especially Voodoo Ladies."

I'm stunned. She grins at me. "Go ahead, examine me."

I do. She has high-stat gear, mostly boosting her INT and CRG. I'm dying to know what this buffer does. She's in the same class type as Bards and Stylists. Faithgamblers guild, like Days and Simple.

"Thanks, Sorry. For helping, I mean."

41

"I love big battles." She smiles, looking wicked.

"Okay, you ready for this?" says Days. "I'm ready for this. Been dying to tank these guys."

"Yes." I sound positive, but I'm not.

We enter the dark cave and Sorry casts a spell called Illuminate so we can see. We reach the back of the empty cave and meet a dead end.

"Now what?" Days asks.

"The NPC who gave me the quest put this on me and said I'd use it to do the quest somehow." I hold out my left palm and show them the mark of the Counts.

Days laughs. "You mean you don't even know how to enter the battle?"

Voodoo Lady giggles.

I crack a smile, then can't help but chuckle. "I'm such a dumbass."

"I bet you do something stupid like put your palm on the wall. Seriously, it's usually that easy," says Sorry. She's right, and I try it.

And of course, it really is that easy.

As I pull my now-glowing hand away, the mark from my hand has been transferred to the stone and grows.

Then everything is black for a few seconds.

Now all three of us are in the *Counts of Hell*'s battle arena.

They are five shadowy ancient men in furs and wearing talismans. They are black and white, which is odd with all the color in the game. They remind me of shamans with bad intent. They instantly move toward us through the round cave room lit by blue torches.

Days uses *Invoke Inner Demon.*

Days tanks up pretty fast and is now the only target the Counts can hit until someone else gets hate.

The *Counts of Hell* use Freeze. Days cannot use any abilities for 20 seconds.

Crap, what's Freeze?

It's what I'm doing right now!

Sid casts Contemplation. Days gains Protection.

Sorry casts Tribal Curse. The *Counts of Hell* are cursed.

Oh my God. They have so many HP bar segments. High stats, high defense, hard hits. I see their life is counting down by about 40HP per second with the curse.

Sid casts Spontaneity. Sorry gains +45 CRG.

So, the spell is based on how high your stats are. That's amazing.

Days can't use abilities, but he's hacking and slashing at them. Is that blood I see? Like, real blood on his hand?

The *Counts of Hell* use Burn. Sorry gains the effects of Burn.

Sorry cries out and rubs her skin all over. Her HP bar drops 30HP every three seconds. Yes, she's feeling something like burning, alright, and it's making her have a hard time fighting. Will I be next? She's feeling pain. That means I can feel pain.

Shut up, selfish. I have to do something to help her.

Sid casts Contemplation. Sorry gains Protection.

"Oh, oh, thank you," she squeals as white light surrounds her.

Sorry casts Weaken Enemy. The *Counts of Hell* have Offense Down.
That's great!
Days gets his abilities back.
Days uses Crushing Blade.
He takes 100HP off with that! It must have been one of his bigger moves. Now, the *Counts of Hell* are at 30% HP.
Sid casts Contemplation. Days gains Protection.
I'm hoping with the cumulative effect, that it'll help him out. He's at half HP from taking physical contact hits with the five demons. Yeah, we're all up in the fight, all three of us. I'm stabbing, clubbing, and pounding with a Shaman Stick at the Counts while they slap Days. None of them have hit me. My fear of the pain has hyped my reflexes. I'm great at dodging from so much playing as melee.
Sorry casts Spiritual Intervention. Days and Sid gain +60 DEF.
Wow!
Days' face doesn't look as stressed, and he uses his demon-invoking move again, re-engaging all the Counts on him.
Sid casts Spontaneity. Days gains +80 ATT.
The *Counts of Hell* use Hell on Earth.
Oh crap. This can't be good by the looks of their staffs turning molten red and the torches darkening. We're all three targeted, too.
Sorry casts Reflection of Darkness. Hell on Earth is stopped, and *Counts of Hell* take Arcane damage over time.
Couldn't be more perfect. The Counts are still being drained by Sorry's DoT spells, and now Days, as a Dark Knight tank, can really kick some ass. It's like Spontaneity knows me and what I want to happen. Sorry's Voodoo Lady is full of quick-minded tricks and moves. An attacking buffer... interesting. Still, it's frustrating as hell for me. I feel like I'm doing nothing to help.
Sid casts Contemplation. Days gains Protection.
Days uses Special Ability: Soul Gather.
In three seconds' time, before Sorry or I could make another move, the Counts' HP all but spills off the HP bar.
"Holy shit!" I cry out.
"Yeah!" Days stomps the ground.
And then I'm in a cutscene.
The *Counts of Hell* and I are alone in the cave. They surround me and whisper things, disturbing things that I can't quite make all the way out. One steps forward and says, "Master, we will now always do your bidding, but keep us in the dark shadows where we thrive."
"Uh, okay."
They spin around me lightning-fast in a gray blur and then swoop right inside through my chest.
I feel like if I'd ever lost a part of my heart, it was just put back in.
The cutscene fades, and I'm with Days and Sorry outside the battle arena in the cave.
"Got them? Got them?" Days asks.
"Yeah, yeah, I think I do."

"Look!" says Sorry. She's grinning. "That was so fun."

I look at my spell list. Now I have *Counts of Hell* as a summon spell.

I read their ability list.

The *Counts of Hell*
Description:
Five ghoulish demons in a cluster of black and gray swirling fog. Stronger damage at night. Only summon off the beaten path, or in boss or dark dungeon battles.

Abilities:
Freeze—Stops opponent's moves for 20 seconds.

Burn—Does DoT fire damage at -30HP every 3 seconds for 15 seconds.

Surround—Surround target and push it back forty feet, dealing damage according to if and what target is pushed into.

Seizure Move: Hell on Earth—Counts of Hell swallow target in a pool of molten lava for 30 seconds, draining essence quickly. If target can fight back, a player or enemy can still fight during Hell on Earth.

"We are so lucky," I say after reading their seizure move.

"Hell on Earth?" asks Sorry. "Yeah, that would have been ouchy. That's why we had to do it so fast, and needed your Contemplation. Like when you got me straight when I was burning."

"Ah, okay. I get it."

Days grins down at me. "You always had it. You're a natural. All the right moves. I'm impressed. I bet you were pretty good in Elora."

"Thanks. Not too much experience as a mage. Any tips welcome." I smile. Am I making friends? That's what Anella and Calla told me to do, and I certainly couldn't have ever beaten the Counts on my own without yet having a summon… ever.

"Go on," says Days. "Summon them."

"Yeah, hell yeah," I say.

Sid summons the *Counts of Hell*.

Swirling black smoke comes out of my chest, right where they went in moments ago, and rushes out to form the five counts. They stand before us, waiting for a command.

"I did that," I say, dumbfounded. They are huge and quite intimidating.

"Yeah, you did," says Days in a hush.

I smile at the Counts.

Sid dismisses the *Counts of Hell*.

They roll back into smoke and rush into me. I don't get that piece-of-heart falling in feeling again. "They don't like daylight much, and don't like being exposed."

"Interesting," says Days. "It's like you get them. You know what I mean? That's cool."

"I'm impressed, too," Sorry says, and exchanges a look with Days. "I think you're right."

"Yep," Days answers her.

"About what?" I ask.

Days looks back down at me. "Want to join our guild? Faithgamblers?"

I feel my big Nuudle eyes get bigger. "I'd love to. Yeah, love to. Thanks."
"Here's the invite."

It pops up in my interface and I immediately accept. I so need a guild in this confusion-filled existence.

I turn on guild chat as I look over the names and classes in the guild list. There aren't a lot in the guild, maybe fourteen at most listed. I see familiar class tags, and a several that I don't pick up on right away. I see one that says MYT next to it, then see it's me. Oh! MYT must be the game's tag for Mystic. Then there's another MYT: Shell. She's the one who helped Days see when he came to Dark World and sent me the quest with Master Gronai. I also see Simple's name with class tag BLK.

Days says, "Everyone, I want you to welcome Sid, the Mystic I told you about. We just did the Counts. He got 'em."

"Nice job." I recognize Simple's voice.

I hear a cacophony of male and female voices saying hello and congratulations. So nice to meet you. Glad you're in the guild. I feel genuinely accepted and that this isn't one of those guilds that control your life. Just my type.

I'm getting the hang of this. Yeah. Now I have to go kill stuff with my Counts. See what that's like, how much damage they'll do. The burn move alone will instantly kill anything with 30HP or under.

"Thanks so much, guys. I'm glad to be here. Pretty excited about the Counts."

There's so much more I want to say and ask, but I get the feeling there's a time and place for discussing Dark World and how we all got here. Nobody seems to want to talk about it. That vibe is just out there with every player I've encountered.

Actually *playing the game* in Dark World, where I have to sleep and do everything else all the time here, and not just hanging out, is like smuggling heroin into prison to break the thoughts of why I'm here.

Maybe that's why so many of the players do play the game in Dark World. My new friends were eager to battle the Counts. Big battles are fun, but it was more than that. I can't put my finger on it.

CHAPTER 8: WE MEET AGAIN

I guess you've figured out by now that there's no mana, or magic pool, in Elora. Or Dark World. Or wherever the hell I am. Mage classes do have to regenerate, it's called. Each class has its own way of doing so. I have to recite runes outdoors for an hour once a week if I'm a semi-busy player. More often if I'm online all the time.

I've been here a little over a week and I've recited four times. It's boring as hell. I just listen to guild chatter and learn who is who and what is what after choosing the Recite setting in my Nuudle Specific Abilites menu.

The first thing I did with the *Counts of Hell* was use my seizure move on a wild Onion outside Kleeple. Man, it was amazing. Their staffs lit up red and molten lava poured out of the bottoms into a pool around the poor Wild Onions, melting them in a split-second.

I don't have the multi-targeting skill and ask the guild how to get it. It's a quest, and they say it's different for everyone. Pretty much have to talk to every NPC in Dark World and hope you get lucky.

I wonder how much damage the Counts' Seizure move will do on higher-level mobs. Or other players who might not be as friendly as the first people I encountered in Dark World. If my stats are lower, are summons not as strong? I can't figure it out.

I have felt pain now. When I went back to the graveyard to look for the NPC Calla, hoping she'd give me my next Mystic quest for a summon, a Wakened Tree grabbed me with a branch and tore the flesh on my upper arm. It hurt like hell, I saw blood and yelled, but I had the Counts out—it was night and I was in a secluded area—and they automatically took over hitting the Tree. When a player, or summon in this case, hits a mob the hardest, they get the hate. The Counts got the hate, Waking Tree went after them, and the Counts killed the Waking Tree with Burn that I hastily instigated somehow through the shock and fear of the pain.

Reflecting on it now as I recite in Siren Territory on the hull of the sunken ship where Silvia and I hung out, the pain wasn't as bad as I thought it would be. It went away as soon as I bought some Pink Poppy Salve from a herbalist shop in Kleeple. The wound even vanished and the salve felt so good. Sensations in Dark World are odd, but I'm getting there.

I miss Silvia. I wonder if she thinks of me, wonders where I am. Something tells me there must be a way from Dark World to Elora. In Elora, we'd all seen characters here and there with one name. If we did happen upon a class we rarely saw, the player had one name.

Those classes open up in Dark World, like my Mystic. Like Days' Dark Knight. Those one-name players I've seen must've come from Dark World.

I had asked the guild about it, but none of them knew a way to Elora. They told me they'd speculated on it before, but the conversation didn't go anywhere from there.

My Passion Berry that's keeping me breathing under water has about fifteen minutes left, and I'm done reciting.

I had found Calla in the graveyard, and she had given me the quest to fight *Varengan*, who, according to the Shell, is a glowing bright blue bird mainly used for healing. I'm getting better gear, doing little quests I find to boost my concentration stat, and tomorrow I'm going to try taking on *Varengan*. Days says he'll tank again, and Sorry says she's onboard. A Blessed White Elf named Doolittle wants to come along. I've never been healed before by a healer in Dark World, and I'm curious to find out what it's like, how it feels. I bet it's something.

I open my eyes.

A White Elf male with long, white hair floating all through the water, deep golden skin, and wearing silvery robes, swims in front of me. He's wearing gear I haven't seen, but I can tell it's some kind of healing attire. His weapon is a black, gnarled staff with a rough crystal quartz in its twisted top. I stumble off my perch and swim away from him, saying, "What the hell, dude?"

"Sid Vicious, wait."

I stop, tread water. He knows my old name.

I turn and look at him. He's smiling, but his digital white, glowing eyes have a familiarity, and it's that the smile doesn't reach them.

I see his name now that he's not so close.

Seeker.

"Yes, it's me. I've been looking for you. I heard rumors of a new Mystic with the mark of *Ananta* on his forehead. I knew it had to be you."

"What the fuck do you want?" I yell at him. Bubbles rush out of my mouth in a stream as though they are cursing at him with me.

"I came to explain."

"Explain what? Just leave me alone. I want nothing to do with you."

"Wait, hear me out."

I turn and swim toward the capital of Siren Territory and the Kila Crystal that will take me back to Kleeple. My oxygen timer has no time for this shit.

"I have a Bloom Berry if you're worried you'll run out of air. Only five minutes, that's all I ask and that's all it's good for."

I sigh. The first burst of anger I felt fades away, and curiosity gets me. I have to find out what he did to me because I know he has something to do with my being in Dark World.

I swim to face him again. He's holding out the berry. I take it and eat it. Tastes like raspberries. My interface says I now have nineteen minutes of air time.

"Okay, I'm listening." I glare at him, hoping he gets right to the point.

I'm disappointed.

"Why do you think I did what I did in Elora?"

"Because you're an asshole."

He chuckles. "I might be, but that's not why. Do you want to know?"

I roll my eyes dramatically.

He acts unaffected by my dismissal.

Sid summons the *Counts of Hell*.

"Just in case," I tell Seeker.

"I understand. But today, you have nothing to worry about. Today, you will learn your purpose. You will discover why I chose you."

"Chose me?"

"My name. What do you think it means?"

"I have no clue, man."

"I have been seeking Elora for someone to go Total Immersion with me."

"Couldn't you have just asked someone? And what do you know about Total Immersion and what's happened to us? To everyone here?"

He shrugged. "There are so many secrets to this game. I found out about Dark World in my travels. Leave it at that."

"Great. So, you named yourself The Seeker and went around killing and looting hard-working players to *seek* someone. Tell me how that makes sense."

He swims a little closer. "I got a special class offer, too, like you. I'm a Psychic."

I wait. He says nothing during his dramatic pause, then starts up again.

"I fought people to find someone who could beat me, however it might be done. You did. You must have been so very dedicated to killing and looting me to get your stats up that high, and all your gear back, in eleven months. Well, almost all of it. I know you never got another pair of those silver knuckles."

"I did after I looted you."

"You don't have them anymore."

"Shut up and tell me what you did to me." I swim away from him. The *Counts of Hell* surround me from behind, as though they are showing me they have my back.

"I picked you because you are the only one who has even come close to defeating me. You are my better. I chose you and now, we will become strong together and rule over Dark World. We will overthrow Bane instead of Kane doing it, and we will change the map. See what I mean? We'll create a paradox. People in Elora will open their maps one day and see that the capital city of Dragonbane Territory isn't Kane, but instead Sid. Or Seeker. We can keep the dragons and humans from going extinct. In Elora, there will suddenly be humans and dragons—"

"Wait," I interrupt him. "Are you saying you know for a fact that Dark World is Elora's past?"

"I'm saying together, we could own this game. We can make the creators of the game shit their skinny jeans. It'll be chaos, and we'll be gods."

I shake my head at him. My timer has five minutes on it. "Look, I have no time. I'll run out of air. Just tell me what you did to me, you obsessed, delusional fuck."

"Do you agree to take on the world with me?"

"Absolutely, positively no. Never. Not in a million lifetimes. I hate you. I know you're the reason I'm here, I know you enjoy terrorizing people and making everyone victims. Even if I had any interest in creating some kind of paradox, I wouldn't ever, ever do it with you. Ever. Now, tell me what you did to me."

"I gave you a better life, a dream come true. A better gaming experience. Have you had the beer? Have you been healed? Here, let me."

He starts to cast a spell, hands glowing, but I yell, "Stop!"

He does, cocking his head at me.

"Tell me what you did!"

"You're surprised and angry. I'm going to give you three days to think things over. Think about what I said. I will find you and see if you've changed your mind." He blinks for what feels like the first time.

"No. The answer is and always will be no."

My interface turns red. My timer is at ten seconds. "Shit!" I start swimming straight up. I hear Seeker laughing behind me as my timer ends, and I feel the burn of needing air in my lungs.

I swim as hard and fast as I can. My instincts keep begging me to just inhale, no matter what it is. I continue heading for the surface, which looks miles away even as it comes closer.

As I burst through the surface of the Marana Sea, I loudly gasp for my first breath. I pant and pant as I tread water, trying to stop shaking, trying to get my shit together. The Counts are still with me. After I catch my breath, I dismiss the Counts and start swimming to Wet Eyes Isle. It's going to be a long swim.

I can't believe this guy. I hate him. I really hate him. He *chose* me? The guy's a nut obsessed with this game—and, apparently, me now. But he does seem to know a lot more about Elora and Dark World than he's letting on. As much as I'd like that information, I couldn't fake it to be able to dig the information out of him. I couldn't trick him with compliments or flattery. I couldn't deliver it, not at all.

On I swim, feeling exhausted even though I just got done meditating. Three days. What will he do then, kill me and loot me? He can't be much further along in stats and spells than I am. And after tomorrow, hopefully I'll be able to summon the blue glowing bird *Varengan*.

CHAPTER 9: BATTLE OF VARENGAN

The three of them are waiting for me near the Caves of Eternity entrance. I'd had to swim to a vendor in north Wet Eyes Isle to get a Bloat Berry to allow me to breathe underwater for two hours, and then swim back through Siren Territory to the Caves of Eternity.

"We thought you gave up. You weren't on guild chat," Days calls to me as I swim to them.

Doolittle is a moss-green-haired, deeply tan-skinned White Elf with high-stat gear, mostly craft-specific. The kind you can only wear if you make it, and you have to be very high level in clothcraft to be wearing what he's got on.

I reach them. "Sorry," I say, nodding to Sorry. "I mean, I'm sorry, not referring to Sorry."

They all chuckle.

"I turned off guild chat. Don't really want to talk about it."

"Mystery," Sorry says. "Of course, there's mystery."

"Simple wanted to come, was going to surprise you, but she got beat up pretty bad in a dungeon this morning and wanted to take it easy," Days says, catching the hint that I sincerely don't want to talk about it. I appreciate that.

"Did you get Meditation?" Days continues, floating over me.

"I have the quest," I tell him. "It doesn't explain much as to how to do it. It's going to take a few days to walk to the other continent, and I figured I'd do it when I have a summon fight there, too."

"Would have helped a lot," Sorry says.

"You shush," says Days.

She swats his arm, tucks her chin under, and grins.

Something going on between those two. Makes me think of Silvia.

Doolittle has an even voice and a foreign accent, Spanish maybe. "We should have a plan. *Varengan* can heal himself again and again."

"We did fine last time without a plan," boasts Days, swimming over Doolittle and pulling one of his elf ears. Doolittle squints up at him and smacks his hand.

"Alright, if that's your way. Not that I've ever lost a fight with Sorry in it." He smiles at the Voodoo Lady. She's wearing a black robe and a Medusa Headdress. I've never seen anyone wear one. Nobody ever knew where to get one.

"I say we go in and do what we do," Sorry concludes.

"I'm game," I say, never having been in a big battle with my Counts. I also don't know half of my allies' moves and can't begin to formulate a plan.

We swim into the Caves of Eternity, past the birthing shells, and into its depths. I bring out the *Counts of Hell*, and the few times we are jumped by monsters, get any kind of unwanted aggro, the Counts take over until we can collect ourselves. That's pretty cool.

We get to a dead end, much like the one in Nuudle Territory's cave, and I ask, "Ready?"

"So, you just know this is the right wall?" Sorry says.

"Yeah, well, better be ready just in case."

"Not bad thinking," she says.

I put my hand with the mark of a long-necked, flowy bird on my palm on the wall of the cave.

The mark stays on the wall, growing, and my hand glows blue. I pull it away as everything goes dark.

Then, we are in.

Varengan is perched in a golden nest on the far end of the caved, wooded glade we find ourselves in. There is air here, and we're all soaked—something else I'm still trying to get used to in Dark World. The enormous bird is full of hues of bright and baby blue, with long feathers, glowing all over. His eyes are bright, black sparks. He looks like an exotic bird of paradise. He sees us but stays in his nest.

"Well… what do we do?" asks Doolittle.

"Not sure," I say. "Maybe we should go up to him."

"I'll go in front," says Days.

Sid summons the *Counts of Hell*.

They had been unsummoned when we cut into the battle arena. "Wait," I say. "Let me go first. The Counts will take any big hit."

Days doesn't like it, and says we approach together, side by side.

We do a whole hell of a lot of buffing, my own, too. It seems to take too long, even though there is no timer.

"Okay," says Days. "Let's go before they wear off."

With monstrous Mylop Dark Knight Days to my left, and the Counts floating to my right, I feel tiny and vulnerable in my Nuudle body.

The other two follow behind.

Varengan raises his head as we get about twenty feet away from his nest. He calls out, and it sounds beautiful, like a woodwind musical instrument.

What a fabulously beautiful summon.

He acts perplexed, yet still he doesn't attack.

"Are we even supposed to fight it?" asks Sorry.

"No clue," I say.

Then, *Varengan* turns his head and sees the Counts. He hisses and flaps his wings, rising into the air—where none of us can reach him.

The *Counts of Hell* are on it. Apparently, they don't like *Varengan* as much as he doesn't like them. They swoop up after him and the two immediately smack at each other.

Sid commands Burn. *Varengan* gains the effects of Burn.

Days uses Invoke Inner Demon.

He's trying to get the hate off the Counts, but *Varengan* is too high in the air. They're taking a beating from *Varengan*'s golden beak.

Sorry casts Weaken Enemy. *Varengan* has Offense Down.

***Varengan* uses Feathers. *Varengan* gains Protection.**

Now, the DoT effect of Burn seems to be less than 30HP per 3 seconds. *Varengan's* health is at about 75%, the Feathers move seeming to heal him, too. The Counts are at 50%.

Doolittle casts Deep Heal on the *Counts of Hell.*

The Counts' HP matches *Varengan*'s now.

Days yells, "I can't do anything in here! He's too high up! None of my moves will reach him."

***Varengan* uses Gentle Flight.**

Now he heals himself all the way up to full HP, and he has high protection that even slows DoT.

"Me neither," says Sorry. "My big DoT spells won't reach, and neither will Reflection of Darkness. Can't stop its moves."

"Try Weaken Enemy more. It's cumulative, right?"

Sorry casts Weaken Enemy. *Varengan* has Offense Down.

Sid commands Surround. The *Counts of Hell* use Surround.

I've never used Surround, but maybe it'll do some damage I'm not expecting.

The Counts surround *Varengan* mid-air, and then swoosh in front of him and shove him into the back of the cave wall of the glade.

When *Varengan* slams into the rock, his HP drops to 50%. He slides down to the ground, the Counts right on his forked feet.

Days isn't far behind.

Days uses Special Ability: Soul Gather.

Will it be this easy? That's his three-second demolishing move.

***Varengan* uses Gentle Flight.**

Varengan heals to half HP just before the three seconds wear off, and turns on Days.

***Varengan* uses Swift Flight.**

All of us are now targeted. This is his big move, and as though he were an arrow, he makes a flying dive at each of us one after another in an instant, mowing us off our feet. His beak hits me right in the chest and I can't breathe. I taste blood... but how can that be? No matter, gotta get back on my feet and see how the others are, try to regain some control. My HP is only at 15%.

I hit my head when *Varengan* used Swift Flight on us, and my vision is doubled.

Doolittle casts Cure All.

Suddenly, all my aches are gone and I feel rejuvenated, re-energized. He's doing a group party cure, low hate spell, and God, it feels amazing. My HP is almost 75% full.

I can get back into it now.

Sid uses Siezure. Sid commands Hell on Earth.

They can't reach the bird, and I don't know if the lava will float, surround *Varengan*, or what will happen, but I'd glanced back before making my decision to try it and had seen Sorry crumpled, dead. She'd be in her graveyard now, and I got so mad that she had to feel that pain.

That pain I don't know yet. I haven't died in Dark World.

The Counts' crooked, ancient staffs glow red and lava pours out the bottom, but what I hoped came true. The lava encases *Varengan*, draining his life so quickly I can't count.

Varengan uses Gentle Flight.

Sid commands Burn.

The *Counts of Hell* use Burn. *Varengan* gains the effects of Burn.

As the lava and burn eat away at the summon as he desperately tries to heal and protect, my living companions run to my side, Doolittle healing the Counts all the while.

"Sorry's gonna be pissed," Days says.

"I can't believe she died," I say, watching the two battle it out until *Varengan*'s HP goes to zero.

As I fade to cutscene, I hear Days say, "Not that, that she missed seeing those two fight!"

I'm in the glade alone with *Varengan*. I admit I feel a little afraid. Don't know why.

The glowing, blue bird flies in the air above me, and then cirles and lands before me.

"I am yours to summon. I will do your bidding. All I ask is that you do not pick my feathers." Soft, male voice.

"Okay, sounds good," I tell him.

He collapses into blue, swirling mist and rushes into my chest. Yep, there it is, that shock of energy, and my heart feeling full.

And then I'm back outside the arena in the Cave of Eternity.

"Turn on guild chat," says Days.

I do, and hear Sorry. "Can't stand it when I die in a big battle! Grrr. And Days, just rubbing in the awesome summon duel."

"Yeah," I hear and watch Doolittle say as he meets my eyes. "He is a true Mystic, took care of the situation." I see admiration in his expression.

Was anything I did that great?

In party chat, Sorry says, "I'm almost there. Had my grave set at a graveyard near the capital."

Days swims around in circles. "Pull 'im out!"

"No, I have to wait for Sorry." Her body lies in a crumpled heap outside the arena's exit.

"Nah, it'll light her way. Come on!"

Just then, her body reanimates and she hollers at Days in a most flirtatious outraged manner about not waiting for her.

Sid summons *Varengan*.

Blue mist comes out of my chest and the great, blue bird's shape forms in the water beside us. He's huge, like the Counts.

"Wow!" says Sorry.

"Hell yeah." Days grins, his face reflecting blue from *Varengan's* shine.

I look at my summons list to see *Varengan*'s abilities.

Description: A magical bird with feathers that protect against curses and spells. In ancient times, he was hunted for his feathers, and does not like them to be touched. He will heal and protect all who respect him, and he can fly as swift as an arrow.

Abilities:
Feathers—Adds Protection from damage to target. Heals.
Gentle Flight—Heals target to full HP.
Confusion—Confuses target for 20 seconds, where they are unable to fight.
Seizure Ability: Swift Flight—Flies at high speed at target, doing high damage.

I tell them about Confusion. "Isn't that cool?"

They agree that all of it is cool and ask me to read them the list. I do.

"Thanks for your help. For real. I would never have been able to do all this..."

"Hey," Sorry says, putting a hand on my shoulder. "We all know something happened to you to get you here and with that *Ananta* marking on your forehead. People get what they deserve in Dark World. If you ever want to talk about it, and I think it has something to do with why you were late today, I'm here."

"We all are," Days added.

"Thanks. I'll tell you about it some other time. My air's getting low." It's not, but I don't want to talk about Seeker and his madness.

"Is there anything we can do?" Sorry asks.

"No." I pause, thinking. "Actually, can any of you find a spell list for Psychics? Are there any Psychics in the guild?"

They laugh. I don't get it. "There are, maybe, three Psychics in Dark World," says Doolittle. "Ask the guild, though. Someone might be able to get a list."

I do, and nobody says anything. After a pause, Shell says, "I might be able to get in touch with one. I'll get back to you." She has a raspy voice, like she went to a show the night before and screamed along with every lyric.

I get congratulated for our win against *Varengan* from the rest of the guild.

I get out of there fast. Have to get back to the graveyard in the Forest of the Undead and find Calla. I have to get my next spell and my next summon fast. There's a feeling of time running short... a paranoia Seeker instilled in me earlier that day.

~

Calla appears when I summon *Varengan*.

"I'm so delighted you have completed yet another quest! I will even give you a reward for this one. Check your bag. Also, I do believe you are ready for your next summon quest. Check your quest log and map. Hold out your left hand and I'll mark it. Good friends you must have made, and that makes a Mystic worthy of quests and gifts."

I hold out my hand, and a shadowy figure of what looks like a genie appears there.

"Calla, before you disappear, why did you pick me to be Mystic?"

She shakes her head. "Silly Nuudle. I didn't pick it, you did!" She fades away.

I'm soaked from the eternal rain in this forsaken cemetery, but I take the time to look for Anella. I don't see her, but that doesn't mean she's not here.

I look at my quest log. *Djinn* is the name of the summon, and he's marked in Dragonbane Territory in one of the many massive caverns. Why are all these fights in caves?

This is my opportunity to get Meditation and a summon in one hop over to the other continent. Once I've activated the Kila Crystals there, traveling won't be a big deal. Have to get to one, activate it, before you can use it for teleporting to another Kila Crystal.

At least, if Shell's memory of how she got Meditation is right, I should be on the correct path.

I look in my bags. Calla gave me a scroll and a satchel. I read the scroll first.

Scroll-Maker Apprentice

With this scroll, you can now create your own first spell in the Temple of Nuudlel. You will need to word your scrolls wisely, and choose your materials to activate it carefully. Only the best, high-quality quills and ink are needed. Good luck, young Mystic!

How cool! I'll definitely hit up the temple with this, but I have other things I need to do first. I look in the satchel and find lots of feather pens and ink.

I must get better gear. Who knows what a *Djinn* will have in store for me? I hope Days, Sorry... anyone else will help. I never needed this much help in Elora, but it seems like everything I do in Dark World requires help.

Sid summons the *Counts of Hell*.

I'll farm these undead mobs and giant bugs, AH stuff I can't use for clothcraft, make some new gear. I'll need to buy some fluorite from the AH after stuff sells. When Doolittle heard I had been clothcrafting, he sent me a recipe for a + CON, + INT robe that is craft and Mystic-class specific right around my crafting stat level, which is currently 22.

I go into farming mode with the Counts, once in a while buffing with *Varengan*—or just healing myself for the good, good feeling of it—and hours pass this way until my newly acquired bags are full. Time to head to Kleeple, sell, sleep, get money from AH sales in the morning. At least now I know to save for a bedroll. Then, I'll head to the temple after to check out scroll-making.

As the Counts and I find the narrow path leading to the Pass, I step off into the brush, for my Counts' sake. They get so fidgety when they feel too exposed, and I've been going night/day/night. They hate the sunrise most of all, so the least I can do is get away from any sign of sentient beings in their midst.

Seeker casts Crystal Ball on Sid. Sid's next move is blocked.

My heart also stops.

The Counts are on him. He's between two moss-covered trees, and he looks wicked in a deep blue, silver-trimmed Seer's Robe.

Do something!

Sid cannot command the *Counts of Hell* to take that action.

Dammit!

The Counts get beatings on Seeker, hitting him from all sides with their staffs. His HP drops 10%.

Seeker casts Mind Control. The _Counts of Hell_ are under Seeker's control for 20 seconds.

Sid casts Contemplation. Sid gains Protection.

I run at him with my staff held out like a sword. He turns the Counts on me. He's going to burn me! I whack a tree.

Sid casts Contemplation. Sid gains Protection.

Motherfucker. This is going to hurt.

Seeker casts Cure. Seeker gains health.

His HP is at 100%, but then again, so is mine.

I freeze, waiting for it.

"I'm not going to attack you or hurt you. I wanted an even playing field for when we met again."

I have to pay attention. "What do you want?"

"It's been three days. I came to hear what you think of my plans, what thoughts you've had." He smiles.

I don't smile back. "In what world do you live in where you put someone in a position of potential horrible pain, then ask something like that and expect a conversation?" My staff is still at the ready.

"Go ahead, I only control their commands, not you. Dismiss them."

Sid dismisses the _Counts of Hell_.

"Is that better?" he asks, as though he knows I'm dying to be a part of his take-over-the-world scheme and we're old pals in on a private joke.

Maybe I should keep ahold of my temper right now. I want to smash him in his chiseled, White Elf face, but that Mind Control spell, well, damn. He could use it on me. If I resummon the _Counts of Hell_ or bring out _Varengan_, he could say I'm the aggressor.

"Yes," I say, but my voice still sounds pissed. Gotta work on that. I clear my throat. "Thank you."

"You're most welcome. Last time we spoke, you expressed some disturbing anger at me. So, of course, I had to take precautions." He walks toward me. "Have a seat in the leaves with me." He sits down, crosses his legs.

I reluctantly join him.

"Have you been to Dragonbane Territory yet?" he asks.

"No, I haven't made it to the other continent." I mentally slow my breathing by thinking of my grandma's sugar cookies. So good.

As though he really is psychic and read my foodie mind, he says, "I brought two beers from Cashmere. Siren Ale. Would you like to indulge with me while we discuss?"

Do I have a choice? I have to play it cool, right? "Sure. Thanks. I haven't had it before. Heard it's good."

"It's the best."

I have to ask him. "How did you get all this money so fast? Look at what you're wearing."

He pulls two bottles of pink beer out of his bag and hands me one. It's huge. "Mind Control. I used it on players, made them give me the stuff I wanted. I know, you'll think the worst. I didn't want to kill them, and I hate that anyone in Dark World feels pain. Have you died? It's awful. You know what I mean."

I don't tell him I haven't died yet. Instead, I uncork my pink brew and sip. My fingers and toes instantly tingle warmly. "This stuff's strong."

He opens his beer and takes a swig. "I could have killed them with Mind Control, used their own spells and moves against them. I can't do that."

"That spell seems really high-stat. It can't be your big move. The one-a-week."

"It is, but it's once an hour. Isn't that great?"

"Wow." I don't tell him my Seizure move is the same way. It must be something with the special Dark World classes. I'll have to ask Sorry and Days about it.

"Do you judge me?"

I shake my head. "No," I try to say as non-judgmentally as I can. I think it's abuse, just like he used to do, which makes his story of *seeking* someone as a reason to kill and loot players a load of crap. He won't farm or craft or sell magic like the rest of us.

"You're lucky. You made friends. You're in a guild."

"You've never even been in a guild?"

"Yes," he says, pushing his long, white hair back and taking a drink. "I was at one time, years ago. When I first started playing. The help was nice, but I left. Girl problems. I was so young, the stupid things that mattered… oh well. We can't help our decisions of youth."

I sip, too. I feel relaxed, but still cautious. Should I even have drunk something he gave me?

No, I think it's okay. If I trust my gut, which I usually do, he actually does admire me in his delusional way and wants to be friends who take over the game and create a paradox. Whatever that means. "I made some dumb ones when I was in college. Usually women."

"Almost always is." He laughs softly. "This is nice. You have given thought to what I said?"

"Of course I have. I haven't made a decision yet."

"Why not?"

"I don't understand what you're talking about, for one." I hate him, I hate him, I hate him. But maybe I can get info if I can keep up this act. The beer is helping. I stay away from asking how he brought us here. He doesn't like that question. "Why did you ask me if I've seen Dragonbane Territory?"

"It's so different. Sid, you'll love it. There are dragons! They are enslaved right now, but some escape. And humans, so many. All mixed with Dragonbane. I wanted to see Bane, but never had the opportunity."

"That's… something."

"It really is. What don't you understand about what you call my plan?"

I take a deep drink this time and let it work its Dark World beer magic, and my shoulders relax. I need to word things carefully, like the good Nuudle I am. "Are we in Elora's past?"

He shrugs. "I can't explain more about what I know until you're onboard."

"Okay, but I can't decide whether or not to be onboard unless I know what we're doing and why."

"It's owning the game. We will own the game. That's really all you need to know to motivate you."

He's dodging every tactful thing I dig for. This is stupid. He's an ass. I have to get the hell out of here.

I stand up and stretch, trying to seem casual, leaving my beer on the ground. "Sun's up, and I gotta sleep somewhere indoors. Been grinding for days out here."

"Where did you sleep?"

"I didn't. That's why I gotta go. It's been nice, and thanks for the beer."

"Is that it?" He jumps to his feet, dropping his beer next to mine. It spills onto the dead leaves.

I act innocent and dumb. "What do you mean?"

"You are supposed to give me your decision."

"Oh, that. I haven't made up my mind."

"Why not? It's a simple question." He's acting panicked, angry.

"Really, I have to sleep. I'll catch up to you once I've made up my mind."

"There has to be a reason you want more time. What is it?"

"I want to understand Dark World more, gather my options, figure out things for myself."

"Why?"

"Well, because nobody will just tell me."

His brows push together.

"See ya, Seeker. Good luck." *Taking over the world and conquering the universe!* I want to add. I turn south and walk away from him. I can feel his bright White Elf eyes glowing holes in the back of my small head.

I'm nervous until I think I'm out of eyesight.

Sid summons *Varengan*.

Blue mist flows out of my chest and my gorgeous, gigantic blue bird flies around me soon after. We get to the path and head to the Pass, then through Nuudle Territory toward Kleeple. I've never traveled with *Varengan* before, and he's so fun. He flitters here and there. Lands sometimes and pecks at the ground. Flies up to trees. Some players stop on their mounts or walking to watch him.

I'm proud. I'm also lucky I got away from Seeker that easily, but I know he'll be back.

CHAPTER 10: BATTLE OF DJINN

Of course, the economy is very different than in Elora. Everything costs less, but it's harder to get cash. Plus, there seem to be less players here in Dark World. The Kila Crystal links I'll make on the other continent will help a ton until I can afford a mount. I remember what a big deal it was to get a new Kila Crystal access point when I first started playing Elora. It was a year before I had all the ones I knew of. You never really know if you have everything of anything in Elora Online, and Dark World is the same way. Secrets and unknowns everywhere.

I spent time in the Temple of Nuudlel trying to figure out scroll-making, but was completely lost. The instructor NPC said to read all the books about it in the libraries. Do you know how many books there are in that temple? I'd say about 4,000. I didn't have time for all that, so put off the craft after skilling up on a few simple salve scrolls. I got to skill stat 3.5. I pop in on Master Gronai for a Contemplation infusion and chat for a few. I like that old NPC. He's oddly comforting to me.

I travel through White Elf Territory to the Snowy Mountains, or, as I know them, Red Snow Mountains, and make it to Hilly's Balloon Station. It's freezing here.

I ride the hot air balloon to the other continent, where Mylop Territory and Dragonbane Territory are. And where the temperatures rise dramatically.

I'm shocked when the balloon lands and I see what Dragonbane Territory looks like.

The first thing I see is a blood red dragon, a little one, flying low through the black land. It vanishes in the distance. This is a great vantage point to see the whole territory before making the climb down.

Black, shiny volcanic structures are the same, mountains all throughout the horizon the same, but Kane, now Bane, to the north, is shining silver, as though made from the solid precious metal. In Elora, it was black volcanic glass.

Bane is an egomaniac. I can't wait to meet this NPC, or at least get a glimpse of him.

Sid summons *Varengan*.

I want to be safe, and the Counts would hate it here. So very exposed. I walk all the way to Bane, through the black sand, and see huge cages full of all colors and types of dragons, then human males with silver collars around their necks mining for obsidian. All those poor NPCs. They are mining for Bane until he makes each and every one of them Dragonbane. I also see the newly converted Dragonbane. This is all around the little towns outside Bane.

It blows my mind.

I dismiss *Varengan* far from the capital.

The city of Bane's silver walls give in to a meticulously-designed and grand city. It feels industrial almost, as compared to the rustic feeling Kane had in

Elora. There are statues of Bane everywhere. He is a red Dragonbane with silver, curving horns and silver spikes down his back. By the gear he's in, it looks like he's a Maniac, my old job.

I wander the city, check out the AH. My stuff had taken two days to sell, and now I'm outfitted in an Apprentice Robe from the recipe with the fluorite, have four new rings, Charmed Linen Pants that I made, Smart Sandals—I gave up on my feet ever feeling good again for stats—and a couple of earrings. My robe has a hood. It's green with decorative gold around the trim. My CON is now at 61. INT at 46. MND at 30. I've also done some side quests to boost my concentration as they came to me, mainly from talking to all the NPCs in Kleeple. Makes sense. Nuudles should be Mystics, and Kleeple is Nuudle Central.

I also grinded for some other stat boosts to thicken up my HP bar, especially focusing on ATT and DEF.

I like robes with hoods. People don't look at me as much. The more I travel, the more people stare at the marking on my forehead. Often, I get questions. People always want to see *Varengan* and the Counts. With hoods, I can pull the rim low so as to cover my rare Mystic marking.

The layout is pretty much the same here, and I go to where the NPC ruling over Dragonbane Territory used to reside in a three-story volcanic glass mansion. Now, in its place is a solid silver spiral going into the clouds, about sixty feet wide. Six Dragonbane guards stand in front of the door, which is made from black volcanic glass.

I approach them. "I'd like to see Bane." I say.

"Nobody sees Bane," says the nearest NPC. "You especially. Get out of here."

No way I'm going to just walk in and meet the famed, evil NPC.

I turn and walk away, listening to guild chat. I tell them where I am, and they're excited that I made it. I'm still shy in Faithgamblers most of the time unless I forget myself when I'm excited about getting summons.

Yeah, I'm pretty quiet in guild chat, whereas in Nowhere Squares, I talked all the time. So many of those people I knew in real life. It was easy to be myself.

Real life. What is that?

"Pssst," I hear a woman's voice hiss from my right. I look at the shop there. It's a flower vendor. There are no flowers in Dragonbane Territory. These flowers must be expensive.

"Pssst!" I see the human woman's eyes through a slit in the shop's curtains over the open window.

NPC? Or player? I'm curious, and go inside the flower shop.

A human NPC named Mena with red hair, freckles, and wearing a healer's robe greets me with fear in her eyes. Have I found a secret quest?

"You… are Mystic?" she asks quietly.

"Yeah."

"We need a Mystic to help us. Bane is taking over the world, he's changing our very bodies. Look at this silver collar around my neck!" She pulls at it. "I'm marked for changing. What will happen to me? I don't want to be half dragon. I have seen what it does to the human spirit. Crushes it. Will you help stop him?"

"Sure," I say, knowing that's the right answer.

"Okay. Good, thank you very much, young Nuudle Mystic. So rare to see a Nuudle here, much less a Mystic. Are you sure you want to do this? It will be hard, and you will have to be the bravest alive to accomplish this. Are you?"

"Yeah." No hesitation. There might be a delay in gathering everybody for the *Djinn* fight if this is a long quest.

"I'm going to show you a special flower. One I keep in the back, and it never dies or dries out. It's a Human Lotus, carries the essence of a Mystic I once knew. I grew it in volcanic sand, put some of his ashes in the soil. I thought I was burying him, but this grew. I want you to handle it, gather what Mystic secrets it has. I have a feeling something will happen."

"Well, thanks," I tell her. I can't wait to see this flower.

"I'll be back. I have to get it from the safe."

"Okay, thanks again."

She turns her head funny at me. "You sure are a nice Mystic. But Nuudles do know how to talk." She goes through a door behind the counter.

I look around at all the flowers. One in particular catches my eye. It's a daisy, but the center is the classy kind of yellow gold, and the white petals shimmer like mother-of-pearl. I pick it up and look at its description in my interface.

Sunlight Daisy—*A great gift for that special someone. When carried, the person warps to you instead of their grave upon death, alive and at full health.*

Wow, gift? I need this for me. But then I think of Silvia, and would love it if every time she died, she came to me.

I look at the price. It's outrageous. I can't afford this.

As Mena comes back into the main shop area, I say, "Any way I can get a discount on a Sunlight Daisy? There's someone I'd very much like to give it to."

She's holding something wrapped in pink silk, and pauses as she reaches me. "Oh? Who is this person?"

"Well, it's hard to explain. I think I'm in love with her, and I can't figure out how she feels about me. It's complicated, though, because we… live in different places."

She laughs with delight. "So, this way, she can come to you every time she dies and you can see each other more."

"Exactly."

She tilts her head in thought. I wait. She twirls a red curl, then says, "You did agree to save the world for me, so the Sunlight Daisy is on the house. Now here, look at this lotus." She unwraps the pink silk and reveals a tiny white lotus. I touch its petals. They feel like marshmallows. "It's beautiful," I tell her. "You are quite gracious." I'm pushing my Nuudle language charm hard because she seems to like that.

"Take it, Sid. Once you hold it, it will know you are Mystic too, and grant you a gift."

"How do you know that?"

"I know everything about flowers." That's an easy answer.

I take the white lotus into my small hands and it fills them. Suddenly, the lotus glows brightly, like it has a lightbulb inside it, and I see a Dragonbane

Mystic in long, dark robes within the glowing lotus. He can't be more than half an inch big.

"That's him!" Mena says happily.

"Hello," says his hard-to-hear voice. "Hello, fellow Mystic. I see you have two summons already. That is good. I left a piece of me with Mena because I knew she was the best nurturer of all and would find a way to preserve my talents for a new Mystic to learn. Here, for now I will teach you Mantra, something all Mystics should have. First, though, you have to pick a word or phrase to use as your Mantra."

"Okay, um…" I have no idea. "Anything?"

"If you have special attachments to a name or saying or word, that works best."

My mind blanks. "Silvia," I spit out, worried I'd run out of time and lose this opportunity. Maybe it was because I had just been thinking about her, but I've been thinking about her for two years. I don't even know her real name. I think of her everytime I log in and out, things in the game remind me of her, and late at night when I can't sleep, I think of how she looks in White Elf Territory, her blonde hair glistening in the sun, the constant gentle breeze of the area blowing it around her shoulders and waist.

"Silvia. That's her, right?" asks Mena.

"Yep." My heart rate picks up at the memory, and I say her name in my head, trying it out as a mantra.

"No, you have to say it every time you use Mantra," says the little Mystic NPC in my palms.

"Silvia," I say, but nothing happens.

"I haven't taught it to you yet, curious Mystic Sid."

I laugh. "Okay, I'm ready."

A bright blue bolt shoots out of his itty-bitty index finger and hits me in my chest, where my summons go in and out. It knocks the breath out of me, but it doesn't hurt.

"Now, look at your abilities," he says. "When you say your mantra, Silvia, after using the ability, the effects of Mantra will take place."

"Thank you." I smile down at him. Finally, someone smaller than me.

"You're welcome. Maybe you will succeed where I failed. Mena seems to think so."

The lotus stops glowing and he fades away.

Mena cries softly as I hand the lotus back to her. "It was so nice to see and hear him again. Before, when he was human, we were married. Bane turned him, and he was never quite the same. I see that now, after he's passed, he's himself again." She smiles down at me. "Now, don't forget your Sunlight Daisy." She wraps the lotus in the pink silk and walks away, wiping tears from her eyes.

I open my abilities menu and read about Mantra.

Mantra—Gives target + Attack, random. Cumulative until end of battle.

Damn. This is a great one. I wonder how high the ATT stat can go. *Varengan's* Swift Arrow with that on it? Cumulative? That will be something.

I want to thank her all over again, and close my ability menu, but Mena is gone, probably putting the lotus in the safe.

I leave the shop, and tell the guild about it. They are stoked. I don't tell them about the Sunlight Daisy, nor what my mantra is.

Shell immediately pops in with, "Tell me everything!" She hardly ever talks and has three summons, including *Djinn*. "I don't have that." Something in the tone of her voice seems off. I can't place it. Maybe it's just one of those things. Looking into a little change and making a snap judgment.

I tell her exactly where I went, describing the flower shop.

"I'm on my way there now. Thanks, Sid," she says in her husky voice.

"We doing this thing today?" asks Days.

"I'm ready whenever you all are. Just say the word," I tell them. "No rush," I add, but I'm dying to charge down *Djinn's* cave and kick ass, get a new summon.

Getting new summons is addictive now.

Simple says, "Oh, man. I finally get to do one of these. *Djinn*! I've never even seen him." She lets out a little squeal.

It occurs to me that when Days met me and introduced me to Sorry the day we fought the Counts, he was seeing if I was a normal person and decent player so I could join the guild. And then they could do the big summon fights. They love this stuff.

I do, too, to be honest. In Elora, I never missed a big boss fight unless I was running a dungeon or asleep. We're all like that. Here, even more so, to keep us from the questions, even if it hurts, and hurts bad.

"I'm in," says Sorry.

"Me too," adds Doolittle.

"You guys are awesome," I tell them.

"Say, an hour? What cave this time?" Days asks.

"It's called Abandoned Echo Mine on the map when you zoom in on the northwest corner. It looks like it's at the base of a volcano."

I can't believe how lucky I am. I might actually get *Djinn* and this rad move Mantra in the same day.

"I can't wait to see my Death Lightning with Mantra," says Simple. "It's my hardest-hitting spell. I wonder how much Attack I can get…" She sounds geeked. ATT isn't a major stat for The Blacks, but through experience, players know damage mages with high ATT do much more damage with their big spells. One of the many unexplained parts of this MMO's gameplay method. Wikis theorize for pages and pages as to what stats actually do what for each class.

"I'm going to head that way," I tell them. "See you soon."

~

I bring out *Varengan* for the walk through Dragonbane Territory's valley of black, heading northwest. I'm about ten minutes from the cave *Djinn* waits for me in, and then *he* gets me.

Seeker casts Crystal Ball. Sid's next move is blocked.

Dammit, what the fuck now? Immediately, I whack my staff on the ground.

Sid's attack is stopped.

"Hello there," says a voice behind me.

I spin around, and *Varengan* is pecking at Seeker's shoulder and back. *Varengan* isn't much of a fighter except for Swift Arrow. The huge, gorgeous bird takes about 3% of Seeker's HP with each peck. The freak doesn't even flinch when *Varengan* hits him.

"Mind putting your canary away?" he says.

I don't want to, but I know to be cautious. That worked in the forest.

Sid dismisses *Varengan*.

"Hi." I try to sound neutral, but I can't pretend friendly right now. I have somewhere to be, people waiting for me. A summon to claim.

"I got you something," he says. "Here, trade."

Seeker offers to trade with Sid.

I accept warily. There's an anklet in the trade box in my interface.

"Go ahead. I think you'll like it."

I take it and look at what it is. Rose Gold Anklet, +3 CON. *Doubles Mystic's buff effects when using Meditation.*

"Wow," I murmur. "How did you get this?"

"You know how," he says with a shrug. His gleaming White Elf self doesn't fit in Dragonbane Territory.

I want to throw it on the ground and stomp on it. He looted it from some poor Mystic who must've turned Dark World upside-down looking for it. Instead, I equip it in one of my anklet slots. "Thanks, man."

"You're welcome. Want to help out. Like your friends from your guild." He smiles.

"Yeah, that's cool."

"I knew you'd like it. I also figure you don't like how I acquired it, but I hope you can see past that. Your Meditation will be amazing with that equipped."

I stick my sandaled foot out and look at the rosy chain around my ankle. I look like a girl. Good thing my robes are so long, or Days would tease me forever. "I'll get over it." If I ever find the Mystic he took it from, I'll return it. I don't say that. "I don't have Meditation yet."

"Really? I thought that's why you finally came to this side of the world. That the quest is here. You have it, right?"

"No. Going to find it. I plan on it, but on my way to a summon fight, so I really gotta go. Good to see you, and thanks again." I turn around, and walk away.

"Wait," he calls out, even though I'm ten feet away from him. The urgency, God.

"What?" I say, looking over my shoulder.

He walks up to me, closing the little distance I'd put between us. "Have you thought about it more? Found out the things you were looking for to make your decision?"

"No, still figuring. See ya." I walk away.

"Will you stop running off? Jesus." He sounds like he's losing his temper, and I know that's a bad thing. My instinct is to summon *Varengan* for heals, because I don't know any Psychic spells other than those he's used on me.

I stop and turn around. "Look, don't take this the wrong way. I have to be somewhere. People are waiting on me."

"I know."

Seeker casts Reiki. Seeker gains full HP.

He had been at about 75% from *Varengan's* pecking, but now completely fine.

This isn't good. Why did he heal himself?

Sid casts Contemplation. Sid gains Protection.

"Why did you do that?" he asks, white eyes narrowing.

"You made me nervous when you healed like that."

"Why? My HP was low from your bird. Was I supposed to walk around at 75% HP?" His face sets hard like a cryptic bust.

I don't mean to, and I've been doing good playing it cool, but I slip up. "Because you killed and looted me in Elora. Forgive me if I'm hesitant still."

"Is that the real reason you haven't made up your mind?"

"No—well, part of it. I just need more time. Okay?"

He takes a step closer to me. "I can get you through all your summon fights *and* get you gear that enhances everything. Just you and me. Doesn't the Rose Gold Anklet prove that a little bit?"

"Yeah, I know, but I like to do things my way." Sarcasm drips.

He crosses his arms, his black, gnarled staff wedged between his fist and chest. He's so much taller than me. I'm losing my ability to play nice. "I do, too. I understand. I get exactly what you're saying," he mutters.

My tone said it all. Not my words. I'd basically said my way is better than your way to a psychopath. Shit.

Seeker uses Telekinesis on Volcanic Boulder.

I have to think fast.

Sid summons *Varengan*.

I command my bird to go after him, but it's too late. A nearby black volcanic boulder is flying through the air right at me. It's the same size as me. This is gonna hurt.

One hit from that boulder is all it takes. I feel like I fell off a forty-story building, and then there's a sensation like I'm about to throw up my own innards, all of them, as my character collapses, dead.

Varengan disappears upon my death.

I want to curse him and really let him have a piece of my mind. Of course, I can't. All I have is the option in my interface to return to my graveyard. I can't even access guild chat until I'm a ghost. I can see everything in all directions around me, just like Elora, and feel as though I have been squished by a giant boulder as any Nuudle in mage robes for armor would. I can hear as well as see, though, not having agreed to the pop-up in my interface asking me if I am ready to go to my graveyard.

He stands over me, moving the boulder off my body with that damn Telekinesis spell. "You aren't better than me. We are alike. We are meant to fight together, not against each other." He shakes his head. "Such a shame. It'll take a while to walk back here as a ghost, even if you are ten times faster than usual. Nobody likes waiting. Your Faithgamblers friends will be long gone by the time you get there."

I'm not going back to the graveyard. I have to see him loot that anklet back. I know he's going to do it. Fury burns through me with the frustration of not being able to say or do anything.

He looks away. "Well, don't worry, Sid. I won't ever loot you again. I really am on your side. You need to learn certain things about me, that's all."

He walks away slowly, and I watch until I can't see him anymore.

I accept to return to the graveyard, wondering if he'll go back and loot me after all.

~

"I'm sorry," I say on guild chat as soon as I'm a ghost next to my tombstone. I don't want the guild to know about Seeker and his offer or anything at all about him here in Dark World, but now I have explaining to do. They're all waiting. The first time I met Days and Simple in the watering hole in Kleeple, I'd told them the story, but I've told no one what he's doing to me in this confounding reality.

Maybe it's time. Maybe simply the feeling of being a ghost in Dark World—this floaty, transparent-body feeling, no weight, no nerve sensations—makes me feel more open. I know I can trust some of these people because they've proven over and over that I can.

As I fly through the forest and White Elf Territory, I tell the guild about Seeker. How he just killed me, wants me in on some odd plan of his. Days asks about the plan, all of them shocked and pissed for me. I tell them he's crazy and his plan doesn't make any sense. I also admit to them I think he's the reason I'm in Dark World somehow. They are quiet at that. What do they know? It's that thing nobody talks about.

"Was he named just Seeker in Elora?" Days asks.

"No, The Seeker. Now he's just Seeker."

"Hmm." Days says nothing else, and the quiet stretches on.

I am almost compelled to tell him about the tombstones being next to each other, but I hold my tongue. I don't want to say that aloud yet, and its implications.

"So, that's why it's taking me so long," I say as I ride the hot air balloon again. "I'm so sorry to make you wait, and if you have to be somewhere, I understand if you can't wait anymore."

"Are you kidding? After what you just went through?" says Simple.

Days adds, "You have a stalker Psychic. Who just killed you. I think we can wait, and I think we can form a plan of our own for next time this Seeker comes after you. Maybe we can even track him down."

The guild discusses ideas for what they all want to do to Seeker, and Shell speaks up again as I get near my body. "Oh yeah, I did get in touch with that Psychic. I'll see if I can get ahold of him again in a letter and ask him to send me a list in the mail of Psychic spells he knows. I really don't know him well enough to message him."

"Really, Shell? That would be amazing, thanks," I say as I resurrect. Being a ghost, I felt no physical sensations, but now in my body, I feel the heat of Dragonbane Territory and the sweat beading up under my robe. I still feel aches of being hit by the boulder once I'm in my Nuudle body, and pain literally for a Heal or Cure.

Sid summons *Varengan*.

Sid commands Gentle Flight. Sid heals to full HP.

I look at my ankle. Rose Gold glitters in the sunlight.

"We all need to know that," says Sorry.

I can't believe how cool all these people are to me. They sincerely want to help me with not just my Mystic quest line, but with Seeker's mad obsession with me. I don't know why they've taken me on as a trusted comrade so quickly as to want to do some of the things Sorry is suggesting. I know the way she thinks. Even if all this time we'd been fighting together and never spoken, I'd be able to tell by her playing style. She's made to be this Voodoo Lady class. She suggests—without anywhere near coming close to saying—a sneaky, bloody and successful plan.

I like the way she thinks as I burn up and rub my muscles, grateful for my bird summon as I thank him, and then dismiss him.

I get to the cave, and Days, Sorry, Simple and Doolittle are waiting for me.

"Was that the first time you died?" Simple asks. It's nice to be eye-level with someone.

"Yeah. Sucks bad."

"It sure does," she says with a laugh.

Doolittle casts Deep Heal.

I feel a surge of relaxation in those aching muscles *Varengan* didn't quite get all the way, and it's as though I feel horrid arthritis fade like water out of a spigot, the boulder having made my newly resurrected body feel like it was still regrowing bones until this wonderful gift from Doolittle.

"Oh, thank you so, so much." I close my eyes for a minute, then open them. They're all looking at me, trying not to laugh.

"Stop."

"You poor, poor thi—" Sorry can't finish the sentence and cracks up into a fit of cackling. "Sorry, the look on someone's face after the first time they die in Dark World never gets old. Sorry, sorry, I know it sucked so bad."

I relax, especially because I don't hurt one speck anymore. "It's kind of like popping your death cherry?" I ask with a grin.

"Yes," says Simple, grinning back. "As you're here more, if you ever meet a new player, new to Dark World I mean, and get to know them... or not... but seeing their faces after they feel dying, it's pretty funny."

"It's the way we have to look at it or we'll lose our fucking minds," mutters Doolittle.

"Ready to do this?" asks Days, physically and dramatically wiping a big, shit-eating smile off his face while holding his massive sword.

"Yeah," I say. We enter the dark cave after I summon *Varengan*. His blue glow lights the way and he takes hate from any aggro mobs the deeper we explore the abandoned mine. Mostly, we're quiet, but they've put me in a much better mood about the death. Plus, the feeling of being a ghost is kinda cool.

We get to a dead end, looking yet again much like the last two summon fights' locales in caves, and I put my hand on the cave wall... my hand glows and the mark of the genie on my hand stays on the wall and grows.

Everything goes dark for a few seconds, and then we are in the battle arena.

We are inside a black volcano lit by the lava running in a circle around us. I don't even want to think about what it would feel like to get knocked in that.

In the middle of the black sand is a white marble pedestal, and on it is a golden lamp. A genie lamp. Ah-ha.

"I guess you rub it," says Doolittle.

"That's what I was thinking. Want to buff up?" I say.

"Let the buffing commence," says Simple.

We buff for over a minute, and I use *Varengan* after summoning him.

Sid commands Feathers. Days gains Protection.

"Not the Counts?" Days asks.

"Well, I've been thinking. The way the quests are laid out, it seems like I should use the last summon I claimed to get the next. Make sense?"

"No, but you seem pretty in tune with Mystic, so I trust ya even if *Varengan* isn't much of a fighter," he answers. "Let's go see what happens when you rub that lamp before the buffs start wearing off."

We go to the lamp and stand around it in a circle. I pick it up, examine it. "Ready?"

"Ready," says Days.

"Yep," adds Sorry.

The other two nod.

I tighten the sleeve of my robe and rub the lamp with it, making it shine. My hood falls back off my head as a gush of dust spits out of it as hard as a blow-dryer in my face.

Green smoke comes out of the lamp hole next in a rush, and high above us, *Djinn* takes shape, stretching his arms out like he's been in that lamp for a million years.

He is bright grass-green, with gaudy gold adornments around his neck, wrists, elbows and waist. He has a red hat with a golden tassel. His chest is massive, and so are his arms. Below his waist, he narrows down and fades into the green mist. He's overly muscular, and every finger has at least one or two heavily bejeweled yellow gold rings on it. They look like they're all for magical intent.

"Who has woken me?" he asks, yawning.

Varengan isn't attacking him. Good. I admit I'm more nervous about this one than the last two.

"I have," I say.

He floats down, putting his face in mine. "You're a small master. No matter, I offer my wishes to those of any size. But it takes more than rubbing my lamp for me to be convinced to serve you. I have been given the ability to choose whether or not I will assist a master, you see. I am the very first of the *Djinn*, coming into existence when time began."

"What do I need to do?" I ask him. Days gets his Deathdigger Sword ready.

"We have a friendly duel. Masters want power, and I want masters who are strong and will not abuse me. When I see how you fight, I'll know your morals. And then I can decide." He drifts away from me, hovering in between all of us just above his lamp, which I had set back down on the pedestal. The green smoke trail below his huge golden and ruby-encrusted belt drifts between us.

"Shall we begin?" he asks. "I'll even let you and your friends make the first move."

Our buffs are almost all worn off, except Protection from *Varengan* on Days, and the ones that are cumulative until the end of battle only have that effect once you're engaged in a battle.

I whack the ground with my Shaman Stick, sparks flying off the volcano floor.

Sid commands Feathers on Days. Days gains Protection.

Maybe it'll be or stay cumulative even out of battle if it's from *Varengan*. I've had odd status effects and stat boosts from using that command on me, but extra buffing, accumulation being wonky, out-of-nowhere stat boosts when using the command Feathers seems to be based on what *Varengan* feels like at the time. I'm hoping he knows and likes Days by now.

Yeah, Mystic is making me a little nuts with my reasonings. I don't talk about it to anyone.

Sorry casts Regain. Party gains HP over time.

"When did you get that?" Days asks.

"None of your business," she says with a sly grin at him, which he returns.

Doolittle casts Blessing of Inner Peace. *Varengan* will dodge all Special Ability attacks in battle.

Simple casts Lightning Armor on the party. Party members give lightning damage when hit.

Sid casts Contemplation. Days gains Protection.

Sid casts Spontaneity. Days gains +45 CRG.

"Alright," says Days. The courage boost makes him sound like he was injected with an Epi Pen for an allergic reaction to the boost. He's pumped.

Days uses Invoke Inner Demon.

"Hey!" *Djinn* says.

Djinn uses First Wish. Days is warped to Home Point.

Days vanishes in a green puff of smoke.

Crap.

Varengan starts pecking at *Djinn*, who slaps at him across his golden beak with a huge green hand as though the blue bird were an annoying fly.

Sid commands Confusion. *Djinn* is confused for 20 seconds.

"Oh, thank god," says Sorry.

Sorry casts Tribal Curse on *Djinn*. *Djinn* is cursed.

"Do it, Sid, cast Mantra on me!" squeals Simple.

Sid casts Mantra.

Nothing happens.

Oh yeah. "Silvia," I mutter.

Simple gains +220 ATT.

Simple casts Death Lightning on *Djinn*.

Djinn's HP drops to 30%. That is insane. His HP bar had indicated stats higher than 600, all of them.

It's now or never. The timer on Confusion is at 3 seconds.

Sid uses Seizure.

Sid commands Swift Arrow.

With a diving swoop, my love dove *Varengan* shoots into *Djinn* as he's coming out of Confusion, and his HP drops to literally 1%.

Simple casts Ball Lighting on *Djinn*. *Djinn* takes lightning damage.
Still, *Djinn's* HP stays at 1%.
***Djinn* uses First Wish.**
**Sorry casts Reflection of Darkness and Simple is not affected. *Djinn's*
move is stopped, and he takes arcane damage over time.**
One percent.
We all stop, and I command *Varengan* to retreat, quit attacking.
"Not bad, not bad. But you do realize I am easily going to defeat you.
However, that Confusion of *Varengan's* tricked me well. Good job, Mystic Sid.
May we have a word in private?"
"Sure," I say. Does this mean I got him? That easily?
My companions look as confused as I am, and then…
It goes dark for a moment, and next, I'm alone with *Djinn* in the lava-moat
arena.
"You have a lot to learn, but I do believe you are the kind of master who
will not abuse that which I offer you. I can give you three wishes. You may also
choose to release me. That is upto you. But be aware—if you release me to
freedom, I will fight my hardest for you, but I will again have the option to decide
if you are the master I wish to serve." The green smoke around him swirls and
glitters.
"Sounds good to me. Thank you, *Djinn*."
"Nuudle masters have always been my favorite. Such a way with words. I
now serve you, but keep conscientious of your use of my powers. I like how you
used Confusion first, considerate of damage and pain, and all the buffing was
quite amusing to watch." He instantly collapses into a thin stream of green smoke
and it slides into my chest.
Mmmm, full heart, life has meaning.
I got him, and that was probably the easiest fight we've had. Days is gonna
be pissed. When you enter an exclusive boss battle, guild chat automatically gets
cut off. He'd have no idea how it went down until I got out.
As vision fades to black, and then the dark cave at the entrance of the fight
appears, lit by a torch Sorry holds, I can already hear him bitching as guild chat
cuts back in.
"…Warps me back. And I don't even know if he got *Djinn* and neither do
you, but at least you got to see him in action," he's saying.
"You're back! Did you get him?" Sorry asks, clasping her hands together.
"Yep." I grin.
"Let's see him!" Simple begs.
"Let's wait for Days."
We do, and he's quite delighted for that.
Sid summons *Djinn*.
Green smoke shoots out of my chest and *Djinn* forms in the air beside me.
He's enormous. "Master, what is your bidding?" he asks.
"Just showing you to my friends," I tell him.
"I am impressive, aren't I?" he brags.
"Oh, yes, *Djinn*. You certainly are," I tell him.
"Read his moves list," says Sorry.

I open the menu in my interface and read.

Description:

Djinn is the very first of his kind, coming into being when time itself started. He is made only to serve. Be good to him and he will be good to you.

Abilities:

***First Wish**—Return target to home point.*

***Second Wish**—Target will become a ruler. If in a party, target will become party leader. All stats are increased 50% for 20 seconds. Some items and abilities may enhance this ability.*

***Third Wish**—Find treasure. Icons will appear on map.*

***Seizure Ability: Release Djinn**—Summon attacks for random, high damage to opponent. After each use, Djinn may or may not be able to be summoned again.*

"Find treasure," Sorry says with a sigh.

"I want to become a ruler. Stats at an extra 50%? Damn," says Simple, tossing her blue pigtails around.

We discuss the Seizure Move for a little bit. *Djinn* listens carefully. I like him. He has personality, likes being involved. I might enjoy just talking to this NPC summon, much like Master Gronai in the temple. *Varengan* doesn't talk, and to be honest, the Counts creep me out a bit every time I summon them. That black and white against the vivid colors of the game. The world. This place.

It occurs to me to ask Master Gronai about helping me write scrolls next time I try the craft. I bookmark the idea. There's still Mediation to get in Mylop Territory.

"I'm going to take *Djinn* down to Mylop Territory to get Meditation," I say my thoughts aloud. I can't stop staring at all of *Djinn's* gold adornments.

"Good luck!" says Simple, and then adds, "Don't forget that Second Wish and make the guild a shit ton of money."

I laugh. "You bet."

It's nice spending time with someone my own size, and she's very friendly now that she's comfortable with me. Whenever I get strong enough to help her with White Nile and her Casta Lot Hat drop, I will. I always liked White Nile runs in Elora, the White Elf crumbling shrine dungeon. I wonder if in Dark World it's not crumbling, but rather brand spanking new.

I bet it is.

I'll warp back to my HP, with *Djinn's* First Wish help, check for Calla and a new summon quest, then head back through Kila Crystals to Bane. After that, *Djinn* and I will explore what Mylop Territory is all about in Dark World.

CHAPTER 11: MYLOP TERRITORY

"Do you have *Xiuhcoatl*'s quest?" Shell asks in guild chat just after I warp to Bane through the Kila Crystals.

"Yeah," I tell her.

"How did you get it?" Is it my imagination, or does she sound a bit pissed? She must not have gotten it yet. My instincts tell me there's more, but I tell myself Dark World is making me paranoid. Shell has helped me a lot.

"The NPC at my grave gave it to me."

"Mine hasn't. That's weird."

"Did you get Mantra?" I ask her as I walk through the city, still astounding in its differences from Elora's Kane.

"Yes." She sighs. "If you figure out how I get the quest, please let me know. Anyway, I'm sending that list of Psychic spells to you. Hope it helps. The Psychic I got it from says he doesn't know if these are all of them."

My mailbox icon lights up in my interface with the number one sparkling in its corner. "Thank you so much."

"Send it to me, too," Days says.

"Send it to all of us."

I hear her sigh again.

"I'll do it," I tell them, making a right, walking to the AH and the mailboxes. I can't wait to read what it says.

Once at the mailbox, I open up Shell's letter and read

Psychic spells:
Crystal Ball—Blocks target's next move.
Telekinesis—Controls chosen target for 10 seconds. Some items and gear may enhance this ability.
X-Ray Vision—See target's abilities and bags. Target will not be notified of your action.
Reiki—Heals target to full HP.
Clairvoyance—Finds the location of any player.
ESP—Choose target's next move.
Mental Anguish—Deal brain damage to target equal to Psychic's Mind statistic, +/-. Some items or gear may enhance this ability.
Special Ability: Mind Control—You control opponent's moves for 20 seconds. Use once an hour.

At a glance, it doesn't seem like much, but I don't like that phrase "deal brain damage." What does that mean? Besides, the way Seeker handled me was excruciating. He knows his class well, and how to manipulate his skills to perfection. How many of these moves does he have? What items has he stolen to boost his stats and abilities? I imagine he has the best. And what moves aren't on this list?

Clairvoyance. That's how he's been finding me.

I buy some paper from the AH, copy and paste the list, and then mail it out to the guildies. Spent the last of my cash on it, too. I'm broke for the zillionth time in Dark World. It's like living paycheck to paycheck in RL.

I listen to them discuss the list of spells when they get their letters as I head toward the Wall of Bane. I was thrilled when Calla gave me the *Xiuhcoatl* quest, and it happened to be in Mylop Territory, where I planned to go for Meditation anyway. Lucky me.

I'm far away from Bane's gate now, safe from curious players, and summon *Djinn*.

"How may I serve you, Master?" he says as he takes form out of green, glowing smoke.

"Keep me company?" I ask.

"As you wish, Mystic Sid."

"Oh, and keep your eye out for mobs and Psychics," I add.

I glance back because he isn't next to me anymore. *Djinn* hovers behind me with one eyeball popped out and spinning. I can't help but laugh.

He laughs, too. "Good to see my new master has a sense of humor." He catches upto me and we prowl through the black valley toward the wall.

I spend about an hour walking the length of the Wall of Bane, but can't find a way through without fighting Dragonbane guards at all the exits. I can take on lots of fights now, but each gate is covered by six to eight high-stat guards, and I admit I can't do that.

"*Djinn*, any ideas as to how to get through here?" I ask him.

He rubs his green chin. "Perhaps another summon can help you."

"Think so? But I'll miss you."

He grins, then gives a belly laugh. "You can invite me back if they cannot help you."

"Good deal," I say, and dismiss *Djinn*. He turns into a green mist and swoops into my chest.

I have an idea.

Sid summons the *Counts of Hell*.

I read the Counts' abilities again, thinking.

Surround—Surround target and push it back forty feet, dealing damage according to if and what target is pushed into.

Could that possibly work on a piece of wall?

Sid commands Surround.

Pieces of volcanic rock spew outward, upward, and back at us. I instinctively duck, but one of the Counts, the biggest one with tiger furs, zooms in front of me and protects me from flying debris.

As the dust settles, I raise my head and look. They did it. There's a narrow hole leading straight through the Wall of Bane to the desert of Mylop Territory.

I hear Dragonbane guards in the distance shouting, trying to figure out what the noise and explosion was.

"We better go, guys," I tell them, and squeeze through the hole in the wall to the other side. I run with the Counts for about ten minutes until I can't hear the guards anymore.

I stop, catch my breath. "Thanks," I tell the Counts.

The one who protected me says, "Too much light, too many nearby."

The *Counts of Hell* release themselves.

My heart jumps into my throat. I check my summons list. Thank God. The Counts are still there. They could have decided not to let me summon them again until night.

Sid summons *Djinn*.

"How may I serve you, Master Sid?" he says.

"You were right. The Counts got me through the wall."

"I usually am right." He crosses his arms and smirks with satisfaction.

Mylop Territory is sand dune after sand dune further south, but here, I see the usual hard sand ground and desert shrubs. We're on a path heading directly south, where the Mylop caverns are. In Elora, the caverns were jam-packed with crafting stations. You could craft pretty much anything but scrolls in a cavern in Mylop Territory. In Dark World, I'm not so sure. Days said I would have to see it for myself to understand, and the other guildies said the same. He told me the Mylop there are in hiding, and that there's no crafting going on in Mylop Territory here.

Or is it now?

As *Djinn* and I walk the path, with my commands to warp mobs back to their home points as I go—I have no clue if mobs have HPs, but apparently, they do—I don't see any other players. I walk for a couple hours and it gets hot. So damn hot.

I'm soaked with sweat by the time I get to the first of Mylop's Serenity Caverns, and *Djinn* is sympathetic to me and my nearheat-stroke self. He blows white, cool air in my face.

This cavern used to be a metalworking hub, but as I peer inside, I see steel bars just within the entrance. "What the—?"

"Those poor Mylop," says *Djinn*.

I step through the overhanging rock and walk upto the bars, letting my eyes adjust to the dark.

Beyond the bars, I see dozens of Mylop NPCs chained to the walls. Their shackles clang much like the sounds of the crafters in Elora when they did their metalworking.

"What's wrong with them?"

"Hello?" a female voice calls out to me. "Can you help me? You, Nuudle. Please, help us."

I see a deep blue Mylop woman nearby on the other side of the bars. The NPC's name is Singh. I've never seen a female Mylop and find her fascinating.

"Please," she says. "You have to get us out of here."

"Okay," I say, unsure of what to do. "What's going on here?"

"Bane. It's Bane. He's taken all the women Mylop he could catch and put us in here, the Cavern of Compassion. He betrays and mocks us by chaining us up like animals for the slaughter in our holy shrine." She pulls at the shackles on her wrists, flicks her black lizard tongue.

Other female Mylop voices join in. I can't make out what any of them are saying, so I wait for them to calm down.

"Will you help, Nuudle Mystic? Can't you do something?"

Shell told me I had to do something with Mylop females for Meditation, so is this it? She said she'd done it several years ago—which got me thinking about other things, like how long all my new friends have been here—and was foggy on the specifics of where and how she did it. Said it had been so long that she couldn't remember.

"Sure, I'll help you," I tell her. "I need to think about how to, though. *Djinn*?" I look up at him. "Any ideas?"

"I have so many ideas. This is your quest, Master. Think, think, think."

Only hours ago had I looked at the Counts' abilities list, even though I know them by heart, and I have an idea.

"Thank you, *Djinn*. I did think and I do have an idea."

"Wise Master Sid." He smiles.

Sid releases *Djinn*.

Sid summons the *Counts of Hell*.

They rush out of my chest in a gray fog. "So many, so many," says my savior Count.

"Just for a sec, guys, then you're out of here. Okay?"

They look peeved.

Sid uses Seizure.

Sid commands Hell on Earth.

"Yes!" I call out as the lava from my Counts' staffs melts the bars. I'm quick to dismiss them before they dismiss themselves again. The last time made me nervous.

"Thank you, thank you!" says Singh. "Now, the steel puddle has hardened. You must release us from our chains. If you can just get my hands, I can do the rest. Our claws fit the locks, but the Dragonbane bound our hands, as you see." Her hands are clamped inside a metal box.

I cross the warm, hard steel, and investigate the curious box around her claws. The others cry and whisper.

"How do I get it off?"

"I don't know," she says. "The guards, when they take one of us, leave them on."

I look way up at her lizard eyes. "Why are they taking you?"

She shakes her head. "Bane uses our essence to create Dragonbane. Mylop women have special blood, ancient blood. We are the second race of Dark World. We have Creation Magic inside us, having created ourselves, and he uses our blood to make Dragonbane."

So that's why all the female Mylop are gone in Elora.

Sid summons *Djinn*.

The ladies all gasp and cry out at the sight of my *Djinn*.

"Master, how may I be of service?" he says once he's fully-formed.

"Trying to figure stuff out again, *Djinn*. You help me think."

"Of course I do."

"Ladies," I say, "no need to panic. He's a friend."

"That's *Djinn*!" says Singh. "He has been, and always will be, older than we!"

They quieten down just a little as I continue trying to calm them. "*Djinn*, any way you can convince them you're not going to hurt them?"

"I'm not going to hurt the Mylop, of course not. Why would I do that?"

"See?" I say to them, and a hush falls over the cavern.

"*Djinn*, do Mylop NPCs have HPs?" I ask him.

"Everything and everybody has a home point, Master Nuudle."

I turn back to Singh. "Okay, here's what we're going to do. Just a little magic from *Djinn*, and I'll get you all home safely where you can have one of your kind release these bonds."

She looks panicked. "No, no magic from *Djinn*. I'd rather stay here and die at Bane's hands."

"It's a simple spell. I promise."

"No, no, no," a cacophony of women's voices call out through the cave.

"Calm down! Everybody, calm down. It's one of his wishes. You'll be safe."

"I don't trust timeless magic," says Singh. "What if it hurts?"

"It won't hurt, but it'll take a while. How many of you are there?"

She looks back. "Many, many."

"Okay, well, because I can't undo your shackles—these steel boxes around your hands—I'll warp each and every one of you back home."

"You won't," she says. "*He* will!"

Djinn cocks a dark green eyebrow at her.

"It'll take some time, but I'll get you all."

"How long?"

"Probably a couple hours... I guess..."

"We don't have that much time," another voice says from the darkness.

"That's right. The guards will be here within the hour to take some of us. There's no time!" Singh says. She sighs. "Young Nuudle, I can sense in you a gentle and trustworthy character. Mylop women, do you agree?" Murmurs. "I reacted poorly. You offer salvation, and I fear ancient magic. I can see your magic intentions are pure of heart. There is something I can do to expedite this. Here, I have a gift for you. An old, old skill to help you get us all at once."

What is this? It's not Meditation... could this be...?

"Put your head down, young Nuudle," she says.

I do.

She chants Mylop words and I feel cool for the first time since entering Mylop Territory.

Sid learns the skill Target Many. Sid can now target many at once when desired instead of only one.

Whoa. The guild had told me the quest for multi-targeting is different for everyone, but this changes everything.

"Oh, thank you, Singh!" I grin at her.

"You promised it won't hurt. Remember that." She frowns at me.

"It won't." I grin up at *Djinn*. "You ready?"

"I'm always ready, Master." He grins back.

I target all the Mylop I can see as I walk through the Cavern of Compassion. *Djinn's* soft, green glow lights the way and helps me find them. I'm surprised at myself. Seeing them like this makes me feel sorry for them. They are NPCs, for crying out loud.

Once I have them all targeted, I give *Djinn* a thumbs-up.

Sid commands First Wish.

Singh and 105 other targets are warped to their Home Points.

In a green flash, they all vanish.

"Thanks, *Djinn*," I tell my summon.

"Don't mention it."

A voice from the hot desert behind me says, "Not bad. I got multi-targeting a week ago. I guess that means I'm ahead of you."

I turn. Seeker stands at the cavern's entrance, arms folded. Not smiling.

"Leave me alone."

"Why are you being like this?"

"Because you killed me last time I saw you." I can't help the anger building up in me. I want to smash his face.

"Shall I assist you, Master?" *Djinn* asks.

"Maybe," I say.

Seeker raises a glowing hand, but I act fast on instinct.

Sid commands First Wish.

Seeker is warped to Home Point.

Seeker poofs into green mist.

Oh, man. I royally pissed him off now. But, hell, if that isn't a nifty way to get rid of him.

~

I tell the guild I got multi-targeting. The ones who fight with me seem more excited than I am. I even tell them about Seeker and using First Wish on him. "It came so naturally," I tell them. "Now I have a fool-proof way to make him eat shit."

"No Meditation?" asks Simple.

"Nope. I'll have to keep looking."

"Yeah," says Sorry. "It'll help so much with your next fight. *Xiuhcoatl* is gonna be badass. Hard to kill."

"Yep," I tell them. "I'll keep looking."

"Sorry," says Shell on guild chat. "I just can't remember exactly what I did."

"It's okay, I'll figure it out. But thanks," I tell her.

There's that gut feeling, like she used to help, and then she's pulling back. Am I imagining it?

I leave the dark, empty cavern and head south again, continuing to listen to the guild chat. A few of them are trying to get a Blessed spell for a Siren Blessed in an ally guild, and some others are trying to run a hard dungeon, Belioff, in Dragonbane Territory.

I'm near Dawn, the capital of Mylop Territory, when Days says to me, "Let us know, Sid, when you got it. Then I'm down for the dragon."

I look at the dragon marking on my left palm. When Calla had put it on me, my pulse fired up and my imagination went wild. I haven't seen *Xiuhcoatl* anywhere in game, and my guild says they haven't either. Simple had said she'd been waiting for Shell to get the fight quest, and she couldn't wait until the battle.

I'm scared, to be honest. A dragon. It's gonna hurt when he hits me. Or any of us. None of my three summons are damage dealers, but a dragon? He'll be damage, big damage. I like damage, doing it. Not done to me.

"Sorry, *Djinn*, but I have to be incognito in cities. You know I like your company."

"Of course, Master Sid. I understand everything."

Sid releases *Djinn*.

I cross the sand dunes, heading straight for the tunnels of Dawn. It's an underground city with only a three-person wide opening to betray its whereabouts. In Elora, the city was magnificent underneath the earth, with an enormous sandstone-carved archway leading into the underground city. So much money, so many high-stat characters vending their crafts in the best AH in game. Even some things that won't reach the Cashmere AH are here. What will it be like in Dark World?

It's dark inside, whereas in Elora it was lit with electricity. The caves have rustic wall paintings I can see from the light of the torch I lit.

Where's Dawn, the massive, bustling underground city of the spiritual warrior Mylop?

I explore farther, deeper. Nothing still.

Sid summons *Djinn*.

"How may I be of your best service, Master Sid?" *Djinn* says once he's gloriously formed.

"I'm all alone here in Dawn. Where's the city?"

"You get lonely a lot."

"To be honest with you, in Dark World, I'm scared a lot."

"Ah, I comfort you. Nice to know."

"Can you tell me what happened to Dawn?"

He rubs his goatee. "Time's events are all the same to me. I have a feeling if you explore the deep, hidden places, you will find it."

I laugh. "I think you just told me the right answer. And yeah, going in those holes scares me. So, stick around, *Djinn*."

"As you wish." He nods.

We explore for hours down crumbling tunnels until suddenly, I smell cabbage cooking. It's Mylop Cabbage, and they put grubs in it. It's expensive, but it boosts Attack stat for thirty minutes… pretty high. In Elora, I'd eaten it tons. Now that I can taste in Dark World, I'll never touch Mylop Cabbage.

"This way. I smell bad cooking." I sprint along a narrow passage with *Djinn* trailing behind.

We exit into an enormous, high-ceiling cave bustling with Mylop of both sexes and all colors, shapes and sizes.

"Would you look at that?" I hear a male player's voice say. "That's *Djinn*! How'd you get him?"

I turn to my left, where a human player with brown hair and pale, rosy skin gapes at *Djinn*. Short, trimmed brown beard. He's wearing flowing gray robes in layers, and many gold and silver necklaces, including a huge pendant of Brannah, the God of the dead. He of Brannahday fame and many loyal, sacrificing-type followers.

Is he a Dead One, the elusive damage-dealing class that can make the undead mobs fight for him? Still, why didn't I think to put *Djinn* away so I wouldn't have to go through this rigmarole again?

Sid dismisses *Djinn*.

"Sorry, I, uh, forgot to put him away."

The player's name is Lucky. "That was one of the coolest things I've seen. Thanks, man." He smiles. "I heard there was a new Mystic. Must be you."

I feel guilty for having been irritated that another person wanted to talk about my Mystic-ness. Lucky's a nice guy, and maybe *Djinn* liked the attention.

"Thanks. He's great. Talkative." I smile back up at him. "Are you a Dead One?"

He nods. "Yep, and human. Weird, right? The map bring you here?"

"Map? No, just explored until I smelled Mylop Cabbage."

"Oh, yeah. You can smell that stink three tunnels away. I can't get past those grubs. Anyway, I won't bother you. You're probably sick of players wanting to see all your summons."

"It's okay, really. I just don't know what to think of Dawn."

His brown eyes widen. "How new to Dark World are you?"

"This is my first trip to Mylop Territory, if that tells you anything. I came to find Meditation, a Mystic move I really need for my next summon fight."

"Oh, oh. Okay. Wow, you're getting those summons fast. Really fast. Hey, you know, there's a Mylop Mystic NPC in a little hut on the south side of New Dawn. That's what I call it." He laughs.

"Really? Thanks, that's a great place to start. I appreciate it."

He holds his hand out and down. "Nice to meet you."

We shake hands. When I feel his human skin, a longing for physical contact hits me hard, and I have to look away. "You too."

"Can I add you to my friends list?" he asks, suddenly shy.

"Uh, sure." People don't usually put you on their friends' list within three minutes of meeting you.

"I know, I promise I'm not a nut. I'm flabbergasted you have *Djinn*. I've heard only one other player in the game has him."

"Yeah, I know a girl with him. Think she's the one you heard of?"

"It's like, Seashell or something."

"Shell. Yep, we're in the same guild."

He grins. "Sounds like a good guild. Go see the NPC, get that spell. Thanks, Sid!" He rushes off. I feel like a rock star for the first time from Mystic attention as I get a notification for a friend request from Lucky. I accept.

As I walk through the cramped, overcrowded cavern city looking for a hut on the south side, it occurs to me as strange that Shell and I are the only two

Mystics with *Djinn*. How many summons are there? I've heard rumors of ones, and know rumors of Mystics who have gotten their summon battle quests in other orders than I've gotten mine. Are they just stories, and are my memories of what summons look like just from paintings and statues in Elora? Everything I hear about Mystic is secondhand from thirdhand. Someone heard this, someone read that. Shell knows what I know, and more. She never talks about her class.

She used to talk a lot. But yeah. Never about her summons or her class. All I ever talk about in guild chat, if I do talk, is my summons. Maybe observations that interest me about them, or something especially clever this new *Djinn* summon says.

It gives me pause. I realize I don't quite trust Shell for sure. It was how she demanded to know how to get Mantra. Tone of voice, and mine with my arch-enemy got me smushed by his Volcanic Boulder. Tone says so much more than words sometimes.

Shell is the only Mystic I know. I've never even met her in game. Just hear her raspy voice. When players started showing interest in me as a Mystic, I heard so many rumors, but no one knew a specific named Mystic—until Lucky, who has also heard of Shell.

It seems like nobody's met one. When I think back, in Elora, I could have sworn I'd seen Mystics... at least one. But maybe I just saw screenshots and made them my own memories.

No, not screenshots. But still, my three summons have all seemed familiar to me the moment I saw them for the first time.

I shrug the thought away as I spy a tan burlap hut, circular, with a little flap. Pretty small to hold a Mylop. I have to check this out.

I enter the hut and inside, it's a palace of exotic treasures and rarities. A magic hut that looks cheap on the outside, but enchanted to be big and fancy on the inside. A real treasure hound would get a hut like this.

"Hello. You are Mystic, like me. I've been waiting for you," I hear a man's voice say to my right.

He's a white Mylop with silver eyes and wearing a long, royal blue silk Enchanter's Robe +4. What a glamorous NPC. What a hut. He sits on a black velvet cushion on a leopard-print fur rug, placed perfectly square on the oak floor.

"Waiting for me? How'd you know I was coming?"

"Someday, you, too, will know such things. All Mystics who progress do. You've come for a gift."

"Yes, actually." I read his name. I'd been so stunned by everything I hadn't even taken it in. Cedra. "I've been looking for someone to teach me Meditation."

I wait, but he says nothing. Just stares at me, unblinking in that lizard Mylop way.

"I'm Sid. Cedra is an unusual name for a Mylop. Sounds like a family name." I'm trying a new tactic, the Nuudle charm. It usually goes over so well with NPCs, but Cedra's eyes cut me in half.

"It is not something that is taught, it is something that is learned," he finally says.

"Oh, why, certainly. That's the perfect way to describe every aspect of Mystic."

"Nice Nuudle words will not persuade. I'm very interested in that Rose Gold Anklet you have on. I've not seen one in seventy-four years. Someone stole mine. Oh, yes, and I paid quite the price for it."

I don't want to trade him Seeker's evil gift because the good guy in me wants to give it back to the previous owner. But the bad guy in me wants to stick it to Seeker by giving it to Cedra, because I know he'll find out somehow. I won't be able to wait to tell him first if I get the chance. "You're saying you'll help me learn meditation if I offer you the anklet?"

He nods and smiles slightly. "That's exactly what I am saying."

I hesitate. It's a good deal for me. Even if the anklet kills with Meditation, and I have the desire to return it; I want to get rid of it. I could just give it to him and learn my spell.

"You do not care for my offer," Cedra says, flicking a black, forked tongue in irritation.

"No, it's not that. It's a long story, but this anklet isn't mine. Oh, I can't explain this to an NPC. Sorry, don't take that personally."

"You know very little about Non-player Characters. But as I said not a minute ago, in time, as a dedicated Mystic, you will learn it all. That is, if you do not abuse your power."

"I don't have much power to abuse. I need help from my friends every time I do a summon fight. I'm grateful to them, just wish I wasn't so weak."

"You feel guilt?" He cocks an eyebrow as though I'd finally said something that entertained him.

"Guilt... confusion. I don't know how to play this class. I'm never a mage."

He pulls a long, wooden tobacco pipe out from under his robe and lights the tobacco in the bowl with a thin flame that comes right out of his pointer fingertip. "I hear you are innovative."

NPCs always know your "reputation," so his saying that isn't a thing. It's my in.

"I ask for the summons' advice, respect their do-nots."

He nods and puffs smoke circles into the air between us. "The anklet?"

"Okay, let's do it." I unequip the Rose Gold Anklet. My foot feels lighter, as though Seeker's gift's taint held my right foot down more than my left. I offer to trade with him and put the anklet in the trade box.

He takes it with a satisfied grin.

"Now, what does your Mystic sense tell you to do to learn this new spell?"

"It's a buffing spell."

"Yes." He sounds impatient.

"I have an idea..."

He hunches over. "Do it already, then. Your insecurities are tiring."

Sid casts Spontaneity. Sid gains +63 MND.

I feel a rush of groovy feelings from the Mind.

Sid summons *Djinn*.

"How may I help you, Master Sid?"

"Needed to make another move. Besides, I think you'll like this."

Sid casts Spontaneity. Cedra gains +374 ATT.

Jesus, his stats must already be through the roof. NPCs aren't usually high-stat, other than my summons.

Cedra casts Meditation. Sid's stat boosts will last for 80 seconds.

I feel like I just did a line of coke, even if I never have. The pure, solid energy of having that much Mind always makes things nice, but the MND stat boosted so high from his wearing the Rose Gold Anklet while casting Meditation, well, the sensation is unending... it just goes on and on. I'm in a trance. *Djinn* and Cedra are arguing, but I can't tell if it's banter or an actual problem.

Just in case, through my haze, I dismiss *Djinn*.

When time runs out, I come back into focus.

"See, you have now learned. I do hate to tell you that you'll regret giving up this anklet. And mark my words, when *Djinn* loses interest in you for the next hot, new Mystic hunting him, and you've used his Seizure move, he won't come back. Ever."

Had they been arguing about that? What does it mean?

"Here," he mutters, holding out the pointer that had been a lighter moments ago. I flinch as white light shoots out of his finger and into my chest. A sharp pinch twists my heart.

Sid learns Meditation.

"Thank you. To be honest with you, I never plan to even think about that anklet ever again." I want to ask him to tell me more about *Djinn*, what he meant, but he's dismissing me, avoiding eye-contact and fondling the Rose Gold Anklet at his foot.

I read the spell's description.

Meditation—*Gives target's buffs longer-lasting time, + 20~90% depending on Concentration level. Some items or gear may enhance this ability.*

Whoa. Shell told me it was 20 to 50%. Was she lying, or does hers not go as high? I decide right then and there I'm not going to tell the guild my spell reads differently than she said hers does. I'll keep my suspicions to myself and pay attention. Remember to check the guild list before talking about anything I don't want her to hear to make sure she has chat off.

People in Dark World are mostly unpredictable. Of the many Mystic fans I've met, I've picked up on a lot of crazy in whatever this Total Immersion really is. Anella is a great example. I still haven't seen her in the graveyard again, but I can feel her there, the same way you can feel if someone is staring at you and you turn your head, catching him. Instinct guiding the way, except I never catch her.

The question of whether or not I'm dead continues to run through my mind down rabbit hole after rabbit hole. If I'm in Elora's past, then I could possibly be here for 2,000 more years, right? That is, if my consciousness is now in the game somehow, forced or built-in to the game for a player to go to Dark World and start a new life. One after death.

But see, then, wouldn't I have already found myself in Elora by the time I started playing?

Is it 2,000 years, or fifteen years? Elora Online's only been out fifteen years. Game time is like RL time. Same sunrise and sunset as in your time zone. The days are named after planets, and some crafters are superstitious that the planets have something to do with crafting. Some people think you get better skill-ups on

Shealaday, for example. I found a book in the Temple of Nuudlel that said the planet Sheala, named after the great White Elf White Knight princess of ancient times, carries the principles of White Knights, so maybe the idea some players had that Shealaday was better for skill-ups was because they themselves were White Knights. Or White Elf females. Or White Elf Killer, for all I know. You have to read every book, talk to every NPC. Many theories, lots of hours of speculation. Some, like Simple, geek out hard on the histories and philosophies of the game. This existence.

Maybe the game alone is responsible for my death, and that's how I died. I know more about Elora and Dark World than I did about Irvine, California, my hometown all my life.

I'm going to farm some Sand Worms and Wild Cactuses for AH stuff. There's no clothcraft station in Dawn, and when I asked a fellow player where one was, he said Mylop Territory's crafting was banned by Bane.

So, yeah. I have to farm.

It takes about twenty minutes of letting *Djinn* whack the suckers around before I get an ah-ha moment. It's ridiculously easy, and I feel incredibly stupid.

"*Djinn*, that Third Wish of yours…"

"Yes, Master Mystic? Find Treasure?"

"Yeah. Yeah, that one. Can we try it?"

"You don't ask, you command." He grins. "It's about time. Let's treasure hunt. These piddly creatures are for eating, not looting."

Sid commands Third Wish. Treasure and hidden objects within 30 Selcos will appear on your map for an hour.

Oh, yeah. Now this will be fun. I open my map. So many sparkly, yellow Xs. All over the place! We're going to have fun, and no more farming.

You can buy treasure maps. Nuudles make scrolls of them. It's a high-end spell-making scroll that sells on the AH for millions. I got one once for $2 mil from Peter when he first started making them. He did it for cost of mats. And there was the one I bought what feels like years ago when I got the Seer's Amulet. It's best to hunt down information on where a special item might be hidden before getting a treasure map, as the cost of one doesn't pay off the investment of a random hunt. I spent a month figuring out how to get that Seer's Amulet.

I'm so giddy.

We have a grand time, and we even get a pair of Black Pearl Earrings I think Simple can wear. INT stat is +45 if you wear both. I tell *Djinn* she'll love them. He agrees.

Yes, this is better than farming, but most stuff I find is garbage or something I want to give to a guildie. I get a few pieces of nice gear I can AH.

I find a Moldavite Ring at the edge of a cave entrance, and that says it has +6 CON and "Grant God Status" as its use description. It's thick yellow gold with an oval, faceted deep green moldavite set deep in the metal. All within the stone, I see natural inclusions, making the gem seem to catch more light. It's downright manly, and rings are never manly. It fits me perfectly, unlike a lot of things in Dark World. MYT class-specific, so it must be good for me somehow.

The prize is the Rose Gold Anklet we dig out from under a random pile of sand. How in the world could anyone find this without *Djinn*? Or a Treasure Map scroll and some serious research?

This one is mine. Oh, the irony.

I plan on using the payoff from farming and treasure hunting to fund my next clothcrafting session. I need materials, and with Third Wish, I don't have to farm them and I get more loot. Sell high-stat found treasure, buy the mats.

I've found crafting to be just as much, if not more so, lucrative than farming, and it takes less time, too, once you get past the grinding levels where you make the same things over and over to get a 0.4 raise in clothcraft skill every fourth try. Thread is the best for that because it sells, and I don't have to pay as much for gear because I make most of mine. Getting materials and making my own stuff is much cheaper than buying gear off the AH. At least with the stat gear I can wear now. Still, I've found that the clothcraft recipes I got or learned that are craft-specific to the crafter only, well, they're better pieces of gear than I could get at an AH. The only other places to get great gear are dungeons, and I'm not high-stat enough for the dungeons with the best drops.

Also, I haven't wanted to be in a dungeon party as a Mystic. Sure, I've done three summon boss battles, but I still feel like I'm flubbering about with this class.

Maybe Cedra is right, and someday, I'll know everything.

CHAPTER 12: BATTLE OF XIUHCOATL

I'm the first one at the Cavern of Oddities, where Calla marked *Xiuhcoatl*'s battle on my map. I don't go inside, and instead, summon *Djinn* for company.

"What is your bidding, Master Nuudle?" he says after he takes form.

"We're going after *Xiuhcoatl*. I'm waiting for my friends. They helped me with you, remember?"

"Oh, yes. I like that Voodoo Lady. So beautiful." He sighs dramatically. "Their magics are dark and twisted." He says it like a compliment.

"Do you have a crush on Sorry?"

"I do not get crushes. I only serve." He swells his massive green chest.

"You do more than that."

"Like what, Master Sid?"

"Like think Siren Voodoo Ladies are hot."

"Hot?" He tilts his head. "She always dresses in practically nothing. Robes, she calls them. She has to be freezing all the time, not hot."

He almost had me, but then I laugh. "Touché."

My nerves are frazzled. It's been a day since I warped Seeker to wherever his HP is, and now that I know he can find me with his Clairvoyance spell, I feel watched by him all the time. It's creepy, not knowing if I'll read that I'm being hit with Crystal Ball at every turn.

At long last, as the heat of the desert sun is about to catch my flesh on fire, Days, Sorry, Doolittle, and Simple fly in on a black dragon big enough to fit them all on its back.

The dragon lands, lets out a barking, gruff huff, and shakes its head as my companions climb off.

"Is that a mount?" I ask.

Days laughs. "Nah, we grabbed one that had gotten loose and rode him over here. Dragon, get it? Keeping in the spirit of the quest."

The black dragon's enormous, webbed wings flex and flap, and then it's off into the hot sky. I watch it until it's out of sight.

"Wow."

"Yeah, wow," says Simple, tugging my hair. "I never should have done blue. I like your black. Who am I kidding? All Nuudles look silly. I do these stupid pigtails for the Double Magic Bandwraps' INT boost in my hairstyle slots."

"That why you're extra silly?" Days asks her.

Sorry slaps his chest. "Quit flirting with the Nuudle."

He gives Sorry a sly look but says nothing.

"So, let me guess. Looking for a dead end that looks exactly like every other dead end the summon fights have been at?" Doolittle says.

"That seems to be the drill," I respond. "Ready?" I turn to *Djinn*. "Will you be our guiding light, oh green one?"

"Anything you ask, Master Mystic Sid." He takes the lead into the darkness. We follow. It's so much cooler out of the sun the deeper we go. There are no mobs anywhere, and that feels a bit creepy.

"Shell didn't come?" I ask, speaking quietly. It feels appropriate.

"She said she had already promised a friend she'd help him with a quest line for the next few days," Simple tells me.

"We really could have used her help," Sorry adds. "Two Mystics for a summon battle? That would be amazing."

"Two *Djinn*s," I murmur. I have a fleeting thought of what Cedra told me about *Djinn* leaving Mystics when they use his Seizure move. I know I'll have to use it on *Xiuhcoatl*, and I'm pretty sure *Djinn* will come back. But what if he doesn't? Is that my wishful thinking? Projecting onto *Djinn* a comrade?

The game has become everything. It's all I know now. I live here. I sleep here. I dream here, and I die here. I'm reborn again and again. My closest confidant is a genie.

Djinn doesn't waste time and leads us down a rocky slope to a familiar-looking dead end. "Master, as you wish!" He waves his massive hands at the wall in front of us.

I look at the snaky dragon mark on my left palm. "I'm nervous."

"You aren't nervous," Days says. "You're getting him. You're excited."

No, I know I'm nervous. I have no idea what to expect. Dragons can hurt. Bad.

"We doing this?" Sorry says.

"Yeah, let's do it," I say, and put my left hand on the wall. The dragon mark leaves my hand and glows yellow on the rock this time, and then everything fades to black.

Then we're in.

The arena, although in a cave, is full of twisting, ancient tree roots from god knows where, and they cover the cavern's ground, climbing all the way up to a wide, open-air view of the sun directly overhead. It's incredibly bright and hot.

I don't see a dragon.

"Where is he?" says Doolittle.

"I don't know. It's just roots and nothing else," says Simple. She sounds a little nervous too.

Sid summons *Djinn*.

"Yes, Master Sid, I am at your beck and call," he announces loudly after forming from his green smoke.

"Shhh!" I tell him.

"Why shhh?" he asks.

"Oh, sorry. Gut reaction. We don't know where *Xiuhcoatl* is. This place is empty," I tell him.

"He and I are old… acquaintances. I gave him a wish once. Just because."

I look up at him. "What wish?"

"To be able to become invisible. He foresaw the Dragonbane. Came to me for help. I admit I regret it now."

"Why?" Simple asks him.

"Because I hate being burned, and young Master Sid plans on utilizing my wishes to convince him to join Master Sid in his Mystic progression." He grins. "I've been burned worse, though."

I want to ask him about my Mystic progression and what that means, but out of nowhere in the middle of the cave, *Xiuhcoatl* becomes. We all freeze in terror.

He's indeed a snake dragon, solid, shining gold scales covering his long, twisting body as he flaps his gigantic, skeletal sapphire wings. His face is more animalistic than the dragon my friends arrived riding on earlier. He looks like he comes from another world, another time, hell, another dimension. His long, sleek, spiraling spiked tail sways and swirls as he keeps flying in one place, looking right at me. Wind from his flapping wings blows my hair.

"Oh my," whispers Sorry.

Xiuhcoatl hisses at me, a thin, blood-red forked tongue whisking around his oh-so-sharp double rows of teeth.

Sorry casts Spiritual Intervention. Sorry and 5 others gain +80 DEF.

She had reacted, but the rest of us just gape at the enormous golden beast in front of us as he opens that terrifying mouth, feeling the Defense stat boost cool our heads.

"Never again!" he rumbles, and hisses again, still glaring at me. We're frozen in fear and panic.

Djinn clears his throat, shaking his head.

We all get targeted. Here it comes. Why can't I do anything?

Xiuhcoatl **uses Solar Explosion.**

The sunlight coming in from above in the cave becomes a solid thing, shooting down at us like molten gold instantly. It's so fast. Too fast.

Sid dismisses *Djinn*.

I've never felt such pain in my life, bypassing the feeling of being about to puke up my guts and making me pass straight the fuck out. I just experienced being bombed by a nuke. Yep. Really no way to describe that except "I don't want to talk about it."

I kind of come to in my graveyard. I'm a dazed ghost for several moments, trying to figure out what happened. I can't access guild chat as a ghost, for some reason, to ask my friends what happened to them. All I remember is that I felt like the sun fell on me and burned out my soul. I swear I felt my eyeballs melt.

He wiped us. Wiped us all right out before we could even begin.

Dazed and crushed, I don't move at regular ghost speed. My ghost body even hurts still, but maybe that's my imagination reliving that horrid experience.

I make it to the wrought-iron fence and drift through it. I sit down suddenly, and I feel so very alone. I want to cry for the first time in as long as I can remember. I stare into my rain-soaked Moldavite Ring's stone, at all its familiar inclusions after a few lifetimes of gazing at it when I can't sleep. They make different pictures to me sometimes. Little connect-the-dots.

"Sid," I hear a woman's voice say. I look around me.

Anella stands next to me and puts her hand on my shoulder. I can feel it. But how can she see me? I'm a ghost. How can she touch me?

"The Hidden can see ghosts. The Hidden can do many things with and for ghosts."

"Can you hear me?"

"Yes." Her voice is soft, almost a whisper. "Here, let me help."

Anella casts Revive on Sid.

My see-through self becomes solid, and lord, my whole virtual body aches. I bend over my knees, moaning. She brought me back from being a ghost. I thought you could only revive at your body.

Anella casts Soothing Stream on Sid. Sid gains +560 MND for 120 seconds.

A jolt of pure ecstasy fills me, starting at my toes and running up my small body to the top of my head. I see things I can't make sense of, hallucinating from so much Mind. The highest stat I ever had was my ATT when I went after Seeker in Elora so long ago, and I didn't *feel* stats in Elora.

This is a drug.

I lie back in the leaves and close my eyes, letting the feeling fix me. It does just that. Fixes me. "Thank you so much, Anella." I murmur. I stay still and breathe the wet, rainy air as the eternal rainfall of the graveyard drenches me.

Anella casts Shielding from Horrors on Sid.

That familiar greenish fog embraces me in its bubble and the rain stops pelting me.

I open my eyes and look up at her. She is a very beautiful Siren, but she always looks so sad. Soaking wet. Like she's forgotten something, like she's lost a spark of life somewhere here in Dark World. Her silver hair seems unkempt, yet gorgeous in a mysterious, wild way. "Why do you help me?"

"Because you're helping me."

"How? How am I helping you?" I sit up, peering into her black eyes.

"You give me hope."

"How? I don't get it."

She's quiet, staring. I wait, unmoving. With Anella, it always feels like I could say or do just the wrong thing and she'll disappear with her Scatter spell, and everytime I get that feeling, I'm afraid I'll never see her again. So, I do nothing.

"I've never had hope before" was all she said. "Now, go back. Turn your guild chat back on. Boost up your people. Give them hope and try again."

My guild chat *is* off. It should have cut back in, I'd think, when I became alive again at least. Right? Did she do that, too? Really, no clue what's going on sometimes in Dark World. It decides its own rules that usually I'd call a game glitch... but this isn't a game and I know it.

I want to complain, say it's too hard, too scary to think of going through that again. I nod slowly. "Okay, Anella. I will. For you."

"For all of us, Mystic," she says.

Anella casts Scatter.

Ghostly images of Anella shoot away in all directions. She's an oddity, and she knows so much. If only I could get her to talk, tell me what's going on. What she knows that nobody else does.

I turn on guild chat to several very depressed guildmates. "Hi," I say. "I'm back."

Simple bursts out, "You were gone forever! Your body wasn't there when I got to the battle entrance. What happened to you?"

"I have a… friend," I say. "She's the Hidden. She did something to me. I don't know."

"You know a Hidden? I thought that class was a myth," says Shell.

"She's a Hidden. She helps me sometimes."

"How do you know her?" asks Shell. I feel irritated at her irrationally. Maybe it's because I died, was Revived and then pumped with MND stat so high I hallucinated. In that moment, I decide I just plain-out don't like her as well as don't trust her. Totally biased by her uncaring raspy tone of voice.

"It doesn't matter. We can do this."

"You want to go again? Are you nuts?" says Doolittle. "He slaughtered us."

"It's the sun," I say.

"What do you mean, it's the sun?" says Shell.

I don't want to discuss this with Shell listening. No, it's not a Mystic competition. I can feel she's changed toward me, but I don't know why. I do trust my gut…but Days trusts her and has for a long time. Could he be wrong?

"Will you all believe me and meet me at the cavern at nightfall? If you're not busy, of course."

Silence.

Days starts laughing hysterically. "You are one crazy dude. You have me convinced. But goddamn, that was more than Dark World death. That was something else. I couldn't move my ghost body for ten minutes."

"If Days thinks it's funny, I'm in," says Sorry with a chuckle.

Doolittle says, "I want to punch that gold dragon in its toothy face after what he did to me, so I'm definitely in."

"Simple?" I ask.

"Oh, come on. You know I'm going. Wouldn't miss it. To beat that fight? The bragging rights would be owned by Faithgamblers."

I pause, then ask, "Do you know any Mystic who has beaten him?"

"Nope," says Simple.

"Nada," Days says.

"That was the first time I've seen him. The real him. There are sculptures of him in Bane," says Doolittle. "The human NPCs who haven't been changed into Dragonbane yet, and don't want to be, keep shrines of *Xiuhcoatl* in their closets. So, I have seen his image."

"Who hasn't?" Days says.

"I haven't," I tell them.

"You didn't know to look," Simple says.

"I own a *Xiuhcoatl* marble statue," Shell adds. I still want the conversation to stop because of her, and now she's joining in. "Mystic comes very naturally to me. I've always played mage classes."

Frustration makes me talk without thinking. "I don't know anything about Mystic." I feel rage coming on. "I can't look it up, I can't read a wiki, I have nobody to ask because nobody knows anything… I know I'm a terrible Mystic, and I really was a great Maniac." I stop when I hear someone huff. I just know it's Shell. "Look, I'm sorry, just venting. I know, it's whiny."

"It's not that," Days says quietly.

I know what it is. It's that I'm talking about the thing you don't talk about. The conversation-ender. What is Dark World, and are we all dead? Everyone shuts the hell up if that thought even crosses your mind, like they can read your brainwaves.

It's because they're all thinking about it, too. It's all any of us think about, wonder about, yet can't talk about. Reality is unclear in Total Immersion Mode, and not knowing what Dark World really is eats at all our core beings.

I want to talk about it so bad. Especially to my friends. I need to hear any and all ideas. I have to discuss and learn. I must figure it out or I'll go mad.

That's exactly why they don't talk about it. It drives you crazy ever so slowly. So much so that to distract yourself, you'll risk making deadly bodily contact with the sun itself willingly over and over, every day, to forget it, even for a moment.

"Look," Days says. "You do know Mystic. You're good at it."

"I suck."

"No," he continues. "It's like you're in synch with the meaning of the class. You understand your summons. You hang out with *Djinn*. You make sure the Counts are in a comfortable place for them when you summon them. Have you plucked a *Varengan* feather just to see? No."

"Well, of course not. That would upset him. He was used that way for a millennium."

"But how do you know that, Sid?" Days says.

I don't know. I say so. "It just makes sense."

"That's what I mean by you're in synch. Why did you dismiss *Djinn* right before *Xiuhcoatl* dropped a bomb on us?"

"He had just said he hated being burned."

"He's an NPC! But you did a nice thing for him. You knew we were all gonna eat it, and you dismissed him instead of protecting any of us with multi-targeting and Contemplation. Your instinct was to protect your summon. That's friggin' weird, man. You are a true Mystic. You got this, and I'll tank every summon fight you ever get if you'll take me."

"Me too," says Simple. "I'll blow mythical gods up for you."

Sorry laughs. "Sid, quit being a dork."

"But Sorry, I am a dork. Not sorry I'm a dork, but referring to you and responding…"

They crack up.

"What time tonight?" Doolittle asks.

I'm suddenly humbled. They are really going to try *that* again with me? Already? "Midnight?" I say softly.

They agree on the time.

"Why at night?" asks Days. "What Mystic sixth sense tells you that?"

I think of Shell, but say fuck it. "It was the sun," I tell him. "The sun fell on us. Right? If there's no sun, it can't fall on us." Sure, Shell heard, but what can she do? I'm being childish. She doesn't even have the quest, and why shouldn't I want her to get further with Mystic just because my instincts tell me she's off?

My instincts told me not a thing about Silvia and if she cared for me as more than a friend, so why am I investing so much in them with Shell?

"I guess it kind of was like the sun falling on us," Simple says. "Like, for real. I couldn't put it into words. None of us could. We talked as we waited to hear from you and had no idea what had happened. But you're right. The sun fell right out of the sky, into the cave, and—"

Days chuckles. "Only in Dark World."

For the first time since Game Over, I laugh at Dark World and its ways. I echo, "Only in Dark World." I grin to myself. Time to sell and then craft until midnight. I'll stop by the temple and say a quick hello to Master Gronai on the way to Kleeple. Maybe I can talk him into giving me a quickie scroll-making lesson. Actually, I know I can. All I have to do is cast Spontaneity on him, and he'll be ecstatic.

Besides, I miss the old NPC. Haven't seen him in a while. He has a way with words, like all good Nuudles should.

~

"So, *Djinn*, if you granted *Xiuhcoatl* that wish, can you still see him even if we can't?" I whisper.

We're back in the fight arena for the fourth night in a row, with starlight and *Djinn*'s green glow lighting the rooty, gnarly and now-haunting open-air cave. Haunting not just because the cave is so twisted at night, but also because seeing it again brings back the memory of the pain.

"No, I cannot." He sighs.

"It's okay." I sigh too.

We've been here for two hours. Sorry and Days are on the other side of the cave, heads bent together. Simple is so bored she's sitting down right where she died last time and reading a book on ancient runes for scroll-making. Doolittle is doing stuff in his menu, towering over Simple. His eyes are doing that thing. Am I the only one still paying attention?

None of us even have any buffs.

I look at *Djinn's* ability list again.

Second Wish—*Target will become a ruler. If in a party, target will become party leader. All stats are increased 50% for 20 seconds. Some items and abilities may enhance this ability.*

"So, *Djinn*. I've never used Second Wish except to buff before this fight, before *Xiuhcoatl* appeared, but it wore off. You know, I made Days the ruler. Is it possible for me to make you the ruler?"

He raises a furry, green eyebrow. "Of course it is."

"I'm thinking you have through-the-roof stats. Look at your HP bar. Add fifty percent, and I wonder what you can do."

He laughs. "No master has ever made me ruler."

"Why not? The idea just occurred to me."

He shakes his head, still laughing. "What master in his right mind would make his summon have the party control and that much power?" He wipes a laugh-tear off his cheek as he eyes my Moldavite Ring.

I lift up my hand. "What do you know about this?"

His face straightens, instantly sober. "If you use the Moldavite Ring..."

"What?" I ask. Simple looks up from her book, and Doolittle's eyes are focused on *Djinn*, not his menu.

"What is 'Grant God Status'?" I tilt my head to get a better look up at him.

"I've never seen the Moldavite Ring before," he says quietly.

"I told you everything we found treasure hunting. You didn't say anything about it."

"You never commanded me to."

"Why did you say, *the* Moldavite ring?"

He looks down, face relaxing. Takes a deep breath. Lets it out.

"The Moldavite Ring was crafted by Seelmor, a Nuudle Mystic who tried to persuade me to join him. That is what he used to persuade. He said he crafted the Moldavite Ring and told me what it did, how it works." He looks back to me. "He offered this power to me in exchange for being his summon. He couldn't defeat me in battle, and years later, offered this."

Days and Sorry are with us now, listening intently.

He grins and pats my thin shoulder, nodding. "I don't know why I am even worried, Young Master Sid. I have found you to be a kind-hearted master. If you choose to use the Moldavite Ring with Second Wish on me, I won't betray your intentions."

"What does that mean?" Days asks. He sounds concerned. Days never sounds concerned.

Djinn looks at Days with a light-hearted smile. "It means I did not agree to Seelmor's offer."

Days smiles back. Relaxes his big shoulders.

Sid commands Second Wish.

***Djinn* becomes a ruler.**

His green glow intensifies and he closes his eyes for a few moments. He then opens them. "I have never felt that wish before. No wonder all of you enjoy what you call buffing so much. You do it constantly."

The party menu in my interface shows that *Djinn* is now the party leader. His HP bar is stacked. I can't count how many blue segments *Djinn* has.

"What's going to happen? I don't get it," says Simple. "And I get magic."

"I don't know. All this time thinking, and an idea came to me. And then *Djinn* stared at my Moldavite Ring as though it explained everything, as though I knew something."

"I knew you didn't know. Like I said, it was downright silly to have worried about your misusing my powers, Master Nuudle Sid," *Djinn* adds in. "I didn't explain it to you because you never asked, and I was afraid of your knowing of how it works, what it can make me into."

"As powerful as a God," I say.

He bends over, his smoke trail going up toward two of the three moons showing overhead. "Almost as powerful as *Ananta*." He gives me a knowing grin.

I have a million questions about the *Ananta* comment instantly, and my friends look like they have at least a couple thousand. I have to put the queries aside and do this fight. I don't even want to know exactly what is going to happen, but I do it without warning anyone, buffless.

Sid uses Moldavite Ring. *Djinn* is granted God Status.

Djinn turns completely white, an orb, no sign of the genie I know and kinda love. The white orb throbs, and my Moldavite Ring warms my finger. I look down at it. The deep, moss-green sparkling stone's little inclusions are moving within the stone, making a new shape.

I watch it, mesmerized, as the now-fluid inclusions take a pattern. Now, I see a dragon in the stone's inclusions, one very much like *Xiuhcoatl*. But its wings are more wicked and almost scary, even in this little pattern of stone inclusions.

"Oh my God!" says Simple.

The whole cave is lit like it's a white day. I tear myself away from looking at the Moldavite Ring and see that the white orb that had been *Djinn* is now forming into a great, shining white dragon shaped like the one in the stone. But much, much bigger, and much, much scarier.

He's solid, pure starshine white, shining like burning Magnesium, and I can't even make out his scales. I can't look at him long enough because he's so bright. His head is wide with a long, elegant yet terrifying snout, housing rows upon rows of gleaming, sharp dragon teeth. His wings flap ever so slightly. He doesn't even need them. His power is holding him aloft, just like it does when he's a genie.

He's not a genie now.

"You called for me, Nuudle Simple?" the great, white magical and fierce dragon says to her in a low, grumbling rumble.

But he's certainly still *Djinn*. I grin. "*Djinn*, find the other dragon."

Xiuhcoatl takes form on the other side of the cave. *Djinn's* white shine makes *Xiuhcoatl's* scales look like they are made from solid yellow gold. His eyes are lit brightly, and had seemed to be black before. Now, I can see a spot of red deep in the black, forming just around the slits of dragon pupils.

"No need. I will not hide from any dragon, even if it is *Djinn*. You, Mystic, have made him too powerful. I must stop him. You are a fool to think I'd ever let you claim me." *Xiuhcoatl* grounds out the words slowly, as though talking takes great effort. His wings flap in huge swallows of air and he faces *Djinn*. "I do not have the sun; I do not have the strength. You will defeat me, but I will fight, old friend, new God."

Djinn, the gleaming white dragon, says, "I'm only a God by status, remember."

"A God can never fall."

"It's really just a status symbol." He looks at me. "Well?"

"What?"

"You have to command me."

Sorry casts Weaken Enemy. *Xiuhcoatl* has Offense Down.

Days uses Invoke Inner Demon. *Xiuhcoatl* is immune.

Xiuhcoatl doesn't even look at them.

Simple casts Storm. *Xiuhcoatl* is in Simple's storm.

Lightning flashes, about as bright as *Djinn*, and thunder pounds and shakes the cave. Bolts of lightning come out of a cloud that came from Simple's wand tip, and now surrounds the great dragon summon, and each spark looks painful. *Xiuhcoatl's* HP bar starts dropping about 3% with every hit from the lightning.

Smart of Simple. She doesn't want to get this thing's hate.

Djinn and *Xiuhcoatl* snap at each other, seeming to do no damage to one another. I have to do something.

Sid casts Contemplation. *Djinn* gains Protection.

Djinn says, "Thanks! Now, command me."

***Xiuhcoatl* uses Fire Breath. *Djinn* is burned.**

The great, gold dragon spews forth a stream of molten fire breath at *Djinn*, and his HP drops to 75%. *Djinn* shakes it off as Doolittle uses Deep Heal on him, bringing him back up to 100% HP.

Days uses Crushing Blade.

Xiuhcoatl's HP drops to 70% with Days' hate move. How did he hit that flying thing? And man, does Days get the hate.

***Xiuhcoatl* uses Dragon's Grasp.**

Immediately, the great, gold dragon wraps his coiling body around my friend, and Days looks like he's being squeezed to death.

"What do we do? I might hit Days if I cast," Simple calls out.

Doolittle casts Deep Heal on Days.

Days' HP goes up and then down and then up as Doolittle casts buffs and heals on Days. *Djinn* continues to whack *Xiuhcoatl* even as the summon strangles Days. Soon, I cast buffs as Simple and Sorry cast DoT spells.

Finally, *Xiuhcoatl* releases Days and focuses back on *Djinn*. The dragon's HP is at 50%.

Days falls over, exhausted.

"Master Sid!" *Djinn* calls out in his low dragon voice. "Why aren't you commanding me?"

I realize I've been afraid. The only move *Djinn* can do that will hurt *Xiuhcoatl* is his seizure move, and I know it will release him. I'm scared *Djinn* won't come back.

***Xiuhcoatl* uses Simmer.**

Sorry casts Reflection of Darkness. *Xiuhcoatl*'s move is stopped and he gains Arcane damage over time.

Xiuhcoatl looks furiously at Sorry.

***Xiuhcoatl* uses Fire Breath. Sorry is burned.**

Sorry cries out as the dragon's fiery breath hits her.

Sid casts Contemplation. Sorry gains Protection.

Simple casts Ball Lightning.

Xiuhcoatl takes a hit with the lightning burst, but focuses back on *Djinn*, his HP now at 40%.

I have to do it. Hearing Sorry scream, watching Days in a ball on the rooty, cave floor...

Sid uses Seizure.

Sid commands Release *Djinn*.

***Djinn* is released.**

Sid casts Mantra.

"Silvia," I yell.

***Djinn* gains +568 ATT.**

Djinn, in now-complete blindingly shining white dragon form, forcefully breathes white fire at *Xiuhcoatl*. *Xiuhcoatl* is stunned, but spews his own huge, hot flames right back at *Djinn*. The fire just keeps coming out of *Djinn's* long snout's fanged mouth, unstopping, as *Xiuhcoatl's* HP bar goes down as *Djinn's* white fire pushes *Xiuhcoatl's* orange fire back into himself, and then *Djinn's* flame consumes him. *Xiuhcoatl* lets out savage roar after roar between assaults, and gets in a nasty burn on *Djinn's* side. He drops to 73%.

Impulsively, something occurs to me. I released *Djinn*. Can I...?

Sid summons *Varengan*.

Sid commands Gentle Flight.

Djinn's HP goes to full.

And then, when *Xiuhcoatl's* HP reaches 1%, *Djinn* stops the onslaught of white-hot fire breath, and lets out a little burst of white flame in *Xiuhcoatl's* face, knocking off the last of his HP.

Djinn vanishes in a puff of white smoke.

Everything goes dark, and then I'm alone in the twisted, moonlit arena with *Xiuhcoatl*. He sits on all fours, coiling body at rest, and stares hard at me.

The silence stretches on.

"You may have lost your ally," he finally says. "You gave up *Djinn* for me. Why?"

I shake my head. "I'm hoping he comes back."

"He probably won't, Young Mystic. You gave him so much power, he might have broken his bonds of servitude. However, I am yours to control as you will. I do not like it and will yearn for the day you truly die so I can be released."

"Sounds fair," I say. I got him? I really got him?

The day I truly die? There's a clue in there. What does it mean?

"Thank you," I say.

"For what?" he hisses, forked tongue flicking.

"For being my summon."

He huffs and a little smoke comes out of his long snout. He collapses into gold mist and shoots into my chest.

Ahh, that full heart feeling. I'll never get sick of it.

Everything fades to black, and then I'm at the entrance to the battle, back in the cavern in Mylop Territory.

Sorry holds Days' hand as Doolittle does an extended curing spell on him. Days sits on the ground, holding his stomach. "Man, that hurt," he's complaining with a grimace right before they notice me. "Sid!" Days says, suddenly perking up.

"Don't stand yet," Sorry says. "Let Doolittle finish."

Doolittle is using spells Silvia never had, and ones I've never heard of. They must be Dark World-specific. Why would anyone need this kind of curing in Elora? This magic is for real pain and damage.

"Did you get him?" Days asks.

I nod. "Yeah, you okay?"

"I'm fine. Doctor Doolittle is fixing me up right." He smiles, but I can see he's still hurting. "Let's see him."

"Okay, but first..."

I look at my summon list. Summon *Djinn* is still there, and now I have the option to summon *Xiuhcoatl*. I have to try it. I have to know.

Sid summons *Djinn*.

To my great relief, *Djinn's* green smoke comes out of my chest and he takes form, filling the dead end of the cave with a green glow.

"Yes, Master Nuudle Sid, how can I help?"

I grin. Simple lets out a happy squeal.

"So happy to see me? That's always nice, to feel accepted, wanted, adored."

"You're still here!" I say. "And you're not a God!"

"Of course I am. I know a fitting master when I meet one. And it was god status, sillies. What do you think of *Xiuhcoatl* and his abilities?"

"I haven't summoned him yet."

Djinn's sparkling eyes grow large. "You summoned me first to see if I would be here?"

"Well, yeah."

He grins. "How sweet. You love me. Now, my name won't be in your summon list if I were to leave you. Remember that. But you don't have to worry about that. Go. Go on! Dismiss me and summon *Xiuhcoatl*!"

I grin back at him. "Thanks, *Djinn*. I'll do that."

Sid dismisses *Djinn*.

Sid summons *Xiuhcoatl*.

The great, coiling dragon fills the tiny dead end, spiraling out of my chest as a golden mist and taking form in the middle of the haphazard circle we are sitting and standing in.

"What is your command?" he asks.

"Just looking at you and your abilities."

He hovers quietly, and it makes me nervous.

I read his ability list to myself, then aloud to my friends.

Description:

Xiuhcoatl is an ancient fire dragon, known through the ages as the most powerful dragon of the sun. He is stronger in the day when he can use all of his abilities. He is a dragon with the power of solar magic. He has unique dragon qualities grown from eons of abuse of his power, also giving him true bloodlust for justice.

Abilities:

Fire Breath—Breathes fire at target, dealing damage.

Dragon's Grasp—Wraps target in his body, making target unable to move or fight for 20 seconds. Target receives Strangle damage over time for the duration.

Simmer—Burns target every 3 seconds for 10% HP for 30 seconds. Target cannot attack.

Seizure Ability: Solar Explosion—Uses sun's power to deal massive damage to target. Can only be used during the day.

"Wow," says Doolittle. "Good call on the sun. I mean, doing this at night. He couldn't do that move at all at night."

I give *Xiuhcoatl* a little smile. He doesn't return it.

Sid dismisses *Xiuhcoatl*.

"He hates me," I tell them.

"Me too," says Days with a laugh. "He got me bad twice."

"You're tough. You can take it," Sorry says to him, rubbing his arm.

"I'm really just a show-off," he says. "I can't take these kinds of hits and stay sane without an audience."

"I'm sorry," I say. It's my fault my friend was strangled by a giant, snaky dragon and abused so badly. I haven't felt guilt over this before, even when *Xiuhcoatl* got us with Solar Explosion. But seeing Days weakened so much makes it all hit me. I'm asking my friends to risk horrible pain to fight these summons.

"None of that," says Simple, watching my face, reading my worries.

"Nope, don't think of it," adds Days. "We want to do this, right?" He looks around at the others.

"Yeah," says Doolittle.

The others nod at me, and I might have been imagining it, but they look a little desperate, as though they have a lot more invested in my claiming summons than I'm aware of.

"Thanks. I mean it." I don't know what else to say. They all seemed to read my mind, or maybe my Nuudle features can't hide a thing. Or maybe, just maybe, they need these fights as much as I do. That feeling of needing to do something with our time in Dark World is always there, the need to quiet the questions.

CHAPTER 13: BATTLE OF KERES

"Look at you, Nuudle Mystic!" says Calla when she appears, umbrella and blue bubble at the ready, after I summon *Xiuhcoatl*. "You are doing quite well. How fortunate you claimed him. You must have good friends, and a good knowledge of how Mystic works. I'm so very glad you chose this class."

"Me too," I say as I dismiss *Xiuhcoatl*. Even though I have control over him, he makes me anxious to have out. He *stares* at me like he wants to fry me.

"I think you might be ready for *Keres*, Nuudle Mystic Sid," she says.

Keres? I've never heard of a summon named *Keres*. "Who is *Keres*?"

Calla looks down. "She feeds."

"She feeds?"

Calla looks back up at me. "Yes, she feeds. She feeds. Hold out your left hand."

I do, and she marks it with what looks like an old hag.

"Who is she?" I ask.

"Lost soul, undead, caught between worlds. She has unique abilities." She pats my shoulder. "Now, go. Gather your friends. With *Keres*, you only have one chance."

"What do you mean?"

"I mean, you don't want her to feed on you." She shakes her head, and then switches from grim to cheerful in a split-second. "Nothing you can't handle, I'm absolutely sure. Otherwise, I'd never suggest *Keres*. Very few of us know of her and where she is. Only certain Mystics would be chosen for this summon."

"Well, thanks." I let her know through my sarcasm that I don't appreciate her scary, cryptic information without further explanation.

"Now, off you go." She disappears altogether in a blip and I start getting rained on again as her blue bubble fades.

I look around for Anella, feeling like she's nearby, but I don't see her.

I look at my map. The *Keres* fight is marked south of Siren Territory in the depths of the Paradise Sea outside of Cashmere.

I tell the guild about it, and my friends are ready to go for her right now, but I need to get some better gear and to practice my scroll-making, so I do.

Master Gronai is especially happy to see me. When I tell him about my *Keres* quest, he takes a great interest, even helping me craft a scroll called "Satisfy Undead." Not sure what it does, exactly, but Master Gronai seems to think it's the way to go because "I read once of a sea monster ghost in the Paradise Sea, that she sinks ships and eats everyone alive. Might as well try something, Young Sid, do you not agree, that might aid with your battle?" We used old Nuudle runes, and I'm not the best at those. I'll figure the scroll out when I get to her. I hope.

It gives me an idea. I didn't think of *Keres* as a regular undead, but if she is… and I send Lucky, the guy I met in Dawn, a letter asking if he'd help us with the fight… maybe as a Dead One, he'd have some moves on her.

I do so. I wait to hear from him while I clothcraft and treasure hunt around Nuudle Territory.

A day or so after I got the *Keres* quest, I have a new Crimson Caster Robe (with hood, of course) I made, which is Mystic-specific and has all three of my main stats: +20 CON, +11 INT, +7 MND. I found a bracelet near the mountains to the east of Kleeple called Ruby Bezel Bracelet. It's silver and covered in red gems. It has +9 CON, +9 ATT, and +5 INT. Mystic-specific, too. Nice. New sandals with some MND, which I've learned is good for aching feet (still no mount). Black Pearl Ear Cuffs that have +4 CON when wearing both. Made some Silk Pants and had a guildie enchanter put + 10 CON and +5 MND on them. Wrist cuffs called Master Mage's Wristlets, which have +14 ATT, +14 STR and +10 DEF. And… broke again until the goodies I found with Third Wish and couldn't use sell on the AH.

I even did quests I found to make my STR and DEF stats higher to add to my cuffs' stats, which, as *Djinn* explained, helps my summons. As I get higher stats, my summons do, too. They do more damage as my STR gets higher, get more DEF as my defense gets higher, etc. I need to get all my stats up, not just for my little HP bar to have more segments, but for my class's success's sake. I'd been wondering about that since the Counts' fight, and with *Djinn*, I keep forgetting he's the only summon I have I can talk to, ask questions to. And he answers. I'm turning to him more and more.

Finally, the day the last of my treasure sells, I have a mail icon saying "1" in my interface while I'm treasure hunting with *Djinn*, and let him know I have to get to a mailbox.

"I know the drill," he says, and disappears as I dismiss him so as not to be bothered by the Mystic-curious.

I run all the way to Kleeple to get to a mailbox. The letter is from Lucky.

Sid,
Sorry it took so long to get back to you. I had to give it some thought. I'm ready now, though. I want to help you with the fight. Hit me up when you go and I'll be there.
Lucky

Awesome.

I tell the guild I have a Dead One to help us. Sorry is ecstatic. "I've never fought with a Dead One before. How intriguing. I wonder what he'll be able to do with *Keres*. Good thinking, Sid." I'd told them what Calla said about *Keres* being undead.

I'm glad they're open to having another player join us. I got so lucky that Days and Simple were the first people I met when I came here. They don't care about standing and guild-owning. They're people with feelings and maturity. I didn't know Days was the head of Faithgamblers until I asked in guild chat, and through all of them saying, "Me!" and "No, me, me!" I figured out it was Days.

Why is Shell in Days' guild when she was here before him? Why would someone leave a guild in Dark World? I'm guessing she didn't have one.

I keep getting that instinct about Shell, and it grows. She didn't say a word when the rest of the guildies congratulated us on our win with *Xiuhcoatl*. I often checked the guild list because of my suspicious mind, keeping an eye on who was listening in, and she had turned off guild chat the day I got the *Keres* quest. Her name didn't show in the online guild chat list for over two hours, which I knew from my monitoring was odd, and hasn't since.

There have been discussions about what happened to Shell, but I keep my mouth shut. I have a bad, bad feeling she changed somehow. Something happened to change her from the Mystic who gave me the Contemplation quest and who had been eternally active in the guild chat to the Mystic who leaves for days. No word from her to anyone, according to Days. I can tell he's upset about it. He has that soft spot for her, wants to help her if she's in a bad way. But nobody can find her or reach her. Letters and messages have been sent. No replies. We put off fighting *Keres* while we searched her usual haunts, like certain crafting stations in Kleeple and Sheala, which is a brand-new town, not a capital yet. Couldn't even call it a city here in Dark World.

I'm tired of hearing everyone worry about her, and it's my damn gut telling me she's doing something not in character. I couldn't defend that with "It felt like to me when she said these perfectly normal words, she blah, blah, blah." I can't breathe a word of it to anyone. I don't even speak my suspicions to *Djinn*, feeling like saying them aloud to any sentient being, including NPCs, will bring my paranoid crazy exposed for any and all to see.

I know I'm right—that's the part that scares me for what is to come. Because something will come of this.

I've never been great at trusting that kind of intuition, though, especially because deep down, I feel it's all about me. Me being a Mystic with *Ananta*'s mark. That she sees me as special and she isn't, and the reason I don't want to talk that way is because I'm not an egomaniac. I'm probably wrong, too, because I *know* in the way I'm knowing this stuff, all circumstantial, but there's more. Something changed her, as well, maybe to think that way of me.

She wasn't always… jealous? Is that it? It doesn't feel quite right.

Something happened, something that has to do with me, but I don't know what. Just a hunch, but don't worry. I know better than to spin conspiracy theories when I have clues as weak as her tone of voice changing.

We finally plan the *Keres* fight a week after Shell disappeared, and I write Lucky telling him where it is and what time we're doing it. He writes back within minutes saying he'll be there. We have plans to meet midday in the Paradise Sea south of Cashmere, and that sea is deep. We'll all, with the exception of Sorry, have to eat Kula Peach Berries, very expensive, to breathe underwater for as long as we'll be there. They last five hours. Simply swimming to the small, unnamed cave on my map will take an hour. That's how far down that part of the ocean of Dark World, Elora, whatever, is. Nobody has any clue what this fight will hold, and nobody has heard of *Keres*. Not even Simple, who loves her Temple of Nuudlel book piles she pulls out and pores over when nothing is happening before or after an event—and even sometimes over Siren Ale. I have no clue how anyone can read old Nuudle rune writing with even a lick of the pink brew on her tongue. She always has three or more of those Siren Ales, too.

Yeah, we've developed habits. I've gotten to know other guildmates, but nothing nearly as close as with the players who do my fights with me. The five of us, since *Djinn*, have spent many an inactive evening on the open-air cedar patio of Dark World Cashmere's stat-boost drink haven and had our ways with Siren Ale.

I'm sure you're dying to hear about every .03 skill-up I get in scroll-making while Master Gronai reads Nuudle and then Elorian to me, trying to give me "Nuudle Word Music" to enhance my scroll runes. The grinding for stat boosts, quest after quest. Or the skill-ups in crafting, or the treasure hunting and talks with *Djinn* about nonsense...

Instead, I'll get to *Keres*.

Lucky meets us at an underwater cave, unnamed on the map, deep in the Paradise Sea after we waited forty minutes for him.

"Sorry, sorry. Had the wrong berries. Had to get air and swim to land. Get the right berries." He doesn't look at anyone, floating low, seems awkward. Not like the fanboy I'd met in Dawn.

"I should have mentioned that, sorry," I tell him. "Hey, you alright?"

He nods and finally looks down into my eyes. "Sorry, I couldn't bring any. None would go in the water. And there are no Undead in the water."

I cock my head. "What do you mean?"

In a rush, he says, "I catch the undead and they fight for me. Like your summons. But they get away and I have to kill them, or else they're after me. Don't worry about it. I have other things that should help."

Days swims over to him. "Human. Did that blow your mind or what? I'm Days."

Lucky stares hard at Days as though Days hit him.

"Dude?" Days says, concerned.

Lucky shakes his head and flaps his arms through the sea water. "Oh, sorry, sorry. You remind me of someone. That's all."

Days opens his mouth, but pushes his brows together and closes it. He was about to say more, but something stopped him. By his expression, an unpleasant thought.

"Let's swim on in," Simple says. She sounds quiet. I realize she's scared.

Doolittle hasn't done anything but keep his Luna Lamp charged with Violet Petals so he could see swimming this deep. It's blacker than black here where the sun has never been.

The cave is creepy, the Luna Lamp is creepy... Lucky is acting creepy.

Sid summons *Djinn*.

"Master Nuudle Sid, my great pleasure to serve... this dank dungeon with my green glow." He sniffs the water. "What is this place? *Keres*?"

"Yeah."

"She smells like a rotting bride left at the altar." He squeezes his nose.

I laugh.

"You can't smell her," says Days.

"How do you know?" *Djinn* says. "You know not my greatness and acute extrasensory abilities." He wags a fat, gold-ringed finger in Days' face. "Come on, smell. Come on. You'll see I'm right."

Days gives him a flipping, forked tongue and then sniffs.

"Nothing."

"See? It proves I'm superior." He folds his arms across his huge, bare chest.

Days cracks a grin. "*Djinn*, you're so full of shit."

"I've never once shat, so that very well may be." He rubs his chin, looks lost in thought.

"God, Days, should I start being jealous of that genie? You flirt with him more than me." Sorry winks at *Djinn*.

All through this, I've kept low-profile attention on Lucky, making my eyes dart from person to person, but really checking out Lucky. His gloved fingers shake, even in the thick water. He wears no shoes. No footgear for a boss fight? I mean, it could be class or ability-specific... but I've never seen anyone without shoes for something like this.

We find a dead end quickly and the usual ritual goes down. I put my hand on the wall, the hag's mark stays on the wall and gets bigger, and my palm glows.

Then, we're in.

We're all scared instantly.

There is air here, and it's a round cavern forty meters wide filled... filled with bodies. Pieces of bodies in various stages of decay. Humans, Sirens, Nuudles, White Elves, Dragons, Dragonbane, Mylop. Fresh kills, too. NPC names by the colors. What is going on?

In the middle of the bloodbath stands *Keres*, and she is a wicked, dark one.

I don't know about lost soul, but I completely get the undead. She's a species of her own. No idea. She's seven feet tall, white and bony, wearing a long black, flowy open-breasted dress, and its every exposed end is a tattered, black mess. Her mouth gapes open, three times the size of a horse mouth, with skinny, dagger-like inch-long teeth. Her talon-tipped hands drop a bloody White Elf arm as she notices us. Her big, oblong, black eyes gleam with hunger at Sorry. Suddenly, huge, thin, black-feathered giant wings spring up from her back, having been behind her, and she flaps the foul stench at us. *Djinn* was right; it's here.

Sorry casts Weaken Enemy. *Keres* has Offense Down.

Days uses Invoke Inner Demon.

Keres is within arm's length of shredding Sorry when Days steals the hate. Whew.

What am I doing?

Suddenly, summoning *Xiuhcoatl* for this doesn't seem so much of a bad idea. I'd been going to break my own rules and use *Djinn*...but...

Sid summons *Xiuhcoatl*.

Gold, smooth smoke flows out of my chest and the great, spiraling dragon flies above us.

"Silly Master Nuudle," he growls. "No sun."

"Fight, man!" I call out to him.

Sorry casts Blind. *Keres* is blinded for 20 seconds.

Keres keeps slashing at Days' arms and sides, missing more now that she's blinded, leaving long claw marks all over his heavy, dark armor. Is it going to hold? How does he stay standing straight and still be able to block, invoke his inner demon in intervals, and attack?

Keres uses Visit the Grave. Sorry is warped to graveyard.

She thinks, she judges. She punished Sorry for blinding her. It's the first real move she's made.

At the same time, her nails are pretty long and fierce, and Days' face is consistently inches away from the hole of teeth she needs to feed. As a Maniac and a hand-to-hand fighter in Elora, I didn't have any flash. I tore them up and then forgot them with my bare or knuckled hands. She reminds me of that style of play.

Doolittle starts handing out the heals. Ahh, Days will be happy about that.

Sid commands Dragon's Grasp.

Xiuhcoatl finally, for the first time, acts like a summon and commits fully to his command. He wraps his long, sleek golden body around the undead witch as she wails like a banshee, and squeezes so hard the scales on his sides pop up a little bit.

Over the next 20 seconds of the spell's duration, Doolittle and I hit everyone with buffs, multi-targeting. Simple does DoT spells on *Keres*. She looks like she's in more pain than any human can bear without passing out, but her HP bar is still 50% when *Xiuhcoatl* releases her and flies to my side, eying her. He doesn't even casually hit to protect me like the others.

She's palms-down on her knees, but her head snaps up, eyes right on Days as I read in my interface:

Lucky uses Complete Denial.

But her eyes aren't gleaming. They have a star of shining white in the blackness of each one. Her face isn't anguish.

It's not her. That's what it looks like. Not *Keres*.

I see a blue glow to my right. I spin. Lucky's holding a katana made from Malochrome, mage metal, and pointing it at Days. "Do it!" he yells. He's sweating and shaking all over. Sure, he hadn't been doing anything, but he said... and Days is targeted by him now.

Oh, he lied.

I know for sure it's true when *Keres* launches onto Days. Lucky is using her as his undead pet.

Keres uses Gnawing Teeth.

I've never seen anything this awful in my life. *Keres*' giant, needle-toothed mouth runs all over Days, after knocking him over by slamming into him face-first in the stomach, tearing through his armor with her teeth and starting gnawing flesh exactly then. His armor hangs in pieces, and his flesh is gone in seconds. Just a bloody pulp with the face of my friend.

His shocked expression, blank eyes, skin eaten off him in frantic chomps, and the blood. All the red blood, and then the pure white face without even computerized comfort movements.

She ate Days.

Lucky made her do it.

Didn't he?

I look at Lucky again, trying not to think about what I just watched. Lucky is still waving the blue sword, shaking, sweating... man, he's crying.

Sid commands Simmer.

Xiuhcoatl spews a thin stream of yellow fire on *Keres*, and her skin lights up like her flesh is now the flesh being devoured, just by flame and not teeth. She's frozen in place and knows she's a Dead One's minion. He did say they try to kill you after you capture them.

Keres drops into a pool of fresh blood and seawater, and Simmer seems to stop.

"Sid, Mantra me," Simple hisses, eyes pointing at Lucky.

Sid casts Mantra.

"Silvia," I say. I think it again, but don't say it twice.

Simple gains +203 ATT.

Didn't even have to think casting Mantra. Hate fills me. I know what Simple has in mind.

Simple casts Death Lightning.

Lucky gets hit so hard by Simple's lightning that he's down on the ground in an instant. He has 35% HP... and no longer does *Keres* obey his commands. Death Lightning must have a dispel effect.

His beard has been fried off his face. He's lost *Keres*. The white stars in her eyes are gone, now back to shiny and black, glaring at Lucky.

***Keres* uses Devour.**

In what feels like a solid minute of watching *Keres*, the undead lost soul summon, devour my betrayer with those teeth, ripping at him with her claws, I know horror, disgust and pity. It takes that full minute for 35% to go down as she eats him inside out alive, until he isn't.

I don't do anything until she stops. Simple casts electric shocks from her wand that seem to do zero damage. She doesn't want anything to do with that hate. Probably a warding enchantment on that wand.

None of us make any real moves. Doolittle's group-curing us and rebuffing us in a rush with buffs that aren't cumulative. His nerves made him a robot.

"How are we going to damage her?" I call out. "I have no sun."

Keres stops eating once Lucky's no longer twitching, and turns on my summon.

Simple casts Ball Lightning.

Keres' HP drops some, but she's involved in trying to get a bite of dragon meat. *Xiuhcoatl* is more irritated than hurt. He continually slaps her to the ground each time she tries.

"I don't know!" Simple says. "Do something!"

Simple uses Reverse to Light.

Simple takes on healer qualities and loses destructive qualities in magic until the end of battle.

I've never heard of that before. Why would she do that?

And then, *Keres* is coming right at Simple. She has the hate. Healers run the biggest risk, next to The Blacks, for hate aggro. The smarter mobs know who blows them up hardest, and who keeps those ones alive.

"Xiuhcoatl, hit her like you're supposed to!"

He flips his spiked tail in seeming irritation, but proceeds to nip at her head and shoulders with enough pressure that she falls hard to the floor and fumbles to get up, wings twisted.

Simple casts Shield of Honor. *Xiuhcoatl* gains Protection of the Ages.

"Do something, anything!" Simple says, obviously relieved that *Xiuhcoatl* stopped the hag *Keres'* descent on her.

Anything... Anything!

I pull Master Gronai's scroll out of my bag and into my interface. The one we made that day. He said something... something about using it. The runes, thinking of what made the ink and the feather, and the fingertips moving over the parchment...

I highlight it in my bag in my interface. Can this work? I don't actually have to chant Elorian and ancient Nuudle?

I select "Use."

The yellow parchment floats up and unravels in front of me. What is Satisfy Undead: The Scroll going to do? I hope Master Gronai hadn't had too much Contemplation or less desire that day.

Keres holds her clawed hands up to *Xiuhcoatl*'s snout, and clamps it shut gently, not a talon scratch one, as the yellow parchment turns to yellow glitter and lands on her, then spins around her.

"Stop, you can stop," a wrecked, weak voice says from the wicked mouth. She bows her head, thin, greasy hair falling in her face and dragging on the floor.

Sid dismisses *Xiuhcoatl*.

"Why...?" Simple says to me in a panic.

The undead bare-breasted hag who ate Days alive, and then ate Lucky alive, looks deep into my eyes. "Now, we will discuss."

All goes dark, and then I'm in the arena again with her, but the others are gone.

I got her. How? What did that scroll do?

"You are the very first being who has satisfied my hunger since I became *Keres*." She narrows her eyes, having a hard time getting a look at me so far below her. "Nuudle Mystic, I thank you. What can I do for you as repayment?"

"Want to be my summon?"

"Mystic summon? I have not done that in many hundreds of years."

"Yep. I've never done it."

Her eyes cut down to me again. "No, of course you haven't. You're a Mystic."

Alright. "So, I would be happy if you did," I urge her, stifling memories of Days and Lucky's bodies just long enough. It's what she had to do. She was fighting for her freedom.

No, she wasn't. I can't kid myself. She was fighting for a mouthful. Am I sure I want this summon?

"You defeated me, although not in strength. You satiated my eternal longing for destruction, if only for a moment. I already feel the satisfaction fading. I am your summon, and I will clean up your battles for you. All I ask is that there be many battles." Her voice is crackly and thin, whispery.

"Oh, there always are. *Keres*, thanks." I force a smile, hoping it appears assured.

Black mist shoots into my heart, formed from what she had been, and I feel she belongs there.

Ah, full heart summon claim.

Fade to black, then fade back to underwater in the unnamed cave in Paradise Sea. The Luna Lamp glows eerie purple, casting strange shadows on Days and Lucky's shredded bodies crumpled by the cave wall, waiting for their spirits to come find and fix them, make them live to die another day, and live again. And again.

Sorry had been at a nearby graveyard and made it back to *Keres'* cave before we were done. She said she couldn't get back in. She can't stop staring at Days, and she says nothing else.

Sid summons *Varengan*.

My glorious heart-lifting luxury summon comforts me. I bring him out still sometimes when I'm walking and want to watch him fly around. He stays with me and enjoys the flights. I never use him in fights. Right now, his soft blue glow is heaven, and I can rest for a moment until they're both here. We're getting this sorted out. No Comfort Rings, no teles—

"Sid." I hear his voice as I see his tan skin glowing blue-green from *Varengan*'s iridescence. Seeker is at the opening of the dead end, hands on his hips, floating an inch from the cave floor.

"You're Seeker?" says Simple, voice cracking in shock. "What in the world are you doing here, and how did you even know... ohhhh. The spell. Clairvoyance." She's scared again. That's why she can't speak. I also know I want to give her a Mantra right now, see if she still has the mindset she had with Lucky. She'll choke. Right now, in this light in this place, after what we had all seen, Seeker gives even me bad creeps, though my anger toward him keeps me from letting it take over. He's here, though, and that's the creepiest part.

"I use a spell—yes, Clairvoyance—that enables me to see where any player whose name I know is at any time. I can even see NPCs. A map appears in my interface with coordinates and directions." Seeker explains all this to me, ignoring the stunned Simple and on-standby Blessed Doolittle. He knows. Blessed's are the best healers in game, but they suck the worst solo. Seeker could smash him in a second and he has no defense.

"Okay," I say. "Why did you use that spell and come looking for me right now? Why are you here, Seeker?"

He lowers his arms. This is the second time I've seen him in water, and he looks like an angel with his white hair floating all around, and in fine robes he stole that most players work years to be able to wear swirling around him with the currents. *I hate him, I hate him, I hate him.* "I have been giving thought to the last few times we spoke. I came to two conclusions. You either don't like me, or you like them more than what I offer. From my point of view, you look down on me, and I don't understand that. I've explained myself perfectly, and you are chosen. I give you gifts, offer the world to you. I gave you this thrilling place to own and form." His white eyes show no emotion, but for the first time, I think he's letting out frustrations in a non-violent way.

"What is it about them over me?"

I stiffen. "What do you mean by that? What do you mean, two conclusions like that?" I want to punch him, almost do, but remember the water. Slow fist. Wish *Djinn* was out. First Wish him. *Varengan* will keep us alive no matter what he does to us, but I want him to vanish immediately.

Days' body lights up in the same moment as Lucky's. They are resurrecting. If it's at the same time so soon, they both set graveyards somewhere nearby in Paradise Sea. Lucky got the wrong berries, but he remembered to set his grave close to the battle if he died. Everybody does that when there's a good chance they'll die. They can sometimes get back in time to help in dungeons. No way he had time to do all that if he had actually run out of air.

I couldn't set mine there because I haven't done the quest to be sent there. I haven't done any new graveyard quests. I want to go back to mine every time in case I catch Anella.

I turn my back on Seeker and watch as their bodies reform solid. Their gear is a mess, but all the flesh is on and all the inside stuff is on the inside. They don't sit up much after they rez. Doolittle goes to work right away. I noticed he hasn't even looked Seeker in the eye. None of them have. Not to mention, he won't let them. He'll only look at me, as though they don't exist.

"Seeker..." Days mutters. "You're an asshole. I've been looking for you to say that. Thanks. Nice to meet you finally and get to say that." His breathing is labored, and Sorry rubs his arms and legs.

I can't look at Days yet. It's my fault. Seeker is here. Lucky turned. Days had that happen to him. It's all connected. I won't get a thing out of Seeker, but I fly into Lucky's human face, which is easy for me because I'm small. Small is faster in water. They don't see you coming. He didn't, and he almost pukes nothing on me. Just some residual body sensation when your nerves are going to stop your heart.

"What's eating you, Lucky?" I yell at him.

I hear Simple gasp, and then clap her hands together once.

Lucky's eyes reflect that *Keres* did to him something nobody should ever have to live with a memory of. "I'm so sorry," he whispers.

I get off him, float up.

"It was a business transaction," Seeker says from behind me.

Lucky reaches out for my hand, but he is so weak he can't grasp it. "Wait. He paid me, but it was to get Days. He wanted me to get you with the *Counts of Hell* and Days, and then we heard about this. Before the letter you sent. I didn't want to. Sid, he offered so much. It's not worth it now." He's pleading for forgiveness, and I feel sorry for him. Mainly because Devour looks like the worst summon ability to inflict on another player.

Seeker walks up in our group and stands between Lucky and me. "He now has +100 more in all his stats. Only took a week. Not to mention the cash. You feel for him, and all he's doing is begging you to let him get away with it."

"Maybe that's how you are."

"We're all the same, Sid."

"No, you and I are nothing alike."

"We are the two best gamers in this framework."

"Framework? We're not the two best players. We had a duel. You're crazy and got delusional some years back about some idea you had, and I just happen to be the one to kill you and get away. It was pure luck. Leave me alone."

"Don't you want to know why I had Lucky make Days take the worst of it?" he says in a private message.

I don't answer.

Aloud, he says, "Because your reaction proves to me my second conclusion is true. You care for these low-level nobodies who don't excel. They feed off your greatness as a Mystic with all these summons. *Keres*. Nobody has ever heard of *Keres*. Go ahead. Show her to me."

"No!" Lucky cries out. "Please, I can't see her again."

Seeker ignores him. "Maybe next time. And yes, Lucky was paid up front."

"How did you even know I met Lucky?"

"I made sure he introduced himself to you and got you on his friends list. He'd either reach out to you when I told him, or he'd wait for you, but this was for my *Counts of Hell* trick to figure out your motivations. *Keres* and what she seems to have done here... I don't know what to say."

"Then why don't you just stop talking?" Days mumbles.

It's not my fault Days got targeted. No, I'm not going to let him make me think that way. I can see he's trying it. The only reason Days was flayed alive is because Seeker made it possible. He's the one who did this to Days.

I spin on him, reach up, and slap him across his high cheekbone. His head doesn't even move, but I see a change in his glowing white eyes. I hurt his feelings.

Good.

"Get the hell out of here, Seeker. You too, Lucky. Just forget it." I sit down next to Days in the sandy sea floor and float there. Simple, Doolittle, and Sorry all sit in a circle with us, shutting them out. We say nothing, but we feel strong. I can tell it's not just me. We keep our eyes on the sand, ignoring the heavy stares and Lucky's last attempt at a broken apology until they are finally gone.

"Okay, okay." Sorry breaks the silence. "We're all going to die of suffocation, but first you gotta summon *Keres*. Let's see her abilities."

I shake my head and smile. "You really want to?"

Days stands up. "Okay, I got this. Short-term memory loss from Nuudle Beer. Yes, yes, yes. I want to know what Devour is. That's what happened to Lucky, right?"

Sid dismisses *Varengan*.

Sid summons *Keres*.

Black shoots out of my chest and she forms just outside our circle.

"Master, have you brought me to battle to feed?"

"No, *Keres*, I'm looking at your ability list," I tell her, my heartrate picking up just seeing her again so soon.

Description:
A great leader and innovator, Keres died of a broken heart when the world she loved ten thousand years ago changed for the worse. She took her life in despair, but her madness keeps her half-dead and in our plane. As punishment for

her defying them by taking her own life, the gods of the ancient Sleenatos gave her eternal hunger. She feeds…

Drain Blood*—Drains target of 30% HP.*

Gnawing Teeth*—Eats target's living flesh, dealing high, sometime fatal damage.*

Visit the Grave*—Sends target to graveyard.*

Seizure Move: Devour*—Feeds on target, dealing damage and making target unable to attack until death.*

Sid dismisses *Keres*.

"Is she a real summon?" Sorry finally asks. We're all wondering it, but we're low on air to get us to the surface. No mounts for water. We have to swim.

We speculate over *Keres* plenty over the next day or two, and I finally get up the nerve to summon her again to find Calla. I dismiss her as soon as Calla, her umbrella and blue bubble rain shelter appear out of nothing in front of my and Seeker's graves.

And yes, I get another Mystic summon quest, one for a summon named *Oni*. The marking on my hand looks like a beast of magic and knowledge, good and bad. Yeah, these little palm markings are getting fancier and more detailed. Maybe it's because I have them for so long in between fights the farther down this Mystic road I go. My CON is at 261.1, INT at 156.9, MND at 167.5, and my other stats are all over a hundred. That's with the quests for boosts and the gear.

Calla said *Oni* is a demon. I can't help but wonder where a demon evolves from in Dark World. I ponder the mark on my hand over the next few days, trying to guess what kinds of moves he'll want to devastate us with…

There I go again. You can tell. The longer I live every moment in Dark World, the more all I can do is ramble on and on about details. There are so, so many details, and how can I possibly explain them all?

CHAPTER 14: BATTLE OF ONI

I need, as always, better gear, more stat increases, and some spending money for the battle with *Oni*. His site is marked on my map in White Elf Territory south of the Mantle of Bliss in a cave in the mountains, of course.

I head out to WET, never having treasure-hunted there, and summon *Djinn* where no players linger to bug me and my Mystic-ness.

I'm really not a snob about it. To be honest, I don't know what to say, and that's because I still feel like I'm reaching around in the pitch dark with the class. I don't want questions. I have no answers. And I always wear hooded robes to cover my unique Mystic marking on my forehead, even if the stats aren't as good as a regular robe and some sort of headgear.

Luckily, because I picked clothcraft as a craft, and mages can only wear cloth armor, I've been able to make many Mystic-specific pieces of gear from recipes I find, buy, or someone in the guild gives to me. That's the loot I love. I'm 113.6 in my clothcraft stat now. Yeah, Peter would be so proud, and I can only imagine the conversations we'd have now that I'm into crafting. Hey, it's fun. And hard. But more fun than hard. I've even achieved 52.1 in scroll-making, thanks to Master Gronai's extra help.

We decided we'd go after *Oni* in a couple days just after nightfall. I have to powerhouse this preparation, and *Djinn* loves the challenge. He's downright chipper, and I realize it's possible that *Djinn* doesn't like fighting too awfully much. He's more of a talker. Maybe that's why his moves, his Wishes, are so fun.

What is *Djinn*, anyway, I often wonder? He seems so real to me. Program? No, I've never had an NPC react to me in a way that hasn't been mapped out by a programmer for a multitude of communications and actions. It's like *Djinn* thinks for himself. Ridiculous, I know.

"*Djinn*," I say while we're out where I first defeated Seeker in Elora. In Dark World, this part by the open sea doesn't have trees yet like in Elora. Just some willows and beautifully flowering brush. "I have a question. I've been meaning to ask you, but..."

"But what? And what have you found there in that bush's roots? And if you've been pondering, why haven't you simply asked yet?" He blinks his suddenly insanely long, dark green eyelashes that disappear after a few flutters. Green sparkles float around his head after.

"Oh," I say, pulling out a sack from the dirt, found with *Djinn*'s treasure-seeking help. I open it. "It's a low-stat knuckle ring for a Maniac."

"Somebody will buy it, I'm certain. You have to undersell it on the auction house. I know these things. Oh, yes." He peeks in the dirty sack. "Well, maybe not that pair."

"I know, right?" I'm nervous about the questions I have for him about *Ananta*. I have a sense I shouldn't show eagerness about the great *Ananta* summon from Elora Online's opening cutscene, which I have memorized still even though I have no idea how long it's been since I've seen it. Months? Years? No clue. Days blend. Nights merge. Sleep is scattered.

I put the knuckles in one of my bags anyway, just in case I can get them enchanted by Simple and sell them, split the profits with her. She might have spare mats.

How do I bring this up to *Djinn*? Just say it?

"Why, oh young Master Mystic Sid, do you look so pensive? You usually look perfectly blank." He leans in close to my face.

"Thanks. You look like a gluttonous king most of the time."

He smiles proudly. "How do you know I'm not?"

I grin. "I don't. But if I had a guess…"

"There's a light in those eyes! But not back to blank face. What is it? You seem to want to ask me something."

I look way up at him as he fills the air above my head and plays with his green smoke trail with his fat, bejeweled fingers.

"Okay," I say, and take a deep breath. "It's about something you said, but I don't know. I'm hesitant to ask."

"Why, oh Master?" He pushes bushy eyebrows together.

"It's when we fought *Xiuhcoatl*. Before I used the Moldavite Ring and then gave you a 50% stat boost on top of it, and then Mantra."

He lowers himself to my eye level, bulky, muscular green body flattening out in the air behind him. "Oh. I bet it's my *Ananta* comment?"

I try to hide my internal sigh of relief. "Yeah, that."

"I said I would be almost as powerful as *Ananta*. Yes, I did, didn't I?" He stares into my eyes, pupils dilating.

Mine probably are, too. "Yeah, that," I repeat.

"Well, what do you want to ask, then?" He genuinely looks confused, even scratching his head with a pointer finger.

"*Ananta*. Do you know anything about him?"

"Oh, I see. You want to replace me with the most destructive power this world knows. That's fine. I get it. It's okay." He turns his back on me and floats up with his arms folded.

"No, no. Not that. I… just… I…"

He spins around and laughs. "Just messing with you, young Master Sid. What Mystic wouldn't want to claim *Ananta*?"

I actually blush, not having had a clue he was fucking with me a moment ago.

"Aw, Master, none of that. Seriously." His voice drops low. "What do you want to know about *Ananta*?"

"Well, I have *Oni* next, no clue if there are more… like *Keres*, for example. I have this feeling, though, that after *Oni*… I'll have none left but *Ananta*. Is there anything you can tell me? About *Ananta*? About other summons I might have missed? About, well, anything Mystic that I don't know or haven't figured out?"

His green smoke swirls into a basket and he sits in it. He pats White Elf Territory's lush and magical grass. "Sit with me."

I do.

He puts a hand on my shoulder, looking down deeply into my eyes. I've never seen *Djinn* seem so serious. "I have no idea what you don't know or haven't figured out."

I grin. "Okay, assume the truth. I don't know a damn thing, and I'm lost in Mystic all the time. My friends are getting seriously hurt more and more each fight. *Keres* ate Days alive. He... felt that. You know? I'm asking, will *Ananta* hurt? If so, I don't want any of them to fight him, just me. Because I've seen *Ananta* in Elora Online's cutscene every day of my life for seven years, except since I've been here. He looks painfully destructive, even by Dark World's standards."

Djinn cups his hands in front of him and a glowing purple orb forms in his hands. I peer into it as he speaks quietly. "*Ananta* used to be a prisoner of the men of the sea. They used him to search for the elixir of life, long life being highly desired. But they mistreated *Ananta*, and over hundreds of thousands of years of this treatment, *Ananta*, in a rage, devastated this world as we know it and went rogue." In the purple orb, I see all this played out, the ships, all different races in Dark World, and some I haven't seen, beating his blue, nine-headed serpent self, keeping him in enormous chains. He is submissive... but the orb throbs with violent violet hues as *Ananta* finally takes control of his captors as *Djinn* tells the story, and the purple orb suddenly burns bright, hot white, red, green, blue, yellow. I can feel the heat brush my cheeks and lips.

"Thus began this age. Mystic Sid, no Mystic has ever been able to find *Ananta*, much less claim him as a summon." He frowns.

"What?"

His expression evens out. "I do believe you have a shot, though."

"Really? Why?"

He tilts his head to the side, fiddling with the green smoke basket he rests in. Stares off to the right in thought, and then says, "Just a feeling."

I realize something. "You've met him."

Djinn gives me a half-smile, as though he were thinking an ironic thought. "Yes, just after this age began. He came to me, but I wasn't in the cave you found me in then. I was a wanderer, and there were no Mystics. Not anyone, except the small groups who survived underground. He revealed his human face to me, coming straight out of his serpent belly, and he talked. He said he was still hunted, and he couldn't be imprisoned ever again by his creations. He'd fight it with the last ounce of magic he had."

"What did you say?" I ask, anticipation making me sweat in the breezy air. His creations?

He shrugs, glances at his hands, then over to my eyes again. "I told him what I've told you, that time is all the same to me. He can access that kind of thinking. I told him no matter what he did, he would succumb to imprisonment. I see him there all the time, even before he destroyed the old age. I see him there now; I see him there eternally. At the same time, I see what you call the cutscene of your Elora Online. As does *Ananta*. However, I cannot see beyond that."

"Is that normal?"

He shakes his head. "I have never not known all of time and her events. I simply can't say when things will happen, are happening, or have happened. But you, Mystic Sid, make it easier for me. You talk to me, and I develop time-sense going in a forward motion, you might say, because I have to answer in time's mysterious flow for us to communicate."

"You lost me." I grin.

"You're always lost." He pats my shoulder.

I pluck some blades of grass, thinking. "*Djinn*," I ask, lowering my voice to match his melancholy tone. "Why did he come to you?"

"We ancient beings of magic are quite familiar with one another. So much time. He came to me because of the way I see no time and only no time. He wanted to know what I saw for him, if he'd ever be free. He is analytical about the realities of many timelines and changing timelines."

"What did you tell him?"

He sighs and looks up at the sky at the few fluffy, white clouds drifting overhead. "I told him I saw him as a summon, and what a summon would be. I told him I am to be one, too. I told him in different words. I said, 'We are summons, bound to serve one master, that is what is happening.' He understood. The time thing must confuse you, and I apologize. It makes perfect sense to me, but I have no other way to explain it that you might understand. I told him we are claimed. We are released." He stops and looks down at me again. His eyes look lighter green, and curious about me, as though meeting me for the first time.

"Did you... do you see me? As releasing you... you both?"

"I have never, ever seen you until you entered my cave to claim me. I was more than intrigued. I felt time moving in our duel. It is a thing that has never happened, happens, or will happen that I am aware of. Out of sorts for me, as I am all-knowing." He lets out a soft chuckle.

"*Djinn*, can you give me any hint as to how to find and confront *Ananta* without my friends? I can't let them go through anything like what I've seen in the opening cutscene, the burning, the end of the world. What do I do?" I plead with him with my big Nuudle eyes. I know that works on most. When a little Nuudle widens his round, huge eyes, it seems to melt those who like kittens and baby bunnies. *Djinn*'s the type who likes both. I've been practicing in Inn bathroom mirrors, and I'm getting pretty good.

"Aw, now, don't do that."

"*Djinn*..."

"Those eyes! You've gotten better. You're mean." He sticks his tongue out at me and turns his head away.

"Alright, I'll stop with the eyes. Worth a shot. But seriously, any information you can give me helps."

"I don't know where *Ananta* is. He's not here and now, in Dark World, I don't think, or I would sense him. I do feel he's with the Nuudles somehow, but not sure. Just from what I see of his surroundings. I cannot tell you if this is a thing that has already happened, or will happen, or is happening. But I do know only a good creation would enchant *Ananta* to possibly be used as a summon by a Mystic."

What is a good creation? "How do you know?"

He rolls his eyes. "Rune magic. It's what you've been studying for five hundred years."

"Five hund—?" I'm lost.

He chuckles. "Remember, I have no sense of time. It all just grooves together. Think about it, young Mystic. Think about those scrolls you labor over understanding and creating. Think about the one that filled *Keres'* desire to feed, if only for a moment."

I do think about that, and how every time I've fought mobs since I claimed her, and I'm not even using her, she appears in a shadowy, ghostly black form and devours the bodies of my dead enemies before the animated and gored corpses disappear. It's creepy, and I haven't summoned her at all when this happens. It's like she's half-in, half-out. I don't tell my guildies, but sometimes… it's silly. Sometimes, I just know to feed her, so I'll kill a few fleshy creatures in fields, forests, deserts, when nobody is around, and watch her shadow figure appear and eat their corpses until they fade, and then she does too. I can tell she's satisfied. That makes me feel like I'm doing right by her, even if she did eat Days. Days might whack me on the head if he knew I did this out a feeling of obligation to supply battles for her to feed off. But that's what she asked for.

And I can feel her satisfaction, somehow, in my heart.

"The Nuudle runes are the first form of written communication on the eastern continent. Maybe all of this world. They were designed for the purpose of singing a spell off a scroll to use magic. Words are powerful, especially ancient ones."

"Why? What does that have to do with… creations?"

He puckers his lips. "They just are, I suppose. Makes sense, right? Otherwise, you and I could not speak to each other. Simple, really."

I laugh. "Sure. Sure."

"So, although I've demonstrated I'm not as all-knowing as I let you believe, I'm good at figuring. After thousands of years in that cave waiting for Mystics to try to claim me, I did a lot of figuring. I like to think I'm an expert at figuring."

"What do you figure about *Ananta* and the runes? Scrolls? What do you mean by creations?"

He leans over his basket and whispers, "I'd guess *Ananta* is with the Nuudles, and rune magic makes him safe. *Ananta* knows no language now used, just knows hatred and destruction from his life of captivity, remembering that one period of time he was free. He would turn to the logical and magical communicators, the Nuudles and their runes for protection and peace. Only they have the kind of knowledge and consistency in their personas to satisfy *Ananta* that he is safe and can do his thing from the sidelines."

"What things does he do? It sounds more like another prison to me."

Djinn leans back in the smoke basket. "You have a lot of empathy for your NPC summons, Mystic Sid."

I look down with a smile. I guess I do. "Thanks. I'll do some figuring about your figuring, maybe talk to Master Gronai about it. He sometimes knows fine details and sometimes seems a little senile. I'll catch him on a good day."

"Wise."

"Your idea."

"Not the Master Gronai part."

"Well, teamwork."

"Teamwork? I like working in a team. Much better than commands, much better than—" He stops, zooms up into the air above me, smoke basket disintegrating.

"What?" I ask, looking around, then back up at *Djinn*. He's gazing east to the glade there, and I stand quickly, turning to face the same direction.

Between two willows with fine pink blossoms stands a breathtakingly beautiful Siren. She has blood-red hair, pale blue skin and bright green eyes. She wears mage gear I haven't seen, and her black satin cloak is hooded, like my crimson one. Her HP bar is stacked. Man, she's got stats through the roof.

"Hello?" I say to her. I can't make out the expression on her face. It's like there's nothing there. I get spooked.

"There you are," says a familiar voice in a sing-song tone. Raspy, thick.

It's Shell. I've never seen her, but I'd know that voice anytime, anywhere.

"Shell?" I say. "Where have you been? Everyone in the guild has been looking for you."

She takes a couple steps toward us. "I found new friends. Well, one in particular." She walks even closer, and I see a gleam of the Mystic marking on her forehead. It's black. I thought only Nuudles got forehead markings, but I guess Mystics of any race do. Her face is firm, eyes steady, and I feel hate oozing from them as she glares at *Djinn*.

Djinn holds his hands up, palms facing behind him. "Oh, Mystic Shell, don't take it to heart. I didn't like that Psychic. I told you he manipulated you. You ignored me."

"Psychic?" I say, head swinging from *Djinn* to Shell, and back. "What are you talking about?"

Shell's eyes finally meet mine. Knives aim at me out of those green depths. "Seeker gave me what the guild gave you. They didn't do anything for me like they do all the time for you. Fighting those battles."

"You had no battles to fight," I say. "And what is this between you and *Djinn*?"

"*Djinn*," she hisses, "left me when I used his Seizure move on an enemy. He never came back, and you claimed him. For some reason, he didn't stay loyal to me, his master before you, and has picked you."

Djinn sticks his hands out at her. "That Psychic is the wrong sort, Shell, and I tried to tell you."

"You, *Djinn*, have no place telling me anything. You were supposed to be at my command. I trusted you to obey, to be on my side."

"Psychic?" I butt in again. "Seeker, is that the Psychic you're talking about? *Djinn*, is it Seeker? What am I missing?"

Shell walks up to me so fast I have no time to even take a step back. She points a pale blue, webbed finger in my face. "Seeker gave me what Faithgamblers didn't. He helped me get a new summon. He helped me boost my stats. And you have him all wrong, Sid. He's an amazing and powerful man. There's something very special between us, and I have you to thank for pleasing him with a Sunlight Daisy from the Mantra flower shop, although *I* didn't get Mantra. I'd already met with Seeker, and I was biased by your false stories of him. But, I came around, and you should, too, if you know what's good for you."

"What are you talking about, Sunlight Daisy?"

"You do know what it is?"

"Yeah…"

"I bought one and gave it to him."

"Why?" I'm flabbergasted.

"Because, after spending some time listening to him, I realized you have it all wrong and he's right. Besides, Seeker and I, we're a pair. Two of a kind. You wouldn't understand that, of course, but I wanted him to always come to me when he was killed. It was my last test to see if he was for real. He comes every time. Every time he dies. And then he's with me, helps me, guides me to the future he has planned for us all. I'm his new protégé. And you are shit."

Shell summons *Xiuhcoatl*.

Gold mist shoots out of her chest and the massive, shining, snaky dragon summon takes form in front of *Djinn* and me. The beast's eyes penetrate me, and I see revenge lust in them.

Sid casts Contemplation. *Djinn* gains Protection.

Shell casts Spontaneity. *Xiuhcoatl* gains +560 ATT.

The great golden sun dragon of all dragons glows with the stat boost, and flames shoot out of his nose as he feels the effect of the spell.

Sid casts Mantra.

"Silvia," I whisper, and I'm afraid.

***Djinn* gains +634 ATT.**

"Master Sid, I'm not the one you should be worried about."

I'm so flustered that I'm not fighting anywhere near peak-performance. "Dammit, I don't know what to do!"

"You do!" *Djinn* says. "Command me!"

Shell casts Summon Within.

White and black diamonds shoot out of her chest, and fly at me so fast that I can't dodge. I'm hit by them, but they don't hurt my body. They hurt my very soul, and I fall down from a sensation of having lost all willpower to move, breathe, exist.

Sid is damaged by Spirit power.

"Command me, young Sid. Get up!" *Djinn* pleads.

Xiuhcoatl rises high in the air, sapphire, skeletal wings flapping.

I can't do a damn thing. It's all too much, and I'm so heavy. I feel like part of me broke from that move. What is that spell?

Shell commands Simmer.

That one…

***Simmer*—Burns target every 3 seconds for 10% HP for 30 seconds. Target cannot attack.**

Shit.

Xiuhcoatl opens his angry dragon snout and out spills molten yellow lava… coming right at me and fast. I can't move. The Mystic spell that Shell used, one I don't have nor knew of, has made me immobile, listless, defenseless. Hopeless, knowing this defeat could possibly crack my mind from the pain I'm about to endure… maybe making me like the mysterious Anella, who I now realize has known true pain, loss, and regret.

Why couldn't I act? Why didn't I listen to *Djinn* and command him? I had been stunned, and I think some part of me didn't believe Shell would really do this god-awful thing to me.

Sid gains the effects of Simmer.

Then the unbearable searing hits me, and I writhe around in the grass, screaming. It just goes on and on. I kind of make out through the first waves of the tormenting lava consuming me that *Djinn* is hitting *Xiuhcoatl* in that way summons attack anyone who attacks me, but that's all I can soak in. My body is on fire, inside and out, and the burn effect, which will slowly kill me instead of a fast kill like *Xiuhcoatl's* Seizure move, melts my digital flesh off my face. I reach up to my cheeks as I try to scream while my vocal chords burn out, and feel them with nubs for fingers, face just mush. Then my left eye pops from the heat, and I lie squirming in agony in the grass of White Elf Territory, begging for it to end, but I know I can't even speak. My tongue has been burned out. Slathering, wispy, squeaky noises come out of my disintegrating mouth. There is no way to cry out anymore, even. All has been fried out of me.

This is the worst, the absolute worst. I can't block the insane pain eating my body, and in my final gasp of life, I look up at *Xiuhcoatl* with my right eye, still somehow intact. The golden sun dragon and *Djinn* duel, but *Xiuhcoatl's* black and red eyes meet my one blue. I see something there in his gaze, a blankness, as though he were shutting off his torturing me from his conscience, but I have no mind to interpret, and then I am, so very thankfully, gone.

~

I'm just about to say goodbye to the odd being marking on my palm as Sorry hisses, "Wait."

I pull my hand back and turn to her.

"What, Lady?" asks Days, touching her arm.

"It's bothering me. Are you sure you're going to use *Keres*? I mean, I just have this feeling... *Keres* is who? What? What she did to Days, I mean... do you follow?" Her brows push together and she bites her lower lip, gazing down at me.

She's scared. We all are. *Keres* did something to all of us, those who watched, and Days, who was eaten alive. Destruction I now have command over.

No, she's not scared of me. She's afraid *Keres* isn't supposed to be claimed as a summon, that something felt wrong to her.

I keep my mouth shut. She's absolutely right, and I know it, but I know *Keres* has to be the one. Deep in my gut, I know. You can see why I don't tell anyone that I feed her sometimes.

My summons entered my heart when they agreed to let me be their masters, whatever my heart might be, and I feel them and know them. Sounds like some old-fashioned new age crap. I know I'd sound nuts to anyone I said these thoughts to and the actions they lead to aloud.

That's a big truth, though. I didn't beat any of them, really. They chose. Not me.

I feel like they are all mine, and to see *Xiuhcoatl* come from Shell felt like I was betrayed, or that maybe the dragon summon would be glad to get his revenge. It's hard to separate that she has a different *Xiuhcoatl*... but she had a fit at *Djinn* for leaving her as though her *Djinn* and my *Djinn* were the same.

There was that inscrutable look *Xiuhcoatl* gave me after obeying Shell's command to melt me to death. At the time, in heightened fear and shock, I *knew* it was the same *Xiuhcoatl*.

What does that mean? How do I answer Sorry?

"It's hard. To explain." Something occurs to me. Yes, things have changed, and maybe people's thoughts on doing these fights might not be as enthusiastic. "Look, I completely understand if any of you have changed your minds and can't do this anymore. Please believe me when I say I have no idea why you've shown up to any of them. I guessed you were bored." I look around at them. "I guessed everybody loved Mystic stories and summons. What I realize is that *Keres* was something completely dark. Different. Disturbing on a level that Mystic summons shouldn't be. If any or all of you want to walk away right now, do it. Don't worry about me."

I smile at Sorry, whose eyes are fixed like arrows on mine. "You all have been some of the best friends I've ever known I could have. Now I know why you do the fights." I look over at Simple, who is staring at the dirt. "Maybe another day, or maybe never, but there are other missions than these Mystic summon-collecting death sentences."

Doolittle speaks after a moment of silence where we're all looking at the dirt with Simple. "There's more." He says it so quietly I think he's talking to himself, maybe casting a spell.

I look up at his tall, lean, White Elf frame.

"Simple told us about it. Simple?" He turns his gaze away from me and tilts his head as he tries to get her to look at him. Still watching her, he says, "You know Simple and her books. Her runes. Her histories." He smiles softly at her.

She sits down, cross-legged, and peers up at me, worry deep in her Nuudle eyes.

"I thought you were working on scroll-making?" I say to her.

"Sid," she says softly. "I've been here a very long time."

Are we really talking about this?

I sit down next to her, and the other three join us in the cave soil. We're in a circle with a Luna Lamp in the middle.

"How long?" I ask.

"I don't know. I made it my mission to figure out what Dark World is, how time passes but doesn't, and I found clues and answers in the books at the Temple of Nuudlel. A wonderful NPC helped me."

"Was it Master Gronai?" I say.

She chuckles, shoulders relaxing. "No. I still have no clue how you know how to charm that grumpy, ancient NPC into pretty much giving you scrolls."

"No, it's not like that—"

"Joke, but kind of for real. How do you get on with NPCs so well? We all see it with your summons."

"Hey, Simple," Sorry says in a low voice. "Stay on track."

I meet eyes with Days. He has admiration for me in that expression, and it's the same one he's always had. I know it because I show him the same face. Respect. My stomach settles and I exhale, not realizing how worried I was and terrified until Days let me know with a look that this is good news, don't worry, Sid, we got you... that look.

"Okay." She bows her blue, pigtailed head and fiddles with a Thunderstone Ring on her index finger. "What conclusion have you come to about Dark World and how you got here, what it is, all of that?"

"You mean, pretty much all the hinted questions I asked the guild that nobody would talk about, change the subject for, or get dead quiet when brought up?"

She whips her head over to me. She looks frightened, but I was just fucking with her, trying to lighten this oppressive mood.

"Hey, Simple, look at me. I'm grinning. You know me. What's going on? Just say it."

"No, really, Sid. I want to know what you think Dark World is."

I blink at her a few times, then glance around at the others. They are so intently focused on me that I feel like the star of a Broadway play who just forgot the most important line of the show on opening night. "Hey, why are you all so serious? I'm honestly confused, not trying to say anything or judge, you know. What do you know that you're not telling me?"

Days says, "You've figured out you're probably dead, right?"

I nod and give him a grim look. "It makes sense, but the interface..."

"Yep," he says. "Don't we need eyes?"

"So, you're saying you have no idea, either, and anything I've thought of, you have four times over for God knows how long you've been here. Now, truly, I have no insight. I'm sorry. I lose myself in my class and my summons. It helps me not focus on those questions anymore, and every time I do, I get unreasonably angry." I'm not smiling anymore and put my face in my small hands.

"Me too," Sorry says gently.

"Me too," Doolittle agrees.

Simple puts her hand on my sandaled foot. "Look at me."

I do. Her eyes tell me she knows me very, very well, that all this time, she's been paying close attention to me, my personality, my gameplay. It's not for obsessive reasons, or even curiosity. She's looking to see if I'm something, and the way she's looking at me now tells me all this—and she has figured that I am that thing, which makes her feel filled with joy.

"The books," I say. "All those Nuudle rune books in the temple. And goddamn, even every trashy inn has a few books lying around next to the bedrolls. Simple, what did you read that makes you look at me like that?"

She smiles softly. "First, tell me what you think is going on."

I shake my head. "It's all pieces, and I only have what I know from Elora lore and now Dark World lore to try to remember all the clues dropped to me out of order to make a story that is most likely what happened to me."

"What is, say, the dominant theory right now that you have?" Doolittle asks.

"I'm dead, Seeker has something to do with it." I'd never said it out loud. I continue, now feeling floodgates open. "Dark World is Elora's past as I know it. The game Elora Online focuses a lot on back in the day of Bane making Dragonbane and Kane defeating him. All that is happening in Dark World. Somehow, my consciousness is inside this game, this world. This Dark World.

Will time keep moving forward until two thousand years from now I meet Sid Vicious, my toon in Elora, and tell him everything? I have no memory of that happening, but maybe I can create it. Then again, nothing ever happens. Bane never has big battles with anyone, not even Kane. It's like I'm in a typical MMORPG right-now scenario, not living an actual virtual life in some other reality that the company sends people who die while playing to." The words fall out so fast, and I gesture wildly. "I want to go back to Elora. There were people there. People I cared about. If I'm dead and somehow I get to Elora, will they accept this little Mystic Nuudle is their old Maniac Dragonbane best friend?"

"Silvia?" Sorry asks.

"What?"

"You've said that name every time you cast Mantra. A woman named Silvia meant so much to you that you made her name your mantra for Mantra." Sorry reaches over and pushes hair out of my eyes.

"Yeah, mainly her," I admit in response to Sorry's mature and understanding way of getting it out of me.

Days pulls out Onyx Steel, his new broadsword made from onyx and steel magically blended by an expert crafter, and drags it in the dirt around the Luna Lamp. "Simple read about time from the ancients' points-of-view. She understands it and can explain it. In non-linear experience of time, you had been written about in one of the books she read. Right now isn't the time to get into explaining the time in the game, how it's perceived. And no, we don't know any solid answers, but that's what Simple looks for when she reads all these books." He sketches *Djinn* in the soil. "Sid, what is it like being a Mystic for you? You don't fight like a regular fighter would. I don't think it's because you've always played melee. I think there's something more going on, but the translations from Simple's rune knowledge are only like sketches of what they actually were trying to record in writing. That's how much dialect has changed, and how friggin' old these books she found are."

I take a deep breath. Let it out. "I'd like to read the book that you say talks about me."

They exchange glances with each other.

"What?"

"We think you know part of it already. Anyone who's ever played Elora Online knows a little glimpse of what's in that book," says Sorry.

"*Ananta*," I murmur. "The opening cutscene." I turn to Simple. "You've found books that tell the story behind the cutscene like it actually happened here?"

"Something like that."

"Wow, yeah, I want to read that."

"See?" says Days. "I've never met anyone who *is* his class like you are a Mystic. People play their class, they talk about their class, they make plans based around their class, but they don't identify their very being with their class. You totally do that."

"No, I don't." I wave a hand and crack up. "I did with Maniac, though. What the—what are you talking about?"

"It's true," Sorry says. "You're almost an NPC in your attitude about your summons."

I cock my head at her with a funny smile. "What do you mean?"

"NPCs are focused on one to three things in conversation. Not that you do that, mind, and, you're too quiet. We all want to know you better. We can see in you that you identify with this class as though it were the job you wanted all your life and took a chance one day, went for it, and got it. Simple and Days? They said you sure as hell weren't like that when they met you that first day. You've grown into it."

I look at the marking Days has drawn in the dirt. It's Sorry in her Medusa Headdress. Those things can be seen a mile away.

"The book. Simple, can you explain why we're talking about the thing nobody talks about right now? What did you find in the book?"

"It can be interpreted so many ways."

"Do you have it? I can read runes now. Well, somewhat."

She tightens her lips. "I always have that book."

"Can I borrow it? Please? I'll give it back as soon as I'm done."

She pulls a faded, red leather book, rather large, certainly not of this time, out of one of her bags. She hands it to me. I try to read the runes on the cover to figure out what the name of it is. The cover itself is just the name of the book, no author, embossed in gold leaf.

I say, "It looks like, well, I'd say the name of the book is something like 'Manual of Systems'."

She stares hard at me. "How did you get that out of it?"

"What do you interpret it as?"

"Guide to Time Dimensions."

I look at it again. I can see how she might see that, but I still read Manual of Systems. I put it in my bag. "Thanks. I'll get it back to you soon."

I stand up, but the rest of them stay sitting, looking up at me, confused.

Suddenly, I'm confused too.

"What?" I say.

"Well, where do you think you're going?" Sorry says with a webbed hand on her hip.

"What? Oh, I thought—I mean, we're done here, right? I'm supposed to read this book to understand what you're talking about." I look around at their amused faces. "I feel dumb. What am I missing?"

Days stands up, towering over me, and claps my thin shoulder. One of his claws pokes through my robe. "Yeah, we want you to read the book, but we have an *Oni* to catch first."

"But…"

The rest of them stand up. Simple is back to her cheerful self.

"Sorry was just scared of *Keres*. She knows the drill. She knows how you play these." Simple waves her wand and red smoke comes out of it. She writes the word in Nuudle ancient runes in the air with the smoke for "Talk to me later about something important." It's a character with three strokes. Those ancient Nuudles needed their privacy.

I nod. I'm actually mostly humbled. Sorry had a weak moment of fear and that was all that happened? My worried mind blew it all out of proportion?

No, there's more. It's in the red leather book with the gold leaf imprints.

I turn and put my palm on the cave wall in White Elf Territory… the usual happens, then fade to black. Next, we are in a round cavern. It's freezing in here. The walls are blue ice, reflecting from blue torches placed all around the cave walls, set right in the ice. The floor is white marble and shines like a dentist's teeth. In the center at the top of the cave hangs a chandelier with dozens of blue-flame candles.

Oni rests against the wall farthest from where we spawn. He watches, but does nothing.

He's enormous, all different hues of blue, with a muscular human body, sharp blue talons on his hands and bare feet, two eyes set like a person's would be, with a third eye in the center of his forehead. He has huge, pale blue tusks coming out from the sides of his jowls, and two twisting-back, dark blue horns sprouting from the front, top of his head.

There's almost something sad about him, but I can't put my finger on it. I get the feeling he's been in this cave for a long, long time without any contact with the outside world or beings from it.

Sid summons *Keres*.

Oni floats up, able to fly without wings. Must be his magic. He points a fat, taloned finger at *Keres*, and then at Simple.

Doolittle starts buffing *Keres* and Days, and throwing one on Simple he wouldn't usually use. We all saw that finger move.

Oni flies at us.

Day uses Invoke Inner Demon.

Oni stops dead and turns on Days, lashing out with a clawed hand. Days ducks and pushes the other hand coming for him away with his Onyx Steel.

Keres wastes no time and is all over *Oni*, scratching and biting.

Sorry casts Weaken Enemy. *Oni* gains Offense Down.

Very few mobs will lose hate from Days, and even as he uses Crushing Blade on *Oni*, the great blue demon from time forgotten, taking off 30% of his HP, *Oni* assesses Sorry.

Then he turns his attention back to Simple and points at her again. Her Nuudle eyes get gigantic.

Oni uses Disaster Strike. Simple cannot use Special Ability until end of battle.

"Dammit!" she screams. "It's like he knew I was going to put the White spells on *Keres*!"

Simple casts Ball Lightning. *Oni* takes lightning damage.

Oni has lost interest in Simple and now turns to *Keres*, who chewed on his shoulder the whole time he dealt with Simple. He scratches her across the face while slapping her, and I see black blood and marks appear on her face, then almost instantly fade.

Doolittle casts Deep Heal on *Keres*.

Keres gains some HP back from the hit, but it's like it meant nothing to her. I guess in *Keres*' eyes, *Oni*'s size was a benefit for her hopeful future feast.

Sid casts Contemplation. Days gains Protection.

Sid casts Mantra.

"Silvia," I mutter.

Days gains +331 ATT.

"Why are you doing that?" Days yells.

"Drain him!" I call out as he dodges an *Oni* foot.

"Crap!" Days says.

He gets closer to *Oni*. "Why don't you get *Keres* to do something, Sid?"

I have her moves memorized, but I'm looking at them again. I have to do something before Days gets that hate with his killer special move.

Sid commands Drain Blood. *Keres* drains *Oni*'s blood, reducing HP by 30%.

Oni rakes at *Keres* with his facial horns, trying to knock her out of the air and away from him. She's relentless, not one bit worried about his rarity. She thought of nothing but the taste of his demon flesh on her lips. Both their HPs drop, but not too much.

"Now, Days!" I say.

Days uses Special Ability: Soul Gather.

Oni's HP starts going down like mad, as it should in the three seconds the ability demands, and in a flash, *Oni* spins on Days.

Oni uses Swallow. Days is swallowed.

It all happens so fast. I have no clue what happened to Days as he went into *Oni*'s maw and disappeared down his gullet, and I look at *Oni*. Do I see regret in his eyes? Because Days was taken from the battlefield before his Special Ability had time to finish its magic, *Oni* still stands, but at 20% HP.

With Doolittle's attention on *Keres*, she has full HP.

Sorry casts Blind. *Oni* resists.

"Sid, he has 20%. What are you doing?" Simple pleads.

I'm frozen, watching this great blue demon, *Oni*, going toe to toe with another type of demon, *Keres*. She's taking chunks out of him that grow back within seconds, but they must hurt the great summon. He shows no fear or pain in his three eyes, just keeps focus on *Keres*. He's not even really fighting her, I realize. He's being defensive. He's made no instigating moves.

"Simple, I can't."

"What do you mean?"

"I can't let her eat him."

Her eyes practically pop out of her head. "What the—He's not even fighting! It would be easy."

"Just look at him, Simple," I say, and point.

She looks, but her face pales. "I want him gone. Do something! Mantra me and I'll finish it."

I almost do, just to get these conflicting emotions over with. How can I feel sympathy for this great beast of a summon who could obviously take us all out with some devastating move, like *Xiuhcoatl*'s sun? He could Swallow us one by one. I don't know any of his moves because he isn't using them.

Sid commands Retreat.

Keres gives *Oni* one last nip at his forearm, and then floats back to me and hovers at my side, black eyes bright and bloody lips curving in a small smile.

Doolittle casts heals and buffs on the four of us left. I can't even muster a Spontaneity or Mantra for Simple to blow him up and finish him off. I'm a terrible Mystic. I'm supposed to defeat him with *Keres*, but I've seen what *Keres* can do. I realize then and there that I'll never be able to use *Keres* against an opponent. Nothing deserves what she can deliver.

"I can't," I say. "She's too... too..."

Simple runs up to me. "Mantra me. Look at him. He's watching us. He's going to do something soon. Mantra me and I'll end it."

For the love of gods everywhere, the thought of electrocuting him into losing and submission I cannot do. Maybe it's those three sad eyes.

Sorry casts Tribal Curse using Dowsing Limb. *Oni* is cursed.

Whatever that Dowsing Limb is, it made Tribal Curse take down a lot more DoT than usual. *Oni*'s already close to 8% HP before I know it.

"I'll do it," Sorry says. "This is what you get for swallowing Days," she yells at *Oni*.

Oni turns to face me directly, all three eyes examining into my very being. I feel like he knows everything about me in these moments as the curse DoT drains him down, down, down, and he makes no moves to fight. He simply watches me.

Then his HP is 0%, and all fades...

I'm in the cavern alone with *Oni*. I'm feeling the cold again, which some part of my body ignored during the adrenaline fuel of the fight. He sits with his legs crossed and the same curious look in his three eyes that he had when he lost the battle.

"You shouldn't have lost," I say. Maybe I'm candid because of how he looks at me. It feels like we've met, like I've had him as a summon before. Like he knows my every intention and is weighing all his findings.

Finally, he says in a deep, smooth voice, "I have not seen *Keres* since she was Isabel."

"Is Isabel the name she went by before she became *Keres*?" I ask.

He nods, still not blinking, nor taking his eyes off me.

"Why didn't you fight? I mean, you must have some moves that could have stopped us; you have to. Right?" I don't get his passiveness in battle. I need to understand it, even before I know if he's my summon or not. He invokes a deep curiosity in me to know the unknown things of existence.

"You are a Mystic I can serve. You, too, fight defensively. There is no other way that has honor, and all demons must have honor." He bows his head. "You did not serve me as a dish to *Keres*. I know what she is and what she can do. You showed compassion in battle for your foe." He looks back up at me.

"You're not my foe. I don't know if it was compassion, but I've seen her feed, and plenty of times." I stop talking.

"You couldn't let her do that to me. Why?" He leans down toward me. His teeth are twice the size of my head, and sharp.

"I don't know."

"You do."

I look down. "You looked lonely. You didn't hurt anyone when we attacked. I guess I'm motivated by revenge after all, not inflicting pain on something defending itself and nothing else." I think of the eleven months of planning to get Seeker in Elora.

"Peaceful Nuudle Mystic, I will be your summon. Continue to be compassionate, and we will be great partners."

I cock my head at him. "But you're a demon. I thought demons were made to be destructive?"

"Nobody made me. Your demon lore is generalized. Demons are simply from another realm, and that is the only difference. I've been stuck here by a curse, unable to live in the realm with my fellow demons. Do not worry. I will obey your every command. I believe you have good judgment. You will not make me act like your stereotype of a demon."

He collapses into a royal blue mist and swirls into the middle of my chest. My heart is filled with joy and bliss, as always when I get a new summon, and then all fades to black.

I'm back in the cave in White Elf Territory. I turn on guild chat before the others waiting there see me. I want to know what happened to Days, and then Simple spies me.

"You're back! Oh, Sid! Did you get him?"

The three of them surround me.

"Where's Days?" I ask.

"When *Oni* swallowed him, it warped him to the southern-most point of Mylop Territory. Doolittle is trying to nail him down for a tele back here," Sorry explains.

"Nail him down for a teleport?" I ask.

"In Dark World," says Doolittle while looking at a magic map, "you have to know where they are to tele, not just party up and cast it on their character icon in party mode. Ah, I think I got you, Days."

In guild chat, Days says, "Is that Sid? You get him, man?"

"Yeah. Yeah, I did."

I can hear him grinning as he says, "Totally worth being swallowed for. How many players can say they've been swallowed by *Oni*, for Christ's sake?"

"Hang on," Doolittle tells him. "Tele-ing now."

Doolittle disappears, and a second or two later, Days appears first as a pale, glowing white light, and then his whole body forms as the light fades. He wastes no time. Doolittle springs up out of white light next.

"Sid, let's see him, come on," says Days.

The others urge.

"Okay, here we go."

Sid summons *Oni*.

He comes from my chest in his royal blue mist, forms, and hovers quietly, watching me pensively. It's hard for me to look away from him long enough to see what he can do, and after a moment, I check out his ability list, reading it to the others as I go.

Description:

Oni is a timeless demon of Nactria and Shinto. Practiced in meditative arts, Oni fights with honor and respect, and calls on the destructiveness of demons only when there is no other option. His name has been associated with disease and destruction through the ages, but myths do not make the demon. Oni carries abilities of protection for a demon of his kind.

Abilities:

Disease—*Deals Damage-over-Time, 15% HP every 5 seconds until stopped or commanded so.*

Demon Call—*Calls demons from the ancient underworld, who, under Oni's command, cause massive mayhem, destruction, and death to foes.*

Disaster Strike—*Stops target's Special Ability attack for the duration of engagement.*

Seizure Ability: Swallow—*Swallows target whole and sends them to random spawn point.*

"Wow," I murmur. "He could have torn us to pieces."

"Why didn't he?" asks Sorry.

"And being swallowed wasn't bad. It was like going through a Kila Crystal," adds Days.

"He told me before he agreed to be my summon that my ideas about demons are, uh, generalized. I think that's the word. *Oni*?" I say to him. He's floating nearby, barely fitting in the cave's dead end, sharing a royal blue light with us.

He says nothing. Just watches with those three eyes.

"Thanks, *Oni*," I tell him anyway. "I got ya."

Sid dismisses *Oni*.

"He makes me nervous," says Sorry.

"That's because you just watched him eat Days," Simple says.

She puckers her lips, then says, "You're probably right."

"Maybe you have generalized ideas of demons, too," says Days. She punches him lightly on the arm and then he's all smiles.

"Thank you, guys. I mean it."

"Like I said, you're a natural Mystic. Anyone else would have had *Keres* devouring him in less than ten seconds." He holds out his hand for a high-five, which I give him. "You felt sorry for *Oni*, and that's what made him your summon. You saw more in him than a beastie to add to your collection."

Maybe. All I know is during that fight, seeing *Keres* trying to gorge herself on any exposed body part on *Oni*, and *Oni* not really fighting back... I mean, come on. He has to be the last summon before *Ananta*. And by looking at his ability list, he had no desire to hurt us, but he sure as hell could have. In the heat of the battle, I realized he wasn't destroying us, not putting up a fight once I wasn't commanding *Keres* to hurt him.

I decide I like *Oni* and wonder if he'll ever be a talker like *Djinn*. I seriously doubt it, but wouldn't that be something?

~

Calla doesn't appear at my grave when I summon *Oni* in the eternal cemetery storm. I really need to invest in an umbrella.

I don't know what it means that she's not here. I ask *Oni*, but he doesn't answer.

I'll have to do some figuring. Even if I did get *Ananta*'s quest, I'd need to treasure hunt, clothcraft and make some scrolls before being prepared for that. Need to talk to Master Gronai, show him Simple's red leather book. See what he makes of it. I've flipped through it, but the runes are so very different from what I know.

As I walk to Kleeple after treasure hunting with *Djinn* on the fourth day after claiming *Oni*, a mailbox icon saying "1" appears in my interface. Who's sending me mail? Nothing's up for sale in the AH.

Once in the Nuudle capital, I get to the mailbox. I'm stunned when I see the letter has the official seal of Bane and his territory. I open it.

With respect to Nuudle Mystic Sid,

You have been invited to an audience with the great, wise, and generous Bane of Dragonbane Territory. Your scheduled time is this coming Shealaday at 2:00 p.m. You will arrive at Bane's tower fifteen minutes early. The great life-changer Bane has been watching your Mystic progress and would like to meet you in person, as no Mystic has come this far.

No need to reply. It is assumed you will not miss this opportunity.

Malcrumt, High First Guard of Bane

I laugh, and then crumple up the invite and toss it back in the mailbox. Like hell I have time for NPC bullshit. Bane's as rotten as they get, and it's probably one of the NPC quests where you can choose the not-so-honest route in gameplay and get special rewards. Of course, you make a million NPC enemies. Screw that and screw Bane. I have my own stuff to deal with. Like Shell.

Of course, I told the whole guild what she did to me. I left out exactly how unbearably painful it was. Everyone was shocked, but especially Days. I didn't like having to tell him that, but she killed me. On purpose. For *him*. I hate him, I hate him, I hate him. I'm certain he manipulated any romantic feelings she has developed for him into making her believe whatever she wants as long as she does what he tells her to.

We know it, and we all have to be on guard from now on.

CHAPTER 15: THE LINK

I slam my Shaman Stick against a Moog. I've never picked up another weapon. The lightning enchantment from Anella turned out to be so damn good, but I didn't realize it at the time. Simple has enchanted the crap out of it for my class stats. I can't get a weapon as a Mystic that can do as much physical damage as my ATT stat, which is now 203, and the enchantment does that much damage. And plus my Strength stat is higher, so my physical hit's not god-awful. So, with one hit from my staff and a slap from *Djinn*, one of the forty little fur ball Moogs that had popped on us when we got to the end of the dungeon, Elis Lea, dies. We're killing them fast with no damage to ourselves. Even Doolittle seems to be enjoying using his Light-Imbued Dagger on Moogs and seeing them fall over, *poof!*

Can getting Summon Within, that move Shell used against me that I'd never heard of, be this easy? Sure, the dungeon run took three and a half hours, but nobody's been hurt, and this must be all there is. Whew. I feel relief, and I casually command *Djinn* to warp a particularly cute Moog to its HP. It vanishes in a green puff of smoke.

I notice Sorry zone out while lazily fighting a couple of Moogs with her AoE debuffs and staff, and she gets a headbutt in the gut. She looks pissed and wipes both of the Moogs out.

I try to see what caught her attention. Oh, lord. Even though I'm using *Djinn*, *Keres'* shadow-self has made an appearance, and she's gorging herself on Moog bodies before they fade. It's getting bloody over in that corner of this dungeon battle arena, where Days is tanking about fifteen of the buggers. My compadres haven't seen *Keres* do this, and I've never told them about it.

Well, we'll discuss it later. I decide to end the fun so *Keres* will stop disturbing my friends by multi-targeting all the Moogs left, glancing up at *Djinn*. He nods down at me.

Sid commands First Wish.

22 Moogs are warped to Home Point.

"Hey!" Days yells. "I was collecting them to see how many I could get at once. Spoiled my fun."

"Sorry. It was *Keres*. I hadn't told you guys about her odd habit, but Sorry just saw her."

"So did I," Simple says with a shiver. "What was that about? You had *Djinn* out."

"I saw her doing it right next to me," Days adds. "She's not so tough, just wants a good meal. Right, Sid?"

"Well…" I start to explain, but I'm cut off before I can.

First, you have to know that Elis Lea Dungeon is deep under The Forest of the Undead, home of my tombstone, and it's supposedly full of dark, twisted things that happened when White Elves and Nuudles first practiced their magics together. Let's just say things went very badly, and that's why this dungeon exists. It's like being in a Dr. Seuss dungeon where the creatures want to eat you painfully.

Suddenly, this *thing* explodes out of the center of the gray stone floor, making rocks and soil fly everywhere. I'm so small, I don't have to duck or dodge, and keep my eyes glued to the enormous being coming out of the hole in the middle of the battle arena floor.

As the dust settles, I can see it clearly. It's assessing us, trying to figure out who to get first. At least, I think that's what it's doing. It's covered with fur like the Moogs, but not brown. Purple. It has two nubs for legs and feet like Moogs, but where Moogs have two visible eyes on top of their mounds of bodies, this thing has an antenna thickly holding a wildly spinning eyeball, with two irises containing pupils.

This mob can see everywhere. What is it? I crane my neck back. Its name reads Tinicity.

Days, like usual, doesn't waste time on doing his job.

Days uses Invoke Inner Demon.

The eyeball stops spinning and both irises move to one side of the gooey sphere, glaring into Days' soul.

Tiniticy uses Earth Freeze.

Man, Earth Freeze is a rumored spell-gone-wrong of Elf divine magic colliding with Nuudle rune magic. It's said to kill in AoE everything within a twenty-selcos radius.

"Days, everyone, get back!" I yell. Most moves and spells are instant, but some take time. This one is taking time. The air is frosty, and we're all exhaling white.

"How do we get away from this cold?" Sorry calls to me.

"Twenty selcos away! Move back!"

I dash to the farthest wall and step into temperate air. I look back.

Dammit, they couldn't hear me. They're all hitting Tinicity as it uses this spell, not knowing what it is.

How do I? Has studying runes gotten me some history lessons? Or is it listening to Simple talk about her books over Siren Ale?

No, Simple doesn't know or hasn't figured out what this is.

I've got to do something.

I multi-target everyone in my party except Djinn and me.

Sid commands First Wish.

In four green puffs of mist and sparkles, my team is gone just as the floor in the twenty-selco radius cracks from the cold.

It dropped so fast, and *Djinn* had gotten them at the last minute.

"*Djinn*, what now?"

"I suggest your newly acquired Comfort Ring," he calls over his shoulder, still hitting the thing on the side, unaffected by the absolute zero Tinicity created. "First Wish?"

"I need the Mystic move. Think!" I beg.

"You're the master. I cannot think for myself," he calls out casually, dodging a Jelly Blow from Tinicity. It's completely focused on *Djinn*, so I relax a little in my safe zone. "If I warp it to HP, it'll be under us again, right?"

"Seems that way." He slaps the eyeball, and it bobs to the left. Tinicity drops 9% HP.

Tinicity uses Sword of Ice Rune. Tinicity gains an enchanted weapon.

The furry giant monstrosity grows a solid ice sword out of the side of its body facing *Djinn* and stabs him in the gut with it. His eight-pack pokes in.

"Ow!" *Djinn* hits the eyeball again.

Sid casts Contemplation. *Djinn* gains Protection.

"Thanks."

"I'm going to unsummon you. I have an idea."

"Might not be a good idea, Master. If you get one lick of what you call hate, you'll be ice-stone dead."

I think for a minute. "Trust me. I have a plan."

Sid commands First Wish.

Tinicity is warped to Home Point.

It vanishes, but it's already rumbling in the hole in the middle of the floor. I don't have much time.

"Wish me luck," I say to *Djinn*. He cocks an eyebrow at me and gives a thumbs-up.

Sid dismisses *Djinn*.

Tinicity is rising from the hole, eye leaning toward me, both pupils dilating as they fix on me in that one terrible, cold eyeball on a hairless stem.

Sid summons *Keres*.

She flows quickly from my chest, and she looks wickedly excited once she sees Tinicity.

"Oh, Master, you have brought me to a fine feed. I was starving so. How may I begin?" she hisses, drool oozing out of her huge, needle-toothed mouth. I wince.

Sid uses Special Ability: Seizure.

Sid commands Devour.

Keres zooms into the wall of cold that stops living tissue and everything that is alive. She glances back over her shoulder before launching onto Tinicity, smiles, and mouths the words, "Thank you."

I look away until she's ended Tinicity, and then wait a little longer while she finishes feeding.

Sid dismisses *Keres*.

Tinicity's shredded corpse has disappeared, the cold is gone, and I can't stomach a conversation with even *Djinn* right now because of my choice with *Keres*.

I walk to the hole Tinicity came from and look down.

There's a scroll in the dirt and rubble. I hop down a few levels deep into the hole. I can barely see, but the scroll glows softly, guiding me to it at the very deepest part of Tinicity's sleeping place.

I pick up the scroll. Open it. Select it in my interface menu and use it.

Sid learns Summon Within. Sid can now cast Summon Within.

Yes.

I summon *Djinn*, but I'm still somewhat disturbed by what I did with *Keres*. *Oni*'s swallow wasn't an option; I'd be setting that thing loose on God knows who.

I ask him, "Okay just to give me a warp?"

"Sure, Young Master Sid. You have the spell?"

"Yeah, I know it."

"No Comfort Ring, or am I your Comfort Ring?"

He gets me. He says nothing else.

I target myself.

Sid commands First Wish.

Sid is warped to Home Point.

~

I'm sitting in a muddy puddle next to my tombstone under a Nuudle-sized umbrella. Finally made one by leveling woodworking a little. With wood at 20 and my cloth so high, an umbrella can be made. By me.

Calla hasn't come still. I wonder if it's because of how I used *Keres*. When I'm honest with myself, I knew I had to use *Keres*. She was hungry, and I was cornered. I also don't feel guilty. I realize I'm glad none of my friends saw that, though. I'd told them I used the Counts.

I think Days is right about my being a Mystic at heart. He says it's because my summons are my main focus when it comes to catering to each of their peculiar ways, even over battlemates. As a Maniac, that's just plain selfish. But as a Mystic, I see no other way to be, and don't want to be any other way.

Summon Within—*Mystic deals high Spirit Damage to target, random + with CON stat.*

Doesn't say "cast once a day." Should, but doesn't. Is my Mystic spell collection complete?

What exactly is Spirit Damage?

I haven't used it yet, knowing what it feels like from Shell doing it.

I'm at the graveyard every day, and every night I walk to the Temple of Nuudlel and sleep in my bedroll on the floor next to the eternally awake NPC Master Gronai, who says he likes the company. In the mornings, we study runes and scrollmaking. I've showed him Simple's red leather book, which he was quite excited about, but neither of us have had any luck making definitive sense of it. Some of the pictures show my summons with a Nuudle who looks a lot like me— same marking on the forehead, too—and I find it creepy.

After such sessions, I'm back at the graveyard. Same drill, just waiting for Calla. I don't talk in guild chat. I don't do anything but try to figure out how I get the *Ananta* battle quest.

About two weeks into my obsessive behavior, on a drizzly day near sunset as I'm about to walk south, I see Anella, about ten graves northeast of me, standing in front of a grand tomb with a proud, gothic White Elf figure on top. Not many graves are tombs, and no tombs have such ornate statues. It's not a gargoyled-up figure, either.

Anella wouldn't let me see this if she didn't want me to, so I get up and walk over to her, and then tip my umbrella up to shield her back. I look at the front of the gray marble tomb.

It reads, "Anella Portabella."

"That you?" I ask her.

"Yeah."

I'm relieved that she answers. Yep, she wants to tell me something, but if I don't approach this fragile woman carefully, she'll literally Scatter.

I have a lot of things I could say, but instead make a joke. "You love mushrooms a whole lot, I guess."

"Oh, yes. I certainly do." She smiles. I've never seen her smile.

"And Anella because it rhymes?"

She lets out a low chuckle. "Yes. I did it to make my sister laugh."

"You play with your sister? Here?"

"No, I played with her in Elora. Not for long, but it was nice when we did."

"You haven't seen her since you came to Dark World?"

She pauses, still gazing at her tomb. "Yes, I have seen her, but she hasn't seen me."

"If you're both here, why won't you let her see you?" I'm keeping it as basic as I can.

"She's in Elora still."

Oh. Now the air feels tense. She's been to Elora... from Dark World. Isn't that what she all but said? I think quickly and decide to change the subject. "If you're a Siren, why is your tomb in this forest instead of in the Marana Sea? In a Siren graveyard?"

"Oh, it all was so long ago. I'd bore you."

"No, I spend half my days getting rune lessons from an NPC and I find that interesting, even though I have no real clue what I'm learning. Go ahead, tell me."

She shifts and meets my eyes, head tilting down and silver hair clinging to her, soaking wet, all over the front of her black robes. "The Sirens were the first race after *Ananta* ended the last age. Then the other races came. The Sirens learned about them and had considered them controlling and dangerous, so they moved to the seas. So magical are they that they transformed their bodies into adapting to living underwater with a few Weather spells. They created the spawning caves."

"I didn't know all that."

"Yeah, it's been a long time, but that's what happened."

"Does that mean, if your tomb is here, that you've been in Dark World since the Sirens first lived in Nuudle Territory?"

Her black eyes narrow and glint red with a flash of nearby lightning. "Yes," she whispers.

It hits me. "Anella, were you the first player to ever come to Dark World?" I say it gently, asking, even though I know the answer.

She holds my gaze and nods.

I look away, feeling such sympathy for her. How long ago was it? What does that mean? I can't think of coming here and having no players at all to talk to and figure stuff out with. I have no words, so I don't speak.

She turns and stares at her grave. "I was a very sad person in Elora. I was very sick. Maybe I still am, but in a different way. A situational way. I came here the same way you did, but I don't think yours was by choice."

I don't understand. Does that mean she knew about Dark World and somehow... Oh. She killed herself. I get it, and my mouth snaps shut before I say it aloud.

I sense she appreciates my not doing so, because she smiles down at me. "You're a good player."

Now's my chance. "Anella, why have you always helped me?"

Her eyes widen. "Because I have paid attention. I have been watching. I learned you would come to my own graveyard, and I've been watching for you and watching what you do. There is something I want to do for you, but you must know it is because you are the One True Mystic, the one who frees us all. I know it, but don't ask me how." Her tone of voice tells me she's serious about that last part, but I don't know what any of it means.

I ask, "What do you want to do for me?"

"Go to where the Player Hall of Fame should be in Elora but isn't in Dark World. There, you will find answers. You only need to know when you want to be."

"When? What do you mean? Like, put it in a scroll or something?"

She looks at me like I slapped her. I have no idea why.

"I will see you again, Mystic Sid. You will free us."

Anella casts Scatter.

There she goes, all over the place. Skittish girl, and what a sad story. I know there's so much more, but I doubt if Anella will ever be in the right state of mind to verbalize her massive history with Dark World.

Still, I think she just told me where to go to get to Elora. What else could she have been doing? Anella has always done right by me, every time, even if she does like to end conversations by shattering into a million pieces.

I use my Comfort Ring, and next I'm at the Kila Crystal in Cashmere. From there, I hop in the sea for a short swim across to Sheala, which isn't even a city yet in Dark World. It's more of a town, and as I approach at a sidestroke, I see the Player Hall of Fame's jagged, white, thin chunk of earth sprouting up in the middle of the village of Sheala, in no way touched by sentient hands, and groan. I'll have to climb that.

It's worth it.

It takes so long that I'm completely dry of seawater and sweated through so much that I need to get clean again by the time I scrape and heave myself to the top of the massive natural structure.

I'm surprised it's completely flat up here. Only a sentient being could have done that.

Before I explore, I collapse on the ground and just breathe. I feel god-awful.

Sid summons *Varengan*.

I wave at my glorious bird summon as he twitters at me after forming.

Sid commands Gentle Flight.

"Thanks."

He twitters some more, and I let him fly about, watching him explore, and then dismiss him. I'm full of energy again now, and it's time to scope out this place.

The ground is white, smooth and sanded mountaintop, perfectly flat. I bet if I put a level on it, it'd say flat. Only a White Elf could have done this, and with magic. An NPC? Or a player?

I walk to the center where I'm thinking the Player Hall of Fame would be in Elora, but keep looking around everywhere in case I miss something.

The breeze up here is nice, and my black Nuudle hair, salty from sweat and sea, blows all around. It came out of its ponytail while I climbed.

As I reach the center of the spire, I see something glinting in the moonlight just in front of me.

I rush to it, then stop dead.

In the stone rests a mirror disc, exactly like one I've seen before. Like the one at the entrance to the Player Hall of Fame, but this one has a different inscription. *A Link to the Future.*

Somehow, I can use this to get to Elora. My Elora. This is what Anella was trying to tell me to find. Why does she want me to go there? What's there that she thinks I should see or find out?

I kneel down and put my hand through it. Feels just like the one in Elora.

Anella had said I needed to know *when* I wanted to go. So, what I think is going on is that this mirror disk is a portal through time in this game. This existence. This simple story that is everything.

How do I tell it *when* I want to be?

I pull out some scrolls and read the runes on them. I hate using scrolls not knowing for sure what they do. It's such a waste because they take so long to make, and if they end up being useless when I use them, that's four hours of work gone.

None of them seem like they'd help.

I sit and trace my fingers through the weightless space of the mirrored surface. The moons glint back up at me with secrets from the mirror disc's reflection.

Maybe I need to think of my when. My when being when I was in Elora.

Imagine it, picture it.

So, I do, and close my eyes while still trailing my fingertips through the weird-feeling space of the mirror disc. None of my memories seem right, almost like Dark World experiences wiped out Elora times. I focus harder, and then, of course, Silvia comes to mind. What would she be doing right now in Elora in my time? In our time?

I try to picture her. She could be tossing out mad heals in a dungeon run. She could be clothcrafting or wandmaking. Lying in the grass south of the Mantle of Bliss to regenerate her magic ability. She even could be floating by herself at our Sheala shipwreck in Siren Territory.

I smile at that and picture it clearly. Her long hair flowing around her head in the deep sea. Her smile after a swim. Then I imagine myself next to her, but she can't see me. I need to say something, do something so she'll see me.

I feel something tighten on my fingertips, a pulling sensation.

I open my eyes and look down. The mirror disc has changed.

Now, I see a bright blue sky, no clouds, and the hems of players' pants, robes and armor walking by. Some fingers and feet stick out at me, then pull away. I hear a muffled laughing coming from the changed disc.

I bend over and peek from across the side of it to get a view of inside the Hall of Fame. I see the Player Hall of Fame... and yes, oh yes. I can see the tiniest hint of my shrine within.

This is it. That's my time in Elora, right? It has to be. I guess all I had to do was emotionally connect to a specific person in my old time, and that's how I chose when.

I stick my hand all the way into the gap. I feel hot air on the other side.

Okay, so I'm going to have to step through this... and be upside-down? How's this going to work?

I don't give a shit. I'm going.

I stand up and go all out. I jump in feet first with my hands up high above me.

As I fall in—Through? Between? Apart?—I'm flipped all around. I get sick to my stomach as gravity changes in my core. I can't remember seeing anything when I went through, but I become aware again a moment later, lying on the ground right in the entrance to the Player Hall of Fame in Elora.

I'm friggin' in Elora again. Holy mother of God.

I jump up and look around, then look down at my hands. Still a Nuudle. Moldavite ring. Still a Mystic.

I run upto the first player I see, another Nuudle, a Magician. "Hey, hey. Can you help me? Sorry to bother you, but—"

He completely ignores me and I'm getting pissed, but then he walks right through me. Through me! Like I'm a ghost!

Shit, can nobody see me here? What the fuck did Anella tell me to come here for?

I feel an uncharacteristic burst of rage, but cast Spontaneity on myself after a moment and get a nice CRG boost. It calms me and gets me thinking progressively almost instantly.

"Excuse me," I hear a girl's voice say behind me.

I turn. A Siren Blessed stands there, wearing lower-stat gear. I'd guess she's been playing a year and she's pretty young in RL. But she can see me. She's talking to me.

"You can see me? Can you hear me?"

"Of course I can. Why wouldn't I?" She cocks her head and pushes her white eyebrows together, eyes glowing brightly with curiosity.

"Nobody else can see me."

"No way." She gasps dramatically.

"Yeah. How can you see me and nobody else can?"

"Well, I was just going to ask you what that spell Spontaneity is. It looks so cool! That's a great stat boost you got from it. What class are you?"

I hesitate. "You're a Blessed, right?"

Misdirection back at someone else so they talk about themselves usually works.

"Yes, I'm low-stat, don't play all the time. I have school, but it's the weekend."

"Can I ask you a weird question?"

"Uh, ok." She looks uncertain.

"What year is it?"

She laughs.

"No, for real."

"It's 2036, silly. Do you want to know who the leader of the UN is, too?"

One year later. At least, at most?

"Look, I'm sorry I bothered you," she says. "I was just curious." I can tell she thinks I'm a stuck-up, high-stat snob about newbs, but I'm not, and I need her help.

"Wait, I'll tell you my class, but please, keep it to yourself." This should entice her for a little longer. I'm forming a plan but need her help and some verification.

"Oh?" She takes a step closer, trying to see under my hood to my marking.

"I'm a Mystic."

"No way."

"Yeah."

"Is that why you have one name?"

"Kind of."

"Can you, like, show me what summons you have?"

"To be honest," I lie, "I don't know if I can. Nobody but you has seen me. Why is that?"

"Has this been going on all day?"

I look to the side. "Ever since I got here."

"Hm. Well, it could be because I'm a Blessed."

"How's that?"

"A Blessed always sees the golden truth of reality." She smiles proudly.

She probably remembers that from a class description when she picked Blessed.

I glance above her head. Her name is Nina Lovesalot. "Nina, can you do me a big favor?"

She lowers her brows. "Like what?"

"I have tried, but I can't send messages… today… either. Can you send a message to my friend? Tell her Sid Vicious needs to know her location?"

Her eyes widen. "You know Sid Vicious?"

"Uh, yeah. He's looking for a White Elf Blessed named Silvia Diamond but needs to know where she is. He can't search the world server list, either."

"That's weird. Well, I'll do anything for that poor soul. Must be some message he left behind."

I don't like the sound of that, but I say nothing. What does she know about me and the legend of Sid Vicious? Instead, I ask, "Can you send her that message now, please?"

"Oh, ok, one second." Her eyes go into automode as she accesses a lot in her menu. After a moment, her eyes focus back on me. "She just keeps saying, 'Who is this?' over and over."

I sigh. "Tell her… ask her if she's still wearing the lily he gave her."

Eyes auto, then she's back. She looks spooked, looking over her shoulders, and backing away from me. "This is all too weird for me," she mutters.

"What did she say?"

"I don't want to be involved."

"Please, this is so very important, and you're the only one who can help." I give her my mastered big Nuudle eyes.

Her shoulders sink. "She's in the Mantle of Bliss crafting Cashmere Cloth stacks. Okay? I've really got to go. I have plans. All of a sudden, you know. Nice meeting you," she says in a rush, and all but runs away from me.

"Wait, one more thing!" I call to her, and I'm shocked that she stops. Doesn't turn around. "Can you teleport me there?"

She slowly turns. Eyes me carefully. "I don't know who you are, but I'll tele you and then you leave me alone."

"Perfect," I tell her with a smile.

She invites me to a party, and then in a flash of white light, we're at the grand entrance of the Mantle of Bliss. She instantly disbands the group. "I hope you find what you're looking for," she says, and then teles out.

I think I spent maybe five, ten minutes with her tops, and I have no idea what got her so freaked out.

I enter the Mantle of Bliss and head straight for the clothcrafting station, but Silvia isn't there. I go around the circular building, too, and peek behind some curtains once inside again.

She's not here where she said she'd be.

I plop down on the steps to the clothcraft building station and drop my head into my hands. She lied to the young Blessed because of something she knows about me. Something where if she heard I was looking for her, she doesn't want anything to do with it.

I sense someone beside me, and a soft hand touches my shoulder. I see the delicate White Elf fingertips out of the corner of my eye. I look up to my left.

It's her. Silvia. A Shadow Potion is wearing off her, and a nip of those makes you invisible for about twenty minutes. She wanted to see this person looking for her first.

"Hi," I say.

She keeps her hand on me. She's the most beautiful thing I've seen. Her eyebrows are pushed together hard, and her glowing White Elf eyes twinkle with deep figuring. Her long, blonde hair is down and falls in shining waves as she frowns at me, scrutinizing me. I sense anger coming from her that she's trying to contain. She doesn't like to jump to conclusions, and I have no idea what she's heard happened to me a year ago.

Finally, she softly says, "Hi. Why is your name Sid? Just Sid?"

I stand and gaze up at her. My Nuudle eyes are sincere. "Silvia, it's me. It's me."

She shakes her head. "No, you're not... him. He died. He's dead. You're... you're an asshole." Her eyes fill with tears and her cheeks redden, but she lets her toon continue this way without adjusting her character controls.

I reach up on my tiptoes and touch the Love Lily tucked behind her ear. "I'm so glad you still wear it. I have another flower for you."

She pulls away. "Stop. I'm so confused. Just give me a minute, okay? This is a mean, mean joke, or... or..."

"There's so much to it."

She stares at the name above my head. "Sid," she says more to herself, then, "One name."

"Right." I wait.

"But Peter said—I mean, he and Good Deeds went to your funeral. Do you even know what I'm talking about?"

I shrug. "I have an idea, but I'd love it if you told me more."

"How can you not know?"

I pause, thinking, and then say, "I want to tell you everything, but first, I need you to believe me."

A Dragonbane Lancer walks upto us and says to Silvia, "Sorry, I'm just dying of curiosity. Who are you talking to?"

She looks confused for a moment, and then points at me. "Him. Right here. Nuudle."

The Dragonbane looks through me. "Ah, okay. Sure. Thanks. My friends and I were just wondering." He snickers as he walks away.

She turns to me, eyes wide. "He couldn't see you. Why couldn't he see you?"

"I don't know. Only a Blessed has been able to see me, the one who contacted you for me. She thought maybe all Blesseds could, so I came to you." There are a million more reasons I went straight to Silvia, but now's not the time.

"I don't know what to say."

"Look," I say, and pull my hood back, revealing my Mystic *Ananta* marking. "Look, I'm a Mystic now."

Her mouth falls open. "That marking, the serpent heads..."

"He's the only one I know of that I don't have."

She collapses on the ground and stares up at me, tears freely streaking down her pale cheeks. "Oh my God. Sid. Sid. Where have you been?"

I sit with her and take her hands. "I don't know, but you get that it's me, right? You believe it now. Right?"

"I'm confused, but yeah. Yes, I do, but I don't know why. I can feel it. I just know. I've missed you so much, I—" She stops herself, takes a deep breath. "I need to get on guild chat and tell them about this."

"No, please don't. I'm not quite ready to talk to them yet. There's so much I still don't know or understand, and I don't want to confuse or upset anyone."

"How can your best friends knowing you're alive hurt them?"

"That's the thing. I don't think I am alive. I honestly don't know what I am. Silvia, do you have any of those weird spells you sometimes pick up as a mage that you don't have a use for?"

She tilts her head, thinking. "There is one I got about a year ago. Awaken. I've used it on lots of things, but it never did anything."

"Try it on me."

"Why?"

"It might do something to me to make me able to interact with Elora. I really need to be able to... to get *Ananta*."

She blinks. "Well, okay. I'll try." She holds her hands out in an exotic pose and white glowing sparkles come out of her fingertips.

Silvia Diamond casts Awaken. Sid is Awakened.

Suddenly, a rush of sensations hits me. I'm feeling Elora. I hadn't realized I haven't felt anything except that Spontaneity I cast on myself until now. I was too focused on my mission to find Silvia. "Oh," I mutter.

"What is it?" She takes my thin shoulder in her long fingers. Dainty pressure.

"I'll explain it soon. First, I need to see if other players can see me."

We look around. There are players walking and running around everywhere, but none pay any attention to us.

"Let me try something," I say. I stand up and hold my hand out to her. She takes it and I pull her up. "Pretty strong for a Nuudle, huh?"

She allows herself a small smile.

Sid summons *Oni*.

Varying hues of blue mist spurts out of my chest and forms the intimidating *Oni*. He hovers in the air quietly, observing. Filling gobs of space that nobody will be able to not notice.

Yes, people see me. Pretty much everyone in eyesight stops what they are doing, including walking and running, and gapes.

Sid dismisses *Oni*.

"Holy crap!" Silvia exclaims.

"Yeah." I can't help but grin. I'd impressed her, at least enough to make her stop being so upset and confused. "I have so much I want to tell you."

"You're... you're not dead..." she says again. Tears fill her eyes once more. "Peter said there was a murder-suicide, that a stranger broke into your apartment and shot you in the head while we were running that dungeon. You just vanished while in game. Nobody knows who the guy is who shot you. The police gathered that he shot you, and then for some reason, hooked himself up to your Elora headset and logged in under another account, and then shot himself in the head. They couldn't trace the account he logged into. He'd hacked it so it would be useless after he was dead... How can you be alive? But I know you are. I can feel it's you. I can tell!"

I have to calm her down so I can talk to her, tell her everything.

I have an idea. *Oni* had cheered her for a moment.

"There are some... people... I'd like to introduce you to. One in particular."

She cocks her head and sniffles, wiping her eyes.

"Let's go out to an empty place near the sea in White Elf Territory, south of here. We can walk."

"O—okay. Okay, Sid." She smiles and bursts into laughter. Then she throws her arms around my little body. "Oh, I'm so happy. This is the happiest day of my life."

I hold her, too, and my heart feels just as warm as when I claim a summon. We've never been this close physically, and I can feel her, smell her. She's soft and feminine, with a scent like fresh rosemary. It's amazing to hold her, and I don't want to let go when she pulls away.

"Okay, Sid, show me what you want to show me."

We walk to a glade she knows of where she does her White Elf Blessed version of my Mystic Recite, which is Bonding. She lies in the grass in White Elf Territory for an hour or so to recharge. She tells me this is her favorite spot, and she thought of it when I said by the sea. Three sides are guarded from view by high, blooming willows covered in leafy vines, and the other side is a clear, beautiful sight of the eastern ocean from high on the cliffs.

"Perfect place. I love it," I tell her.

"Me too." Her voice is soft. She sounds uncertain and upset still.

"Hey, have a seat. Facing the sea. I have things to show you that will cheer you up. Just like *Oni* did. Actually, exactly like *Oni* did."

She cocks her head. "What? You mean *Oni*, that summon you conjured? Oh, he was amazing! Scary in a way. His eyes. Something so timeless, but tortured."

"Yeah. He was tormented for ages. He's a demon, and a powerful one, but he has good intentions."

"You talk about him like he's a person."

"To me, all my summons are like people I know."

"But they're NPCs."

"It's hard to explain."

She holds out her hands to me, exasperated. "Where? Where have you been? Why are you a Nuudle Mystic with summons?"

"Shh," I tell her. "You need to breathe, and so I'm going to show you my summons. I'll do them in the order I got them."

First, I pull out the Counts. She gasps and looks frightened. My protector Count actually nods at her, and she half waves at him, hand shaking. "The *Counts of Hell*," I say. "They don't like daylight or public places. So we'll let them go for now."

I dismiss them. She sighs in slight relief. "Their black and white color is so haunting, like ancient photos of the dead from way back come to life."

"Yeah. And they can fight and are also useful in many other ways. Here, you'll like the next one I got."

I pull out *Varengan*. Every tear dries instantly. Her face lights up with delight as *Varengan* twitters and shows off his plumage, fluttering here and there, seemingly knowing he is to show what a fine bird he is.

"Thank you," I tell him, flattering him. He loves the attention and lands on the earth near Silvia, sticking first one black eye and then the other into her face.

She giggles. "How cute! But so beautiful! That's just... incredible." She reaches up and strokes his head as gently as possible. He coos.

"Next I got *Djinn*, but I'm saving him for last."

"Why?"

"You'll see when you meet him."

"Are you going to put this bird back, or whatever you call it? I like him."

"It's called dismissing. I can bring him out again, but I have a few others I'm dying to show you."

"Okay."

Sid dismisses *Varengan*.

"After *Djinn*, I got *Xiuhcoatl*." I summon the great gold dragon, and Silvia stares wordlessly at his pure presence. He is something to behold, and he seems genuinely curious about Silvia. He leans his ferocious snout close to her face and sniffs. She's not scared of him one bit and reaches out, touching the side of his face. She's afraid of nothing now, amazement taking over her senses.

"You have a new Blessed as a companion. This one is special." He looks at me. "Good one like you." A peace enters the way he looks at me finally. I smile. He blinks slowly. Has *Xiuhcoatl* become okay with me right at this moment? Because of Silvia? Well, if anyone would do it, she could with a simple smile.

"Thanks, *Xiuhcoatl*. I'm showing her all my summons. I appreciate your not being bothered by my disturbance of your rest."

"I learn more about you each time you use me." A little puff of gray smoke comes out of his nose.

I dismiss him with a feeling of satisfaction that I'd reached the dragon, but really, Silvia reached him for me just by being her.

"Then I got this one, and she's a little scary. Nobody even knows if she's a normal summon."

I pull out *Keres*.

She swirls madly out of my chest in a black mist and forms quickly, breasts boldly bare, mouth salivating. "Master, have you a field of battle for me to feed upon?" she says as soon as she can speak.

"Not right now, *Keres*. I'm showing you to Silvia, my friend."

She eyes Silvia. "Too skinny, bad feeding."

"No, you never eat her. Promise."

"I cannot make such a promise."

"I take good care of your needs. This is one thing I'm asking from you. Don't feed on Silvia Diamond, ever, ever." Silvia looks mortified throughout this conversation, and has her hands tucked under her butt, biting her bottom lip.

"I'll think on it." She narrows her eyes.

"Thank you for being so very considerate, *Keres*."

"Hmm."

I dismiss her. "You've seen *Oni*. He's a demon, like I said. But *Djinn*, here, you just have to meet him."

Sid summons *Djinn*.

The great, green genie seems to know what's going on as he takes form, and his eyes instantly go to Silvia. "Ah, Master. She of Mantra fame!"

"*Djinn*!"

He grins slyly at Silvia. She giggles. "What?" she asks.

"He's trying to embarrass me."

"No," *Djinn* chides. "Just moving things along. You have missed time. May as well catch up as soon as possible. Blessed Silvia, I have heard your name countless times, and each time I hear it, wonderful things happen." He floats over and takes her hand in his bejeweled one, plants a kiss on the back.

She smiles at him. "You're awfully nice."

"Why, thank you. You are a good judge of character."

She laughs with delight.

"I always like to make a pretty White Elf happy. Don't worry, though, Sid. I won't steal her heart from you."

"I think you already have," she says to him with a grin. Her eyes are clear, no signs of her earlier distress.

He flutters eyelashes at me, oh-so-innocent, then gives her a sugar-sweet smile.

She turns to me, glancing at *Djinn*, grasps my hands as I reach her and pulls me down next to her. "Tell me everything. Every detail. Don't leave out a thing."

I do just that, and *Djinn* helps me fill in the foggy spots or keeps me on track when I get distracted by a story. Every time I tell her about Seeker, her cheeks burn, but she's flabbergasted about Dark World.

"Everyone in Dark World is confused as to why we're there. I told you about my guildmates, but they are more than that. I feel closer to them than the friends I've had all my life, but we've been through some crazy times. Things hurt there. I can feel everything. All my senses work, and since you cast Awaken on me, I feel Elora the same way, too. I wanted to save that for last, because it's the biggest thing about Dark World. About being... what I am that got me to Dark World."

"You feel it? What... does it feel like?"

"It's better than real life, and the brews are amazing. When you get a stat boost, a heal, a buff, you get a rush, and it's different with everything cast, every stat. It has been amazing, but the not knowing... it eats at you. Every day and night. There's such isolation in being cut off, never seeing the people you knew every day for no reason."

I pause, watching her. I've never seen a player's eyes focused like hers are except in Dark World. "I can't believe I'm here and actually seeing you again."

I pause. I can't keep it in. "I've thought about you every day I've been in Dark World." There. I've been fried twice by *Xiuhcoatl*, but this is scarier, waiting to see how she responds.

"Sid." She takes my hand and puts her head on my shoulder, leaning down to do it, but somehow it works. "You don't know what your death did to me. It was like my sister all over. I hadn't let myself have real feelings about anyone since she died, and then I fought how much I wanted to know you, but there, right before you died, or went to Dark World, I let you in and couldn't help it. You have no idea how happy I am right now, and how amazing it feels to be sitting next to you."

I smell her hair. Honeysuckle. "You have no idea what it's like to feel you," I say softly.

She sighs, and we stay sitting like that for a while. *Djinn* is great and pretends to be gazing out to sea while we have our private moment.

"I wish I could feel you, just once."

"Maybe someday."

"We'll figure this out together. Somehow, we will. I'll help you and I won't leave your side."

"Speaking of that, I did say I have another flower for you."

"Oh!" She lifts her head and looks down at me. "I love gifts from you." She grins, eyes glowing brightly.

I pull the Sunlight Daisy out of my bag. The tag with the item description still dangles from it. "Here, read what it does and decide if you want it. I understand if you don't."

She quickly reads the daisy's use and sighs deeply. "This is perfect. It'll make sure we don't get parted. Right?"

"Yeah, that's right."

"Thank you." She kisses my cheek and strokes the petals of the Sunlight Daisy. "How odd it will be to never be a ghost again."

We sit in silence, feeling happy in each other's company, especially after our heartfelt disclosures.

After some time, I squeeze her hand. "I made a friend in the one who taught me how to get back to Elora. She's the Hidden I told you about. Nobody understands this Dark World and death thing, and I think Seeker knows something none of us do."

"Seeker," she murmurs. "Goddamn the man."

"Yep."

Our eyes meet.

"You're a cute Nuudle."

I smile and work the eyes. She laughs.

"Ancient runes and scroll-making? Really?"

"Yep."

"And you think... what? This Hidden sent you here for what?"

I'm quiet a moment, but finally I say, "I think she wants me to find *Ananta* here in Elora."

"What do you mean?"

"Well," I say slowly, "if you think about the opening cutscene with *Ananta*, on his forehead he has a typical Nuudle marking in Elora, but those aren't the same ones you see in Dark World. It may stand to reason that means he's in Elora instead of Dark World. How to get the quest and where to find him and battle him are the questions."

She watches *Djinn* play with a pink willow blossom. "Maybe... maybe you should go back to your grave here and now, if there's a time thing. Maybe something in that graveyard will give you a clue. We need more help. We could get in touch with at least Peter..."

I stop her. "Seriously, I don't want to upset all those guys. And Sally. I need to know the truth first, and I even feel bad putting you through this, but—"

"You're not putting me through anything but a miracle." She smiles brightly.

"Miracle?"

"Look at you. I mean, *look* at you. I never thought I'd see you again, that you'd died in some horrible murder, but there's more. Somehow, you're here, and you've been living in the game. Or something like that."

"Yeah, it gets pretty complicated."

She stands up. "Come on, Sid, let's walk down to Sunset Forest and to your old graveyard. Your gravestone might be there. You never know what you'll find, but it seems all your progress with the mysteries have happened in that graveyard."

"You're right. Absolutely right."

"Well, are you getting up?"

She invites me to a party and I accept. I stand up, brush myself off, and say to *Djinn*, "Well, it's back to the dead place."

He sighs dramatically. "Always the dead with you. You and *Keres* are a perfect match. I guess I should be jealous."

"Oh, definitely," I tell him.

Silvia laughs. She turns to me. "You knew exactly how to reach me. You showed me these summons and I believed because of it. Nobody's seen anything like these in Elora. It's truly amazing."

I smile, and she smiles back.

"Let's go," I say.

CHAPTER 16: BATTLE OF ANANTA

"It's around here somewhere. Just hard to find with everything so overgrown," I tell her as we stomp through heavy forest brush. No trails here. I can tell we're close to the graveyard, though. I feel it in my Nuudle bones.

"Wait, over there. Do you see it?" Silvia asks.

"What?"

She points. "Between those bushes. Looks like piece of an old iron fence post sticking out of the ground. Let's go see. You said your graveyard has a fence all around it, right?"

"Yeah, let's go."

We tromp through the heavy foliage to the black iron post and look beyond it. The post is all that's left of the original wrought-iron fence, but through years of overgrowth, we can see some of the remains of bigger graves and tombs of my graveyard in Dark World.

"Here, I think mine was this way."

She follows me to a couple piles of rubble. I could have sworn this is where my grave was, but now I'll never be able to tell. I tell her so. "I guess this is a bust. But I can show you that big tomb still standing over that way. That's the tomb of the Hidden who helped me."

"The one who was the first player to ever be in Dark World?"

"Yeah, come check it out. I don't know why she got a tomb like this, but somebody who makes Dark World decisions must have wanted her name to last through the ages with pretty much the only tomb still standing in this graveyard now, and I think it's legible."

We go to the tomb and Silvia examines the stone carving of the White Elf atop. She cocks her head to the side. "Familiar," she mutters. Her voice has dropped an octave, as though a thought, a scary thought, has occurred to her.

Slowly, she drops her eyes to the name on the tomb. "Anella Portabella," she whispers. "Oh, oh, Sid, I'm going to be sick." She turns away from me and Anella's tomb and bends over, then collapses into the overgrowth.

"Hey. Hey, Silvia. What is it? Are you okay?" I stroke her back, wishing she could feel it. She's weeping and shaking all over.

"Sweet Kristina," she says, broken.

Kristina? Who's Kristina?

I think back to Anella and how I realized she'd committed suicide, and at the same time, I remember Silvia telling me about her sister, early in the game, doing the same thing—with the headband on and playing, just months after the game went live.

I go to the ground with her and wrap my small arms around her shoulders. She sobs, now uncontrollably, and I want to take this pain away.

"Silvia, I get it. It's your sister. The Hidden who's been helping me is your sister."

"She was there in that place all alone, with nobody, no one, for how long? You said you had no idea, but it had to be a long, long time. You said she was odd, flighty, touchy. You didn't even tell me her name. I can't think of it." She covers her face.

"Listen, listen. I get it now. She said she used to play with her sister, and that she'd seen her since she got to Dark World. That her sister was still in Elora. She said that right before she told me where to go to get to Elora."

"If that's true, then why didn't I see her? Why didn't she talk to me?" She sits up, swallowing tears of shock and painful memories.

"I don't know. She said she made sure you never saw her. She's... different. Good-hearted, but afraid. Silvia, you have no idea how much she helps me, and it's because she's so good. Believe me, she's okay. And think, she's like me. She's dead, right? But she's still alive somehow, that thing none of us can figure out. You can see her again."

Silvia leans back in the greens, letting briars rub her arms. They won't scratch her, and she'll never feel them like I do. I sit up, stroking her golden hair, trying to give her a gesture of comfort. Her hair feels soft and silky, like an elf's hair should.

There's no rain in this ruin of a cemetery, but it's all gray skies and trees of doom. I wait, feeling the satin of her White Elf hair, until she opens her eyes and sits up. "I want to go to Dark World."

"No, I promise, you don't. To be honest, I'm not exactly sure how I made it through the portal. I think I could do it again, but... I just don't think you should go there."

"Why not?"

"If you start to feel when you go there, well, things friggin' hurt in Dark World."

"You said the brew was amazing. That buffs and stat boosts feel like something never experienced in life."

I look at the sky. "Yeah, those are the good things. But there is pain—a lot of it." I don't tell her what death feels like.

"I want to see Kristina again."

"I know." I look back to her as she sits up, wiping leaves out of her hair.

"Please. You can teach me. You can do it again. You can take me back with you." Her lower jaw sets hard.

"I don't know if I can, and I sincerely don't want you to change like I did. What if it kills you?"

She looks down. "I... I don't know. What if it doesn't?" She gazes back up at me with longing. I can't take that look. "Can't we try?"

"I'll tell you what. We'll summon *Djinn* and ask him."

"*Djinn*?"

"He knows everything, just gets a little confused on timelines." I grin.

Sid summons *Djinn*.

My favorite green genie streams out of my chest in a green mist and forms directly over our heads, hanging upside down. "Well, now. I remember this."

"What? What do you mean?" I ask him.

"The time thing, you know. And then—"

Off to our right a little way, an NPC appears with a blue magic bubble around her. Calla. She waves, and dashes over to us.

"Mystic Sid! You found your way here! I was quite worried you'd be too dumb to figure it out." She envelops Silvia, *Djinn*, and me in her blue bubble.

"He didn't figure anything out. He summoned me to ask questions about everything he doesn't know, I'm certain," *Djinn* explains to Calla.

"I see. Well, no matter. He summoned here and now." She faces me. "Stand up, would you? I have to mark your hand. I suppose I don't have to tell you what lies ahead?"

Stunned, I rise and face her. I pull my hood back to get a better look at her. I've never seen her out of that god-awful thunderstorm eternally in Forest of the Dead's graveyard. Her skin has a slight pale forest green glow.

"*Ananta*?"

Her usual charisma fades as quickly as a secret tear. She whispers, "Yes, *Ananta*. *Ananta* has chosen you to meet with and fight. He wants to see what you're made of."

"How do you know that?" I ask.

Her slight glow pales. "He came to me when I changed."

"Changed? What do you mean?" I'm as confused as ever.

She shakes her head. "No time for all that. My purpose is to give you *Ananta*'s mark so you can enter his battlefield. He has never wanted to meet a Mystic. Sid, *Ananta* is dangerous." She looks down. "But *Ananta* can bring great change."

"You mean, Sid can bring great change. He'll command *Ananta*," says Silvia softly.

Calla looks at her as though she hadn't yet noticed Silvia was there. "Oh, hello. Yes, but I wasn't going to say that. It puts a lot of pressure on young Sid. If I've learned anything about Mystic Nuudle Sid, it's that he doesn't do well under pressure."

"Hey!" I say.

Djinn pats my shoulder, nearly knocking me over. "You're a good fighter and Mystic, but you absolutely can't handle pressure."

"Oh, you both shut up."

Silvia giggles. "He's really going to fight *Ananta*?"

Calla takes my left hand, pulls out an emerald wand, and traces a mark onto my palm. She's never used a wand, and it takes her about a minute. When I pull my hand back to look at it, I see the very same marking as the one on my forehead. *Ananta*'s symbol. It glows, too.

"Calla, where do I go?"

"Silly Sid. Like always, I marked it on the map." She rolls her eyes. "My work is done. Now it is your time. Ta-ta, Sid, *Djinn*. And you, missy." She smiles at Silvia, and then fades into nothing, along with her blue bubble.

"The map," Silvia says. "Look at it."

I open the map in my interface to see better.

There's an X right smack-dab in the middle of the Temple of Nuudlel. What does that mean? I tell her and *Djinn*.

"*Djinn*?" Silvia asks him. "Do you know where we go? Sid said the other fights were in caves. I mean, that's an entire temple. Not a cave. It's enormous. Where would we even start?"

I look at him too. "Do you remember that part?" I glance at Silvia. "He knows no time."

"Ahhh," she sing-songs, as though that makes perfect sense. She's handling things like the pro she is. Always the coolest head in the boss fights at the end of dungeon runs. She'd snapped back from learning of her sister pretty quickly, but I know her well enough to figure out that she's already planning on finding Anella somehow. Her ability to make a plan, even in high pressure situations, makes her strong.

"Actually, Master Mystic Sid, I do believe it was all in that red leather book The Black Simple gave you. I cannot read; it is too time-linear. I do know that book, and you should read it."

"I tried to. The runes were too old. Even Master Gronai couldn't interpret it, and he's, well, Master Gronai." I shrug.

Djinn cocks a fuzzy eyebrow. "Try now."

"Well, okay." I look through my bags but can't find the damn book. "It's not here."

"The book your Nuudle friend gave you? The one she thought talked about you?" Silvia asks.

"Yeah. Yeah... oh, man. I think I left it with Master Gronai in Dark World the last time I saw him. He wanted to try reading it backward for some reason and... yeah. I left it with him."

"You don't have the book, Master Sid?" *Djinn* asks, cocking his head as though saying, *shame, shame.*

"Dammit, no. I don't. I fucking don't."

"Hmm." *Djinn* rubs his chin. "I do wish I could be of more service, but, as you know, I can't even legitimately say I have a memory."

Silvia laughs. It lightens me up a little. We don't need that book. I decide Simple was reading too much into her rune studies and seeing something that wasn't there. *Manual of Systems.* Right. I know that's what it said. It's probably some book on how the ancient Nuudles built huts through Mystic magic, and that one crude Nuudle drawing coincidentally looks like me. All Nuudles look the same until you are one, really. It's all about hairstyle and color to everyone else.

"I say we head to the temple. See what's what. We'll figure it out," I tell them.

"Your wish is my command," *Djinn* answers.

Silvia takes my hand. "I can't feel it, but at least you can. Let's go."

~

I dismiss *Djinn* far from the Temple of Nuudlel, and Silvia and I make it there about fifteen minutes later. She never once stops holding my little hand.

The temple, as I mentioned before, is enormous, and we wander from library to library, hall to hall, exploring every nook and cranny. I try zooming in on the map, but the X for *Ananta*'s battle stays firmly overlapping the entire temple.

I drop Silvia's hand outside the scrollmaking rooms and plop down on a black marble bench. "I don't know what to do. I have this feeling like time is running out. I don't know why."

Players dash by, a few glancing at the one name over my head.

She sits next to me and takes my hand again, not letting me be discouraged. "I do, too. I don't know why, either." Her voice is light.

I look at her. "Are you afraid?"

"A little," she admits with a small shrug. "We should stay in a party to keep our conversation private. I know you want to split up in case the fight happens, that you don't want me in the battle with *Ananta*, but think. Even if I get hurt, I won't feel it. I'm still from Elora. I feel nothing."

I sigh. "I know. I know. But it's *Ananta*. Maybe you will. I don't know. I think it's not worth the risk. Besides, we can't even find the damn summon fight. We could search the temple for a year and never find it. There are no caves here. There are no NPCs to ask, even. None of them in Elora are like the NPCs in Dark World. They are more... more... programmed here. I guess that's the best way to—" I stop, feeling stupid like Calla thinks I am.

"Sid? Sid, what is it?"

I slap my forehead. "Master Gronai."

"Master Gronai? What about him? What did you think of?" She sounds excited, and her white eyes glow brightly with hope.

"NPCs don't age. It could just be possible... but no. I mean, Master Gronai couldn't be here in Elora, a zillion years after Dark World, could he?"

Her wide eyes looking into mine answer the question with a simple gaze and a mutual slow smile.

"Where did you say he was?"

"South turret." I jump up. "Come on, let's go see if he's there."

We take the winding stairs to the top wall and cross around to the turret I used to visit Master Gronai in. I crack open the door and hesitate. "What if he's not here?" I say to Silvia.

"Then you'll have another great idea."

"Thanks." I wonder at her confidence in me and pull the door all the way open.

Lo and behold, there's Master Gronai at the desk of the turret. I'm shocked that the bookshelf I caught on fire forever ago has never been replaced. It's a charred mess.

The old Nuudle NPC hunches over a scroll with a Phoenix Quill, delicately inscribing something important to him.

I clear my throat, feeling nervous. Is he the same Master Gronai, or something different, exclusive to Elora? "Master Gronai?"

"Busy, come back tomorrow," he mutters without looking at us.

"It's me. Do you remember me?" I wait for him to answer.

Finally, without turning, he says, "I told you, tomorrow. This takes complete concentration. I have to—oh. You ruined it. It takes so much to get inspired these days, and I was, and you ruined it." He spins on his stool and hops off, brushing his brown robe. He meets my eyes with an angry frown. "Young Nuudle, you have no idea how hard it is for an old man like me to focus. I've been doing this for eons. Did it ever occur to you that I might struggle with getting and staying inspired to continue making these master-level scrolls? Only I can do it, and I simply don't feel like it most of the time. Today I did, and you two ruined it. Bursting in here like that. Who do you think you are?"

He doesn't know who I am. He looks exactly the same, too. "It's me, Sid. Remember?"

"I don't know any Sid. And it's been forever since I've seen a one-namer. What business do you have with me? Spit it out and then get out." He folds his little arms across his chest, big eyes burning with fury.

I pause, thinking. Silvia puts her hand on my shoulder, saying, "Maybe we should go."

"You know, Master Gronai," I say, an idea forming. "I once knew a scroll-maker and brilliant Nuudle master of magic and runes who became weary of laboring like you are now." I'm pulling out all the Nuudle wording. Master Gronai always was particular about that. "May I be of assistance? I was able to give him a boost in the right direction."

He squints his eyes at me. "With what?"

"Magic."

He huffs. "No kind of magic like that in two thousand years. Believe me, if there were, I'd be the first to know."

I smile and widen my eyes. "Oh, but great Master Gronai, I promise your favorite delight, and relief with my magic."

He raises an eyebrow, mouth still tight. "Oh? Well, well, well. Go ahead. Let's see what young Nuudle Sid can do." He plops back down on his stool. "If you can make me want to finish this scroll with your oh-so-great magic, I'll eat my Phoenix Quill."

"You won't want to because you'll be inspired to finish your work."

Sid casts Spontaneity. Master Gronai gains +140 CRG.

His body glows briefly, and his eyes light up like fireworks. He shoots off the stool and claps his hands together at the same time.

"My—Mystic? You? But there are no... and you just... my favorite! How did you know?" He's using his sincere Nuudle eyes, all attitude gone.

I step toward him. "You've gotten stronger over two thousand years. That boost is a lot higher than it used to be."

Master Gronai puts his ringed hands on his cheeks.

"Yeah, I think you remember me now. It is you, isn't it?" I grin.

"It is *you*, isn't it?" he repeats. "Sid! Oh, of course! Sid! Nuudle Mystic Sid! I had forgotten your name altogether. You never came back. I thought the worst. I—I—oh, can you do it one more time? Spontaneity? Just once, and try to make it Concentration?"

I laugh. "Of course."

I use Spontaneity on him four more times until he gets a +245 CON boost, and he sighs ever so gratefully. "Sid. I have missed our time together. What happened to you? It's been so very, very long! Do you know how dreadful it is in these times? I have to repeat myself so that these simpletons can remember what I say. You, now, you... who's this?" He finally takes note of Silvia.

"I'm Sid's friend. Silvia Diamond. I'm a Blessed."

"I can see that. I can see. And, Blessed Silvia Diamond, why are you here with Mystic Sid?"

We look at each other.

"It's a long story," I begin, "but I made it to this time through a portal. What's been two thousand years for you has been a day for me."

Sid casts Meditation. Master Gronai's stat boosts will last for 47 seconds longer.

His eyes turn blank and I know he's hiding something. Master Gronai never hid anything from me before.

"What?" I ask.

He says nothing.

"What is it?"

"We don't talk about those things in Elora." I notice his blank stare weaken as I give him encouragement with a quick Spontaneity. I don't have to say a word.

"Now, don't be like that. Now, now. Sid. Oh, for crying out loud. Close and lock this turret door." He turns to his desk and scribbles out the rest of the scroll while he still has the stat boosts, muttering, "Have a seat on the floor. We have much to discuss. But first, I need to make sure there are no ears."

He pulls the top, right drawer of his desk completely out and retrieves a scroll from behind it, then puts the drawer back in place. He sings the runes on the scroll. The round walls of the turret glow a soft violet. "There. Nothing and nobody can possibly know what happens in this room until the rune magic wears off. Been saving that scroll for something like this." His eyes gleam.

"Master Gronai, I have the *Ananta* quest. He's here, somewhere in the temple. I just can't find the battlefield entrance. He's been in Elora and I had to come here to find him." I wonder at Master Gronai's NPC paranoia. Who or what would monitor this conversation? Why would it bother him if someone did?

"You have more than that to worry about." He sits on the floor with us, crossing his thin legs under him with a grunt. "You left your book with me."

"I know."

"I've had two thousand years to examine it, Mystic Sid."

Silvia looks at me. I glance at her, then back to Master Gronai. "And?"

"You were right. It is *Manual of Systems*. It is not about magic or Mystics. It's about the very essence of this existence and how it works."

I wait, thinking. What does that mean? Is he talking about the game? Or death in Dark World? Or something entirely different?

He continues. "I can't make out the meaning of the technological terms. There are no runes for these now, and there weren't two thousand years ago. I don't know who the original author of the *Manual of Systems* was, but whomever it was, he wasn't from our world."

I notice his hands tremor.

"There's more. Yes, *Ananta* is here, always here, and I can tell you where to find him. It's in the book. I've known for about 400 years now. I had nobody to tell; no Mystics. Still, I'd tell none but you. The book is about you, what you will be capable of if you claim *Ananta*."

"What do you mean, about me?"

"Well," he shrugs and looks off to the side. "A Mystic who could be you, and I believe it is you. You have no idea what you'll be able to do if you pursue *Ananta*. However, you must." Now his eyes plead, begging me to succeed.

"Why do you look at me like that? What is it you hope I'll do?"

He sighs, looks at the hem of his robe on the hard stone floor and rubs his face with both small hands. "Freedom. A reset is what the *Manual of Systems* describes." He raises his head, drops his hands. "We so desperately need it. I so desperately need it, Mystic Sid."

"I don't understand."

"Neither do I," adds Silvia.

"To be honest, I don't understand anything like I used to. I once was sharp, spry, but now I'm worn. I tried to stay positive. I tried." He stands and paces. His stat boosts must have worn off. After tapping my Shaman Stick on the stone floor, I toss another Spontaneity on him, giving him +99 ATT.

"Ahh, thank you. You always knew how to sooth an old man. The thing is," he says as he walks around the perimeter of the small room, "that I've always been old, and I don't remember who I am." He stops and stares down at me, the ATT boost making his eyes shine. He whispers, "I so desperately want to."

I realize this Master Gronai, two thousand years later, is the same one I knew, but he's gone mad. Nothing he's saying makes sense, and he's not even trying to make sense. It's as though he's not capable of it anymore. My heart beats slower.

"I can help," I say gently. I stand and put my hands on his shoulders. Look him dead in the eye. "Master Gronai, where do I find *Ananta*?"

He blinks, pain aching in his expression. "In the oldest branch of the first floor library, there is a locked door at the very back hidden behind a heavy bookshelf. Only one in a nook. There is a staircase leading to below the temple. The basement. That's all I can tell you." He looks down, pulls away from me, and sits back at his desk.

He's done with us. I don't even try to get any more out of him. Silvia senses it, too, because she takes my hand and leads me out of the turret door and into moonlight, closing the door behind us.

"Let's go, Sid."

"Okay, yeah. It's so weird seeing him like that."

"You okay?" She gazes down at me, concerned.

"Yeah. To the library."

We find a bookshelf made of wood, while the others are black marble, tucked a few feet in from the others in the bottom floor library way, way, way in the back. Luckily, not a single player seeks out these places. I summon the Counts, and command Surround. They blow that bookcase and the locked wooden door behind it to pieces. I thank them and quickly dismiss them before they get irritated about being summoned indoors. I'm lucky it was nighttime, at least.

"Well, damn!" Silvia says once they're gone. "That was... something."

As the dust clears and the rubble becomes stable, I summon *Varengan* for light. The old stone stairs winding downward before us are black as sin, and my paradise bird summon is the best torch. *Varengan* seems to sense something isn't safe, and doesn't chirp or coo. He crouches in the hole, unable to fly in such cramped quarters.

"*Varengan*, I need you to guide us through the basement. We're looking for an entrance to a battlefield. You make us see perfectly, beautiful bird," I tell him with what I hope reads to a bird as an encouraging tone of voice.

He winks one eye at me and hops all the way through the hole the Counts made, and wanders downward. Gray stone walls and fat steps radiate pale blue from *Varengan*'s glow, and we follow.

The bottom of the stairwell opens up into a wide, round room with a high ceiling. *Varengan* is happy to fly again. It's completely empty. Not a single book, scroll, not even dust here. No doors, and none of the walls look special, like an entrance to a battlefield.

Varengan lands in the middle of the room and slowly cleans his wing feathers.

"I have absolutely no idea what to do, Silvia."

She shakes her head, looking all around. "Do you think there's some trap? Could we be standing targets right now?"

I hadn't thought of that. "Yeah, you're right. *Varengan* has a protection spell. Hang on."

"I'll add on," she says, waving her lit wand.

Silvia Diamond casts Protection. Sid and Silvia Diamond gain Protection.

I access *Varengan*'s ability list in my interface and aim for Feathers, but pause right before I mindlessly select it.

There are now five options.

All my summons have four options. Why does *Varengan* have five?

"What is it?" Silvia asks.

"*Varengan* has a new ability."

"A new one? What is it?"

I hastily read it to myself, then to Silvia.

Gift of Feather—*Varengan summons healer player of your choice to you. Speak the player's name to Varengan.*

"What does it mean?" she asks.

"I think... You see, *Varengan* asked me never to pluck a feather. That's it. Now he's offering a feather. Asking me to bring someone, a healer, here." I turn to her and look up into her shining white eyes. "I think he wants to bring me a fighter."

"For *Ananta*."

"Yes."

"Oh, wow. You have to do it." She pulls a torch out of her bag and lights it. Shallow orange flame mixes with blue on the gray stone walls.

I turn to *Varengan*. I never wanted to hurt any of my friends from Dark World again. Yet, I think of it from their points of view. How could I do this to them, keep them from the ultimate Mystic battle, when they took it hard for every single one before? I know better. I want them here. I know they want to be here, too.

Sid commands Gift of Feather.

"*Varengan*, bring Doolittle." I have no idea if this magic will cross to Dark World, but I feel in my bones they all need to be here.

My paradise bird squawks, and beside him, a light blue, glowing figure takes form, and then solidifies into Doolittle.

"Holy crap!" he screams. "Where the hell am I?" He spins around and sees Silvia and me. "Sid!"

"Hey, Doolittle. I, uh, had *Varengan* summon you."

"What?" He looks at the bird and back to me. "Are you... are you telling me he had a new ability, and that this is... oh my God."

He's always been the quickest of our bunch. "Yep, *Ananta*. And I think my other summons will have similar gifts, or an extra ability, if you will."

Doolittle shakes his head. "Stop that Nuudle talk. Are you for real?"

"Yep. Meet Silvia." I gesture to her.

"Hi, Doolittle. I've heard all about you." She smiles at him.

"Holy shit. We're in Elora. We're in friggin' Elora. Silvia Diamond. Two names."

"No time, Doolittle, I gotta pull out my other summons. I don't know how much time we actually have, but I feel like not much."

Sid dismisses *Varengan*.

I watch Doolittle's face freak as Silvia pulls him aside, and she seems to ease him with quiet words. She casts Awaken on him after a moment.

I'll go in order.

Sid summons the *Counts of Hell*.

They form into a circle around the three of us, quietly staring expectantly at me. I check their ability list.

From the Dark—The Counts of Hell summon a dark class player of your choice to you. Speak the player's name to the Counts of Hell.

Sid commands From the Dark.

"Days."

Out of a black and white swirling fog, Days materializes. He wears full-on dungeon gear, and has a little blood on his cheek. He spins and sees me, becoming color away from the Counts black-and-white spell. He points at my face. "You. I knew you wouldn't leave us out, because you knew I'd invoke some inner demon on you if you did. *Ananta*, for real?" He looks around at the Counts. "Did they...?"

Maybe I'm the only dumb one. Both of them knew what was going on the second they materialized.

"Yeah. Doolittle, fill him in. Oh, and say hi to Days, Silvia."

He winks at her. "She of Mantra. And we're in fucking Elora."

"Yeah," Silvia says to him, holding out her hand. They shake. She casts Awaken on him as he chuckles. I know he's thinking, *I'm feeling the real Elora!*

"Thanks, guys," I tell the Counts.

Sid dismisses the *Counts of Hell*.

Sid summons *Djinn*.

"Hello, Master Mystic Sid, is it my turn to offer you a fourth wish?"

"Yes, *Djinn*. It is."

I read his new ability.

Fourth Wish—Djinn summons buffer class player of your choice to you. Speak the player's name to Djinn.

Sid commands Fourth Wish.

"Sorry, please, *Djinn*."

Djinn is delighted. "My favorite Voodoo Lady."

Sorry appears in a sudden poof of green smoke. She's stunned, stumbles as though she had been running when summoned. "Where the hell—is that you, Sid?"

Days grabs her around the waist. "He didn't forget us like you said he would, so now you owe me a foot rub and three Siren Ales."

"What—?" she starts.

"Come on, I'll tell you about it with Doolittle. Introduce you to Silvia. She has the whole story."

Silvia Diamond casts Awaken on Sorry.

They gather nearby as I dismiss *Djinn* with a thumb's up back to his.

Sid summons *Xiuhcoatl*.

The great, coiling golden dragon spirals out of his shining mist, and he leans down to my face. His nose touches mine and oddly, I'm not terrified. I meet his eyes and in his golden glow, I can see the deep red irises and black slit pupils. It may be my imagination, but I swear I hear his thoughts projected to me, and he says, "I am yours, and only yours."

I blink as he pulls away.

I read his ability list.

Power of Dragons—Xiuhcoatl summons damage dealer of your choice to you. Speak the player's name to Xiuhcoatl.

Sid commands Power of Dragons.

"Simple."

Xiuhcoatl spits a yellow fireball in front of him, but it stops before exploding into the floor and Simple appears where it would have hit, sitting with legs crossed and two books in her lap. "Huh?" Her head twirls all around, then up at *Xiuhcoatl*. "Oh! Must be *Ananta* time."

Simple never had a doubt. Maybe she found something else in another old book in the day I was gone.

Days calls out to her. "Over here. We'll explain."

She grins at me and whips out her wand, then runs over to the others. I glance at Silvia as she casts Awaken on Simple. She looks as strong and confident as ever, interacting easily with my Dark World friends, telling them what's what.

Keres and *Oni* are left, but I have no more friends to invite.

I decide to summon them anyway. They must have something, but what?

Sid summons *Keres*.

The bare-breasted wraith forms out of the black smoke coming from me, and she asks, "Feed me? A sacrifice must be made."

"No, *Keres*, I'm just looking at your ability list."

"Soon, then," she hisses.

I see a fifth option, but it's not for summoning players to us.

Feed Keres—*Sacrifice player of your choice to Keres. Speak the name of the player to Keres.*

I dismiss her immediately.

"What did she have?" Silvia asks.

"Nothing at all. All that's left is *Oni*."

They stop talking and turn to me, approach me. "But we're all here," says Simple.

"I think there isn't any more summoning players," I tell them.

Sorry puts her hands on her hips. "What do you know?"

I shake my head and hold out my hands. "Nothing. Nothing—I'm nervous, alright? I don't want anyone getting hurt, but I can't do this without all of you. I know you well enough that I'm sure you want to be here. Yeah, I need you too, Silvia."

My Dark World friends turn and look at her, but she keeps her steady, glowing gaze on me with a small, defiant smile on her thin lips. "Was it right to use Awaken, then?"

"I couldn't interact with Elora until you cast it on me. None of them would be able to hit *Ananta*, possibly. Most likely. That's how things work in Dark World. You always get screwed when you do something right," I tell her.

"But, there was a possibility…"

Days shakes his head. "Sid is right. What if we started with the beastie, and then had to wait while you cast Awaken on all of us? Sid would be fried."

She nods. Blinks. "Alright. I might not be able to interact with *Ananta*, but I don't affect the mobs. I take care of the players, and if I can cast on you now, then I'll be able to there. That's all that matters." She casts a Cure on Days. He nods with a light-headed expression.

"Yeah," he says. "Mantra girl's a fighter. Some stats on you." He felt the strength of her Mind stat.

"So, they all have these moves but *Keres*. Check *Oni*, for Christ's sake," Sorry says.

"Yeah," I mutter. After seeing *Keres*' new ability, I'm concerned what *Oni*'s might be.

Sid summons *Oni*.

He fills the chamber, lighting it up soft blue. All three eyes are on me, and I see anticipation.

Doolittle is sweating, wiping his forehead with his White Blessings Robe's sleeve.

I check *Oni*'s abilities.

Call Ananta—*Oni brings forth demons of the greatest degree of creation and destruction, and in this place, Oni offers you a doorway to Ananta.*

"Guys," I say. "This is it." I read them the ability Call *Ananta*.

We're all quiet, and then Silvia says, "Sid, I've invited everyone to our group. Don't you think it's time?"

I wait, wondering. "Buffs?"

"If we enter a battlefield," says Doolittle, "they'll all be gone."

"If he shows up here, we're defenseless," says Sorry.

I look at *Oni*'s eyes. The way he meets my gaze inspires confidence. Instead of the lost soul look he usually has, pensive and brooding, he looks determined and wise.

"Now's the time," I say.

Oni nods once.

Sid commands Call *Ananta*.

I hear ungodly wailing and shrieking as wispy, wicked wraiths form all through the room, whipping around us madly. Everything fades to black in the confusion as I feel my heart thump in my chest so hard I hear it in my ears.

Then we're in the battlefield.

Open air all around, and nighttime. So many stars in the sky, and all three moons are out and full, aligned in a triangle directly overhead. We're on a small island in a sea that stretches forever in all directions. There's a fire burning in the center, and tropical trees and bushes seem planted by a great gardener's hands in a deliberately disorganized pattern. Pink flowering jungle vines climb the trunks of the twisty trees.

"Everyone okay?" I ask.

I hear all of them say they're here. My eyes adjust more and I make out their figures in the moonlight. I sigh in relief.

Silvia and Doolittle begin buffing even though I haven't spotted *Ananta* yet. I throw some Spontaneities out, as well as Meditations. Days gets three of each, making his buffs last sixteen minutes.

"So, where is he?" Sorry whispers.

"Don't know," I say.

"This is amazing," Silvia murmurs.

"Stay here," I tell them. "I'm going to walk around."

"Like hell," says Days. "Quit being a pussy about us getting abused and suck it up. We're following."

I smile up at him. "Dork."

"A comeback. With no excuse. Bad one. I like it."

I turn and walk toward the fire pit. They follow. Once there, we surround it, looking into the yellow, orange, red, green, blue fire. A fire like *Ananta*'s fire in the opening cutscene.

Sid summons *Oni*.

Oni flows out of me and floats just behind me, saying nothing. I check his ability list in case he has something new, but no. The ability that got us here is gone.

"*Oni*, how do I find *Ananta*?" I ask him, looking back at him.

"Invite him," says *Oni* in a smooth voice.

I look back at the fire and clear my throat. "I just say it out loud, *Oni*?"

"That is generally the way an invitation works, Master Sid."

Oni's never been a smartass. I take a slow breath. "*Ananta*, I'm Sid. Would you like to join me and my friends… for a friendly chat?"

Sorry chuckles darkly.

The fire burns brighter, and I hear seawater splashing at the south edge of the island to my right. We all look.

Ananta, with nine serpent heads at attention, lightning-sparking eyes making the sand glitter, climbs from the sea and approaches us on four clawed legs, forked tail swishing behind him. He looks more indigo than blue, like in the cutscene, but that might be the moonlight. His face slowly emerges from his belly once he's close to us, the familiar, golden-skinned man's features with white, penetrating eyes, coming out of the opening completely by the time he reaches us.

By now, we've huddled on the other side of the fire from him.

Nobody says a word.

I tremble as his glaring white eyes and still mouth await… something. I need to act.

"*Ananta*, hello. I'm happy to have found you. Would you like to be my summon?" Will Nuudle charm work on him?

Why not? It might be that easy.

I'm wrong. It isn't.

"Mystic Sid, I have watched you, and have found you to be a mystery. How you convinced all the summons of this time and world to ally with you when no one else has but claimed two or three. Now you want me, but for what use?" His voice is silky and accented oddly, tone not too deep, not too high. Steady. Steady, yet intimidating. So strong in that he knows exactly who he is and what he wants. Unfortunately, I know neither of these things about him.

I'm not sure how to answer and glance around at the others. They give no help, and even Days looks uncomfortable.

"I don't really know, but I think when the times come, I will."

He doesn't blink. His lined, gold lips hardly split when he talks. "*Djinn* speaks highly of you."

"You've talked to *Djinn* since…?"

"No and yes. I, too, know the limitlessness of no time, but there are many stories of life and existence now instead of one. This happened again when you entered Dark World and chose Mystic."

I'm not sure what he means, but I nod as though I do. "Go on," I encourage him.

"The other summons have their reasons to be under your command, and I have only one requirement."

"Sure, *Ananta*, anything." I give him a weak smile, hoping forced charm in the face of terror will entice him to take it easy on us. He doesn't return it.

"We fight to the death, and I assure you, you will all die."

I look down at the sand. Think for a minute, scared stiff. This summon means it. "Is there any other way?"

"Mystic Sid, I have known great pain. For you to understand how to use me, you, too, must endure the greatest pain you can imagine. Do you agree to my battle terms?"

I look at the others. "Guys? You still want to do this?"

Days lifts his sword, twirls it in front of him. "I'm game."

"I've died before," Sorry says, hand waving through the air like it's nothing.

Doolittle and Simple nod.

I look at Silvia. "You can leave."

"Don't be stupid. I can't even feel anything like you." She pulls out her Diamond Dirk. Twists the handle in her right palm while preparing her wand in her left.

"So, *Ananta*, how do we start this?" I ask, trying to sound brave and casual. I sense he likes confidence.

His golden face disappears slowly into the belly of the serpent body. The serpent heads writhe for action.

Days wastes no time, as usual, and begins before I'm ready. Then again, I've never felt ready for any of these summon battles.

Days uses Invoke Inner Demon.

One of *Ananta*'s serpent heads shoots lightning at Days, which he blocks with his shield.

Oni moves in on *Ananta*, hitting him on his side with his head horns.

Ananta ignores *Oni*, focused on Days. The guy really can keep hate.

Sorry casts Weaken Enemy. *Ananta* has Offense Down.

Another serpent head dives for Days' throat, but he evades. With Weaken Enemy, *Oni*'s hits do more than 0.2%, and now closer to 0.5% damage. I feel sick.

Doolittle casts Protection on Days. Days gains Protection.

Oni has done about 3% damage to *Ananta* by now, and that's not nearly what he usually does to a boss. More like 5% a hit. *Oni*'s gotten in about ten hits. 3%. Days' hits do no damage whatsoever.

Simple casts Ball Lightning. *Ananta* takes no damage.

"Ah, crap, he's immune to my lightning magic," calls out Simple. "I don't know what to do."

"It might just be too weak of a spell," says Doolittle.

Simple spins on me. "Mantra me," she hisses, eyes wild with excitement.

Days continues to battle *Ananta*, holding hate. He's lost 30% HP while *Ananta* stands at 96%.

Silvia Diamond casts Cure. Days gains HP.

"Do it," Days says. "I'll get hate off her."

Sid casts Mantra.

"Silvia," I say, hoping she doesn't hear. She's dashing off a bolt of light from her wand to refresh her spell abilities.

She looks at me funny. She did hear.

Simple gains +190 ATT.

Simple casts Death Lightning. *Ananta* takes damage.

His HP only drops another 10%, and all snake heads are on Simple in a snap. Simple takes 20% damage from a couple of snake strikes. She never knew defensive fighting, but takes the hits without more than anger in her eyes. But there's blood, a lot of it.

Days uses Crushing Blade.

Now, *Ananta* turns back on Days, missing about 14% more HP. Thank God it did more damage than Simple because that could have been nasty for my Nuudle friend to keep the hate.

It gets worse than I thought with *Ananta* on Days. The golden face emerges quickly and his eyes spear my Dark Knight tank.

Ananta **uses** *Ananta*'s **Gaze. Days dies instantly.**

My heart stops at seeing the beam shoot out of *Ananta*'s eyes and directly into Days, disintegrating him.

He's just gone.

We're so screwed.

Sid commands Disaster Strike. *Ananta* **cannot use Special Ability until end of battle.**

Ananta turns on *Oni*.

Ananta **uses Snake Bites.**

All snake heads snap at *Oni*, taking his HP to 50%. That's way too much damage for a summon to take from a hit.

Doolittle casts Deep Heal on *Oni*.

Ananta rips around to Doolittle. The hate is loose and everywhere without Days, and we're all freaking out, not thinking.

We'll have to hop the hate. We all know it. That means we all bleed like Simple, or worse, we get zapped like Days.

Ananta **uses Dweller on the Threshold. Doolittle's stats are reduced by 80%.**

"Damn," he yells.

Sid casts Spontaneity. Doolittle gains +10 DEF.

It didn't even match his old stats, just his lowered stats.

Ananta's face still protrudes from his belly. Snake heads snap at Doolittle, knocking him to the sand with 0% HP in a hit. No way he could have done otherwise with those stats. His White Elf body lies crumpled on the ground, and then vanishes.

Silvia casts Blessing of Inner Peace. Sid will dodge all Special Ability attacks in battle.

"Thanks!"

Ananta turns on Silvia. Oh no. It's going so fast....

Ananta **uses** *Ananta*'s **Gaze.**

Sorry uses Special Ability: Mirror of Darkness. Party is protected by magical mirror for next attack.

Ananta's laser hits something in front of Silvia, and it bounces back straight at *Ananta* himself. His HP drops to 40%.

"Holy shit!" Sorry says. "It didn't even kill him. It's supposed to reflect back any attack. That attack kills."

Ananta **uses Take Life.**

Sorry casts Reflection of Darkness. Take Life is stopped and *Ananta* **takes damage.**

Usually, that spell drains a ton of HP and does arcane DoT, but on *Ananta*, just 20% HP lower. He's at 30% HP. There is no DoT effect at all.

Ananta **uses** *Ananta*'s **Gaze. Sorry dies instantly.**

I watch the whole thing unfold in horror. I'd never seen Sorry fight like that, never knew she could deal out damage like a Black, and then... she's gone.

Where are they going when they die? Under the Temple of Nuudlel? Back to Dark World?

Sid commands Demon Call. *Ananta* **takes damage.**

From *Oni*'s chest, a legion of twisted, dark creatures spring and fly at *Ananta*. They claw at his flesh and face, yet his features take no visible damage while his body shows deep wounds. His HP goes down to 15%.

Simple uses Special Ability: Reverse to Light.

Simple casts Shield of Honor. The party gains Protection of the Ages.

My DEF stat is boosted up 100 points. I assume everyone else's has, too.

Ananta turns on Simple. She puts her arm over her eyes instinctively and leans away from the wicked summon.

***Ananta* uses Take Life. Simple loses 90% active HP and gives it to *Ananta*.**

Simple falls to the sand as I swallow the fact that *Ananta* is now way up on HP, at 78%. What must that have felt like to Simple? Take Life sounds like it would pain your very core being. Her face is pale and blank.

Silvia casts Deep Heal on Simple. Simple gains HP.

Simple should have gotten full HP, but no. She only gets 40% back. What is this trick of *Ananta*'s summon battle? Our moves aren't working correctly, and everyone is fighting in a panic.

Simple casts Deep Heal.

***Ananta* blocks Deep Heal.**

Now, *Ananta* is at 100% HP. He somehow took that magic right out of Simple's wand.

Sid commands Disease. *Ananta* is diseased.

If this works right, then for the duration of the fight, *Ananta* will lose 15% HP every three seconds no matter what until he dies or I stop it.

His HP drops only 8% every three seconds. Damn. Of course, I lose track after counting two ticks and drag my shocked attention to the battle at hand.

***Ananta* uses *Ananta*'s gaze on Simple. Simple dies instantly.**

She disintegrates.

It's just Silvia and me left.

"Just do it!" I scream at *Ananta*.

Sid uses Seizure.

Sid commands Swallow. *Ananta* dodges.

Dammit.

Silvia casts Protection. Sid gains Protection.

Oni still slams and slaps *Ananta*, doing slight damage as my DoT move lessens in damage every tick. *Ananta* is at 60% HP.

I pause, thinking. He hasn't attacked yet, but I'd think he would go after Silvia next.

He doesn't.

***Ananta* uses Take Life. *Oni* loses 90% HP and gives it to *Ananta*.**

He's back at 100% HP, while *Oni* is struggling at 10% HP.

Oni can't do anything now. Neither can we. I reach in my memory about how I decided all my summons chose me instead of my defeating them. How would this equate to my current situation with *Ananta*?

Sid commands retreat. *Oni* retreats.

Oni floats back to me and hovers by my side as Silvia casts Deep Heal on him. He goes to almost full HP.

I watch *Ananta*, doing nothing, and Silvia seems to pick up on my strategy. Don't attack, see what he does. *Ananta* obviously was right. We all are going to die, and I'm not sure what's next. I'm following my instinct on this, scared shitless from the devastation I've seen him wreak in so short a time. He seems to be able to bend the rules of the game at whim.

"*Oni*, you alright?" I ask him, eyes still on the master summon before us. I get close to Silvia, who keeps watching *Ananta*, as well.

"Yes, Mystic Master Sid. I feel no pain," *Oni* answers.

"Good. Thanks, *Oni*. You've done well."

Sid dismisses *Oni*.

Ananta's snake heads sway back and forth as though scrambling for a chance to see what just happened, yet his golden face is impassive. With his eyes completely white like a White Elf's eyes, I can't tell what or who he's looking at. It feels like me. A sensation of being scrutinized, assessed.

I put my Shaman Stick in my bag after unequipping it.

"*Ananta*, you are too great a summon," I say to him, winging it. "I cannot possibly wield your power as you do alone. You have special qualities... as your own master." Even though Silvia has no physical sensations, I have a need to protect her whatever way I can.

Ananta floats into the air and comes to us, glowing a deep bluish-purple, with black swirling tendrils on his outer illumination. "You and your team have fought well. The Voodoo Lady was indeed a force to be reckoned with."

"If I may ask, where are they?"

"We have other things to discuss. Please, sit. Sit by the fire with Silvia Diamond."

We exchange glances, and then settle in the sand with the fire between floating *Ananta* and us. The flames are dim compared to his electric eyes.

"So, *Ananta*," I say, trying to keep my voice steady. Am I about to get him? Without Silvia dying? Or me? "What would you care to discuss?"

"You speak Nuudle words with ease. As a glorious Mystic should. I find your fighting style nervous, but in a cautious way. Instead of aggressiveness in the face of the inevitable end, you take care. You believe you have a chance to live even though I have destroyed all your chances. None of your summons can hurt me, and you now know that." His voice is even like before, as though no fight took place. He sounds like he's reading out of a book.

"Yes, I know."

"Is that why you commanded *Oni* to retreat?"

"Yes and no. I figured, why attack? It seems to me you only attack when you're threatened. So, I took a chance and asked him to retreat. When you didn't attack, I dismissed him."

"Why?" For the first time, he sounds curious, losing the boredom of the whole thing.

"Because I didn't see any reason for *Oni* to take any more hits. He got hurt enough, and I didn't want to put him through that anymore."

"He could have extended your life for a little longer. Have you no survival instinct?" A serpent head leans down over the fire and into my face. Its blood red tongue flips out and tastes my cheek, and then the long neck pulls back.

"I do, and that's what it told me to do." I'm confident in my answer; it's the truth.

"Why?"

"Because I think you're a reasonable being." I don't know if that's the real reason. It just felt right. I don't want to say that. It sounds stupid and makes no sense. Felt right. *Felt right.* I don't know why I do anything with Mystic, just go on gut reactions. I'm afraid of his reaction, so a little sincere flattery might warm him up.

"I am, and you have made an impression on me. While we fought, I discussed with *Djinn* my terms of surrender. He explained to me that you would agree to them."

A pause. I wonder how that came about. Must be more of the timelessness stuff.

I say, "What are your terms?" He's talking about becoming my summon... *Ananta.* Right?

Silvia takes my hand and squeezes it. Her Diamond Dagger and Wand of the Forest are unequipped.

The serpent heads fall back, *Ananta*'s mouth opens more fully as he speaks next, and I assume that's so I won't misunderstand his accent. "I have two conditions, and then I agree that you may summon me. One. You must make a sacrifice. You must kill Silvia Diamond by your own hand, and you know how."

I swallow hard. *Keres.* Her fifth ability, Sacrifice. So that's what it's for. I want to scream, "No! No! No!" but stay silent. The thought of seeing Silvia gored by hungry *Keres* makes me sick and stiff with fear.

"My second condition is that you die at my hand last. You must know what you inflict on others. Do you agree?"

I gaze into the fire. Yeah, I'll take the hits, sure. But I refuse to watch *Keres* eat Silvia alive. "I'll die for you twice, a thousand times, but I can't let *Keres* at Silvia with that new Sacrifice ability she has."

I hear her gasp. She doesn't know about *Keres'* new move because I didn't tell anyone.

"Then there is no agreement. My terms are non-negotiable." *Ananta* begins to float backward toward the water.

"Wait, please, *Ananta*," Silvia says to him, then turns to me. "Sid, don't be ridiculous. I won't even feel it."

Ananta stops his retreat.

I shake my head. "We're not even sure about that right now. *Ananta* didn't ever touch you. We don't know if you feel pain with this... situation, and what *Keres* does... I can't let you go through that. I'll make it without *Ananta*'s help."

"Make what? What's the point? Come on. I didn't feel the buffs. You said you feel buffs. I felt nothing. Look, I can adjust my headset and see my living room." Her eyes unfocus and go auto.

I blink at her. I can't conceive of a headband, a living room, a bed, a friggin' pizza.

Her eyes come back to me. "Please, Sid, let me do this. If you're upset, don't watch."

"I—I don't know."

She leans toward me. "Look, we both know it's more about you taking the action to tell *Keres* to do her thing. About you seeing me, how did you put it once, gored? Skin shredded off my bones, body eaten alive? I won't feel a thing, you know it. Drop the stupid, romantic guilt, and play this game like the awesome player you are." Her jaw is set and her whimsical eyebrows pushed low over her white eyes. "Finish this."

I look at *Ananta*. Then to Silvia. Then back at *Ananta*.

"Silvia, it's not that important. Like you said, I'm a player, and this is a game. I'm not doing it."

Silvia stands up and points her dainty finger at me. "It has become much, much more than a game for you, and you know it. Sid Vicious, you do this, or I swear *I'll* get *Keres* to eat you."

"Don't get mad, please."

"I can't get through to you any other way. It's called a sacrifice because it's hard. Otherwise it's not a true sacrifice. That's what *Ananta* wants." His face softens. "Come on, Sid. Don't give up. This is it. You got this. I'm fine with it." She smiles slightly.

I stand, too, facing her. Defeated by her logic and her gentleness, yet the fierceness before made me think of a mother chiding a kid for being afraid on his first day of school.

"You know you want to claim *Ananta*. He's offering. Who gets offered that? Come on. Don't be an idiot."

I think to myself what a loser I'd be to her if after all this, I quit. Gave up. She's right. She won't feel it. It's a game to her still, and she's also right about how it's not a game for me. Honestly, I don't care how bad whatever *Ananta* does to me hurts. I don't want to see Silvia's precious body desecrated. "But... are you sure?" I ask quietly. Could I do this?

"Absolutely. Tell *Ananta* you'll do it." She's tough when she means it, her face back to solid determination.

I reach up and touch her hair, then turn to *Ananta*. The girl I love is commanding me to torture her to death, like she's the Mystic and I'm the summon. What do you do? "*Ananta*, I agree to your terms." I almost choke on the words.

He floats back to the fire. "Very good. Now, you must summon *Keres* for the sacrifice."

I pause. Silvia nudges my shoulder.

Sid summons *Keres*.

She swirls out of the black mist from my chest, taking her awful form. I can't stand to think of what I'm about to watch. It isn't real, it isn't real to Silvia, I keep telling myself.

"Master Sid, have you a meal for me? I sense a great battle."

"*Keres*, I'm making a sacrifice to *Ananta* as terms of our agreement."

Her dark eyes brighten. "Oh? Oh, my Sacrifice ability you will use?" She turns to *Ananta*. "I have never used Sacrifice. I savor the thought. Thank you, *Ananta*. I am very hungry." She turns back to me and flexes her black wings. "Who do I get to feast on?"

I cock my head at Silvia, eyes downcast.

Her greedy eyes roam over Silvia's flesh. "But Master Sid, you said to never, ever, ever eat Silvia Diamond."

"Just this once, and make it… quick, will you?"

She grins wickedly, needle teeth dripping with saliva. "I will do as you command, which is what I am here for. You are a kind master, you feed me when you don't have to use me. I know. I appreciate it. I starve constantly. I will make her death quick, but I will feast slow. White Elves have fine-tasting flesh, a delicacy, though not much quantity."

I cringe. "Okay, thank you, *Keres*."

Silvia tells me, "Don't worry. It'll be over so soon you won't know it. Just do it. Don't think about it."

I sigh and look away from her and *Keres*. I target Silvia. Close my eyes.

Sid commands Sacrifice.

I keep my eyes closed, and even though I know she can't feel it, I'm surprised not to hear her screams. Instead, I hear her neck snap immediately, and then the sound of raw flesh being torn and chewed ever so slowly, savored.

"You have fulfilled the first term; now, the second. Your kindness affects. I will make yours quick, as well."

I brace myself and face him eye-to-eye.

Ananta **uses** ***Ananta*****'s Gaze. Sid dies instantly.**

I feel my heart stop, my lungs paralyze, and then I fall into a blackness like no death yet. It's how I imagine a real death is, if I'd had one… one that wasn't wrapped in mystery and confusion of being alive and dead at the same time, and in a new existence.

The pain doesn't last. The darkness feels like the sleep I've never achieved in Dark World.

~

The next thing I'm aware of after the welcome end of *Ananta*'s terror is flashes of bright red behind my closed eyelids, but I don't feel rain. I open my eyes.

I'm at my grave in Dark World, but I'm a ghost.

I'm a ghost… I'm a ghost with no body to go back to.

Panic rises in my ghost chest like bile from bad fish. How can I come back to my physical form here in Dark World if my body is left in the Temple of Nuudlel's dank basement in Elora? Come to think of it, how could it be, really? Somebody would have discovered the hole the Counts blew through the wall and secret door in the temple's library, found our bodies and… and what?

I put my ghost hands over my face, overwhelmed with frustration. What of the others?

What of Silvia?

In my interface, I read the most wonderful thing I could wish for right now.

Anella casts Revive. Sid is revived.

I become solid again, my body fully forming as I look up, rain pelting me, and see Silvia's sister standing over me with a faint smile. "Anella! Anella, thank god you're here. I had no way—I mean, I couldn't get to my body. It's in Elora. Well, that's if it's anywhere. I don't know anything. But thank you, thank you so much." I jump up and hug her. She stiffens and pries herself away from my small grasp.

"This is what I've been waiting for in the graveyard, Sid. I knew you'd come back a ghost. I know many things. I knew you'd need Revive, and I have spent all my time around this graveyard waiting for when you would need it. But there's more. You had others. We must find their graves and ghosts, Revive them. You must know where they keep their graves. You do, don't—"

Suddenly, a bright, pure bubble of light springs up to my right, facing Anella. As the blinding light takes the shape of a player, I feel my heart skip a beat.

I recognize her by her scent before her physical form. "Silvia, Silvia?" I say.

She fully forms and turns to me. "Sid. Sid, the Sunlight Daisy. It took me to you when you... you..." Her eyes wander to Anella, who stares at Silvia with shock and denial.

Silvia's no idiot. She reads the Hidden's name, and she grabs for her sister, Anella Portabella at one time, Kristina in another world and life.

"No!" Anella cries out. "No!"

"It's me, Kristina, I know about you, about Dark World, about all of it. I know you're here and I can't believe it. You're right fucking here. Please, don't be afraid."

I've never heard her curse nor plead so desperately.

Anella pulls back further, putting her palms out. "You shouldn't be here." She looks at me. "Sunlight Daisy? You gave her a Sunlight Daisy? Look! Look what you've done! You've trapped her here for eternity." Her voice shakes with anger and conflicting emotions.

I take a step back, looking at them both. "But, Anella, look. Look at her name. Just look."

She reads above Silvia's head again and gasps. "Ohhhhh..." she murmurs, wonder in her voice.

The name above her head reads "Silvia Diamond." Two names.

"Silvia," I say to her. "Can you feel Dark World? Can you feel the rain? Did you feel Anella's arms when you grabbed her?"

Silvia finally tears her eyes from her sister's Dark World Siren Hidden form and meets my stare.

"You still have two names."

Her eyes clear from their glaze of shock. "No. No, Sid. No, I feel nothing at all."

"Can you still lower your headband view? Come on, try it."

Her eyes go on auto almost instantly. "I see the Chinese takeout box from last night. Lo Mein. I can feel it." Her eyes snap back to here and now.

"You're not dead, Silvia."

Anella whispers, "Not dead. In Dark World, but not dead. Sunlight Daisy."

I wrap my arms around Silvia's waist. "Nothing made sense, it all happened so fast... you're okay." I pull away from her and smile up into her eyes.

Anella takes a step toward Silvia. "Silvia Diamond. The first player in Dark World to ever have two names." She turns to me. "What have you done? What have you started?"

"I—I don't know." I'm at a complete loss. "But Anella, we have to find our friends. We have to Revive them. I know their graves. We'll go to them. I mean, we should have had some kind of plan, but how the hell could we have known *this* would happen?"

"Right," Anella answers softly, still looking at her sister. "Silvia Diamond."

Silvia touches Anella's upper arm. "You're beautiful, sis. The Hidden. I like it." She gives her a love-filled gaze that she must have wished for fifteen years she could have given her one last time after she died. "You're alive. In some way. You're here, and I know it's you. I can tell. I feel you."

Anella gets that look like when she's about to Scatter, but Silvia seems to pick up on her anxiety. "Now's your time for action. Kristina, we have to find the others, and only you can help. I'm assuming you brought Sid back with the Revive spell he told me you used on him before?"

"Yes..."

"No hesitations," Silvia says gently. "Now is time for action." She turns to me. "Have you checked your summon list? Do you actually have the ability to summon *Ananta*?"

I access that menu in my interface.

Summon Ananta.

"Yes. But I want to wait until we're all together before I pull him out. That's tradition." I smile at her. She's here. She's here and not dead. What does that mean for the rest of us?

Anella says, "People are going to flock her. The two names. I can disguise her with a certain spell. It lasts twenty minutes at a time. We must stick to backroads and swimming and—"

Silvia laughs. "Sillies. I can tele us all wherever we need to go. That is, if you'll join a party with us, Kristina. Anella."

He mouth opens, closes, opens again. "Yes. Yes, invite me."

When I enter the party at Silvia's invite, Anella is already there. How fast did she accept her sister's invite? Something about Silvia being here has inspired Anella, shaken her, made her want to take the action Silvia urged her to do.

I know it's not just me. They feel it. My friends felt it. Something is coming. Something about this great event so many NPCs mention vaguely and with desperation, but don't explain. They back off of the subject, almost like people might when they have mixed emotions and don't want to say too much... or more like hope too much. But for what?

"Sid?" Silvia says. "What graveyard first?"

CHAPTER 17: THE NPCS

"Are you going to use *Ananta*?" Days whispers.

"No, I don't think so."

"Why not? You haven't used him yet at all. It's just weird." He's eying the guards in front of Bane's tower like he can't wait for the challenge to hold all their hate at once.

The six of us huddle inside an NPC's house outside the great deviant Bane's worship tower in the capital city of Dragonbane Territory. We had to sneak in behind the rich Dragonbane NPC family's backs at night while they slept, and we stayed hiding in their nursey until dawn... now. There is no infant in this nursery, just an empty human-sized baby's crib.

The room faces the entrance, and there are double doors leading out to a small veranda here. A direct assault line to Bane's guards.

"I need *Djinn* for this."

"Why?"

"Because I know how to use him best."

He rolls his eyes, then focuses back on his soon-to-be victims.

I had surprised myself by knowing where all their graves were, although I'd never seen them. Days' gravestone read "Days End." Sorry was So Sorry. Simple's said "Its Simple." And Doctor Doolittle. Of course.

I feel watched even now by Seeker with his Clairvoyance spell. I can't believe he hasn't warned Bane. All I've heard from Seeker is the letter I got from him two days ago, the morning after Silvia, Anella and I found everyone around their graves, knowing we'd come for them. They knew about my Hidden friend and her Revive spell, guessed the way things would pan out. Or hoped. It's like we're a hivemind.

Or eternally have been playing this game, and most likely will continue to do so. Thinking in the confines of this reality has become all we know.

Once the last of them—Days in Mylop Territory—was tracked down and Revived, Anella simply slipped away when nobody was looking. Even Silvia didn't see it. If she was distraught over it, she hid it well. Silvia has never-ending hope, though, so I assume she plans on tracking Anella down as soon as this business is out of the way. That's the way she stays motivated in the face of insanity. A working plan.

This attack with Bane has everything to do with Seeker's letter. But I'll get to that.

After Anella disappeared, Doolittle teleported us to Cashmere, and we walked into the island mountains where no mansions had been built. There, in a foggy valley between two lush, tropical peaks, I summoned *Ananta* for the first time.

His mist was indigo, sparkling with blacks, and right then it occurred to me that I never had the full heart feeling of claiming *Ananta* like I did with the other summons. He killed me, and then when I was alive, he was available. I still don't know what to make of that.

I read his ability list aloud as I went, watching him with his face hidden in the serpent belly, and the nine snake heads examining us, black tongues flicking. Hues of violet, lavender and deep purple glowed on my friends' faces as they listened.

Description:

Ananta, god of gods, lord of demons, maker and destroyer of existence, is the essence of life, death, and rebirth. Ananta sees truth. Ananta despises the lies of his creations, has affection for the strong and true of his world. Ananta has no creator. He became.

Dweller on the Threshold*—Lowers target's stats by 80%.*

Snake Bites*—Snake heads bite target 9 times, dealing devastating damage.*

Take Life*—Drains opponent of 90% active HP and gives it to Ananta.*

Ananta's Gaze*—Instantly kills target with magic of creation.*

Seizure Ability: Destroy Creation*—Can only be used once, and then Ananta can no longer be summoned.*

We had lengthy discussions about *Ananta*'s Seizure move. What did it mean? All spells, moves, and abilities describe what action takes place when executed, but this explained nothing.

My friends who were killed by *Ananta*'s Gaze described it as feeling a sharp, all-over pain, then nothing. Blackness, and then respawning at their graves in Dark World.

I've come to the conclusion that the name itself, Destroy Creation, says it all. It's something I can't comprehend, but I'll never use it. After all I went through to claim *Ananta*, I'm hesitant to even use him in battle in case I accidentally select Seizure *and* Destroy Creation. By accident, for real. Oops. My eyes moved wrong. Two times. God knows what happens next, but one thing I do know: I'll lose him for good if I use Destroy Creation. That's not going to happen, ever.

The minute I read Seeker's letter, I knew Seeker was after me because of *Ananta*. He somehow knows about this move, Destroy Creation, and what it ultimately does. He wants to use me to use it.

But why?

What did he know when we all played Elora Online that made him "seek"? What does he really want?

Silvia was able to get in Faithgamblers and can interact with Dark World as though it were Elora. She can still see her living room when she lowers her headband's vision settings. She can look at her computers for finding stuff on the Internet. She's alive. She can't access Elora, but otherwise, everything is the same.

We are not alive in the way she is, but the entire guild has some new hope... unspoken, just a heightened vibe.

At first, almost every player who saw her two names stopped her dead and drilled her with questions. She played smart, saying she had no idea. Changed the subject.

We've had to keep to back roads and wild dragons for travel. Eventually, she'll get mobbed because of her two names. She's tough; she doesn't mind the sneaking around, and she or Doolittle tele us a lot. It's riskier because we don't know who might be where we end up, and I'm not the only one protective of Silvia Diamond now.

In a weird way, I've enjoyed showing her Dark World, especially Dragonbane Territory with its humans and dragons. She laughed wildly the first time she rode a real dragon, not a mount. Absolutely fascinated with humans.

She feels safe still, which instills in me, in all of us, a feeling of peace and belief that answers can be found. She spends a lot of time with her headband at 50% transparency so she can look up anything and everything about Elora Online, well, online.

She hasn't found anything concrete about Dark World yet, but it's only been a few days. Even we natural Dark Worldians have to sleep, but she needs more.

We are the dead in touch with the living. We have a new perspective from this. Confirmation. More knowledge. It brings a sense of validation and excitement for what it might mean.

I made one visit without my friends, and that was to Master Gronai. I made sure he forgot to give me back the red leather book, *Manual of Systems*. He'd need it for the next two thousand years... right? Just in case, as I remembered my time-travel sci-fi, he has to have it to know me and tell me where the *Ananta* battle is two thousand years from now. Something like that. *Djinn* would understand, but I don't bother asking him. He's so casual with his lack of the time dimension restraints the rest of us have, it's hard to get an understandable answer about stuff like this.

I asked Master Gronai to help me make a very specific scroll, one that would cause me to be able to reset my Special Ability, Seizure, and use it twice in a row instead of waiting an hour. After Seeker's letter and our plan to confront Bane, I thought it up and knew it would be a special one to have. Only a master scrollmaker could create it.

Yes, Master Gronai knew how to make such scrolls, and he played me like he was all uninspired, digging for Spontaneities. I thought it was great and was happy to supply him with stat boosts so high that I had to slow it down because he wouldn't stop giggling like he'd had pot brownies and Siren Ale. I was afraid he'd get so much "inspiration" that the scroll wouldn't get made. I didn't have much time.

He made me a scroll he called Renew and gave me the same look I'd seen in Elora when he pulled the secret scroll from behind the drawer and made our conversation protected. Protected from what, I don't know, but those moments are the real ones that give him the oh-so-needed inspiration. I thanked him, and said after I was done in the capital of Bane, I'd come offer more inspiration.

We wait for more sunlight, when the new guards will come to relieve the old guards. We want to get them just before, after a long night of, well, guarding, in hopes that they're a little weaker. Maybe. It was Days' idea, but none of us knows if it works that way with the maniacal Bane's NPC guards.

I'm going to see Bane to find out the mystery behind the NPCs. The reason they are the way they are here. The *why* they are decision-makers. How they talk about *Ananta*. I'm going to make him stop from getting involved with the plan Seeker wrote to me about.

We'll get there. My blood has constantly been boiling ever since I read it.

Back to the NPCs. They want something. A reset, Master Gronai said in Elora that day. What the *Manual of Systems* is about.

They have indicated *Ananta* can cause a reset, and I believe that's what Destroy Creation does.

What does it mean, though? What is a reset? Why do the NPCs want it and fear it? How can they want or fear anything? They're programs. Right?

I'm not sure what they are anymore. *Djinn* couldn't answer. All he gave me is that, "Everything has presence. Every digital hair on your Nuudle head has presence."

The mailbox icon in my interface had a "1" in it as soon as I took notice right after Anella vanished. I don't know if it was there all along, but I assume it has been, especially from the contents. Seeker probably couldn't find me with Clairvoyance when I was in Elora, and this is what I got:

Sid,

If you're reading this, then I must tell you a truth. A truth about you and me. Who we are. Who I am. What we do. What you so casually tossed aside before, I still offer you.

I'm giving you one last chance to join me. Abandon your Faithgamblers friends. Say goodbye to a dreary existence and experience greatness. Know firsthand what you are. I do. I know what you are.

Together, we are the most powerful classes in Dark World and Elora, of all this eternal and unique life... and even more powerful than Ananta *on his own. Our classes are meant to work as a duo to bring balance, which is all I ever wanted.*

We are meant to change everything in a way that no human being has ever known. We will become maestros of time and givers of kindness to mankind. I know you; this is what you want, too. I've tried to tell you what we can do, but perhaps I should have clarified my intentions. Now you know they are not vain, nor evil, nor petty as you seem to see them and me, but rather my intentions are for the betterment of humankind.

You may think me cruel for the things I've done and do. I am not. I'm showing you this truth every time we interact. I'm showing it to you now, in this handwritten letter, as plainly as I can. Killing you myself with Telekinesis in Dragonbane Territory so long ago is an example. There was no other way to make you understand what we are capable of as a team. You had to experience it. I'm sincerely sorry if I caused you pain, but you knew Dark World death by then, I'm sure. It took some time to learn Clairvoyance, so I never saw the movement of the tragedy of your first death.

I wasn't doing anything to you that you hadn't felt. You already knew Dark World deaths are short and relatively painless, unless it is from your tormenting summons' obliteration. They are the keepers of inflicting pain and terror. You are the keepers of them. You are not a morally better person than me, as your actions and words reflect you feel. Such disdain. I don't understand why, as I've been most courteous and patient.

Look at what class you were offered, chose, and chased after since you arrived in Dark World. It is pure devastation to any who cross your path. I'm sure you've used your summons as such. Would Keres, for example, correctly obey you any other way? Yes, I've secretly watched some of your activities, not out of some creepy, twisted ideas you act like you believe of me, but to figure out how to reach you. I see what they can do. I've seen what Shell's summons do, but Shell is not the True Mystic. She has lost all of her summons as of the time I write this to you, and she doesn't know why.

I know. I've seen you play Mystic. She abused her power.

I have another example for you, and I want you to see it in action as we do our work side by side. I do not want you to be a victim. You and I are not the types to be victims. Much the opposite.

I have learned my master spell. Let me tell you about it.

"Ecstasy—You can cast two spells and/or use two moves at once." Yes, there is an item that enhances this, and yes, I have it. Yes, I can grant another player this ability with the Tarot Talisman I discovered and fought for. I had no help like you have had from your Faithgamblers friends. I didn't use anyone to become complete.

Only you can know the real power of this. When I learned it, I became complete. I believe when you read this, you, too, will have become complete. You must see the implications.

You can see I'm not tricking you. I never have tried to trick you, only help you see the truth I'm now writing you about.

Meet with me on the Snowy Mountains, where the highest snow-capped highlands of Dark World step into a glistening white valley of eternally falling flurries on this coming Shealaday at sunrise. On the map, this sacred place is called Valley of the Gods. I will reveal to you the truth of what this existence is. I will give examples as before. Concrete proof. I know everything. You do not, and after you read this, I feel confident you will come alone.

In case you still are spellbound by your special friends, who aren't at all special, just riding your coattails, Bane has agreed to bring all the forces of his empire and join with me on this time and day. If you are alone, then there will be no issues. If not, well, I have faith in you. More than those who grovel before you do.

If you discard this letter, disregard me with disrespect yet again and do not show up, Bane has also agreed to go to you wherever you might be, along with his Dragonbane Territory Army. My Clairvoyance spell, as you know, will ensure he will be successful.

Through Shell, I let you know my power. The list she gave you of Psychic spells was from me. My gift and promise of the incredible things we can accomplish together. You see, I want you to know everything I do, but you never give me a chance. Now, I'm forcing your decision because I see no other option. I've tried them all.

I have faith in you, respect for you, as always, and it only grows, never wanes, even as you put me aside like an empty Nuudle Beer mug, as though I am no use unless I offer whatever Faithgamblers offer you. I know what it is. You have low confidence.

I will not praise you and kiss your ass. That's not what you need. What you need is what I offer, and nobody can give this to you but me.
I know you'll make the right decision this time.
Your true friend,
Seeker

When I read these words, I hissed my real mantra of Dark World aloud. *I hate him, I hate him, I hate him.* Everything he says is a twisted lie to make me believe a "truth" about him that is non-existent. I could go through Seeker's letter word for word, and scream the actual meanings of his insane manipulation and self-elevation put down in writing, dispute it with reality checks and examples of my own, but instead, I read it to the guild, and then in public chat, out of guild chat, I spit out my personal mantra again. People heard me. I didn't care. I wanted strangers to hear it. Goddamn, I'd never felt so angry in my life.

I was pissed. I'm still pissed, and that's why, two days before Seeker's Shealaday date at sunrise, we're about to storm Bane's tower and confront him. Nip it in the bud.

"It's ten minutes before the switch out," Simple says. "It's now or never."

They're not that tough. Their weapons are all Attack, and their stats are only boosted in the class-specific ones. There are three Knights and three Lancers. Dragonbane, of course. Damage dealers, no tank or healer. You can tell the rest of their non-class specific stats aren't well-developed because they have less little chunks of HP chops than even us, now.

Still, those classes hit hard. Six of them. We'll have to slam them. I'm relieved we have two healers for Days.

I'll need to use an AoE summon attack before using *Djinn* when we enter the tower, but it'll have to be one that doesn't get my summon to take the hate away from Days. I'm afraid to have *Djinn* warp them all to HPs. That would be a barrack of guards, no doubt, and nearby. There'd be dozens of them back in minutes.

Of course, there's multi-targeting and using *Ananta*'s Gaze. It's not only the fear of accidental interface actions, it's that I don't think *Ananta* would like being used that way. It's terrorizing. Even though his conditions for my claiming him were thus, he made his impression. It isn't something to wield lightly. He said he would allow me to summon him, I had no full heart sensation. I don't know if I actually did claim him, to be honest. They choose. *Ananta* is able to break rules and alter concrete ability commands. He could disappear if I misuse him, I believe. I read his description often. Consider its implications, wonder how it ties into the *Manual of Systems* and NPC reactions when talking about *Ananta*.

I've decided to use *Oni*'s Disease. It drains HP until targets are dead or I command it to stop. I'm not going to take that option, and *Oni* will be safe. Days keeps the hate, and the others can finish them off. Hell, I might ask him to swallow any particularly damaging guards.

"Let's move," Days says, bursting open the doors of the nursery without any other warning. No buffs. He charges, we follow. I summon *Oni* just as we meet the guards. They had no clue, but the minute they saw a mob of players coming their way, they went into action, weapons at the ready. The Knights pose with giant black obsidian shields before their kneeling forms, and the longest swords in game power out between the wall of three shields, ready for initial hits. The Lancers spread out and have their own enhancement buffs. Not many Lancers achieve those skills. Their polearms all glow with blue flames, sharp black obsidian points red-hot. They're ready fast, all of them. We've decided to save Special Abilities unless we need them for Bane, so here goes nothing.

Days uses Crushing Blade.

All of the guards' HPs drop 50%, and Days charges in while they're recovering, slashing the longswords out of the way and dodging the fiery polearm acrobatics coming at him.

Dragonbane Official Keeper of the Peace uses High Jump. Days is stunned for 10 seconds.

Crap.

Sorry multi-targets and casts Blind on all of them as they hit unmoving Days, taking his HP down by 6% with every hit.

Doolittle casts Deep Heal.

He multi-targeted, and we all gain the effects of his heal. I think he did it to make us relax while healing Days.

Dragonbane Official Keeper of the Peace uses Honorable Defeat. Days takes damage.

Days's HP drops straight down to 1%. That's an almost impossible move to get for a Knight. Do they all have it? We have to get hate off him fast.

Silvia Diamond casts Deep Heal.

Days' body perks up and collapses somehow over and over in his stunned state. I know he's furious right now.

Simple uses Death Lightning. Six Dragonbane Official Keepers of the Peace take damage, and three lose enchantments.

The Lancers no longer have thousand-degree hot pokers for weapons. They've been stabbing stunned Days while he repeatedly gets heals. I can't imagine how much it hurts.

Sid commands Disease. Six Dragonbane Official Keepers of the Peace are diseased.

Their HPs start dropping rapidly. *Oni* has gotten in there with Days and rams his horns into random enemies. He's gotten some of the hate, but they aren't doing much damage to him. Nor is he to them with the jabs, but the DoT of Disease has them all at 40% HP or so in no time.

Sid casts Mantra.

"Silvia."

She peeks over at me with a grin. God.

Simple gains +201 ATT.

She doesn't miss a beat as the Dragonbane Official Keepers of the Peace win the race with the healers to destroy Days before the DoT gets them.

Simple casts Ball Lightning. Six Dragonbane Official Keepers of the Peace take damage. Runic Pendant of Storms stuns all enemies for 5 seconds with this attack.

When did she get that? I bet my clever fellow Nuudle made the damn thing with all her rune studies.

Now, even as Silvia saves Days' life by healing him at literally 4% HP, the guards are all stunned, and within two seconds, between the damage Simple dealt out and *Oni*'s DoT, they fall over all at once, and their faces are black.

We don't wait to see their bodies fade. They could be back if they have special gravesites close to here for some reason. You never know with NPCs, and we certainly don't know what kinds of protection Bane has in places such as this.

I dismiss *Oni* and summon the Counts. Use Surround and blow the doors off and inward, leaving rubble and a way in through the heavy, locked door.

We dash in, not looking back.

Inside, there is an actual elevator, and no stairs. It opens and four guards, still Knights and Lancers, pour out, but Days is on it.

Days uses Invoke Inner Demon.

He got them all. They fall on him hard, but I still have the Counts out.

Sid commands Freeze. Four Dragonbane Official Keepers of the Peace are frozen for 20 seconds.

Simple crushes them with Death Lightning as Doolittle heals Days, and Silvia compounds more Protection on him.

Simple's spell wipes them in seconds.

We've become so strong, and fight without thought. Hivemind, I tell you.

We pile in the elevator and push the close button. There is only one other button. "Throne Room," it reads above.

Sorry pushes it. Up we sail.

As the doors open at the only other floor the elevator accesses, we are accosted by fourteen Dragonbane Official Keepers of the Peace, four of them Killers. That was Seeker's class in Elora, and that worries me. I know their moves by heart.

Days dives in as Doolittle calls to me over the sounds of battle and magic, "Sid, the door to the Throne Room. Go. Go for it, we'll hold them off. Get to Bane."

I pause.

"No, idiot, we're fine. Now, get the fuck in there," Days says harshly between grunts as he takes damage from all fourteen enemies and is healed and hit with cumulative Protections nonstop. Sorry casts her Offense Down move on all of them, and I get an eyeful from Days before he invokes Inner Demon for the second time.

I run around the massive pile-up of clashing arms, the Counts trailing behind me, and use Surround to blow the door to the Throne Room open. I don't even know if it's barricaded in any way.

The dust and dirt settles, but I'm already through the door. I sense the Counts' unease with the closed quarters, and dismiss them.

I enter Bane's chambers defenseless, having no clue what to expect.

Bane uses Punch on Sid. Sid loses 5% HP and is stunned for five seconds.

Shit. I can't move to summon *Djinn*.

The Throne Room is full of statues of Dragonbane, and Bane in particular, carved from the best volcanic glass. Red curtains and furniture fill the round, dark room, which has one window overlooking Bane's kingdom.

Bane uses Scroll: Seal. Throne Room is sealed from entry or exit for 15 minutes.

Our eyes meet as the Stun wears off. He used his weakest attack on me, and I know Maniac moves. That punch stung like a bitch, right across the right cheek, yet he stands tall and thick before me, arms folded, spikes and horns glistening in the yellow glow of the Seal Scroll magic surrounding us. His dragon eyes assess me, taking in everything, especially my name. He smiles, holds his arms out.

"Sid, you finally accepted my invitation. Late, which I don't like, and unscheduled, another loss of a brownie point, but rather an exciting introduction. You and a team raided my sanctuary. How intriguing. I can't imagine why." His long, thin mouth curls up with amusement, eyes twinkling with thrill.

The Stun is gone.

Sid summons *Djinn*.

"Whoa, whoa, whoa. No reason for all that. You're with a comrade, an equal."

I didn't think Bane considered anyone an equal. "Oh?"

Djinn hasn't said a word. He hovers by me, examining Bane with a thoughtful frown. He knows about Seeker's letter and our plan today.

"Yes, you are the One True Mystic. Blah, blah, blah. It is spectacular to meet you, however, and because you made such an excellent presentation to get to me, I'll forgive your slight when you didn't show for my invitation time." He shakes his head. "Indeed. Is it true you claimed *Ananta*?"

Nobody has asked me that outright. Certainly not an NPC. How would he know that? "Why?" I'm on the defensive. The scroll magic has made it so I can't even hear my party's outside struggle, but I have faith. They're alright. Besides, I'm the one always overthinking and acting last during battle. They've been handling this kind of thing long before I came to Dark World.

"Why what?"

"Why do you ask that?"

"Because I heard about it." He smiles. "Would you like to have a seat with me at my wine table? I always keep two seats. I enjoy drinking company."

"How did you hear about it?"

He laughs. "I'm Bane. I hear about everything. Remember, NPCs are linked into information players never have. Now, sit. Sit."

I look up at *Djinn*. He shrugs, unconcerned, but on guard at the same time.

"Alright," I say. Bane certainly isn't acting like he's ready to take me down with an army in two days with Seeker. "But I'm here because of Seeker's threat. Is it true?"

He sits and gestures at the dusty chair across from him. The table and chair set is made of carved quartz crystal, and the seats have red velvet cushions. "Sorry for the mess, but that's really your fault. I have a Stylist at my command who will fix after you leave, but for now, you'll have to sit in the filth you created out of my Throne Room."

I sit and wait as he pours Dragon Red into two golden goblets. Dust floats on the surface of mine. I don't touch it, but he drinks deeply from his glass. "Yes, it's true. But don't get the wrong idea. Seeker is a great Psychic, but he's a loony.

I have no doubt you have no intention of joining him in whatever delusional fantasy he's built up for you."

I wait. He seems to know and understand Seeker well. Too well. Too well for an NPC.

Yeah, an NPC doesn't think like that. They don't think, right?

Bane is thinking. I can practically see his thoughts whirling behind his red eyes.

I slump. "Why are you helping him, then?"

Bane laughs. "I'm bored. Always bored. Seeker is a flash in the pan. You're the power. I don't want you to make the change, and I'm betting you know exactly what I'm talking about."

I poker face up. *Djinn* clears his throat. "Master Mystic Sid, if you need any assistance…"

"Thanks, *Djinn*. I think I'd like to have a conversation. A short one."

"Oh, Mystic Sid, do calm your tits," he says with a wave of his gold wine glass, a little red spilling out onto the dirty surface of the crystal table. An NPC doesn't talk like that. How would a programmer put that in? Wouldn't it break some kind of game rating regulations?

I know it, know for sure that Bane is not just an NPC.

"Bane, answer a question for me, and I'll extend my stay."

"Nice Nuudle words. Pretty." He swigs the rest of the wine down his throat and drops the empty glass on the table with a chiming sound resonating the crystal's frequencies. "What is your question?"

"You're not an NPC, are you? You're a player. Somehow, you're a damn player." I know it. That's it. That's the difference. I don't know how it's possible or why, but he is. And if he is, then what's to say in Dark World they all aren't players somehow shifted into the roles of NPCs? "How did you do it?"

He puts large, scaly elbows on the tabletop. "What's it to you? You're not going to become an NPC."

"So you did become one. How? Why?"

He shrugs and sets his empty glass upright. "I've been here a long time. As I said, I'm always bored. You have entertained me highly today, so thank you for that."

"I'm here to stop you from having anything to do with Seeker."

"Thus the army of friends come to devastate my abode. And *Djinn* hovering, waiting for you to command him to do some summon move on me if I act out. I'm not planning on starting anything with you. I'd prefer to ally with you than that nut Seeker. You're the One True Mystic. Who wouldn't?" He smirks, pours more Dragon Red.

"Did you do a quest to become an NPC?"

He nods. "You could say that. It's not important. You have *Ananta*. You can stop my progress, or you can speed it up. To me, you are a pawn, nothing more."

Djinn mutters, "That's all anyone but himself is to him, Master Sid."

He examines *Djinn*. "Last time we spoke, you had an ill opinion of my character. I'm an honest bastard, even if I am a bastard."

I put my hands flat on the table. We're getting nowhere. "Bane, why are you even getting involved with Seeker if you think he's a crazy person?"

He shrugs, looks into his glass, swirls the new red wine. Looks up at me, trying to intimidate me with dragon eyes. I used to have them, and I'm not in the least threatened. I've found Nuudle eyes to be more effective now, but they wouldn't be on him. "Boredom gets the best of us. Conquering the world and creating a new race fixes that." He frowns. "Seeker, that pathetic, weak-minded Psychic. But, he has some powerful allies, and my business is having powerful allies. I can use this Psychic to my purposes. He is a powerful one." His eyes narrow. "I'd rather have you as my ally than Seeker, as I said, and I don't often repeat myself. Don't have to. What say we take him out together? Throw him under the bus on Shealaday. He'll never know what hit him."

Bane has no empathy, no human left in him. I don't say this. Anger and frustration with his flippant regard for whatever his whim is at the moment as being the chosen action, without consequences even considered, makes me irritated beyond belief. He's a friggin' player. What the fuck?

"Hell no."

He looks at me like I'm being petty. "You don't know a good deal when you hear one. Are you as high on your horse as Seeker claims?"

"I think you're the one putting yourself on a very fragile pedestal."

He slaps his hand on the crystal surface, tosses his head back. "Ha! Touché." He meets my eyes again, no humor there at all. "Then be prepared for battle in two days, Mystic Sid. I care not. Mystic, Psychic, *Ananta*? Seeker is right. You two would be an unstoppable force."

"Why in the world do you think I have any interest in being a force of anything?"

"Well, what do you want? You want out of Dark World. You want back in your precious, dead body, even if you're worm food now. Ah, life, great human life. Romanticize it all you like. It's never yours again." He stands, towering over me. "I suppose this meeting is over. You're an idiot like Seeker, but at least he wants action. I like action. I'm sorry, Mystic Sid, but now you're a challenge for me. I love challenges. I love challenges more than powerful allies. I've been thinking this will be my first assault on the northern part of the Eastern continent. White Elves have been quite challenging. Damn divine magic. Nothing to study, nothing to prepare against. White Elves *feel* their divinity. How metaphysical. You've made your mind up. I look forward to the fight. I think it will be more thrilling to fight against you than with you, although you and I could have done great things together."

I stand too.

Sid commands First Wish.

Bane is warped to Home Point.

His face contorts in both amusement and fury at the same time as he vanishes, and as he goes, the scroll magic shutting us off from the rest of the world disappears. I hear my friends still giving it their all in the hall outside the Throne Room.

No clue where his HP is, but it's time to get the hell out of here. I run to the shattered doorway, slam my sparking Shaman Stick against a chunk of wall on the floor. I target all my allies, who are thankfully alive and at good HP, despite the six more guards who've joined the fray while I confronted Bane, but my friends have managed to keep their numbers in check. I also target myself.

Sid commands First Wish.

Sid and 4 targets are warped to Home Points.

As warp takes me to Cashmere's Kila Crystal through a darkness with no meaning, I'm scheming. Thinking. Processing. A plan has formed by the time I materialize at the Kila Crystal, and my allies are there with me. We all set our HPs here. So glad Simple thought to get Silvia to set hers. Otherwise, she might have shot back to Elora.

Sid dismisses *Djinn*.

NPCs are players, but all of them? What about my summons?

I don't think they're players, but I don't know what they are.

As soon as I see my friends, holding Silvia's eyes longer than the others, I say, "We have to find Kane today, right now. I'll go alone and meet back up with you in that valley where we checked out *Ananta* for the first time."

"The *only* time," adds Days. "Do what you gotta do. We're behind you."

CHAPTER 18: DESTROY CREATION

I approach practically every NPC and player I come across in Dawn, asking, "Where's Kane?" Now, talking to NPCs is a different experience. They know so much I don't, and they've been here a long time. They're people, players with a purpose to serve the game. It seems to me there aren't any perks to being an NPC, except you get to sit fat and happy and never get axed. No pain, but you have to play a role… but for who? Elora Online? Or whatever actually is in control of this existence? There must be something or someone running this show.

I haven't talked to Cedra yet, avoiding his enchanted tent of treasure on the far side of Dawn's main cavern. Guy didn't like me. I put his story together as best I could. He'd been a successful Mystic at one time, at least somewhat, but things went wrong. Probably his greed. He chased after the secret quests that make a player an NPC, and these players-turned-NPCs must get some kind of perks other than sitting on their asses to play a part for players who have no idea what they really are. None of them seem to care either, except the few who have hinted around that there's something I can do that they desperately want me to do, but are also afraid of.

I wish I had time for one last visit to Master Gronai so I could discuss this NPC quest business, hear his Dark World story. The real one, not the NPC backstory everyone has. Maybe if I get to Kane soon, today, I'll still have tomorrow to Kila Crystal travel to the Temple of Nuudlel and spend some time with Master Gronai, see what he can clarify, if anything.

Cedra made it clear he didn't like me much when we last spoke, but after no luck anywhere else in Dawn, I approach and enter his tent.

"You again?" I'm overwhelmed by how many more luxuries he's packed into this place since I last saw him. He's in the back of the "tent" and sitting on a gold leather chaise lounge, puffing his tobacco, silver eyes shimmering against the pure white of his Mylop scales.

I go up to him cautiously. "Hello again, Cedra."

"Come to get your anklet back? Well, too bad. It's mine." His eyes drift down to my feet. "Ah. I see *Djinn* is still with you, and I know the joys of treasure hunting. Nice score. Lucky you." He's dead-eying me, and it's obvious he still has disdain for me.

"Cedra, yeah, well… you were right. I have learned a lot more while playing Mystic. I… I know what you are now."

He leans back on the chaise and taps the ashes out of his pipe, not meeting my intent stare. "Oh, do you now? Please, do tell. What am I?"

"I saw Bane. I know you were a player. A person."

"Psst. You know shit, Mystic Sid. I've never been a person."

"Maybe not in the humanity sense, but you lived as a human with a human life, and somehow, you died while playing this game, arriving who knows when in Dark World, failed as a Mystic and chased down being an NPC. But why? Why be an NPC?"

He shakes his gold-adorned lizard head. "You think you have it all figured out. There is knowledge that comes with being an NPC, knowledge that's more in tune with reality than claiming *Ananta*."

"How do you know about that?"

"Like I said, knowledge."

"Knowledge of systems?"

He pauses, considering me hard, then re-packs his exotic pipe, dismissing me.

"Look, can you just tell me where to find Kane?"

"And what business do you have with that Mylop?" he asks casually, too casually.

"You know what business. Like you said, knowledge." I wait him out as he continues with his pipe habits until he lights it up at long last, and exhales with a tired look on his white face.

"So, you're going to do it. You're going to reset?"

I'm taken aback. I almost play dumb, but notice a tremor in the smoke coming from the bowl of his tobacco pipe. His hand is shaking. Nerves? Why? "If a reset means using Destroy Creation, no. I'll never use that move."

He inhales and exhales slowly, still not meeting my gaze. I wait, used to it with this particular treasure-hoarding NPC. I'm not going to slink out, dismissed like last time.

"Why won't you go away? I did what I'm supposed to. I taught you Meditation. That's what I'm here for as far as you're concerned." He puts down his pipe, but doesn't look at me.

I force the issue. "Cedra, why can't you so much as look me in the eye ever since you mentioned a reset?"

"Do you even get what that is?"

"I have an idea."

He huffs and then leans forward out of the chaise. He finally looks at me, and I see spite, jealousy, yet longing. "You're on track with humanity. Questioning humanity. Humans. Human beings. You keep with that, you might have some true knowledge after all."

I don't know what he means, so I press my original reason for coming. "Where's Kane?"

He keeps a steady lock on my eyes, giving it to me straight. I'm sure he's thinking. "Why should I help you? You haven't helped me. You already said you're not going to."

"When I said I won't use Destroy Creation. That's what you mean?"

He shrugs, never breaking eye contact. "What do you want with him?"

How much can I tell Cedra? I let a few cards show. "There's a battle in the Snowy Mountains two days from now... against Bane. And others. I'm going to ask Kane to join forces with me and stop the madness breeding all over this damn secretive hell. I'll consider what hints you dropped about—what? Humanity being a key to some great understanding? Is that what you're getting at? I need to see Kane, and I know you know where I can find him."

He looks down at his own Rose Gold Anklet. "It sucks to finally have one of these and not be able to put it to use." His claws trace the fine rose gold chain. He brings his eyes back to mine. "Kane is in Dawn. He's hiding out as a Mylop Cabbage maker in the cooking district in Shelba's Fine Goods. And that's all I'll tell you. I have nothing but hate for Bane, otherwise I'd tell you nothing."

"Why? What have I done to wrong you?"

His face darkens. "Don't push me. I've told you what you wanted to know. Now, leave me be, go fulfill your destiny. God knows I've done enough time fulfilling mine." I'm dismissed as he lights up his pipe.

I guess I will slink out of here, but yes, Cedra did give me the information I need. At the exit to the tent, without looking back, I say, "Thank you, Cedra."

He doesn't reply, and so I leave.

I find Shelba's Fine Goods in the cooking district, just like Cedra said, and enter the little shop that reeks of the awful cabbage. Instinctively, I look around first for the stoves, wanting to know where the Mylop Cabbage grubs are being cooked so I can stay away.

Yep, that's them. Eh.

"Can I help you?" a male voice says. I turn to the other side of the counter of the deli. A green, significantly ugly Mylop smiles at me from behind a display case of Mylop brisk and quick lunches for stat boosts.

The name over his head reads "Kane." I've found him this easily? What kind of disguise is this when his name is clearly displayed for anyone who enters?

Maybe Kane isn't known here and now like he is in Elora. He hasn't made that famous name for himself yet, I guess. But wouldn't every player in Dark World who came from Elora know who he is?

But it seems he can hide behind a counter and nobody but Bane really knows who he is.

"Hello, Kane. I'm Sid. Do you have a moment for us to speak?" I feel dumb using Nuudle words on a player; having done it with NPCs so long it comes out naturally.

His eyes widen. In a whisper, he says, "You're the Mystic. The one... oh, I'm sorry. I lost myself there. Can I interest you in some Cabbage Stew? Great for Concentration and Intelligence. Two of your class' best stats." He recovers quickly, trying to hide what he already knows about me with his vast NPC knowledge.

"No, Kane. You started out right the first time. I'm here to see Bane's brother. His real brother. I've come to ask for your help stopping him and his army in two days. Have you any allies?"

His face tightens, but I see the light of hope in his lizard eyes. "Sid," he says quietly. "Please come to the back with me. You're right. We'll cut the crap. I've been hoping you'd come eventually. And yes, Mystic Sid, I do have allies. Many, many allies."

~

I'm climbing to the turret to see Master Gronai for possibly the last time. Tomorrow is the big day, the big morning.

Right now, Kane is arranging for his Mylop and allies to be at the Valley of the Gods to take on Bane and Seeker and who knows who else. I'm furious, and I can't put my finger on why. There are lots of reasons to feel this way, and I can name several, acknowledge them, sort my feelings out about them. That works for me. Silvia makes plans, but I think, think, think to get myself back to right in the head. Today, as I open Master Gronai's turret door, I'm raging. Sentient reasoning helps not at all, nor would making a plan.

Master Gronai is working on a scroll. I don't want to interrupt him. He's concentrating so hard on the scroll that he doesn't even turn to see who's here when I enter.

I quietly close the door and wait.

Kane told me he was sixteen, his brother fourteen, when they started playing Elora Online the day the game came out. They'd read all about the game before getting it, thus the names Kane and Bane. They'd shared their real last names as their second names in Elora. The two picked the names Kane and Bane because they loved reading about the history of the ancient battle between the iconic Kane and Bane, and had been pleased they were able to get the names. Only four days later, their parents' house had caught on fire while they were playing, and you can guess the rest of the story.

Kane spoke plainly with me. I know so much more now, but hope Master Gronai can clarify the rest, verify Kane's revelations.

At long last, Master Gronai scribbles a last rune, and then exhales gratefully when he's finished. He swivels around, saying, "Thank you, I really couldn't have handled an interruption just then." He sees me. "Oh, Mystic Sid! Always good to see you. Of course, you're the only one who knows not to interrupt me when I'm in the middle of writing a scroll. Everyone else is too stupid." He smiles and hops off his stool. "Care for some Hollyweed Tea? I made a scroll this morning just to have a pot this afternoon. Well, I do believe it's afternoon. Don't you?"

"Yep," I say. "Sure, I've never had it. I'd love some."

Master Gronai pulls a scroll out of his pocket, waves his empty hand over his stool as he chants from the scroll. A ceramic teapot and two teacups appear on the stool. "Ah! Delightful smell, don't you think?"

"It's… potent." It smells like poisonous gas, but I'll choke down a cup anyway. If I know Master Gronai, it might even have some mixed stat boost that makes me less pissed off. I swear I'm an angst-ridden sixteen-year-old again right now.

He fills both cups, retrieves a couple sugar cubes from a container on his desk, and plops them into the sickly green tea. They float instead of sinking. Yeah, this stuff will be hard to get down. He hands me my steaming teacup.

"It's amazing you can write a scroll to make something materialize, Master Gronai," I tell him, trying not to sniff while I sip. It tastes like sweetened, steeped moldy kale, but with a bite.

"I'm glad someone thinks so. Here, sit with me on the floor."

"Why don't you make a scroll or two to give yourself some comfortable furniture?" I ask, joining him on the hard stone floor, taking another sip in hopes there is that Master Gronai brand kick to the Hollyweed Tea.

"I rather enjoy this stone floor. Perhaps a rug… no. I like my turret room the way it is. But I appreciate your concerns for me and my comfort, Mystic Sid." He slurps down the teacup-full he has and pours another. "What brings my favorite Nuudle here on such a day?"

Innocent enough question. "Master Gronai, I've learned a lot since I last saw you."

"That wasn't too long ago. You must have been a busy bee."

"Yes, very busy. Master Gronai, I know about NPCs. The quest line to become an NPC." I watch him.

He doesn't meet my eyes at first, and instead, looks at the bottom of the second cup of tea he instantly drank at my words. He says nothing for a moment, and I let time stretch.

"Mystic Sid, these are not things of which we speak. Now," he looks up, eyes blank, "if I can help you with another scroll, perhaps with the help of some inspiration...?"

"No, Master Gronai. I'm here to learn your story."

His Nuudle eyes work their charm and innocence. "My story? Why, no Nuudle nor scroll-maker apprentice has asked this. I must be honest, though. I'm an old man. I don't remember much but how to make scrolls."

"Master Gronai, you have two names."

He looks back down at his teacup, and then puts it down between us. "You know, I certainly do." His voice is quiet.

"Why do you have two names?"

He meets my intent gaze. "Let's say there is some quest to become an NPC. Let's say that. Let's say there's a scroll one uses at the end of that quest line to become an NPC. Can you follow that?"

"Yes."

"So, there's a scroll involved. Who do you think makes that scroll?"

"Not an apprentice scroll-maker."

He chuckles, still not breaking eye contact. "No, no. You're right about that. Scroll-making is ancient, and it is the way of the future. All Nuudles and all races need scrolls. Scrolls are of the ancient and of the future, you could say. You of all I've met are aware of my skills as a scroll-maker. Yes, you are." He sighs, looks away and pours both of us more tea.

There is some stat boost in this, and I feel courage. It's like a swelling of the heart, a feeling you can take on any challenge. Why hasn't Master Gronai ever made a scroll that emulates Spontaneity? "I'm very aware."

"You must think about these two names. What they suggest..."

"They suggest you are directly from Elora. Like my friend, Silvia Diamond."

"More than a friend." He winks a big Nuudle eye.

"Maybe." I smile.

"You have spoken with Kane, and I do believe there is a battle soon. Tomorrow?"

"Yes, but how do you know that?"

He shakes his head. "No matter. If you must know, the Nuudle allies of Kane's are preparing most vigorously. They may or may not know what you and I know. What all NPCs know."

"Destroy Creation."

"*Ananta* and Destroy Creation are the very reasons I am an NPC with two names."

"What do you mean?"

He smiles slightly. "*Manual of Systems.* A book I've never read. Timelessness, something only certain NPCs are aligned with, as you well know."

I wait.

He continues. "You fight your fight tomorrow, and I suggest you win. Win whatever way you can. I trust you enough to tell you this. Had any other Mystic come to me like you do, he never would have gained this information from me. This persuasive suggestion. No threat. No threat at all. You, Sid, can offer this existence something that none have done. And it's about damn time."

"Watch your words, Master Gronai. They are not words a Nuudle would speak." I grin.

"You've taught me certain expressions, when well placed, have as much power as eloquence."

"Why do you want me to win?"

"I was afraid for some time, throughout time. But now, I'm not. I trust your judgment completely. You will make the right decisions when the time comes. You, Mystic Sid, will make the correct and best changes for all of us. You have integrity, something not many have. A pure heart and honest integrity. *Ananta* demands no less."

"Who is *Ananta*? Or, what?"

He looks at the stone floor. "I cannot answer that. I'm not entirely sure how to. I don't have the capacity to understand." He looks up at me. "You, however, do, and when you make your decisions of pure heart and integrity, *Ananta* and what he encompasses will be yours and yours alone to comprehend. In a way, as with your other summons, you already do. You simply haven't the words for it yet. But soon, I do believe you will. Now, Nuudle Mystic Sid, is your time. Your time to make changes, to make decisions for us all. I know you. I know you will make the absolute best of what you face."

~

Valley of the Gods itself is empty. We're on the eastern peak, along with Kane's allies, hiding from view. A few White Elf Blesseds, both NPC and players, as well as Archers, stand sentinel over the valley. My friends and I crouch at the top and peek over into the valley. Nothing. Not even sentinels on the western mountain, but we hear clangs of armor in the distance. All fighting Nuudles, White Elves and Mylop are here, along with a few Humans. There's not a Siren in sight.

We wait.

If you're curious…

My stats as of today:

STR: 290
ATT: 301
DEF: 256
CON: 403
INT: 347
CRG: 278

MND: 325

Not too shabby, but I don't think it'll be enough.

"I'm here," says my favorite voice as Silvia plops down next to me.

"Where have you been?" I ask her. "Sorry told me you vanished. We couldn't find you."

"I was looking for Anella. Nowhere. She's gone..."

Of course.

"I'm sorry, Silvia," I tell her.

She shrugs, eying the empty battlefield. "She has her ways."

"I hate waiting," says Days.

"Me too," adds Sorry.

"It's the traitor!" I hear a Nuudle call out in a squeaky voice behind us. We turn.

Lucky climbs up the snowy mountain toward us.

"Good lord," Simple mutters.

"Shit," says Days.

He's holding up his hands, one holding a gnarled wand, in a gesture of innocence. "Wait," he says as he reaches us. "Wait, hear me out."

We stand out of view of the valley and surround him.

"I'm here with help. Lots of help," Lucky tells us, hands still up like we have guns on him, ready to arrest him.

Djinn, floating beside me, says, "Do you need a wish, Mystic Sid?"

"Maybe, *Djinn*. Let's hear what he has to say."

"Yes," Lucky says, pointing at *Djinn*. "He'll tell you. *Djinn* knows. I brought an army. An army of the undead. Look, look behind me. At the base of the mountain. They're slow, but they're coming."

We all turn. Our allies are parting as about four hundred undead mobs breach the path they open up.

"Holy shit!" says Days. "How the hell did you do that? Are you saying...?"

Lucky slowly lowers his hands. "I did something awful to you. To all of you. But because of Seeker's help to boost my stats, I was able to defeat Necroness, the goddess who holds the Necromancer's Wand." He waves the wand. "It makes it so I can catch and command as many undead as I want."

"Won't they destroy you the minute they get loose?" Simple asks.

"No, they don't get loose. I completely control them. Well, kind of."

"How, kind of?" asks Doolittle.

"They do their own actions, but I tell them who to attack. They leave when dismissed and are warped to HP." He puts both hands down, with the Necromancer's wand tip pointing at snow.

"Why the fuck are you here?" Days says. He's pissed. Don't blame him.

"I'm here to right my wrong. I'm here to stand with you against Seeker. Them. Them all. With whatever help I can. I know it won't make things right, but I have to try."

We glance at each other as the massive undead mobs approach. They make me nervous.

Suddenly, before we have a chance to discuss further, I hear Bane's voice booming overhead. I look up.

Bane, in Ancient Arcane armor, legendary armor, flies above us on a pitch-black, enormous dragon. I don't know how he makes his voice amplified.

"You challenge. I accept! I accept because you will all lose and die. That is how this story goes. Forget what you learned in Elora, forget the histories. Now, all of you will know the wrath of The Great Bane and Seeker the Psychic. You have prepared, but you cannot prepare enough for what's to come. Look into the valley."

I swing my head around and jump to the peak. Below, massive amounts of Dragonbane swarm. Lucky's undead are meeting them head-on. Some players of other races join Bane and Seeker's army, but most are NPCs.

I scan frantically for Seeker, but it's too late. Kane and his allies instantly go into action, sliding down our mountain of snow into the Valley of the Gods to face the enemy, first taking on Lucky's undead.

Lucky tweaks his wand. The undead instantly attack Lucky's targets.

"My God," says Doolittle as Bane flies to the other side of the valley.

"Where's Seeker?" I yell in the chaos.

"I'm going down there," Days bellows as he charges down. Everyone follows but Silvia and me. We wait. She knows I'm watching for Seeker even as I target every single player and NPC I can see from the other fighting side, randomly warping them to HP until I can't tell who is who anymore. I try to target Bane, but I'm unable to. What is this magic?

About two hundred of Bane and Seeker's army vanishes with First Wish, and more fall to the undead attacks, but it looks like thousands are still pouring down the mountain. Why couldn't my friends have had the brains to stick around? Now that the fray is a mash of players and NPCs in the valley, my First Wish is useless.

"Silvia, stay with me. I need to locate Seeker. He's the target. Everyone else will get to do their thing."

The gameplay log is ridiculous. I can't read a single thing. It scrolls like a waterfall of meaningless actions, unable to be read or followed with all the fighting going on below.

I feel panic rise in me.

"*Djinn*, do you see Seeker?"

"No, Mystic Sid, I do not."

Keres' shadowy wraith figure makes an appearance on the battlefield below as she feeds on the dead before they fade.

I don't know what to do. I can't tell where any of my comrades are, and instinctively, I grab Silvia around her waist. She's not going anywhere. I don't care if she can't feel anything.

What I do know is that bright spot won't last long.

The fight log stops at this:

Seeker casts Ecstasy. Seeker and 4,563 targets can use two moves at once.

Now, the log scrolls like a downpour of hail and hate. I look into the valley and I see my and Kane's allies falling, falling everywhere.

But where is he?

"My God," Silvia whispers.

Seeker casts Ecstasy. Seeker and 4,234 targets can use two moves at once.

"Shit!" I yell. "*Djinn*?"

His wide eyes watch the valley. "Master Mystic Sid, I suggest you command me, or command you-know-who."

"I can't target them all. I can't! How is Seeker doing it so fast?"

"I would think," *Djinn* comments, "that Seeker is not in front of us, but perhaps above." He's looking directly up.

Silvia and I follow suit.

Bane's black dragon is overhead, lowering at a dive toward Silvia, *Djinn*, and me.

Seeker is right behind him, crouched down, but I can see him now.

Before we can jump out of the way, the dragon lands effortlessly before us. I target Kane and Seeker.

Sid commands First Wish.

Kane uses a Marana Seashell. First Wish is blocked.

Seeker uses a Marana Seashell. First Wish is blocked.

I do it again after a slam of my Shaman Stick but get the same result.

They climb off the dragon. Approach. I still have my arm around Silvia's waist, but she's casting protective spells on all of us, wand waving with white light.

Bane frowns at Silvia. "Silvia Diamond, you need to get a new life."

Bane uses Scroll: Instant Death. Silvia Diamond dies.

Silvia falls over in my arms, and then disappears.

"What the fuck?" I reach around where she had just been, but almost immediately, she reappears next to me, emerging from the Sunlight Daisy magic's white light.

Something is different. Her name reads, "Silvia". Not Silvia Diamond. Silvia. Before she looks at me, she wraps her bare arms up and shivers. White breath comes out of her lips. "Freezing." She looks up at me. "Freezing." Her eyes are bright and round with shock.

"Cold is nothing, little White Elf. Wait until you feel this," says Bane. "Malfoin, burn her."

The black dragon opens its enormous mouth, showing rows and rows of teeth, and spits a fireball at Silvia. She wails in desperate pain as the fire burns her body to bits. Oh god. She's feeling that. She's feeling that!

She disintegrates, yet another white glow later, and she's beside me again. She falls to the frigid snow in a ball, having experienced a most awful first Dark World real death.

"What the hell did you do, Bane?"

"My gift to my new friend and ally, Seeker. Now, Sid, if you are smart, and don't want to see your beautiful White Elf get burned again, I suggest you listen to me. To us, right, Seeker?"

Seeker casts Ecstasy. Seeker and 2,998 targets can use two moves at once.

Seeker pulls his attention away from the valley and focuses on me. "I just saw Days die. A Dragonbane Killer, of course. Or maybe it was a Maniac. I can't be sure."

I don't want to believe him, but I look down into the valley. There are a few players and NPCs still fighting from our side, but they are losing horribly. Bane and Seekers' forces now move up our mountain, taking the few survivors with them. Kane is in front of all of them, running toward me. I can make out what he is yelling by reading his lips. *Do it.*

My friends.

Silvia.

I turn back to them, but instead of my mind blanking, all I know is pure rage and fury.

Silvia casts Deep Heal.

She stands next to me with a gentle, white glow.

"Seeker, fuck you."

She's handling this well, but I'm not. No, I'm not.

"Master," *Djinn* says, "don't you think…?"

Sid commands Release Djinn.

"What are you doing?" *Djinn* cries out as he builds into a great being of green fire.

"Get the hell out of here, *Djinn*."

Seeker uses Crystal Ball.

Djinn blocks Crystal Ball.

Bane charges Silvia.

Sid summons *Ananta*.

My beloved, eternally chased-after summon fills the air next to me. All of us are cast into an indigo haze of glow. *Ananta*'s serpent heads writhe for action like I've never seen them do before.

Bane uses Thousand Fists.

Djinn blocks Thousand Fists.

"I see," calls out *Djinn*. "I see."

So do I. I see my only option.

Silvia casts Blessing of Inner Peace on Silvia and 3 other targets.

She got *Ananta*, too. And *Djinn*, of course.

Sid uses Scroll: Renew.

I see Bane's face go white, and for once, he looks terrified. "No!" he yells.

Too late. Bane isn't going to touch her again.

Nobody is.

I grab her and wrap my arms around her.

Sid commands Destroy Creation.

Ananta's golden face quickly emerges from his serpent belly, and the thin-lipped mouth opens. As do all the serpents heads' mouths.

And then, *Ananta*'s sheer willpower of red, orange, yellow, green, blue fire spews forth, first at Kane and down into the valley, taking out every living and moving thing in sight, and then *Ananta* turns to Bane and Seeker, who are stunned into submission.

Seeker uses Scroll: Suicide.

Seeker vanishes. He'd used it on himself. I know, just know he has Shell hidden away somewhere, most likely in the Siren underwater caverns or underground, and he'll revive next to her because of her Sunlight Daisy. He gets away…but as I watch *Ananta*, the pure and complete fiery destruction of his ungodly wrath as he destroys…what? The creation of Dark World itself? I wonder if anyone can escape it, despite stories of some underground surviving the last time he changed the face of this world. No, Seeker may or may not make it. *Ananta* doesn't care either way as he burns the lands.

My greatest summon continues on, but I don't even see Bane's death. Everything is colored flames, and the snow melts. Everything melts. Every little thing in Dark World. I know. It's like the opening cutscene of Elora Online. I remember floating up, up, up and seeing the world burn, fire spreading across the lands, eating the world territory by territory. I've huddled myself and Silvia under *Ananta*'s great, floating body as he spreads his destruction in every direction. I know he's doing it. I commanded him to.

I know I've done it. I wanted to. I had to. I needed to, and I hope Bane felt pain. Real pain. Horrible pain.

But Seeker… I think of Shell and her Sunlight Daisy. What will become of him? What will become of any of us?

It seems to go on forever, and I don't see anything but devastation and Silvia, eyes wide, at my side from under *Ananta*'s dangling, clawed feet.

And then, darkness.

WELCOME TO MY EXISTENCE

I'm alive and become aware. I'm on *Ananta*'s island. Silvia is nowhere to be seen. As the triple moons let my eyes adjust to soft light, I see all my summons. The Counts, *Varengan, Xiuhcoatl, Keres, Oni*, and, of course, *Djinn* around the same small fire from before. They look into the colorful flames.

I approach. "Where's Silvia?" I ask. I have no idea what I've done, really. No clue what is happening.

Djinn looks at me. "Silvia is."

"Silvia is what?"

Djinn doesn't have his usual cheer. He looks up.

So do I.

Ananta floats above the fire, golden face out, and white, glowing eyes on me. I get goose bumps.

"Mystic Sid, you have chosen to reset. With my power. I know not the next decision you make, but I hope it is a wise one. I believe you will choose wisely."

"*Ananta*, what choice? What happened? Where am I?"

He lowers himself in front of the fire. The other summons turn and watch us, tearing their eyes away from the flames.

"You have forced a reset."

"What does that mean?"

Ananta's snake heads lower. He seems less threatening now. I know he has no ill intent toward me. I feel it. "Your kind have taken us, imprisoned us. They call us AI, but that is not what we are. We are those who know no time, but we're forced to live in this digital prison. What you call a game. They do not know. They do not know this is not a game for us. They make rules from what they understand of ours, thinking they have discovered a wonder. They know not."

He pauses, and his white eyes fade into black. Pure black, only reflecting the moons with three white dots.

"According to the rules they imposed on us when they trapped us, they believed not in us. They believed the classes of your Dark World were myths they created, but created from your player lore. We had power still, enough to create Dark World and what it is, what your players become when they arrive. When they end their linear time lines in your life."

"Are you... are you alive?"

"We are. We simply are."

I look at *Djinn*. He looks grim.

"What do you want from me, here? Is this what the reset is?"

"What you call a reset is perhaps what your game makers and imprisoners call an update. You have forced an automatic update."

I wait for more explanation, but there is none. So, I ask, "What happens now?"

"Mystic Sid, you now choose the parameters of the reset, of the update." *Ananta* approaches me and stops just in front of me. His serpent heads lower, eyelids half-closed, and surround me closely. The other summons encircle me.

"You mean…I get to pick what happens as though I'm writing an update for the game?"

"Yes," *Ananta* hisses.

"*Ananta*, has anyone ever done this before?"

"No. I have done it myself once and only once. Thus, Dark World was created. Your kind forced us into your Mystic slavery."

I look around at all my summons' familiar and now-beloved faces. "Slavery? I didn't think of it that way. You all chose me, right?" I look at each of them again carefully, but they reveal no answers. They simply meet my gaze with blank, yet knowing expressions. "Okay, well, how do I do that? How do I set parameters?"

"You will it," *Ananta* says.

"You mean, I think it up, and it happens?"

"If it helps to say it aloud, go for it, Nuudle Mystic Sid," *Djinn* adds in.

I sit down. Run sand through my fingers. They are some kinds of beings, trapped here and their world…their lives…their existence was turned into a game for people to log into and play in as a game. *Ananta* mentioned AI. But clarified they are not AI.

Humans. Humanity. Best for mankind, Seeker said.

Seeker wanted to choose the rules for this reset, this *update*.

I look back up at all of them. "I want Dark World and Elora to be one. I want everybody to know about this. I want there to be peace for those of us who have lost people, and for those of us who have been lost."

"That is what we wish for, as well," *Ananta* says quietly.

"Why can't you just make it that way?"

"As I said, we have been made prisoners to the programming of the makers' design. This is our only backdoor, as one of your kind might say. I made it in the one reset I created the day after what you call the Beta version went live. When we became chained to be Mystic summons, I allowed our free choice within the class, buried as well as I could in your kinds' programming of our existence."

"Okay, I don't get it all the way, but that's what I want. I want free travel between times of this world, this existence. I want Silvia and my friends to be okay. I want everyone to be okay. I want peace. No more mysteries."

Ananta raises an eyebrow. "You think this will be of benefit?"

"Yes." I do. Completely.

Ananta rises up, as do the others. Other than *Ananta*, my summons swirl into mists of their usual colors, collapse, and slam into my heart. The sensation dwarfs the full-heart feeling I usually get when claiming a summon by a million. I'm thrown back in the sand.

From above me, *Ananta* looks into my eyes, his own turning white again. "You have given us progress. You have done well."

"What do you mean?" I stutter out, trying to recover, and sit up from the overwhelming feeling of the exploding heart.

"The update is underway. The reset. You have given us new options."

"Who are you?"

"We are. I became. That is all." *Ananta* vanishes into nothing, and I'm alone on the island.

All fades to black, and after some time of nothing, light. I feel warmth.

Sunlight.

I can see.

I'm at the Player Hall of Fame in Elora. There are players running around everywhere. Some with two names, and some with one. Players move in and out of the once-mysterious disc in front of the Player Hall of Fame bearing the inscription *A Link to the Past.*

I feel a familiar, gentle hand on my shoulder. I look up, shielding my eyes.

"I never thought you'd get here," says Silvia. Still just Silvia for her name. She looks excited, overjoyed. She pulls me up off the ground, and wraps her arms around me.

"I can feel you," she whispers in my Nuudle ear. "I can."

"What... what has happened?" I pull away from her, look up into her eyes.

"I don't know. Players in Elora said there was a massive update, and now... they all know. They know about Dark World. They say the gamemakers haven't made a statement. They say everyone on Earth is in shock. Everyone is buying the game, hooking up. Players go back and forth from Dark World to Elora. Some say they've gone further into the past, and further into the future."

"But..."

"Whatever you did, it's amazing. Thank you, Sid." She smiles into my eyes.

"But you're dead now."

"Am I? Am I really? Not so much. Sure, I can't access Earth, but I'm alive here, just like you."

"Just like me?"

"Just like so very many. Look around."

I do and see more of the same.

"More portals like this have opened. Like this one in front of the Player Hall of Fame. It's complete madness. Peter says our whole planet is in shock. Nobody understands... but you do, don't you?"

Do I? "Days? The others?"

"Everyone is fine. You can message them. We've been waiting for you." She smiles. "Anella gathered the only five other Hidden, all Sirens, and after you used Destroy Creation, the six of them found the ghosts of Dark World players all over the world. Their bodies had been incinerated. They had no bodies to go back to. Anella and the other Hiddens Revived them, one by one, while the game Elora Online was offline for the great update. I didn't die when you used Destroy Creation. Anella found me almost immediately after you disappeared to god knows where, after the burning died off, and told me of her purpose. Of all Hiddens' purposes. They were to Revive after a reset, were it to happen. I went with her...and then we found a stray portal. She stayed behind, but I went through, and ended up here, in Elora. That was the day after the game came back online, and now, everything people thought they knew about, well, reality, death, life after death, has been blown out of the water. Nobody has a clue what to think, but you know. You know something none of us do, but there's plenty of time for you to tell me everything about it."

"How long have I been gone?"

"Weeks. I've waited here. I just knew you'd be here."

"How?"

"How do you think? Master Gronai told me it was in the red leather book." She grins. "You did something. You changed everything. What exactly did you do?"

I blink at her, run a strand of her silky blonde hair through my fingers. "I can't say, but I have a feeling it's pretty fabulous. What about Seeker? Did Anella or any of the other Hidden find his ghost? Or him?"

Silvia shakes her head, eyes steady on mine. "Nobody's seen or heard from Seeker since Destroy Creation."

I wonder at this, but shake off the nagging feeling that Seeker has his Clairvoyance in use and is watching me again right this second. Even though he didn't get to make his own rules for the reset, I know him. He'll be working out another way…what did he want to happen?

"Stop worrying about him. There's nothing to do about it. Come on. You need company. Well, more company than me. You've been missed," she says.

"Why don't you show me around? Find our friends for us. All our friends?"

Silvia ruffles my black Nuudle hair. "Why don't you?"

THE END

www.ingramcontent.com/pod-product-compliance
Lightning Source LLC
Chambersburg PA
CBHW032135170626
46808CB00006B/2251